THE YOGA TEACHER

Also by Alexandra Gray
Ten Men

THE YOGA TEACHER

Alexandra Gray

Black Cat
a paperback original imprint of Grove/Atlantic, Inc.
New York

For Diane

Excerpts from the poems "Time Suite" and "Cabin Poem" from Jim Harrison's
The Shape of the Journey: New and Collected Poems (1998) are reprinted by
permission of Copper Canyon Press, www.coppercanyonpress.org

Published simultaneously in Canada
Printed in the United States of America

ISBN-10: 0-8021-7055-2
ISBN-13: 978-0-8021-7055-2

Black Cat
a paperback original imprint of Grove/Atlantic, Inc.
841 Broadway
New York, NY 10003

Distributed by Publishers Group West

www.groveatlantic.com

08 09 10 11 12 13   10 9 8 7 6 5 4 3 2 1

THE YOGA TEACHER

Chapter One

NATARAJASANA — Lord of the Dance

Nata (dancer) raja (lord, king), the Lord of the Dance, is one of the names of Shiva, god of stillness, death, and destruction, but also of the dance. It is said Shiva is dancing not to entertain, but to involve the world in his dance and awaken it to the wonder of creation. Shiva, destroyer and creator, is the god within whom all the forces of nature exist. This dramatic pose is dedicated to Shiva, Lord of the Dance and source of yoga. It is essential when holding the pose that the hip bones be parallel. If the practitioner cannot hold the big toe behind the head, the ankle may be held instead. This asana balances the nervous system and builds strength and concentration.

While performing asana the yogi will assume many forms resembling different creatures, from the most insignificant to the most divine. Asana practice teaches the yogi that the Universal Spirit, the source of atonement and unity, dwells in all creatures regardless of their form.

Grace owed yoga much. Sometimes she believed she owed yoga her life. It had all started so simply with a picture of Natarajasana, that elegantly, ambitious balancing pose, on the cover of *Yoga Journal.* Grace had bought the magazine—and the outfit the cover girl was wearing. A yoga teacher came next.

A good yoga teacher is always hard to find, but it was a lot easier when there were only three yoga studios to choose from in the whole of London. Grace rejected the clinically white Iyengar Institute in Maida Vale and the purple saris and *bindis* at the Sivananda Vedanta Yoga Centre in Putney. She chose instead Swami D's yoga studio in Kensal Rise. Today better known as the neighborhood north of Notting Hill, it was, and is, a no-man's-land south of the Harrow Road, three minutes' drive from Grace's house.

Concealed by a wire fence—and lilac in the spring—Swami D's studio was an abandoned Church of England hall, Easternized (before it was fashionable) by Sanskrit scripture and incense. Attracted by a pose Grace may have been, but once she could stand on one leg while holding the other behind her head what kept her coming back was Swami D, one of the few truly wise men in London. He had not always been.

Spells at Wormwood Scrubs and Brixton prison had prompted plain Dave Green, at twenty-one, to pack his bags and escape the criminal future awaiting him in London's East End. He had traveled India, then settled for an incarceration of his own choosing in an ashram in Kerala; he became a devout student of Sri Swamiji, a revered spiritual master. Dave rose every day at five to meditate, then helped to clean the ashram and work in the kitchen. Day after day, he practiced asanas for hours; then, after eating with bare hands food served from a metal bucket, he studied the scriptures. Every evening he meditated before going to sleep on a rush mat. And the purpose of such austerity? To cultivate a dispassionate attitude to all things, to overcome *prakrtic,* or the conditional existence favored by the mass of human kind.

Dave was a willing student and within sixteen years he rose above the conditioning of childhood and culture to understand the God within and was able to say 'I am' with no trace of ego. Finally, Dave desired no more than was necessary for the maintenance of life, and it had long ago occurred to him just how little that was. Then, in his seventeenth year at the ashram, Sri Swamiji told Dave that he had mastered himself and earned the title Swami. And Swami D would have been content forever with ashram life. His teacher, however, saw contentment creeping in. He advised Swami D that his dharma—the desirable action leading to heaven—was to take yoga to the West. For the first time in years Swami D experienced resistance: his desire was to stay forever in India. To overcome his attachment to a simple life, he accepted his teacher's teaching.

Swami D was in his late forties when he returned to live without money or community in London. His dharma felt like a punishment, and every day was an act of faith. To the East End boy in Swami D taking yoga West meant building his centre in West London, which is why he squatted in and finally signed a lease with the Church of England for the hall in Kensal Rise. Things started looking up when he met a woman who persuaded him that the city was no place for celibacy, and that he had forsaken his title for a pleasure it had denied him for almost twenty years. With lean tattooed limbs, ponytail hair, and eyes that glittered from meditation, Dave still looked and behaved the Swami in every way but one. His students affectionately preserved the title.

By his sixties (his age, like much else, was a mystery), Swami D's faith and obedience had yielded two children and a yoga studio full of students who admired him for living by the creed from the *Bhagavad Gita* that was inscribed in gold above his door: 'Hateless toward all born beings, friendly, and pitiful; void of thought of Mine and I; bearing indifferently pain and pleasure; patient.'

Swami D talked with his pupils about their lives, less indifferent toward them than the *Bhagavad Gita* suggested he might be, and he held Grace in affection. It wasn't difficult. Tall and generous looking with long auburn hair, a slender neck, and a strong, flexible body, she had a softness to her mouth that men felt they needed. She responded to Swami D's teaching, accepting his adjustments, trusting the magic in his hands as they eased tension from her. Like a pea on a drum at the start of class, by its end she would sink into the floor as though it was moulded to fit.

For six years Swami D observed Grace's transformation: at first she had come to class as though in competition and all had assumed, including Swami D, that she was the kind of woman whose path through life was easy. Grace was successful at work—something to do with health care was all they knew—and lived with Ted, the man she loved. He would sometimes arrive at the end of class, when Grace slid toward him and away from the rest. Yoga was not Ted's style. He was addicted to action, a foreign correspondent whose coming and going kept them alive to each other and life.

Grace and Ted had been together six years—all good things since the beginning with more to come—when he had caught bronchitis, taken an assignment anyway, and come home with pneumonia. He had refused to see a doctor. It was as if he knew it would be game over. When he was too weak to resist, Grace had taken him to hospital and was there, days later, when the consultant explained that his immune system was depleted, compromised by a strain of cancer—it didn't matter which. Hearing the consultant say: 'degenerative, progressive, terminal,' had been worse, in a way, than holding Ted when he died and all Grace felt was love.

Ted had wanted to be at home for the end, and that's how it had been, three days before his forty-second birthday. In those last months he had protested that Grace did too much for him. She was practical, funny, resilient. She said she wanted nothing in return. At the yoga studio (a world away from Ted), Swami D could tell that something was wrong: Grace was remote but softer, broken, he recognized, but could not have guessed why. She told Swami D that Ted was ill weeks before he died, and only then did she fall apart, because despite what she'd told Ted she *had* wanted something, and what she'd wanted, and secretly expected, was for her love to save him.

The studio became Grace's haven. She was there, every day, perfecting the asanas—the physical postures that limber the body. After class, she would talk with Swami D and he could see that outside the yoga studio her interest in the world, even for living, had waned. Slowly he began the process of persuading her that life alone was the gift and the yogi's path was to advance from the physical to the metaphysical. As Swami D hoped it might, Grace's curiosity pierced her grief. He gave her a copy of the ancient text *The Yoga Sutras of Patanjali*. It was irrelevant that sage Patanjali may or may not have existed, or was perhaps several persons writing under the same name anytime between three hundred to five thousand years ago. Regardless of authorship, the terse injunctions attributed to him, setting out the sacred science of yoga, remained powerful, a little austere.

As Swami D had secretly anticipated, Grace was drawn to *pratyahara*. 'Through the practice of *pratyahara*,' he told her, 'you will learn to control the senses, to turn your attention inward and retreat from the world. It might even revive your appetite for it.' But Grace's senses, dulled by bereavement, closed down with such ease Swami D suspected that she had not surrendered but had cut herself off, falling into overwork and isolation: the twenty-first-century trap. He sensed her agitation, as once again she became withdrawn, difficult to know.

Swami D intermittently warned Grace that she worked too hard. 'Surrender takes a lifetime to master. This retreat into yourself will be tested,' he cautioned. The kind of test Swami D had in mind appeared when Harry Wood walked into the studio one late summer Sunday for the seven o'clock class.

Harry Wood was no yogi but he was also under no illusion either about what he wanted from the studio. He had heard that Swami D's was the best place to meet women that didn't require a bar, a drink, or a fat wallet—essential considerations for Harry at the time. On the day Harry met Grace he was two years and one month without cocaine; three hundred and forty days without a cigarette; and one year, one month, and six days without a drink—or sex, come to that. It had been around the time of his daughter's first birthday that sex with his now ex had felt like hard work; without the substances, it had proved impossible. Sometimes Harry believed that's why he'd moved out of Vicky's four-storey Notting Hill house, and sometimes he remembered that it was her idea that he should leave. It was a grey area, like much of his past.

By the time Harry met Grace, that couples got together at all seemed a miracle to him. Nobody he knew had done it sober, which was the stone cold prospect that terrified him—until he glimpsed Grace through the changing room mirror taking off her business suit. He had kept his focus on his own reflection when he said, 'These Thai pants looked a whole lot better in Phuket.'

'Don't worry. On the mat priorities change,' Grace had said, and hers certainly had when Harry lay beside her, horizontal and so close they might as well have been in bed. It was as though *pratyahara* had primed her senses rather than dulled them. Grace was unsettled by her delayed reaction to Harry's rangy good looks, which she felt she should recognize from a magazine or television, such was his indifference to their effect. When the class had started, as it always did, with Swami D instructing, 'roll your head slowly to the right,' Grace had gazed at Harry as a lover would a sleeping beloved. His refined profile, gentle breath, and the shape of his mouth beside her in candlelight collided with a memory of Ted, and Pandora's honey vase (it never was a box) had opened. Desire, followed fast by hope, had escaped to claim her. Grace was Harry's before he asked her.

Throughout their first class together Harry had been diverted from yoga as much by Grace's beatific face as her heavenly body, which he eyed furtively in all the postures while he attempted them himself. When the agile old Swami had adjusted her forward bend, settling his hips into her upturned bottom and pushing his hands down her back, Harry had felt his own energy surge: he'd wanted to hit him, 'nut the old fucker,' he had later confessed. But even he could appreciate that beneath the Swami's touch Grace's body was granted release, allowing her to nestle her forehead closer to her ankles. At the end of class, when students were told to rest, Harry may have been surrounded by supine women, but cradled by the sound of a sitar and candlelight, he was soon asleep, and was still sleeping when the other students had rolled up their mats. Intent on saving Harry from humiliation, Grace had kneeled beside him and whispered, 'It's time to wake up.'

Two years after her sympathetic whisper, the day-to-day had eroded Grace's romantic notion that meeting Harry at Swami D's was proof of a karmic connection. It broke her heart that he still laboured under the consequences of his past, while labour of a lucrative kind eluded him. At first she had been seduced by Harry's insistence that he had changed his life and was destined for greatness. Grace saw his potential, set him on a pedestal, and supported his dreams of one day becoming not only an actor and a model, but also a clothes designer. So far, Harry had acted for two weeks in total, one of them in Notting Hill's fringe theatre. He'd earned less than £52 since they'd been together.

Once upon a time, Grace hadn't cared that Harry was penniless. She had never worried about money, and refused to start. She was well paid and Ted had left her the house and a bit beside. To rediscover pleasure was all she expected from her time with Harry in their early, loving days. Her London life had been transformed by their walks in Hyde Park and breakfast on Golborne Road where they browsed Moroccan shops, the storerooms crowded with antiques, and the secondhand bookshop. They had always finished at the fishmonger followed by the fruit and vegetable stall opposite, run by the old man from Marrakech. Grace bought the food, Harry cooked it: an apparently innocent switch in the conventional roles. Then there had been cycle rides along the canal path to Camden, and for the first time in years, Grace had taken public transport, where she and Harry stood as equals. Being the passenger in Grace's Mercedes had put Harry on edge; travel cards had been his solution, and her delight, especially when the bus or the underground train swung them together— though this romantic enthusiasm didn't survive the mass of drunken humanity on the last Friday train from the West End. They were back to her car. Letting Harry drive didn't make him more the man, and as the months went by, his dreams of greatness felt like an indulgence for which Grace paid the price. His latest scheme, to film friends' weddings, had lost rather than made money and lately he spent days at home designing yoga clothes. Grace no longer found their role reversal modern: all she wanted was for Harry to get a job—any would do. These days he balanced precariously on the pedestal she had set him on. That he would topple into the baggage that dragged him down seemed inevitable. Harry's load included an adorable five-year-old daughter, Lucy, who could, at times, love Grace as if she were her mother. The woman who actually had that privilege—a destructive force fueled by wealth and celebrity—was Vicky Hope. Her design business was a nineties phenomenon that still thrived in the new millennium. Her second book, *Encore Décor,* was on the best-seller list the whole time Grace and Harry had been together; Grace no longer went into Waterstones on Notting Hill Gate, where multiple images of Vicky's airbrushed face smiled down from the local author's shelf. She had never seen Vicky smile in real life. That didn't seem to trouble Harry as much as Grace felt it should, and he remained as compliant as he had been in the face of her fame, fortune, and motherhood—a potent combination Grace had thought to tempt him from with love and hope and naked nights.

But Vicky's life was a roller-coaster ride Harry couldn't get off, and Grace had to accept that if she stayed with him, she was along for a bumpy ride. Only yoga returned her to sanity. Over the years, it had strengthened her, as she had hoped. What she had not foreseen was that it could subtly undermine her faith in Western medicine, and that wouldn't have mattered if she'd had a different job.

Harry called her 'the drug dealer' and said with perverse pride that only he, reformed addict that he was, could have picked her from a room full of yogis.

'I'm not a drug dealer, Harry,' Grace would protest, weary of defending herself. 'I work in medical health care.'

'Drugs are all the same to me, scored on the street or packaged by Suprafarma.'

The orthodoxy of Western medicine was the liturgy in Grace's family; to work outside the medical profession would have been inconceivable. Her father had been a surgeon, famous for pioneering the 'boob job,' a phrase he decried for demeaning his art and the most sublime of all God's creations. Grace's father had started his career as a breast surgeon, but been lured from this path on a quest to perfect the healthy breast tissue of the rich and famous. His reputation was such that women from all over the world came to London to be enhanced by his hand, long before such procedures were screened on prime time TV.

Grace's mother had been a different kind of doctor, a pediatrician, dedicated to a stream of patients. Grace had seen, firsthand, what it took to be a medic and preferred the theoretical realm; after graduating from Cambridge in natural science, she had joined the pharmaceutical giant Suprafarma. Psychotropic medication was her specialization, and in the lab she worked on the brains of rats and mice, developing compounds for antidepressants and mood enhancers. Progress took time and trouble. Convulsions, paralysis, hallucinations: Grace saw them all—indeed, she induced them—but always within the sanctuary of the lab. She preferred it that way. You could always walk away from a rat. By the time the drugs she had helped develop were tested on humans, her involvement was over. Even so, she respected the men who first tested a drug—the so-called 'healthy normal volunteers,' who were always males aged eighteen to twenty-four, and paid to swallow on our behalf. Grace called them 'phase one heroes'; the pharmaceutical industry was less laudatory, persuading itself that the £3,000 it paid volunteers to enter a trial was money easily earned.

Like distant parents watching a child make its way in the world, Grace and her project team would track the progress of their drugs through multiple trials all the way to the pharmacy—although few ever made it. When one of their drugs reached the market within seven years of leaving the lab, it was considered a record. Only four of Grace's compounds ever got so far but one of them was Procent, a new-generation antidepressant, and the most successful on the market.

When Ted had been ill, to give her time with him, she had given up research to work part-time as a representative promoting Procent to the psychiatric departments of the hospitals in Greater London. No sales rep had ever been as qualified to talk about a drug. Preoccupied with Ted, Grace hadn't missed the laboratory; reaching sales targets became her obsession, an almost soothing distraction. The condescension of doctors took her by surprise but did not intimidate her. Not all her new colleagues were as resolute: one still suffered panic attacks in certain streets in W1 and couldn't say Harley Street without stammering.

After Ted died, returning to research held no appeal. Nothing did. Neither she nor drugs had saved Ted. Too dispirited to find the energy to think, still less to ditch her job, she'd carried on selling Procent. In fact, for a very long time, Grace was indifferent to everything apart from yoga—until she met Harry, and for that she would always be grateful.

But Grace had picked a boyfriend who was opposed to medication and who denounced her work. For that, too, she would later be grateful, though not just then. The job no longer felt like her calling—had it ever been, she often wondered now—but to have admitted that, out loud, would have robbed her of a reassuringly familiar script. Besides, with none of Harry's grand projects coming off, it felt too soon to depart from salaried security. That suited Harry. 'We can't both die of optimism,' he'd said when she'd once hinted at her secret wish to stop working as a sales rep.

This Friday evening, Grace was not reluctant as she once would have been to leave Harry resting at the end of Swami D's class to go into the West End for a Suprafarma sales meeting. The consultant psychiatrist, Dr. James, had been at the Chelsea and Westminster hospital for almost a year; it had taken Grace that long to persuade him to meet to discuss Procent—an appointment he had repeatedly canceled. But that afternoon he had called to suggest Claridges Cigar Bar at nine o'clock. 'I'd like to go there while it's still fit for purpose. What will they call it come the smoking ban?' He laughed. Grace liked his laugh. In fact, she had always liked the sound of Dr. James's voice, and there was a leap in her belly that had nothing to do with securing a sales contract when she agreed that, yes, Claridges would be fine.

New regulations of the pharmaceutical industry (as Dr. James had to be aware) prohibited a sales rep from meeting a possible client anywhere that served food and drink, apart from the hospital canteen. The 'sweetners' that had once been permitted in the industry—business-class travel to exotic locations for half-hour seminars, the latest goodies from Apple, delicious dinners—were all illegal now and there was less fun to be had promoting drugs. Doctors were more reluctant to meet; they had so little time, and could find out about the drugs they wanted from colleagues or online. Pharmaceutical sales reps, Grace guessed, would one day be a rare breed.

On her way to meet Dr. James, Grace was consoled by the pleasure of driving her car—the one undeniable luxury Suprafarma still afforded. The Westway, the direct route to the West End from Swami D's, was her favourite stretch of London road and she accelerated her Mercedes into its broad curve. Grace had liked cars for as long as she could remember. The cocoon of metal and music, the responsiveness to command: cars adhered to reason, their occasional sickness simply remedied—inspection, operation, cure. Easier than people, thought Grace as she accelerated. Driving to meet Dr. James put things in perspective. Deep down, though really not so deep, Grace knew that practicing yoga while promoting pharmaceuticals wasn't a match made in heaven, but nothing was anymore, and she convinced herself it was merely inconsistent to sell medication while being a yogi. The road ahead was clear, there were no speed cameras, the car seat was warming up. All would be well.

Grace entered Claridges ten minutes late. The impeccably dressed man in the dark blue suit sitting at the bar with a margarita and a copy of the *Psychiatric Times* was no doubt Dr. James. From the bar Dr. James spotted his medical rep with equal ease; the tailored suit, elegant heels, and briefcase betrayed her caste.

'Sorry to drag you to the West End this time of night,' he said, approaching. 'I have a patient staying at the hotel; this is my only free time for weeks.'

Shaking his hand, surprised by his courtesy, Grace's diary slipped to the floor. Everything she had filed in the book's back pocket—credit cards, business cards, stick figure drawings of yoga poses, a photograph of Ted, and one of Harry—spilled at Dr. James's feet. Composure shaken, Grace bent down, hoping the doctor would take Ted and Harry for one and the same. The messy dark blond hair, the square jaw: surely in the low light of the Cigar Bar he wouldn't notice they were two different men. The doctor didn't seem to be interested in the photographs. He was looking at Grace. 'Let me,' he said, resting his hand on her shoulder.

Grace watched his hands—elegant and deft—gather the scattered bits and pieces. She managed a closed-mouth smile when he returned what suddenly seemed to her the pathetic representation of her life. 'What would you like to drink?' he asked, mercifully indifferent to her humiliation. Perhaps it was Dr. James's manner that disarmed her, or the effect of her two-hour yoga class, but for a moment, Grace had no desire to push Suprafarma's pill. She edged onto the bar stool and said yes when he offered her a margarita. The cocktail, prepared with swift precision, was served with a short blue straw. Dr. James raised his half-empty glass— a toast, she supposed, to the account he was about to give her. Instead he cautioned, 'always more potent when you suck.' Amusing but patronizing— and perhaps he fancies me, thought Grace.

Grace knew about the straw: it had long been her father's trick to induce a hit. She sucked through the straw, the tequila went straight to her head, and she launched into her Suprafarma pitch, failing to observe that Dr. James was hardly in the mood. He leaned forward rubbing his eyes. 'I'm sorry. It's been a long day. What about side effects?'

Grace edged him the latest fact sheet for Procent. 'Nothing fatal. The usual,' she said, circling the thick paragraph in reduced print at the foot of the page with the tip of her Bic. 'Drowsiness if mixed with alcohol, headaches possibly, weight gain, and our faithful friend, constipation—for which I have a very effective laxative. Ta da!' Grace produced the packet she kept in her pocket for such occasions, aiming for humour without demeaning her product.

'Nice to know you've got a sideline in laxatives. Some of my more medicated patients haven't had a shit in weeks.' The doctor's tired eyes sparkled but Grace refused to be seduced. She liked to control the humour until her work was done. 'I think you'll find Procent surprisingly side effect–free,' she said.

'You think I'll find?' Dr. James pushed away the sheet.

'It's late. We could have sorted this out over the phone. Sitting here with you I'm already in breach of clause nineteen.'

'Ah,' he said slowly, 'the latest code of practice.'

'The very one.'

'If you hold the Procent literature and I take off my tie, can we forget about business?' He loosened his collar and looked sideways at her.

'Okay,' she said, cautious but intrigued.

He pulled off his tie, leaving it curled in his lap. Grace liked how he did that but hid her pleasure. Dr. James turned to her. 'I probably shouldn't say this, in fact I know I shouldn't, but I saw you the other day at the hospital and wanted to have a conversation. That's really why I called you.'

Underhand passes and innuendos from admiring men were easily combated, but Dr. James's honest appeal unnerved her. He was attractive in his Savile Row suit and wanted to talk. Where was the harm?

'The thing is, I'm disillusioned,' he went on. 'I thought I saw that in you, too.' He smiled, a thin line at the corner of his eye creasing deeper than the rest.

'Disillusioned? Where was I?'

'Outside Dr. Carmichael's office.'

'Oh dear. Well. I'm sorry,' Grace laughed. Dr. James's appeal for a response beyond her remit—and his—made her nervous. 'I don't know if disillusioned is the right word. Preoccupied possibly. There's something I need to talk about, but my boyfriend isn't the right person, and I don't think you are either.'

'Is your boyfriend in medicine?'

'No, he isn't,' Grace said, wistful.

'So what does my competition do?' Dr. James was a margarita ahead and surprisingly playful. Impossible as it is for a man who has always worked to imagine one who hasn't, he was unable to see Grace's dread of the subject. 'Is he independently wealthy?'

Grace put a stop to the game. 'Dr. James, what your "competition" does is dream. Otherwise he's unemployed.'

'You shouldn't feel responsible.'

'Thank you, but I do. I feel his responsibilities more than he does.'

'Is that what attracted you?'

'What, lethargy?'

'Oh dear. Is it that bad?' They both grinned.

'Actually I can't tell how bad it is anymore. It's gone on too long. It's all a bit depressing.'

'Do you think you might be depressed?'

'Is this a conversation, or a consultation?'

'You don't have to answer,' he said and smiled softly.

It was then that Grace realized that they were at ease with each other, as if they knew—knew what? Perhaps that they could trust each other—if they dared.

'I'm not depressed,' she said. 'I know what depression feels like.'

'Did you ever take Procent?'

'Not the first time. I was too young.'

'Who diagnosed depression?'

'Me,' she laughed, 'years later. Looking back I see I was shut down and would have been classified as depressed if my father had taken me to a doctor. I'm grateful that he was too busy or too drunk. As hypocritical as this sounds, I'm glad not to have had a medicated childhood. I don't think it would have made my mother's suicide any easier to bear.'

This rare confession was a release, and the last thing Grace expected to say. She would have moved the conversation along, if she could, but no words came. Her dark secret could still rouse her shame—shame at not being enough for her mother to choose life. Dr. James seemed to know this. He waited, then asked, 'How old were you?'

His sympathy made her tearful. She couldn't look at him. 'I was twelve.'

'There should be a law against suicide.'

'And all untimely death,' Grace added.

Dr. James watched her for a second. 'Did somebody else die?'

'Yes. Ted.' She had learned to make light of her hurt, and by the time she looked back at him, she was ironic, resigned. 'Unlucky, don't you think, to lose the two people I loved the most?' Before he could answer, she asked, 'How about you, have you been lucky in love?'

'Sometimes very lucky, but not for long. I got divorced nearly ten years ago. I've been married to my work since. Were you and Ted married?'

'It was better than that, in a way. When I lost him, I lost myself, and as I don't believe suffering has any particular merit, I took Procent.'

'Are you still on it?'

'God, no.'

'Why did you stop?'

'At first it took the edge off. Mind you, so does this,' Grace said, finishing the last of the margarita. 'I gained weight on Procent. Being physically heavier neutralized the benefits of being emotionally lighter, and that tiny pill always felt stuck here,' she said, raising her chin. He watched as she stroked her throat. She looked beautiful like that, with her chin lifted. She dropped her hand. 'Procent didn't suit me, and that was depressing.'

He was aware of the cost to her of such self-disclosure; suddenly aware, too, that he was negotiating his own conflicting emotions. 'So the road to health isn't paved with pharma drugs?' he asked.

'I think we know that, although some drugs do give some people a better life than they might otherwise have.'

'That's the problem right there—*some* drugs for *some* people. We don't know which to prescribe to whom, so it's trial by error, with no guarantees. Isn't that why you're disillusioned?'

'Probably. I still don't want to admit that I am.'

He waited. 'It's hard to be invested in a system you have cause to doubt. I've had a similar experience, and I no longer fight it. I don't tell many people this, but I have an academic training in acupuncture.'

'So you've consulted an acupuncturist?'

'Many times.'

'Is it good science?'

'It's a different science that convinces me. I'm tempted to go to Vietnam to retrain so that I can come back and practice Chinese medicine. In the West we've specialized ourselves out of treating patients holistically.'

'It's not that drugs don't work,' Grace insisted. Dr. James lightly touched her forearm.

'You're right. I shouldn't get agitated. I wish I could walk away.'

'You will, when you're ready. Anyway, as you said, some lives do begin again with medication, although I've known too many galvanized to action by antidepressants and the only action that made sense to them was suicide.'

'The work I did protected me from the reality of patients.'

'You never wanted to practice?'

'I felt . . .' She paused. 'I *thought,* not felt, that to go into medicine would have been hopeless. My father was a remarkable surgeon. Breast remodeling.' She smiled, or started to. 'His reputation would have eclipsed anything I tried to do. My mother was a different kind of doctor; she questioned everything and sought solutions. I think it became unbearable for her when she realized that she wouldn't find them. At least that's how I account for her suicide.'

Dr. James waited, wondering if she would go on. He realized that she needed him to speak, and he did so, softly. 'What does your father think?'

'The day after my mother died, he took me out of school for tea and told me, "Mummy's gone to heaven and everything will be all right." To prove that it was, he dropped me back in time for prep. We haven't spoken about it since.'

'Do you think the right medicine at the right time could have saved her?'

'Believing that it could is why I went into research. I wanted to help people who suffered like my mother, and save a child from what I went through losing her. After sixteen years in this business, such aspirations sound naive. You know, sometimes . . .'

'Sometimes?' Dr. James prompted.

What the hell. Grace no longer cared if it sounded absurd. It was about time she confessed. 'Sometimes I dream of being a yoga teacher.'

'Why don't you?'

'I'm not in a position to give up Suprafarma.'

'Unless you've got no choice,' Dr. James said, gentle complicity in his eyes.

Chapter Two

TIRYAKA BHUJANGASANA — twisting cobra pose

Tiryaka means diagonal or triangular. The pose is, almost quite literally, 'cobra with a twist.' While holding Bhujangasana, cobra pose, direct the gaze over the shoulders diagonally across the back of the body to the opposite heel. The secret of the pose is revealed in its name, which recalls the cobra's strike when its body is coiled and weighted to the ground. As the cobra does, when practicing the pose keep the lower body strong and free the upper body as it rears up. This asana can remove back pain and keep the spine supple. A stiff spine impedes nervous impulses sent from the brain to the body, and vice versa. Improving the circulation of the back of the body will tone the nerves and enhance communication between brain and body. This asana stimulates the appetite, alleviates constipation, and benefits the abdominal organs.

It was midnight when Grace got back to Harry's studio. She stared down the bed at her sleeping beauty. His latest self-help book, *Change Your Life One Day at a Time,* was open facedown beside him and his right foot dangled free of the covers as if he'd fallen asleep mid-getaway. Still too awake to join him, she went to sit on the wide ledged windowsill where, from the darkness of the studio, she had fallen into the habit of watching the couple in the house opposite. Grace liked to think of herself as the unobserved observer but knew well enough that she was spying on a love that seemed young, even though the lovers weren't. Tonight she watched the end of their dinner party. Grace knew the scene and missed it: friends, conversation, red wine, the man across the street wrapping his arms around his woman—as Ted would have done, late at night, loving her. Grace looked across at Harry; she regretted that he had not stayed awake, but would not snuggle beside him in the hope of rousing him. Better to drive home to her empty bed than lie restless beside him.

The following morning, lying in bed, she invited images from last night's meeting to linger: Dr. James sitting at the bar, taking off his tie; his face, animated in conversation; their respective confessions. She shivered suddenly, fearful that she had said too much, but was comforted that he had also confessed to disillusionment. Grace appreciated what they had shared. All she and Harry talked about these days was Lucy and Vicky. She grabbed her mobile and checked the time: not yet seven. Harry would be asleep. Recently he was lying in later than ever, and Grace recognized depressive symptoms. Only last week she had asked him to try Procent; she knew it was a long shot—Harry wouldn't countenance food that wasn't organic, let alone pills unless they were homeopathic. But Grace, tired of carrying the burden of Harry's heavy mood and empty pocket, had procured a three months' supply anyway. She'd asked him to be broadminded and give the medication a chance. 'It's helped hundreds of thousands move on from a debilitating funk,' she'd said.

Harry had thrown the pills back at her and insisted he was not depressed. 'I'm in a depressing situation, that's all,' he'd said. 'There's nothing wrong with me a little luck won't cure.' That luck was Harry's Plan A was too precarious for Grace. Just thinking about Harry's situation made her tired.

She got out of bed and lay down on her mat, unrolled and ready, right beneath the painting. There was plenty of time to practice before returning to Harry's studio to witness the feng shui consultation he'd organized. Plan B she supposed, since luck hadn't shown up.

Grace wondered what Max, the feng shui expert and Harry's new friend, would make of her bedroom. Harry complained that it was over the top with its ornate mirror, classic boudoir dressing table, antique wardrobe, and green silk curtains. But he knew, and she knew, the root of the problem was the painting. Grace remembered the morning she had returned to the bedroom, dressed for Monday, to find Harry in his Calvin Kleins, looking up at the six-foot oil. His 'who's this?' had sounded defensive. 'A Howard Morgan,' she'd said, offhand, tying back her hair.

'I didn't mean the artist, I meant the naked lovers,' Harry said.

The lovers faced each other, the woman's bent leg resting on the man's hip, he about to penetrate her. Grace had continued looking in the mirror when she replied, 'That's me with Ted.' Harry couldn't believe they had posed like that. 'Well, we did,' Grace said quietly, walking out of the room.

The comfort of Grace's house on Oxford Gardens put Harry on edge, reminding him, he had once confessed, of all the things he didn't have. Reminders of Ted did not help. At the foot of the stairs an oil painting showed Ted as a boy, holding a shotgun and standing next to his grandfather, at his feet a retriever with a bleeding bird in its mouth. In the hall, three miniature oils recorded scenes from a nineteenth-century battle commanded by one of Ted's ancestors. The towels in the bathroom bore his initials, as did the robe behind the bathroom door.

The dead can do no wrong, so competing with Ted was hard for Harry, but at least Grace's past *was* dead, however much it haunted her. Harry's meanwhile was very much alive; Vicky and Lucy dominated his world. It all came down to Lucy, he said. She was the reason he could put up with Vicky; in fact, it was why he and Vicky had got together in the first place. Grace knew the story: Vicky was forty-three and childless when she'd met Harry. Within three months she was pregnant. Abortion wasn't an option. Harry would never ask a woman to go through that, and Vicky had no intention of getting rid of her dream come true, which wasn't without complications. Five months into the pregnancy she had said to Harry, 'Sweetheart, around the time I conceived, I got home late, remember?' Harry remembered. Vicky had returned drunk and high at four in the morning, provoking an outrageous fight that had ended with consoling lovemaking.

'The thing is,' Vicky said, 'before I got home, I crashed. I woke up next to Steve.'

'So?' Harry was accustomed to Vicky's idea of a good time.

'We were in bed.'

That was when Harry had raged, and Vicky had cried. Vicky never cried, so Harry had stopped pounding the sitting room door and, licking blood from his splintered knuckles, changed his tone to help Vicky establish her child's paternity. 'Was Steve wearing anything?' he'd asked.

'A condom?' she said.

'No, Vick, clothes. Was he wearing any clothes?'

'I can't remember. I don't think anything happened.' Vicky had kneeled beside Harry with her arms around his neck, hanging or hugging, it was hard to distinguish. 'If you love me, love the baby—even if it isn't yours,' she said, her voice small to diminish the enormity of what she asked.

Harry knew Steve. He was on the scene and he was black. They wouldn't need a DNA test. But Harry made the investment: he decided to love the baby. The ultrasound had revealed a girl, and Harry didn't miss a single prenatal class, which was more than could be said for Vicky. She was ten years older than him and a handful, but she had provided him with a role: he was her partner and a father-in-waiting—in more ways than one.

Vicky had dark hair and eyes. Lucy arrived blonde, blue eyed, his. On the day she was born he had promised to be the father she deserved. That it took another three years to give up the substances was a pity, and it felt like a punishment that sobriety exposed his incompatibility with Lucy's mother. When he moved out, Harry's intention of being the good father suffered a setback, which he was determined to overcome. Vicky didn't make it easy.

For the sake of seeing Lucy, Harry tolerated Vicky's delinquency and told Grace that if she loved him enough she would do the same. Grace was optimistic that Vicky would weary of being obstructive, but it was she, not Vicky, who was bruised by the constant fighting that connected Harry and his ex more convincingly than love.

What Vicky had wanted from Harry, and what she'd got, was a child, but Grace never talked about being a mother, even though she was at the age when most women who hadn't been pregnant were desperate to be. While Harry certainly didn't want another child right now, the fact that Grace wasn't begging him for one was an issue. Grace seemed to him absolute, sufficient unto herself. More than once he had asked her why she was with him.

That Harry was a father appealed to Grace. If it was sometimes difficult to compete with his five-year-old look-alike for his attention, she forgave them both. Grace had always been committed to getting on with Lucy. It wouldn't only be Harry she was leaving if they split. Grace still wanted to believe they could be if not a family, a unit that looked like a family and sometimes acted like one. It didn't matter to her that Lucy wasn't hers; some days it was her love for the child that kept Grace in the relationship. She had even booked builders to convert her attic into a bedroom for Lucy—the first step toward turning her house into their home, even though Harry still resisted moving in.

'I moved in with Vicky too soon, and lost my way in that woman's world. It's a mistake I don't want to repeat,' he said.

Money was the other reason Harry didn't want to give up his studio. He feared that moving in with Grace would disqualify him from welfare and housing benefits—handouts from the government that granted a semblance of independence. Grace couldn't understand his willingness to be on benefit, rather than get to work and take the future into his own hands. At her insistence, Harry had consulted the benefit office to find out where he would stand if he did move in. 'My girlfriend's house and money aren't mine. She's the one with the assets. I'm the one with the kid,' he'd preempted when facing the signing-on woman across her desk.

'All I do is put the information in,' the woman said. 'The computer decides what you're entitled to.'

Harry already knew the exercise was pointless—Grace's assets would disqualify him instantly. There was a way around the system: to deny their relationship, and move in with Grace as her lodger—an idea he had put to her that week. 'The benefit office will send you the rent check that currently goes to Mr. French, and I can keep signing on. It's a win-win,' he'd grinned.

'Harry, it's called benefit fraud. If you need money, get a job,' she'd responded. They were back to that, which was why Harry was counting on feng shui to fix things.

'What good is that going to do?' Grace had asked.

'Defend against Vicky, and boost the positive energies in our lives.'

'Who said feng shui could do that?'

'Max,' Harry said.

Max was mortal proof of feng shui's transformational power. The two men had met in the vitamins and herbs section of Whole Foods, the organic store on Westbourne Grove. Harry had looked up when he'd heard a lowered voice ask the assistant 'what's good for warts?' A shaggy beard could not conceal warts the size of raisins on the big man's face.

'Get them lasered,' Harry said quietly, as he reached for his Rescue Remedy (alcohol free). Max caught up with Harry at the cash register, clutching a bottle of chelidonium.

'Did you have warts?'

'No,' Harry said. 'My ex. She had a wart on her nose, and that stuff didn't shift it.' Vicky's misfortune still made Harry chuckle, which is when Max's memory clicked in.

Max had a mind that filed and graded celebrity pictures with a rigor that caused him real pride, but whose commercial potential had eluded him until enlightened by feng shui. Max had retrieved Harry's face within minutes of seeing him, even though it was four years since Vicky's Ibiza villa had filled eight pages of *Hello!*, Harry in every photograph completing the picture of her perfect life. The magazine hit the stands the week after Harry moved out.

Intent on discussing the laser surgeon, Max had invited Harry to join him for coffee—or Barley Cup with soy milk, in Harry's case. Max eyed the Barley Cup and said he couldn't imagine a more disgusting drink. A one-time car salesman from Chingford, whose real name was Craig, Max wasn't as alternative as the feng shui suggested, and his offer to transform the stagnated energies in Harry's flat, and by implication, Harry's stagnated life, was a spasm of altruism ignited by self-interest. Vicky, famous for creating serene interiors nothing like her own, could make Max's career.

Grace was skeptical about feng shui, but she was intrigued about meeting Max, who was gaining a reputation among the Notting Hill nobility as something of a wizard. Certainly his chameleon progress from Essex show-room forecourt to London W11's stucco terraces was powerful testimony that a transition from the conventional sales sector to the alternative realm could be achieved, if ambition burned.

At half past eight, she called Harry.

'Where are you?' he yawned.

'Home. Sorry I didn't stay last night.'

'Is everything all right?'

'Yes, fine.'

'I mean between us?'

'You were sleeping. I didn't want to disturb you.'

'You could have. By the way, good news—Max has promised to feng shui my place for nothing if I introduce him to Vicky.'

'A great trade when you consider the fifteen square feet you call home.'

Harry grunted acknowledgement. 'He's here at ten, if you want to meet. And sweetheart, pick up some breakfast, would you. I'm starving.'

Harry could have fallen out of bed into Whole Foods, he was that close, but he had no cash. He had long ago assumed that such treats were for Grace to procure.

'You certainly gave up the luxuries,' observed Max, as though Harry had sacrificed much without knowing why. Then Grace walked in with a bag full of breakfast. 'But who cares about that when you've got a woman like this. Love is the finest compensation,' he said, greeting her with open arms, registering her face—and more. 'You know, it isn't so bad in here. I like the high ceilings,' he said, checking his watch as he set to work.

'The light's amazing, but I'm swamped with antiques,' Harry said, setting down three mugs of bitter herbal tea.

'Ditch the antiques and paint the walls in here green. That will shake things up,' Max said, blowing on his tea, delaying the taste of it.

'The antiques are holding me back. They've got to go,' Harry said, convinced that he could count on his landlord to take them away at short notice. Mr. French owned the building and the antiques business on the ground floor, and filled all his rentals with old furniture. Harry and Mr. French got along, Mr. French being a gentleman who liked to mind his own business.

'Sort that now if you can,' said Max.

Harry left Max plotting the studio on graph paper. When he'd gone, Max asked Grace, 'What's your theory on Harry's slow progress?'

'Certainly the past has a hold on him,' she acknowledged, 'but I'm not sure you can pin the blame on the antiques.'

Max's eyes sparkled: if he was going to be challenged, it might as well be by a hot woman. 'Getting this furniture out will make a difference, which is when you'll call me to feng shui your place,' he said, winking at her.

'We'll see about that,' Grace said, skeptical but admiring his confidence.

Harry buzzed the shop door. Mr. French peered from the back to check that it was safe before letting him in. The growing affluence on the street made him nervous. Back in the day, when he'd inherited the house from his father's mistress, the neighborhood had been seedy but honest. He'd preferred it that way.

'Hello, Harry. Anything I can do for you?' Mr. French half expected some kind of problem.

'It's the antiques, Mr. French.'

'One of them broken?' Mr. French winced but kept his voice steady.

'No, no. Nothing like that. It's unsettling to be surrounded by so much history.'

'You want me to change the bed?'

'I'd like to keep the mattress, but you could take the base and the headboard.'

'Are you sure?' asked Mr. French.

Harry was sure. The bed was carved with luscious fruits and exotic birds in imitation of Grinling Gibbons, the seventeenth-century master craftsman, and too ornate for Harry's taste—as were the bureau, the chaise longue, the dining table, and the Chinese lamps. Mr. French stopped writing his list. 'You're getting rid of everything. What's this all about?'

When Mr. French heard about the feng shui he thought the lamps could have stayed, but promised that his son would clear the studio if that's what his tenant wanted. 'The shop could do with the stock,' he reflected. 'And of course, the curtains, you'll want them down,' he said, upbeat. The curtains, a vivid orange with a psychedelic floral print, had always offended Mr. French. His wife had bought them in Portobello market for a shilling and he'd been looking for an excuse to get rid of them ever since.

'The curtains can stay,' said Harry. In Harry's mind the orange print would complement the green he'd be painting the main room, and add to his retro intentions, which, for the moment, he was keeping to himself.

Back in the studio, Max was in a hurry to finish. 'John Barratt is expecting me.'

'Are you talking about *Sir* John Barratt?' Harry lit up.

Max crooked one eyebrow.

'That's serious. *He's* serious.' Grace was incredulous that the recently knighted old actor would fall for feng shui. 'How did you meet?'

'His wife. I bumped into her in Whole Foods.'

'You mean, you stalked her,' Harry laughed.

'Be nice. She wants me to start their house in Holland Park and see how we go. I might have to charge them more than usual.'

'How much is that?' Harry asked.

'Two hundred.'

'A day?' Harry asked.

'An hour. The rich pay double. Expensive makes them feel good. Making people feel good is my job.'

Grace watched Max move around the studio using a compass, sketching ticks and crosses on his feng shui diagram. 'So how long did it take to get from selling second-hand cars to here?' she asked.

'I pestered my feng shui teacher until he promised to teach me everything he knew. And I meditate, which helps on every level.'

Grace glanced at Harry and slyly shook her head. She was intrigued by Max's metamorphosis, but did not believe it had much to do with sitting still with his eyes closed. Grace knew that Max was a chancer, and a charmer, but she followed him and Harry into the bathroom anyway. 'All your relationships will improve,' he was saying, 'once you paint these walls any color in the red ray. Put up a picture of swans, or dolphins—they mate for life. Avoid penguins. Penguins are monogamous, but only for a year.'

Harry was hanging on every word. 'How's my money corner?' he asked as they turned into the kitchen.

'Your waste bin's in it.' Max hauled the bin to a propitious position beneath the breakfast bar.

'It doesn't look great there,' Harry complained.

'That won't bother you once you see money in the bank,' said Max, spreading out the completed feng shui diagram. 'Ticks are positive, crosses negative.'

The map of the flat was annotated with more ticks than crosses, which implied that the energies in Harry's flat, and consequently Harry's life, were better than he—and certainly Grace—had expected.

'Your relationship corner needs the most help,' Max said with the authority of a Chinese master. 'Paint the bathroom as soon as you can, and when you do, have a clear intention of what you want. Use these when you're done.' He handed Harry a purple velvet pouch. 'You need crystals and these are the finest money can buy. The Barratts won't miss a few.'

Harry poured the shining stones into his palm: pink, emerald, purple, and blue. Vibrant colours from deep within the earth. 'Let's paint the bathroom this afternoon,' he said to Grace, turning over the rose quartz.

As soon as Max had gone, Harry propelled Grace to the hardware store as though a brighter future depended on it. He picked out the High Red Ultra Gloss.

'Brave to go for gloss. Are you sure that's a good idea?' Grace asked. Harry was adamant, but hours later applying the paint had left them defeated. The good intentions for the future that Max had told them to keep in mind while they worked were all but forgotten. The depth of the colour somehow left them emotionally drained, while the paint's viscosity had tugged hairs from the brushes and transplanted them onto the walls.

'Emulsion would have been cheaper to buy and quicker to apply,'

Harry said, frustrated. Finally, when the four walls were painted red, Harry moved to the other corners identified on Max's diagram. A raid on Lucy's craft box lifted his spirits. 'How lucky is this,' he said, holding up a strip of cartoon stickers. Dolphins with pink smiling lips jumped in pairs over a breaking wave; Harry stuck one on the wall in the relationship corner. Below, in the bath's corner ledge on either side of Sir John Barratt's rose quartz, he placed two candles. Grace lit them. Suddenly, Harry and Grace seemed mysterious to one another in the dark red light.

It was only four o'clock, but they agreed to share a bath. Perhaps the charade was worth it, thought Grace, while the hot was running and Harry searched for lavender oil to scent the water. The oil eluded him but he discovered instead a condom. He placed it behind the crystal, which ruined the aesthetic but was worth the sacrifice; good sex, they knew, was cement in the kind of relationship they wanted. They lay in the bath, Grace's back to Harry's front, the only sound the dripping tap.

'It's my father's birthday today,' Harry said.

'Did you send a card?'

'No. I should go see him though,' he responded, vaguely. That Harry didn't bother with his father lessened the guilt Grace sometimes felt about neglecting her own.

'Fathers. It's not easy having one,' she said.

'Or being one.'

'I'm glad we've got each other.' Grace rolled onto her tummy. They were face-to-face now, her body half floating on top of his in the warm water. It was good right then, all very good, but when the telephone rang Harry couldn't ignore it. He got up from the bath. It was always like this when he hadn't heard from his daughter for a while. Alone in the water, Grace sank back. A call from Vicky was overdue.

'I'll be over in twenty minutes,' was all Grace heard him say.

Vicky could summon Harry whenever it suited her, as though he were her minion—his response invariably reassured her that he was. 'Have we got Lucy?' Grace said, out of the bath, toweling her body dry.

'Looks like it.'

'You can drive over. I'll come with you if you like,' she said, prompted—perhaps by the feng shui—to present a united front. Grace knew that Harry did not like her to drive him when Lucy was in the car. He'd once confessed the best thing about Vicky was that she'd always thrown him the car keys.

When they were outside Vicky's house on Pembridge Place, Harry called to warn her that he was there—a precautionary tactic to avoid having to go inside, where the risk of a protracted argument was high. This evening, Vicky didn't answer. 'Come on, let's go in together,' he said to Grace. 'I'll keep the in-out short, nothing to worry about.' But Grace always did: just driving past Vicky's road made her anxious. She bit her bottom lip as Harry rang the bell.

To make Harry wait was one of Vicky's tricks, a reminder, if one were needed, of who called the shots. Five minutes later Grace hissed, 'When are you going to stand up to her?'

'She's the mother of my child. It's all the entitlement she needs—'

'To treat you like shit?'

'As long as I see Lucy, that's all that matters.'

Grace held the anger for them both. Her recurring fantasy was to lob a brick through Vicky's window—either the Range Rover's windscreen, or the prized blue-glass windowpane on the first floor of the immaculate house. In her head, Grace would see the brick fly, hear the smash, watch the glass shatter. Picturing herself in police custody was the only thing that stopped her. Such visions evaporated when Vicky opened the door.

'Hi, Ken,' Vicky said under her breath, loud enough for Grace to hear. Lucy had told them that 'the fantastic plastic couple' was Vicky's latest name for them—in the battle between her parents, the child was indeed her mother's free-range missile. Grace was ready to be rude if Vicky so much as whispered Barbie, but Vicky was too shrewd for that. Her dark hair was piled high and she wore a brilliant-coloured caftan that elegantly concealed her weight. Since Harry had moved out, Vicky had piled on the pounds, and her fat had acquired a permanence that would take some shifting. Grace smelled smoke. So that was the delay: they'd caught Vicky with a Marlboro Light. She talked of quitting but Harry said she never would and no longer cared. His concern was for Lucy, who coughed some mornings as though the thirty-a-day habit was hers.

'Dada!' Lucy ran down the stairs.

'In pyjamas already, Loobiloo?' Harry said, lifting her high into the air.

'She didn't feel like getting dressed today,' Vicky explained.

Lucy looked at Grace and made a funny face, as if to acknowledge that she had indeed been petulant. Apart from this quick look, Lucy ignored Grace. Warring parents had made her a minidiplomat and she instinctively knew to conceal her affection for her father's girlfriend until the time was right.

'Daddy, Daddy, Daddy,' she said, skipping around him until he picked her up again. She was skinny, a sparrow. Vicky hovered in the hallway, as if to absorb a little of what Lucy and Harry had. It was love after all, love they all wanted.

'I'm hungry. Mummy won't let me have cheesy pasta,' Lucy said, her too-pink lips to Harry's ear as he rocked her in his arms.

'The homeopath said it's dairy giving her that mouth rash, so no dairy from now on. And I wouldn't mind something toward the doctor.'

Harry carried Lucy upstairs as much to avoid being berated for not paying anything toward her expenses as to get the child dressed and ready. The homeopath had been his idea but Vicky had chosen one on Harley Street; he couldn't afford a tenth of the bill, as they all knew.

Vicky offered Grace a cigarette, fully aware she didn't smoke. 'So you're letting him drive?' she asked.

'He drives the car when he wants,' Grace lied.

'Harry's a good driver, just don't expect him to fill the car with petrol.'

Grace was wary of Vicky's random, negative comments and, over the years, had tried to block them out. But Vicky knew Grace's position better than anyone. Who else would have vibed that the last time Harry had borrowed her Mercedes, he'd returned it empty, so that Grace had been stuck on Bayswater, out of gas, in the middle of rush hour?

'Decorating?' Vicky inquired, casting an eye at Grace's paint-splattered hands. Grace nodded. 'Your place or his?'

'His.'

'That figures. He's good with a paintbrush, I'll say that for him. He should be an odd job man—we'd all be better off. Why don't you come in, have a drink?' A conversation with Vicky was a minefield, and the last thing Grace needed when she was trying to maintain faith in Harry. What's more, she had learned that Vicky's gracious moods rarely lasted from one minute to the next.

'We just had a cup of tea, thanks,' Grace said.

'Don't mind if I shut the door then,' Vicky said, and promptly did so, leaving Grace on the door mat.

Within minutes the door opened again, in time for Grace to witness the group hug, Lucy squeezed between her parents, willing to be squashed to death she wanted them back together so much. Harry explained this as Lucy's need to believe in her parents' love, no matter how many years she might have watched them ripping each other apart. 'Our happy family happened once upon a time, and Lucy wants it back,' he had memorably explained.

In the studio, Harry switched on the electric heater. When Lucy was over he kept the place warm, to hell with the expense. 'Next time you're here, Loobiloo, the studio will be empty. I'm getting rid of the furniture.'

'What about the hummingbirds?'

The birds engraved on the headboard were characters in Lucy's bedtime stories. Hummingbirds fly free of time, Harry had told her. They carried hopes and dreams for love and happiness, and they carried away Lucy's nightmares, too. 'Dada, we need the birds,' Lucy said from the bed, tracing the carvings with her tiny hands.

'Don't worry, sweetheart, Mr. French will look after the birds.'

'But who will look after us?'

'We'll all look after each other,' Harry said, winking at Grace and gathering his daughter in his arms. 'Now how about a hot chocolate?' he said, carrying her into the kitchen for the ritual that started all their winter days. While he prepared the drink—this time with soy milk but with twice as much sugar in the hope she couldn't tell—Lucy drew on the blackboard Harry had put up on the kitchen wall. With Lucy there, he never talked about having a cigarette. Lucy filled him up, he said. Later, they pulled the desk away from the wall to fit the chairs around, and in the electric heater's sorry heat ate supper, or in Lucy's case didn't. The Alternative Cheesy Pasta, with vegan cheese and soy milk, didn't go down well. She filled up on toast made with lashings of butter and honey, sitting on Grace's lap to eat it. Grace was always staggered by the child's ability to switch in and out of modes: one minute loving her mother, the next snuggling up to her as though her mother didn't exist.

When it was bedtime, Lucy stood on the bed as Harry helped undress her. 'Miss you, Loo,' Harry said, carefully easing the pullover over her head. From woolly darkness a small voice echoed, 'miss you, too.' Smoothing the static out of her flyaway hair, he kissed her face. 'You're the best girl in the whole wide world. I love you.'

Grace gathered the pyjamas she'd put to warm on the heater, then kissed Lucy good night before clearing the table. It hurt sometimes, but Grace understood that Harry cherished the bedtime ritual and didn't want to share it. He didn't see his daughter enough as it was and Grace was not invited to step into what he chose to see as his territory.

When Lucy was in bed, Harry stretched out beside his daughter, stroking her forehead as he read the last pages of *Matilda*. Grace turned to the washing up, determined to call her builders the next day: this three-in-a-bed had gone on too long. Lucy soon would be six: time for her own room. What's more, Grace wanted privacy with Harry come the night. Harry didn't see it that way: he may have lived half the time at Grace's, but when he had his daughter, he liked to stay at the studio. The little house, as Lucy called it, was where she had always come to be with him. Grace understood the nostalgic connection, but it didn't make sense for the three of them to cram in together while her big house languished, empty, five minutes' drive away.

Chapter Three

URDHAVA DHANURASANA—back bend

Urdhava means upward, dhanu means bow. This invigorating pose replicates the movement of a bow as it arcs when pulled by the bowstring. With the soles of the feet and palms of the hands set firmly on the floor, the spine arches up, flying free as a bow. This pose benefits the digestive, respiratory, cardiovascular, and glandular systems. It influences hormonal secretions and can relieve gynecologic disorders. This inverted pose places the whole body and nervous system in an abnormal position. It is difficult to raise the body up if the nervous system is not ready. While holding the pose, if the practitioner loses a sense of position in space, or proprioception, strength is also lost.

Grace had allowed herself to be seduced by Harry's conviction that much would change after the feng shui consultation. They were both disappointed when, some weeks later, apparently nothing had. 'I suppose there's only so much feng shui can do,' Grace commented. 'At some point we'll have to change more than your colour scheme.'

'Like what?'

A long list occurred to her, but to steer clear of trouble, she said instead, 'We need to go back to Swami D's. We haven't been for ages.'

'At the gym, yoga classes are free,' Harry countered.

'Don't confuse Swami D's with stretching in a mirrored room that smells of stale sweat,' she said, though no longer surprised that Harry equated her teacher's wisdom and experience with the banalities of the twenty-five-year-old erstwhile aerobics instructor who taught yoga at his revered gym. Harry had been given a free membership by its new manager, a friend from his acting days, and he was spending more time there. Grace didn't blame him. That she paid for his yoga classes and suppers at Swami D's made him feel wretched, which defeated the point of going.

'Harry, so many of our problems come down to the fact that you aren't earning anything. I think, sweetheart, you've got to accept that it's time for you to get a job,' she encouraged.

'Working for the minimum wage is a waste of time. I'm better off signing on, getting the rent paid here,' he said.

'Why don't you drive a minicab and study to be a yoga teacher?'

'I thought you were the one who wanted to be a yoga teacher, once you stop dealing drugs.'

'Criticize my job when you've got one of your own,' Grace said.

'Grace, I can't take this pressure anymore.'

'*You* can't take it?' She sounded like an exasperated mother.

'I'm going.'

'Going?' Her voice betrayed her.

'Going out.'

'Where?'

'The gym,' he said.

Grace had expected him to say the minicab office, and as she watched him walk out it was as though an invisible cord that connected her to him was cut and pinged back into her belly.

When Harry returned to Grace's later that night, he was uplifted. He fished inside a Boots carrier bag and produced a bottle of Chanel, which he gave to Grace with a kiss. 'Things are going to change. They *are* changing,' he said, then went into the bathroom and shaved his head.

In a last-ditch attempt to please the casting directors, Harry had been growing his hair. Grace found the buzz of hair clippers more tantalizing than the sound of his daily blow-dry. The short hair transformed him. It was enough, anyway, to persuade Grace to believe him when he said, 'I'm tired of castings and counting on my looks. From now on I want to concentrate on designing yoga clothes. And you're right. I should be a yoga teacher.'

Harry pulled Grace to him, but deep inside she held back. For a reason she could not rationalize his plan left her deflated, even alarmed: to be a yoga teacher was *her* dream and she feared he would rob her of it.

Harry called Grace late Friday morning. He was sorry, he said, but Vicky's plans had changed at the last minute and he was staying the night with Lucy.

'Babysitting?' Grace asked, upset but not unaccustomed.

'I can't babysit my own daughter,' he said, but Grace knew that's what it felt like and how Vicky intended it to feel.

Grace's night, home alone, turned out to be a pleasure. She cooked, and opened a bottle of wine without the guilt that accompanied every glass she'd ever had in Harry's sober presence. Beside the log fire, listening to *Late Night Junction* on the radio, she relished the bliss of solitude when it isn't all there is.

On Saturday afternoon (Harry had called three hours later than he said he would) they agreed to meet on Queensway, that thoroughfare of Chinese restaurants and raunchy underwear shops between Westbourne Grove and Hyde Park. From a distance, Harry watched Grace walk toward him, then turned back to his newspaper. Sports—the football in particular—was his section. His team had floundered in the league most of his adult life but was now top of the Premiership and winning games in Europe. Finally the Blues were where they deserved to be. Chelsea's success, Harry confessed, took some getting used to. Absorbed in the day's prematch commentary, he leaned against the wall, one leg bent, a foot pressed against the brick as he read. When he looked up again, Grace was right beside him, unsure that she would ever get used to his short-short hair. He looked sheepish, a shorn sheep she thought.

His unshaven face gruffly scraped her cheek but she liked the way he kissed her full on the mouth. He folded the newspaper and stuffed it into the back pocket of his jeans. 'Sorry about last night, darling,' he said, as they walked down Queensway. Darling? Grace softened. She could still want to be his darling.

'I was thinking we'd get a falafel,' Harry said.

Grace was starving. Waiting for Harry to call, anticipating breakfast together, and then lunch, she had missed both. 'What about the Four Seasons?' she said, peering beneath the row of roast ducks skewered in the window of the Chinese restaurant. She wanted to sit down and eat hot food somewhere warm. Before Harry had detoxified, the Four Seasons had been his favourite. 'Half a duck for £5.50 has to be a bargain,' she said, reading the gilt-framed menu outside the door. Instinct told her the dark meat would satisfy; the queue of Chinese people winding its way onto the street was all the confirmation she needed.

'There's a higher price to pay. Duck that cheap can't be organic. Let's stick with falafel.'

The Lebanese takeaway was one of the few places Harry could afford and the first place he had ever taken her. They walked to it, past tourist shops selling British flags, plastic police helmets, and postcards—pert breasts painted with dog faces, nipples for noses, alongside dead members of the Royal Family smiling in perpetuity beneath well-made hats.

'I used to think the Princess of Wales had it all,' Harry said. 'But in the end she was just another desperate parent making all the wrong moves.'

'Not that that should be any consolation,' Grace said, but supposed it was.

The falafel was as good as any food anywhere, even sitting on the stone step of a scaffold-clad building, the cold creeping into their bones. Grace had needed to eat: her humour improved as the fried chickpeas and crisp cabbage settled in her belly. There was tahini sauce in the corner of her mouth. Harry leaned forward to wipe it away. Things were looking up.

'You know, Harry, last night I decided I'm going to give Suprafarma my notice,' she said.

'That's good,' he said, without enthusiasm.

'I hear a *but* . . .'

'The but is money.'

'I'll make money as a yoga teacher,' she countered, aware that she was now on the defensive.

'But when, and how much? There'll be no buying what you like when you like.' He bit into his falafel and stared ahead, chewing. 'I know how hard it is to get a plan off the ground. Look at me.'

'You won't be my role model,' she said, resenting his lack of support. Her approach would be pragmatic, productive. She would not waste time waiting, as Harry had done and continued to do. Resisting the temptation to fall into a childish squabble, she screwed the rest of her food into the tinfoil wrap and aimed at the bin. The silver ball hit the metal edge and fell in.

'That means something good is going to happen,' Harry said, still sitting on the stone step.

She looked up at him. 'I'm about to train to be a yoga teacher and that sounds good to me.' She turned toward Hyde Park. Harry stepped up casually beside her, subduing the urgency she could feel in him. 'What brought this on?' he asked as they crossed Bayswater Road.

'To be a yoga teacher is the only thing I know for sure that I want.'

Harry caught the implication. They walked to the park in silence, darkness falling. 'I missed you last night,' he said, his hand moving inside Grace's coat and under her T-shirt.

'It was good for us to have time apart.'

'Didn't you miss me?'

'Not really.' It was true she hadn't, but accepting his hand on the small of her back negated the subtle hint that she was better off without him.

Harry loved Grace's bottom in her blue jeans; his hand edged lower. 'Let's go to Swami D's if you want, or a movie, then have an Indian at that restaurant behind The Gate. I'll pay,' Harry said, definitive.

Grace looked sideways. Harry never suggested going out, let alone paying, and his new attitude drew her to him. Perhaps she had been right to have faith in him. And then there was the familiarity of skin to skin. 'I'd love to go out this evening,' she said.

'I've been meaning to give you this.' He pressed four fresh pink fifties into Grace's hand. They felt nice.

'Are you sure?' she frowned.

'It's about time I put in the footwork, pay my way.'

'Where did you get it?'

'That tree they talk about.'

'No really, how come?'

'After our minifight the other day, I went to the gym and got back late, remember?' Grace remembered. 'I was with Nick and Joe. I'd sent them some designs, which they liked, but I've waited until our deal was signed and sealed before telling you. They've asked me to work part-time, strange hours, but it's a start.'

Grace smiled widely and right then everything was all right. At the tinkling tone, the sound of a message landing, she checked her pockets. 'My phone?'

'It's mine,' Harry said, consulting the latest BlackBerry.

'Things really are looking up. When did you get that?'

'Vicky. Last night,' he said, reading his e-mail. Grace was losing the habit of needing to know what Vicky was up to—a freedom she had worked hard to achieve. 'Everything okay?' she asked, casually.

'Everything's cool,' he answered, switching the device off, sliding it away.

'That's a first. No interruptions *and* a date.' She kissed his cheek, pressed up close, then kissed him again.

The air was bitter cold. Harry wrapped his arm around her and pulled her to his side. 'I like the park best like this, nothing going on,' he said, his nature to prefer trees without leaves, everything still.

'You're a minimalist right through,' she said, keeping it to herself that she preferred spring's rising, summer's heat, anything but this melancholy time that reminded her of death. Grace walked ahead of Harry, then turned in his path. He stepped up to hold her and kissed her forehead, which was hot.

'This is enough, isn't it?' she said, pulling back to see him better.

'What?'

'This love.'

He nodded and Grace was satisfied. She could overcome the demands of inconsistent fatherhood. She could take Harry for himself, for herself. They would make the future work. Later, in the darkness of her bed, she whispered close to his mouth and beautiful face I love you, and he took her with a passion that was rare. Lying together, the back of her body curled into the front of his, his arm around her, Grace couldn't imagine being without this intimacy.

'Do the yoga training with me,' she said.

'What, come away with you?' Harry's voice lifted, as though he was glad and would come.

'It might be good for us. I can pay.'

He reached to kiss her, and in the dark his mouth quickly found hers. It felt right.

'So you'll come with me?' she asked.

'When are you going?'

'As soon as I find a good school.'

'It's Lucy's birthday next month. I said I'd go.'

'Go where?' The edge was in her voice first.

'Ibiza.'

'To stay with Vicky?'

Harry rolled onto his back and folded his arms.

'Are you really going to stay at Vicky's?' Grace asked.

'With my daughter's mother, where the party is. She invited me in front of Lucy. I couldn't say no.'

'If you go as a family Lucy will be confused. We all will.'

'I'm going because I want to be a good father. I didn't think it would make me a bad boyfriend.'

They fell asleep, a wide space between them in the bed. In the morning the mood was brittle, the quietness between them convenient but uncomfortable and a consequence of all they had left unsaid.

But gossamer threads of hope and expectation bound Grace to Harry tighter than she knew. Lucy was such a pleasure and Vicky was in an unexpectedly cooperative phase. Harry's sporadic work for Nick and Joe was certainly better than none at all, and they paid him cash, so he no longer called on Grace to be the lender of last resort. She didn't mind him driving her car to work in the evening; since he had a job, he always returned the tank full. Who said men can't change? Grace continued her daytime discipline convincing psychiatrists that the paper-thin difference between Procent and rival antidepressants was door-wedge wide in Procent's favour. Driving out of the Chelsea and Westminster hospital car park one time, she had glimpsed Dr. James crossing the Fulham Road. Some part of her felt relieved that he was still in the system they had both talked of leaving. She fantasized for a second about contriving to meet him, but for what? He had placed an order for Procent and there was no reason for her to be in contact for a while.

Most weekends, Grace still trawled the web searching for the perfect yoga training but sensed that Harry could make it to the hallowed ground of yoga teaching before her. His spare time (while he had less of it than he used to, he still had plenty) was spent in practice: every morning, even on Sundays, he put on his Ashtanga Vinyasa DVD, and in front of a full-length mirror, observed his poses. Curled up in the warmth of Harry's bed, Grace heard the DVD slide in. 'You're so dedicated,' she said, eyes closed.

'I can be,' he said.

'Don't forget your Ujjayi breathing,' she teased. Grace decried the American Ashtanga star's approach but could not deny its effect on Harry. In a few weeks, not only had the contours of his body changed, but so had his spirits. The pre-Ashtanga Harry had called nine o'clock 'early doors.' Now he was up before the sun, naturally high.

The studio was cold, but Grace propped herself up against the pillows to watch her favourite sequence. She was amused by Harry huffing and puffing through the dynamic moves in his black Calvin Kleins, which were not so unlike the form hugging shorts worn by the muscle-loaded yoga instructor, but when it came to the splits, he was defeated. Rare among men, the DVD yogi had elastic hamstrings and in a flamboyant interpretation of the splits he balanced on straight, iron-strong legs between two trucks as they took off across the hard, flat sand of an exotic beach. 'Let me know when you get to this bit,' Grace chuckled.

Harry switched off the DVD. 'Instead of mocking, why don't you help?'

'Bring on the trucks,' she said. Laughter played across her face.

'The splits are impossible with hamstrings like mine, but I'm close to Urdhva Dhanurasana.' Harry hadn't expected the Sanskrit to roll off his tongue quite so smoothly.

Grace smiled. 'Saying *Urdhva Dhanurasana* is harder than doing it.'

'Then show me,' he said, pulling the bedclothes from her.

She got up from the mattress. Harry was already on his back, still and beautiful as a painting. She looked down at him, his glacial eyes turned dark, and Grace was mesmerized. Perhaps the back bend was a ruse to get her to touch him, but when she did, Harry turned his face to the ceiling and closed his eyes. She had a yoga student on her hands, not a lover.

Grace stood over Harry, her feet on either side of his head. 'Put your hands on my feet,' she instructed, her voice flat to conceal her desire to kiss him. He pressed tentatively. 'Press harder,' she said.

'I don't want to hurt you.'

'You can't.' Grace leaned forward with her hands on his quadriceps, which he tightened to show their strength and shape.

'Stop that,' she said, slapping his legs. 'The muscles need to be long, not tensed up.'

Harry sneaked a look at the circle their bodies made: his head between Grace's feet, her hands on his thighs, her breasts and belly swooping above him. She moved her hands to support his shoulders. 'Now lift your pelvis,' she said in the same flat voice. As he did so, she lifted his shoulders and Harry's back rose, table flat. His spine from pubic bone to collarbone was rigid as armor.

'My first back bend!' he said, straining to speak. 'Let go. See if I can stay up.'

Tactfully declining to point out that there was no bend in his back, Grace withdrew her hands. Harry's face turned red from effort, the veins bulged blue on his neck, but his back was off the floor and that's what mattered to him. She helped him to land softly back on the mat.

He waited, quiet. 'Nobody's ever touched me like that before,' he said. 'Like what?'

'As though they wanted nothing from me,' he said, his raised eyebrows threading lines across his forehead. Grace thought he might reach out and show her what it was like to receive that kind of touch, but he rolled away to grab the fat yoga book by the bed.

Yoga in the 21st Century was a recent addition to the yoga canon, edited by a fashion-director friend of Vicky's. At £45, it was Harry's most significant investment in his yoga future and he consulted it often.

'What do you think of this?' he asked, opening the book at a marked photograph of a girl sitting in lotus.

'Her knees are too far from the floor,' Grace observed.

'Not the pose, her top. What do you think?'

'It's transparent.'

'But cute. I'm working on the idea for Nick and Joe.'

Grace snatched the book. 'Rumi quotes in grey italics don't make sense scrawled across pictures of models trying to do yoga. This book is pretentious. Chuck it.' They tussled on the bed, apparently for the book, which Grace held to her body like a shield. Harry prized it from her, but let it fall to the floor and, cupping her face in his hands, put his mouth on hers. They stayed like that, focused in fingertips and lips, aware of every breath and touch, until her mouth opened for his kiss and right through her heart she longed for him. Which is when the doorbell rang.

Harry went to the window. 'Vicky,' he said.

'How could she know we'd be here?'

That Vicky could intuit his whereabouts was no surprise to Harry. She'd been at it for years. 'Best get dressed,' he said, and headed for the stairs.

Vicky had parked the Range Rover on the pavement and left the engine running. 'Have a lovely time with Daddy and don't forget to brush your teeth,' she said, kissing her daughter, then rushing back to the car.

'What's going on?' Harry called, tying his cotton robe against the windy morning.

'Tokyo. Got the call last night. I'll be in touch,' Vicky called back.

She U-turned on Westbourne Grove, her wave small and frantic as though she were rubbing him out. To save his daughter from confusion Harry played along, carrying her up the steep stairs while she chanted, 'I'm staying at the little house, I'm staying at the little house.'

'How fantastic is that,' he said. 'Did Mummy say for how long?'

'As long as I like.'

Harry pushed the door open with his foot, feeling the grit stick to his soles, and set Lucy down. He pulled her out of her coat and went back for her suitcase. When Grace emerged from the bathroom, dressed and ready for whatever surprise Vicky had in store, the bulging pink suitcase told her all she needed to know. This was no sleepover. Grace touched the tip of Lucy's chin and said hello. A warmer gesture would, she knew, make Harry nervous, but Lucy smiled to see her. Everyone softened a little.

'Let's go to Lucky Seven,' Harry said, glancing at Grace, even though it was Lucy's approval he sought. The breakfast special at Lucky Seven, Notting Hill's all-American diner, was Harry's affordable treat and Lucy's favourite place to eat.

Harry shook Lucy back into her fake-leopard-skin coat, fumbling with buttons too tiny for his fingers. Thin wool tights, a purple leather mini-skirt, and black boots with two-inch heels: Lucy's outfit didn't make sense on a five-year-old. Loobiloo clumped down the stairs, Harry and Grace behind her. 'She looks like Jodie Foster in *Taxi Driver*. Where does Vicky get her clothes?' Harry said in a low voice.

For harmony's sake Grace resisted sharing her theory that Vicky, too fat for fashion, dressed vicariously through her daughter.

At Lucky Seven, Lucy settled into a red booth by the window, excited to be their first and only customers. 'Not enough room,' she giggled. 'Grace, sit over there.' She pointed to the table opposite. Grace bit the inside of her cheek. Crazy how a five-year-old could hurt.

A young waitress came over, tying her apron, not ready for early risers. 'Cheese toasty,' Lucy said, brightly.

'One cheese toasty,' Harry said, overruling the dairy ban. 'And what would you like, darling?'

'I'll have pancakes,' said Grace.

'Blueberry pancakes for two,' Harry said. That he was the one to order, and pay, was still a novelty that Grace enjoyed.

'Maple syrup with that?' said the waitress.

'Yes,' Grace and Harry said together.

'I don't know why I ask. Everybody has maple syrup,' the waitress said, walking off.

They sat in complicated silence, waiting for the food. It was often like this at the beginning when Lucy came over. The more Lucy loved Grace the more guilt she felt for betraying her mother, and it took a while for them to fall in with each other. A game helped.

'I spy with my little eye something beginning with *p*,' Grace said.

'PT Cruiser!' said Lucy, pointing to the car parked outside.

'I spy something.' She clapped her hands to her face, shaking her head for missing the *i*-rhyme and began again: 'I spy with my little eye, Dada and Grace, something beginning with . . .'

The game went on, the girl setting Grace's name beside her father's and seeming to like the sound of that.

'Toasty?' asked the waitress, back at the table balancing three white plates.

'That's a big sandwich,' Grace said, passing it to Lucy.

'That's a hell of a sandwich,' Harry said.

'The cheese isn't melted,' Lucy whined.

'You won't know till you take a bite,' said Harry, tucking into his pancakes. Grace reached across and sliced Lucy's massive slab of bread in half. The child smiled. Lucy's devotion to her mother was automatic, and she loved her father as a five-year-old should, but in the canny way of a child, she trusted Grace to see what she needed. The big promises her parents made were seldom delivered, but in the two years she'd known her, Grace had never broken a promise. The girl had learned to love her for it.

Lucy wiped her finger through the pale yellow goo oozing onto her plate and, dangling a thread of cheese above her mouth said, 'Look, Grace, a worm,' then bit down on the congealed cheese.

Harry didn't mind Lucy having fun with her food as long as she ate it, and he seemed content as he poured more maple syrup over his pancakes. 'Thanks for going along with the change of plan,' he said.

Grace was gripped with a desire for them all to be happy and she believed they could be. Lucy's unexpected appearance hadn't ruined anything, nor could it: Grace loved the girl. Perhaps it was a maple syrup sugar rush, but Harry was equally optimistic. 'You're wonderful,' he said to Grace, then turned to make a fuss over Lucy, wiping her buttery mouth, covering and uncovering her eyes with his paper napkin.

With Vicky away, life was less complicated. Grace and Harry knew where they stood; they had Lucy and the days unfolded peacefully around the girl. Harry's work, such as it was, was going well, and brought the kind of changes Grace had given up hoping for. The little gifts bestowed by a lover upon the beloved were finally part of Harry's realm, and he was more the man, from opening doors for her to how he made love. If it's true that manners maketh man, Harry having money made his manners possible.

With Lucy with them, they got by for a few days in the studio, but had moved into Grace's house by the weekend. Harry agreed that it was time for Lucy to settle in there, and it also didn't seem fair to leave Grace with Lucy in his studio on the evenings he worked for Nick and Joe.

Then, one evening Grace returned from work to find Harry sitting on her garden step, head in hands. Harry explained, through tears, that he'd been on time for the school pickup but Vicky had beaten him to it; the form teacher had released Lucy when her mother appeared half an hour before the end of class to take her home.

The house without Lucy was quiet, organized. The weekends once again belonged to Harry and Grace. Grace tried to believe she was glad for the freedom, but with Lucy gone so had her joy.

Chapter Four

MAYURASANA—peacock pose

Mayura means a peacock. Just as a peacock can kill and digest a snake without being affected by the poison, this asana helps the practitioner to metabolize toxins in the body. Those who master this pose are said to be able to digest even deadly poisons. Before attempting this pose, purify the system by eliminating all milk products, meats, fats, spices, and foods that are difficult to digest. Eat fruit, vegetables, rice, rye bread, and other simple foods. Within weeks the whole system will be purified and the practice of mayurasana can commence. Perform at the end of the asana series. Mayurasana speeds up the circulation and increases the toxins in the body as part of the purification process, so never practice before doing inverted poses as it may direct toxins to the brain. The female musculature may make this pose difficult, given that its performance is greatly enhanced by a flat chest and a strong abdomen. It is easy to fall forward from the final position and crush one's nose on the floor.

Swami D once told Grace that real change happens only one step from where we are, but there were days, rare days he'd called them, when we can leap forward, and ignore one step at a time. Grace was due such a day and it started much like any other—at home, eating breakfast, checking e-mails. Among them was a government document circulated to all

Suprafarma employees that on any other day she would have skimmed, then deleted. Most government enquiries into the pharmaceutical industry were no more than a wrist-slapping exercise that provided politically correct sound bites seldom backed up by plausible suggestions for reform. Grace had long believed such reports were a waste of time, but for no apparent reason she pressed print and proceeded to read it.

No surprise to discover that pharmaceutical companies were held responsible for increasing the number of patients classified as ill and requiring treatment. Undeterred that the usual pharma suspects were blamed for acting like disease mongers, she read on. The report's call for an independent body to oversee pharmaceutical trials was hardly new: everybody in the business understood the inbuilt flaw of a regulatory system paid for by those it regulated, just as they understood an independent party paying for trials was a utopian ideal. The claim that people were relying too much on pills was the kind of banal generalization Grace had come to expect from the Regulatory Agency. Drug companies existed for patients, and profits were a consequence of their effectiveness—a required consequence, given the £9 million spent every day in the United Kingdom on research and development. Such justifications ran in Grace's blood.

Sending the report through the shredder would have been her standard response but one sentence stopped her: 'Unhappiness is part of the spectrum of human experience, not a medical condition.' Grace shoved the report, with the rest of the day's mail, into her briefcase and went to the coffee shop on St. Helen's Gardens. She sat outside under the gas heater to drink a cup of coffee. At least an article in that month's *Rowing Magazine* (a subscription of Ted's she still hadn't canceled) showed that up to three hundred milligrams of caffeine a day was good for you: it increased performance by 3 percent, reduced the risk of liver cancer, *and* burned fat. She picked up the government report and read on. 'Side effects, including death, have revealed the shortcomings of the Medicines and Healthcare Products Regulatory Agency.' Death a side effect? Grace thought of Ted . . . death was hardly a side effect.

Back at her desk Grace canceled the day's appointments and went online. 'Yoga training' was bookmarked on her laptop and 8,710,000 sites came up. Grace had faith that she would find the training that suited her among the millions and millions of Web sites. She still wasn't resigned to attending the Sivananda yoga centre in Putney—a town of uninspiring convenience on the Thames. If the yoga teacher's training was to start her new life, she wanted it to be more than a commute away. She refined her search. 'Yoga training in India' produced three million sites, the first for Raja Yoga, the yoga of kings. The ashram in Jaipur promised enlightenment and eventual immortality for those who completed the advanced course—a bargain at £2,000. The claims of the next site were less extravagant: an OM sign and flickering candle encircled an old yogi sitting in lotus, as bad translations from the *Bhagavad Gita* faded in and out. Only one of the Indian Web sites that Grace visited featured a woman who wore a sari, lying on her tummy in a cobra pose that looked more likely to induce neck pain than awaken kundalini Shakti. Swami D had already warned Grace that his old ashram was not what it used to be. All the residents from his day were dead or gone—besides, the next teacher-training course was in monsoon season. Grace wasn't going to pay £4,000 to be indoctrinated into Hinduism in pouring rain.

The Eastern Web sites were endearing and mostly genuine in their attempts to appeal to the West but where, Grace wanted to know, were the yoga girls of India? Five thousand years on, India was not the appealing home of hatha. Going West seemed more honest. Grace Googled 'Yoga training in America.' As bad as the Indian sites were with their soft-bodied yogis and naive attempts to seduce with Eastern wisdom, the American Web sites were worse, packed with hard bodies stripped of fat and pumped with ambition. There was steamy Bikram Yoga, Naked Yoga, Laugh Out Loud Yoga, and Fitness in America Yoga. There was Yoga for People who Hurt, in Sacramento; Sacred OM Yoga, in Wichita; a two-year tantric training in New Mexico; and a weekend course in Vermont that guaranteed a teacher's certificate in exchange for $1,500.

Grace didn't want to be a vegetarian Hindu with Sivananda, a Bikram franchise holder, a Jivamukti Ashtanga queen, or an aligned-to-dogma Iyengar devotee. She simply wanted to be a good yoga teacher. She scrolled farther down the list of Web sites and stopped at the Bodhi Tree Yoga

Foundation. The school paid homage to the East but, set in Southern California on land sacred to the Chumash people, its ethos was undeniably Western. Claims for nonsectarian teaching and gourmet vegetarian food sounded promising. That it was also run by a good-looking couple called Garuda and Rita Gold who had been married and practicing yoga together for over twenty-five years, was all the incentive Grace needed.

She called California, where it was six in the morning, and was clearing her throat to leave a message when a soft voice answered. 'You're lucky to catch me. I don't usually answer the phone this early.' The appropriately named Miss Messenger passed on the good news that there were places in the next training that started in two weeks. Grace filled in the Web site application form and paid for the course with her credit card. Then she called her boss.

'I'm resigning.'

'Okay, very funny.'

'Seriously. I'm resigning.'

'When?'

'Right now.'

'Why?'

'I want to train to be a yoga teacher—'

He cut her off with a sharp laugh. 'If you think you can walk away from Suprafarma that easily, you don't know yourself. A yoga teacher? Grace, come off it.' In the silence that followed, he relented. 'Do the bloody training, then come back. I'll hold your job.'

Grace hesitated, tempted.

'Meet me for dinner,' he said.

'I can't,' she lied.

'Lunch tomorrow, then, at the Caprice. We'll renegotiate your contract.'

It was one of her favourite lunchtime restaurants and she was actually fond of her boss. 'Sorry. I can't,' she said quickly, before she changed her mind.

'Grace, you're not helping me here.'

'I know. My mind is made up.'

'Then you'd better drop off the car and our database this afternoon. Keep the promotional crap.'

'I'll be there in an hour.'

'Grace, I still expect you to come to your senses.' He put the phone down.

Grace's hands shook as she cleared her desk and filled a black trash bag with Suprafarma's promotional products: spotlight pens, latex gloves, notebooks, and clipboards—plastic promotions, all stamped with Suprafarma's name and swirling logo. She drove to the Suprafarma head office in Bracknell, a concrete town of roundabouts and office blocks less than an hour from London. She was too angry to care about the indignity of heaving her bin bag of products up the stairs to the glass doors. It would be a pleasure to deposit it on her boss's desk. She swiped her entry pass. The door stayed shut. She was already part of Suprafarma history. Furious at being so instantly cut out, she called her boss—her ex-boss, she reflected. His robotic assistant intercepted the call. He was busy, she said.

'When will he be free?'

'I really can't say.'

Grace called a minicab. When the car arrived she left the black bin bag and the car keys on the steps of Suprafarma's headquarters. A sad legacy after sixteen years. As she headed back to London, the meter registering pounds as fast as miles, the driver asked if the fare was on account. 'Those days are over,' she said, then checked her purse. She hoped she had enough cash. Sitting in traffic on the flyover, she regretted impulsivity. Her boss was right. She should have taken a month off to do the training, then returned to the work she knew. Seeking reassurance, she called Harry. There was no reply.

For the first time in years Grace arrived home early from work. She walked into her empty house and stood in the hall. No car keys to throw down, no suitcase to empty. Nothing to do unless she chose. So this was freedom. Halfway up the stairs she froze. Somebody was in her bedroom. When she heard the shower, terror subsided. It had to be Harry. She would creep into the bedroom and surprise him. Excellent: nothing to do apart from loving her man on a Wednesday afternoon.

On her bed, their bed, she dropped her coat and was unbuttoning her shirt when she noticed Harry's clothes on the floor. The Maharishi combat trousers were new and had to have cost £500. She picked them up. The back pocket bulged with notes. Grace flicked the folded fifties and gave up counting at one thousand. Surely Nick and Joe weren't paying him this much? She dug into the other pocket and found a business card: Harry Wood, it read in copperplate script. His mobile number was engraved below. On the other side another number was scrawled in pencil, and not by him. Grace felt sick. Harry was singing in the shower. She fished his BlackBerry out of a pocket and went to the landing to dial the number. It was registered in his call log to Tricksy.

An American woman answered, and cut right in. 'Told you you'd be addicted.'

Grace listened, waited.

'What's up, baby?' It was the voice of an older woman, with an East Coast money-coated voice, who called Harry baby.

'Who are you?' Grace asked.

'The one who got him to shave his head,' said the voice, before hanging up.

When Grace walked into the bedroom, Harry had a white towel wrapped at his waist and was rubbing his head with a hand towel, Ted's blue initials jiggling at the corner.

'Who's Tricksy?' she asked.

Harry looked up, startled. 'You're back early? Everything all right?' His eyes were blue innocence even as his face reddened.

'Did Tricksy give you this?' Grace held the money out in front of him. As he reached for it, she tossed it in the air. Fifties floated to the floor as she struck him across the face. Harry did not react. 'It's not what you think,' is all he said.

Grace struck him flat and hard again, and only when she tore at his bare chest did he grab her wrists and hold her firm. He held her down on the bed but still she kicked at him, managing to land her knee on his back. He winced. 'Come on, Grace. Stop. You're acting like a jealous kid.'

'Who's Tricksy?'

'She's interested in my designs for yoga clothes.'

'Harry, don't lie to me.'

'Grace, grow up. These meetings are part of business.'

'I've been to business meetings, and I never walked out of one with £1,000 in cash in my back pocket.'

'There are backhanders in your business, too, you'd better believe it.'

'So is that what this money is?'

'The money is a deposit, a down payment. Tricksy believes in me.'

Grace let her limbs relax, all the fighting gone from her. Harry released his grip, pulled on his trousers, then looked at her across the room. 'Sweetheart,' he said, approaching slowly.

'Don't touch me. Get away.' She cowered at the top of the bed like a dog in fear of being whipped. He must not touch her.

'Grace. You're overreacting. Tricksy works in fashion. She wants to buy the yoga clothes, but until we've signed and sealed the deal, I've got to keep it secret.' He breathed easily but Grace could not believe him. 'Don't look at me like that,' he said, sitting on the bed, elbows on his knees. 'It's nothing sinister, Grace. I had lunch with her today, that's all.'

'Where?'

'Nobu.'

'For which she paid you a thousand pounds?'

'For the designs. It's just the start. I can make real money doing this. Grace, we're going to be all right.' He reached out to her. She looked at his extended hand.

'Harry, you're an escort, aren't you?' Only when she spoke was she aware of the certainty she felt. It was hardly a question. Harry stood abruptly, disgusted. She watched him buckle what looked like a new belt, still bare-chested, showing sculpted arms and strong shoulders, but Grace saw no beauty. 'Harry, admit you're an escort.' The assertion was assured, clinical.

'No, Grace, I am not an escort. But you don't trust me, so what's the point?' Bending to pull on his boots, he stuffed a few notes in his pocket. Tying his bootlace, down on one knee, Harry looked up at her. For a moment, and even in this most contrary circumstance, Grace thought he was about to propose. Instead he said, 'How could you think that I'd sleep with an old woman for money—or any woman, come to that?' He was calm, master of himself. If Grace hadn't heard Tricksy's voice, she would have believed him. Harry tied his other boot, secretively gathering extra notes. The money was his (however he'd earned it), but Grace felt that he was stealing from her. Standing up, Harry was defiant. 'You know, it's funny. I was suspecting you,' he said.

Grace picked up her coat and stuffed her yoga clothes into her bag. 'I'm going now. Please take everything that belongs to you and be gone by the time I get back.' Her manner and words were stilted, as though she spoke to a stranger. She was on the stairs when he replied.

'The way you've been lately, wrapped up in your thoughts, cut off. I suspected you had another man in your sights.'

'Harry, you were the man,' she said, which ended their conversation, and everything.

On Ladbroke Grove, Grace waited for a bus. Swami D's was the only place she could face. In the studio, the class had started; she fetched a blanket and lay on a mat in the far corner. She was in the room where she had met Harry, all willingness to believe in love, and in him, spent. Even one asana would destroy her composure, so she covered her body with the thick wool blanket, and drew it up over her face. She lay still and heard Tricksy say, 'Told you you'd be addicted.' Addicted to Tricksy, addicted to sleeping with her. It's the only thing she could have meant. Grace remembered she and Harry had made love that weekend. His body on her and in her, in her bed, the window open, Sunday morning. Three days before. But Grace was convinced that Harry had slept with Tricksy that afternoon for £1,000, showering off his shame as she'd come up the stairs. In that moment, Grace hated Harry, hated herself for loving him, hated him for deceiving her. Swami D's calming invocations ('gently roll onto your side, extend your right leg, and open your arms to the universe') taunted her, his equanimity accentuated her turmoil and hurt. She didn't want to open her arms to anything, let alone the universe. It was pointless to wait until the end of class to talk to Swami D, for she would never tell him, or anyone, what had happened that afternoon.

Swami D sensed her distress but, with a class to teach, let her be. She emerged from beneath her blanket, acknowledged her teacher, and walked out. She wanted water—to drink, to make her clean, to drown in. Absolution to wipe out her memory of Harry. She walked back down Ladbroke Grove. It was cold and wet and gone eight but she would not go home. Harry needed time to pack his things; she prayed that's what he was doing. She couldn't bear to face him again.

With the carelessness of the hopeless she crossed the bridge and took the steps down to the canal path. To be there alone on such a night would be miserable, and just about perfect. Turning left would take her past the orange light of Sainsburys, the mammoth metal water towers now abandoned, then darkness. Right after the skate park, Meanwhile Gardens—an unlikely name that always appealed to Grace—the path parallel to the Harrow Road would take her to Maida Vale with its houseboats. Grace turned right. Fine rain put a sweatlike sheen on her face. After half a mile, when her feet began to hurt, she took off her heels and walked on, toes imprinting themselves on a slime of mud and grit.

It was still and almost silent down by the water, the path narrow. Some way ahead, three figures began to assume shape and purpose. Grace grabbed her mobile, as though being in a conversation could protect her. She scanned her address book and pressed call, fear obliterating trivial concerns, like what to say to Dr. James.

'Hello.'

'Sorry to bother you,' she said, her attention on the approaching men, hands thrust inside their pockets.

'Who's this?'

'Grace . . .' She stopped, distracted by the men, close enough for her to make out their features. Their eyes were down, registering her bare feet, elegant black coat, and Gucci bag: a useful prize.

'Grace, are you there?' said Dr. James.

'Yes . . . Yes, I am.' Her strategy was to be in conversation; she had to say something. 'It's just that I gave up work today—' The men were two steps from her, still with their eyes down.

'Are you celebrating?'

'I should celebrate, let's celebrate,' she said, loud and clear for the men to hear that she was expected and would be missed. And then, from around the corner, a beam of light lanced the darkness: a fast-approaching cyclist. There was a yell—'Out the way'—as the rider sliced the space between Grace and the three men. Grace ran.

'Grace, are you okay? Where are you?'

'On the canal between Kensal Rise and Maida Vale.' Still running, she turned—there was no one behind her. She stopped to catch her breath.

'Are you crazy?'

'Maybe,' she replied and even though she was dismal, some part of her saw that it was funny; she *was* crazy to be walking, barefoot, on a wet winter night, terrified by strangers, dodging broken glass, dog shit, and demented cyclists.

'Do you know the pub on the corner, The Bridge House, right by the canal?' Dr. James said, sanely.

'Yes.'

'Wait for me there. I'll be twenty minutes.'

In a pathetic attempt to neaten up, Grace pulled her damp hair into a ponytail; her feet were too wet for her shoes, so she carried them into the pub.

'We don't do champagne by the glass,' the man behind the bar was telling Dr. James.

'A bottle then,' he said, turning to scan the pub for Grace, who stood behind him, dull with despair. She watched his eyes pass over her; unrecognizable to him, she moved closer and tapped his shoulder. 'We don't need champagne,' she said.

'My goodness, Grace, I didn't see you. What happened?' Dr. James frowned.

'It's been a bad day.'

'You left Suprafarma and you're miserable?'

'It's not just that.' She couldn't even say Harry's name. 'I don't think it's a day for champagne, that's all.'

'We're having champagne. You quit Suprafarma after sixteen years.'

Strange that he remembered her years of pharmaceutical service, stranger still that he was so insistent, almost frantic for celebration. The barman was telling him that he was pretty well out of champagne. There'd been a wedding, or a wake, maybe both, earlier that week. Only Dom Pérignon left. Dr. James ordered it without hesitating. Then, with ice bucket in one hand and glasses in the other, he tucked Grace under his arm and led her to a small round table by the fire. 'We'll drink half,' he said, pouring them both a glass. Such forced merriment didn't make sense, even as they raised their glasses, made unsteady eye contact, and drank. Neither had eaten that day and the alcohol hit fast, which settled them somehow.

Grace took off her wet wool coat, and held her hands toward the fire.

'Seems like your day was as bad as mine,' he said.

If that was the reality, it was better said. 'Let's forget forced celebration. What happened today?' she enquired.

'A patient killed herself.'

'Oh God . . . That's terrible. Are you okay?' The inadequacy of her words struck her as soon as she said them.

'I will be, but right now I'm out of faith with my work, with myself. Your call couldn't have come at a better time . . .'

'It's impossible, as you said, to predict—'

'Forget what I said.'

Grace could see that he felt responsible, that it was pointless trying to console him. 'How old was she?'

'Nineteen.'

Grace looked into the fire. 'So little time to have lived, yet to know she didn't want life.'

'We thought we'd protected her. There was nothing in her room. She hanged herself from the door hinge with a shoe lace.'

'Insanely brave, in a way.'

He wiped his eyes with the back of his hand and then poured them both another glass.

'Of course it's not the first time, but it doesn't get easier. She was a great kid . . .'

They sat in silence. In the heat of the fire, steam rose from Grace's coat. Dr. James moved it to one side and for the first time noticed her shredded stockings. 'You went barefoot by the canal?' he asked, bemused.

Grace nodded.

'You really are crazy.'

'Certifiable. I even enrolled for yoga training today.'

'That's something to celebrate. Grace, congratulations. Maybe it's time for me to go to Vietnam, to train to be a barefoot doctor.'

'What kind of doctor's that?' asked Grace, unsure whether she was meant to take him literally.

'The Chinese equivalent of a junior doctor. They're trained to know sixty-four acupuncture points and sixty-four herbs, which equate to the sixty-four hexagrams in the *I Ching*. You know the *I Ching*?'

'The book of change.'

He nodded, quiet again, and drained his glass.

Beside the fire's flame, drinking champagne with Dr. James, Grace felt safe. Messed up she may have been, but she was no longer shivering from shock and cold.

'If we have any more we won't be able to drive,' he said.

'I couldn't anyway. Suprafarma took the car.'

'Already?'

'First thing they did.'

'Shall we finish this then?' he lifted the bottle. There was plenty left. She shook her head.

'Okay, let's go,' he said. He helped her with her coat, and guided her through the crowded pub back to the street. 'If you put your shoes on, we could walk for a bit. Would you like to?'

It had stopped raining and the streets were shining in the lamplight. Dr. James held out his elbow and Grace linked her arm through his as they followed a Maida Vale avenue that looped around and back on itself, to his car. Grace checked her watch. Where was Harry now? Waiting for her? Or with Tricksy?

'Do you need to be somewhere?' Dr. James asked, sensitive to her.

'No. Just home please. Oxford Gardens off Ladbroke Grove.'

Dr. James opened the passenger door and as bad as the day had been, it wasn't so bad that Grace couldn't appreciate his blue Aston. At the sound and feel of the engine Grace flashed a smile. 'You'll keep the car when you quit. That's the difference between us.'

'I doubt I will. Have you ever driven one of these?' he asked, circling the roundabout before heading onto the Westway.

'I haven't,' she admitted.

'Before I sell it, we'll go for a drive. You can drive me.'

'I'd like that.' She laughed.

When they reached her house, he climbed out of the car. 'Thank you for meeting me this evening. I feel human again.'

'Dr. James, it was you who rescued me.'

Her formality amused him. He gently tugged her ponytail. 'Good night, Grace,' he said. She went to kiss his cheek, but he drew her body to his in a strong hug. She smelled the skin at his neck, warm and something that was just him. They stood apart. Again good night. She ran down the path and turned. He was in the lamplight, watching her.

'Would you mind waiting a second?'

He nodded. He would wait. He did not ask why.

Grace opened the door. The house was dark—and empty, she instantly knew. She waved Dr. James good-bye and shut the door. Dark silence. The car outside roared off, and still she hadn't moved. She wouldn't put on the lights. She would wait until the morning to see what Harry had taken. On the landing she shut her bedroom door; she preferred the smaller room, the unfamiliarity of it, and the single bed where Ted had died. First she showered and scrubbed her body, as though the steaming water that scalded her skin might rid her of memory. Then she lay in bed, naked and aware till dawn, when finally, sleep came.

Grace woke at midday, uprooted, disconnected, half terrified to have nothing to do apart from her yoga practice. Wrapped in Ted's bathrobe, clutching a mug of tea, she walked through the house: Harry had taken everything that was his, even the book he had given her that she was in the middle of reading, but he had left the bookmark, which seemed strange. The money had gone, too, of course.

She rolled out her yoga mat and moved slowly into dog pose. She felt her back open out, her tendons stretch from her ankle, her calf extend, her whole body wake up. Her lungs expanded and it seemed her spirit did, too. She kicked up into handstand, from time to time lightly touching the wall with her foot to balance. Upside down she saw the world differently: what had Suprafarma brought her in the end, apart from money and a way to fill her day? She was even thankful that Harry had finally shown himself to be what he was. Then she thought of Lucy. She wanted to see her very badly, but without Harry she would not make sense in the girl's world. In the end, if Harry had given Grace very little of himself, he had given her the chance to love a child.

Grace came down from handstand and, kneeling with her forehead to the floor, closed her eyes and cried.

Chapter Five

Kurmasana—tortoise pose

Kurma means tortoise. Kurmasana is dedicated to Kurma, the tortoise incarnation of Lord Vishnu, maintainer of the universe. Kurma is also the name of one of the five secondary forms of prana, *or the life force. It is said to circulate in the skin and bones and is responsible for the opening and closing of the eyes. Kurmasana is sacred to the yogi. The* Bhagavad Gita *says, 'When he [the practitioner] can withdraw his senses from association with other objects, as a tortoise withdraws its limbs from external danger, then he is firmly fixed on the path toward wisdom.' In this pose the body resembles a tortoise and the mind becomes calm whether the practitioner experiences pleasure or pain. Eventually the practitioner of this pose will know freedom from the emotions. The pose tones the spine and the whole central nervous system, and stimulates the abdominal organs. The asana prepares the spiritual aspirant for the fifth stage of yoga,* pratyahara, *or sense withdrawal, symbolized by the tortoise.*

The taxi climbed away from Malibu and the ocean, winding up through hills of dry red soil until the side road became a dirt track, and finally a dead end. At the top of a steep drive, in the shade of a black oak tree, a stream bubbled into a pond that held three terrapins. It was a hot afternoon and a warm dry wind came over the land. Grace wrestled out of her sweater, stopping to watch the wide wingspan of an eagle, circling overhead.

As if deferring to the majesty of the landscape and the big clear sky, the Bodhi Tree yoga centre was built into the rocky headland and painted the same sand color. Opposite the glass entrance a man leaned against a dry stone wall, his pale face tilted to the sun. Black hair curled emphatically on the white sheen of his thin legs, and Velcro-strapped black sandals disguised feet of unusual elegance. From behind closed eyes the man said, 'They want us to wait out here.' Grace sat beside him, welcoming the sun on her winter skin.

'You were on my flight from London. I'm Sam.'

Sam was American and taught at the American school in Paris. He had flown through London to check it out, he said proudly, his earrings glinting silver. 'We've traveled far, yet we're here first, and that means we'll get our first choice of where to stay.'

'I left that part of the form blank. I didn't know what a yurt was.'

Sam described a yurt as a round, canvas tent. Bodhi Tree had a village of them, kitted out with heaters, beds, and wooden floors. 'I'd rather stay in a tent at the bottom of the valley,' he said, 'right in the heart of nature.'

'It's more than natural enough for me up here.'

'I don't want to be on top of the yoga centre. Too much going on.' He glanced at her Dolce & Gabbana sandals and well-made luggage. 'My guess is you're in a cabin. Take it as a compliment. Cabins are elite, and would destabilize a teacher's budget.'

Miss Messenger appeared, her gypsy skirt and long red hair at odds with the businesswoman impression she'd given over the phone three weeks ago. She held her clipboard as a shield against the sun as she addressed the students who had arrived in a steady stream. 'Om *shanti,*' she said.

The greeting amused Grace, but was forgivable, given not so much where they were, but what they were there for. 'Please be patient. I will get to you all. First come, first served. You must be Sam,' she said to the only man in the long line.

Sam came out of the building happy. Heaving his backpack onto his left shoulder, he headed off to his tent. Grace was next. Observing the sign to remove her shoes, she walked into the hall, past a life-sized laughing Buddha standing at the entrance with his arms raised. Grace touched his round belly, the red wood stroked smooth by thousands of trailing hands. At the far end of the hall, three women worked silently in a stainless steel kitchen that had floor to ceiling windows looking onto an herb garden. Grace wanted time to absorb the calm, cool atmosphere, but Miss Messenger was waiting.

'I've put you in Yurt Six with three lovely women. Your application forms suggest you're compatible,' said Miss Messenger, getting down to business.

Grace regretted careless answers given in haste to questions she couldn't remember. 'I'd rather have a cabin, if you don't mind,' she said. The last thing she wanted was late night talks with girls in yurts, revealing secrets, reliving days.

Miss Messenger twitched at the unexpected resistance. 'I think you'll enjoy the yurt. Students in yurts really bond.'

'I'm not here to bond. I just want to do the training and learn as much as I can.'

'Then you'll miss out on the Bodhi Tree experience. Anyway, cabins cost extra.'

'Please can I have a cabin? I need time alone to think.'

'Or not to think,' said Miss Messenger, eying Grace above the Yurt Six file. Grace looked back evenly and waited. Miss Messenger unlocked a drawer in her desk and handed Grace a tiny key on a plain plastic tab. 'This is for the cabin at the top of the property where it gets mighty windy, so it isn't that quiet. Neither is it the splendid isolation you say you want. The other bed has been reserved by a student with whom you have very little in common.'

'Apart from yoga,' Grace smiled.

'Let's hope it's enough. Three weeks can be a very long time.'

After signing the indemnity that protected the Foundation from every conceivable (and inconceivable) misadventure that might befall her,

Grace picked up a map of the Bodhi Tree property and went in search of her bed.

The cabin, a garden shed from the outside, was painted white within, and furnished with two wooden beds and an old glass apothecary cabinet. It was a small, good room and Grace was happy. She unpacked her bag and, out of habit, checked her mobile. There was no signal. She felt cut off, from what she wasn't sure, since she had nobody to call. Leaving the door open, she lay on the bed, gazing at the mountains through the mesh curtain that kept insects out but allowed air to flow through. Spinning from twenty hours of travel, lulled by the constant sound of cicadas in the California afternoon, Grace drifted off to sleep.

When she woke the bed opposite was covered in clothes that were stacked in neat rows. On the table between the beds was a note: 'I'm Stephanie, your cabinmate. You looked so peaceful, didn't wake you. Induction at seven. Perhaps see you there.'

Grace liked Stephanie's handwriting as much as her wardrobe. She picked up a white T-shirt (size x-small) that was hand painted and ripped in the right places, just the right amount. Judging by her clothes, Stephanie was a petite original, and, by the books piled on the bedside table, a serious yogi with a big mind. Patanjali, Desikachar, Sri Ramana Maharshi, Iyengar . . . and Jim Harrison? What was he doing alongside such illustrious vegetarians? Harrison, a poet, novelist, and meat eater, was an American who hunted and fished; he was an old favourite of Ted's, which made sense, but he was hardly an obvious choice for a yogi girl. Grace opened *The Shape of the Journey* and read randomly: 'I began my Zen studies and practice well over twenty years ago in a state of rapacious and self-congratulatory spiritual greed. I immediately set about reading hundreds of books on the subject, almost all contemporary and informed by earnest mediocrity. There was no more self-referential organism alive than myself, a potato that didn't know it was a potato.'

Grace laughed. Zen studies, yoga studies; both promoted the idea of liberation, that it was possible to live attuned to something higher. She would have preferred to lie on the bed and read but the Bodhi Tree induction called. She ran to the main hall. The room was full of students, cross-legged on the floor; Grace squeezed in, knee-to-knee, between two women. The second she was still, a man's voice said, 'Let's om to know we're here.'

Everyone closed their eyes to hum, tones rising and falling with a harmony that ended of its own accord. When Grace opened her eyes, she recognized Garuda and Rita from the Web site. They were sitting at the far end of the circle, a bull terrier resting his head on Rita's foot, his tail whacking Garuda's knee. Confident that such a dog would not tolerate a self-referential anything, Grace felt better. In a way, the dog made things seem normal, although right then Grace felt that nothing was. For the first time it occurred to her that it was pretentious to have come so far west to learn about an Eastern discipline. What's more, yoga teaching in England required no certificate. She really didn't need to be here at all. Grace had wanted distance from home to heighten her experience, but now that she was here, all she felt was tired and precariously aloof from the thirty-six women and five men with whom she now sat: a circle of strangers. Grace was glad for the male-female imbalance. Her attempt at *pratyahara* before she met Harry had been wrongly executed. She understood now that she had simply shut down. The Bodhi Tree was an opportunity to reapply herself to sense withdrawal, and while, post-Harry, another man was the last thing on her mind, she was reassured to think that those at the Bodhi Tree would not distract her.

'Congratulations on your journey,' said a lyrical voice. Rita spoke the language of spiritual America, but any word from her would have sounded divine, such was her southern accent. 'I know for some of you the journey started a long time ago. For Garuda and me the journey is twenty-five years old, and it's a treat to be gathered together with you this evening. Over the next twenty-one days we will become a yoga family. It's a dynamic we're already creating.'

Rita was the poster girl for a yogic life with a fine yogi husband. In Patagonia pants and plain T-shirt, Garuda didn't look like a man who would take the mythological name of Lord Vishnu's mount, the half-eagle, half-human personification of courage. He was wiry, blond, inscrutable, and let his wife extend the courtesies. Grace liked Garuda all the same, and supposed she would grow accustomed to his name, although he looked too American for it. Next, Rita introduced Mark, the assistant yoga teacher.

Mark had broad shoulders and a puckish smile and was the darkest-skinned person in a room that was predominantly white-white-white. 'Fifteen years ago I arrived from England and haven't been back since.' His rolled *r*'s and flattened *a*'s were broad Hampshire, the last accent Grace expected to hear. 'My job is to help make this the best experience for you, so don't be shy, and do ask for help.' Untouched by American influence though Mark's accent may have been, his manner and Native American rings and bracelets were hardly Hampshire.

Rita invited students to introduce themselves, requesting that they keep their stories short. About half were married and three were planning weddings. There were several teenagers who had graduated that year and expressed indecision about the future. Only one woman, Frances from Seattle, thirty-five that day, admitted she was counting on yoga as a future career. Many women described husbands and children, and spoke about things that happen in life, and stick. All of a sudden, Grace felt bereft that nothing had stuck to her.

The girl beside Grace drew her heels higher on her thighs to tighten her lotus pose, pulled up her spine and cleared her throat. 'I'm Stephanie,' she said. Stephanie had apparently protected her pure white skin all her young life, but had dyed dark hair and kohl-smudged eyes. She was a California Gothette. Grace regretted not heeding Miss Messenger. For the next three weeks she'd be stuck with a rebellious young woman who shone with confidence, and she didn't feel up to the challenge. 'I was an English major, graduated Berkeley last summer. Right now, I'm between worlds, extending the dreamtime.' Dark as she tried to appear, Stephanie's laugh was as light as a charm. 'I discovered yoga when sports failed me, or I failed sports. People who like sports seemed to be happy people but nobody in my family likes sports. At college I tried every kind of sport, but I was just sweaty and unhappy until I discovered yoga. My yoga teacher trained at Bodhi Tree, which is why I'm here.'

It was Grace's turn. Predicting disapproval, she avoided her career in pharmaceuticals and, with her personal life a wasteland, she avoided that, too. It didn't leave her much. 'I'm here because I want to be a yoga teacher.' The plain truth hit her and she bit the inside of her cheek. Linda, the grand-mother from Kansas ('I want to train so I can give free yoga classes to the wives of men posted in Iraq'), fluttered her hand over her packet of Kleenex. Still, Grace could not speak. Aware they were waiting for another crumb of self-disclosure, she tried again. 'Hatha yoga changed my life.' Grace's voice broke and, afraid to cry in public, she bowed her head with her hands in *namaste*, as Linda's tissue flew from hand to hand toward her.

When all the students had spoken, Rita led them in the name game, each student saying their name and all the names of those before them. Lucky the one who began the round, not so lucky the last. The names that came easily to Grace that night belonged to the people she would, for one reason or many, remember long after training had finished. Stephanie, her cabinmate, was the liveliest. Of the gaggle of girls, Kirsty and Fantasia, locals from Malibu, had been practicing yoga at their after-school club since they were ten. Serena from Las Vegas was the daughter of yogis and was memorable for a composure beyond her thirty years but Grace mistrusted her demeanor and thought she sat too close, too soon, to Sam, the Ameri-can in Paris. A few down from Sam was Mark, who made Grace proud because he was English, even if he had abandoned the land of his fore-fathers. Then came blonde Olga, a Russian model nobody would for-get, and her unlikely cabinmate and physical opposite, the tiny, dark-haired Vietnamese, Sungli. Grace wondered on what pretext Miss Messenger had put them together, although their English grammar was surprisingly simi-lar. Pixielike Sara, with tattooed arms and the hairiest armpits on the planet (forget the room), was diminutive but enthusiastic and had proclaimed, with arms raised, 'I'm from San Francisco and I believe in God!' Her declaration made the circle freeze with embarrassment; explicit reference to God, or money, did it every time. No such exuberance from the troupe of ladies in their fifties who blurred instantly in Grace's memory—apart, that was, from another Linda, who had been a professional ballet dancer, the evidence for which was in her upright body and the way she held her head. And then there was deaf Derek, midfifties, and new to yoga. This was his first time in a yoga studio. 'I hadn't realized yoga was such a girl thing,' he said, genuinely astounded to be so surrounded. Nobody asked what a complete beginner was doing in a yoga teacher training session, but that was as it should be, for as it promised on the Web site, the Bodhi Tree was all-inclusive. Everybody was to be made welcome.

Grace memorized names as best she could, hoping she would not forget, or be forgotten. When Garuda initiated an om to end the day, the class, unbidden, joined in. Grace stared through the glass doors of the hall, down the valley toward a telegraph pole shaped like the symbol of the resurrected Christ, black against a burnt orange sky, while deep within her, the sacred sound resonated on and on.

Grace woke at five the following morning and tiptoed toward the cabin door.

'Morning,' Stephanie said.

'You scared me!' Grace jumped.

'Girlfriend, you scare easy,' Stephanie said, opening one eye. She was sitting cross-legged in the corner by the apothecary cabinet; she stretched out her arms, her shawl unfolding like wings behind her.

'Being in the middle of nowhere amplifies every sound,' Grace said.

'Tell me about it. My meditation sucked. I'm starving. Supper last night was carbsville. I couldn't eat a thing. Time for turkey slices.'

'Where are they? They don't even allow meat in the students' fridge.'

'I hid them in a tofu packet,' Stephanie said, tapping the side of her nose.

In England it was gone lunchtime and, still on that clock, Grace happily joined Stephanie to eat. In pyjamas they crept down the garden path, into the kitchen. They kept quiet so as not to wake the women who slept in the cubbyhole in the ceiling of the main hall, reached by a ladder attached to the wall. Climbing into the cubby required agility and some nerve. A child would find such a place an adventure to reach, yet Miss Messenger had known to put the over-fifties up there. Nestled in sleeping bags, the oldest women in the training had giggled like girls when they'd first climbed up. In the early morning, Grace and Stephanie heard their sonorous breathing; one of them was snoring. Silently, Stephanie prepared coffee and Grace made toasted turkey sandwiches; to their surprise, the divine smells did not wake the ladies, so they returned to the cabin, wrapped themselves in blankets, and ate breakfast on the step.

'You can't beat the wisdom of the stoop, watching the world go by,' said Stephanie, extracting the turkey filling from the bread, wrapping it inside a piece of lettuce.

'Not much world going by here. Give me the city over this nothingness,' Grace responded.

'Read some Jim Harrison. He'll bust the concrete out of your veins. Happily, his tendency to misogyny doesn't appear in his verse. Mind you, stuck here, I could tend toward a little misogyny myself. What do you think about Mark, by the way?'

'The Hampshire boy. I like him.'

'The original, right?'

'Yes. Good old Hampshire, rather than your New.'

'He's incredibly cute, so who cares if I can't understand him—which is not why I'm skipping his trail hike, by the way. Only mad dogs and Englishmen go out in the midday sun.'

'Noel Coward. How d'you know of him?'

'My uncle played me his songs every time I went to London.'

'Does he still live there?'

'You bet, holed up in Cadogan Square, New Jersey boy made good that he is.'

If Mark was a mad dog, and Grace suspected he was, he had that dog under control. On the hike he was courteous and took care of his charges as they followed him around the Bodhi Tree land. Lathered with SPF, and wearing long pants and training shoes to protect them from poison ivy, the students clutched bottles of water as if heading for the desert. Cautious they may have been, but few were sure-footed as they walked in a slow line.

Impatient at being stuck toe to tail, Grace bounded to the head of the group, alongside Mark and Sam.

By the waterfall, Sam pointed out two camouflaged tents. 'That's where I am. Derek's in the other and he's not pleased.' Derek, it transpired, was on the training to investigate opportunities in the expanding yoga market and, whether he knew it or not (and it seemed he didn't), the company of flexible females.

'Those tents are a long way down the valley,' Grace observed.

'It's too far for Derek. He wants to swap your cabin for his tent.'

'What about Stephanie?'

'Derek wouldn't object.'

'I was thinking about her.'

'Either way, he's going to ask. He can't take the hike up from the tent, or the bugs,' Sam said.

'Bugs?' asked Serena, the coy Vegas girl, right behind Grace as they followed the narrow track by the river. Conversation was cut short as they concentrated on clambering over boulders, following Mark to the edge of a deep, wide pool.

'Welcome to the swimming hole. Who's first in?' he said, taking off his shirt.

His torso was certainly worthy of acclaim, but Grace suspected it was his proposal to dive in that prompted the squeals that followed. The distant snow-capped mountains were the source of the waterfall. The pool would be close to freezing.

'Come on! It's never as bad as you think,' encouraged Mark, jumping in mad-dog style. Students stepped closer to the edge as if to better observe an animal in his habitat. Mark looked so at one with his world, Grace wanted to join him. She pulled off her T-shirt, kicked off her shoes, and jumped. She surfaced, teeth chattering uncontrollably, laughing from the coldness of it.

'There's always one. I guessed it would be you. Fantastic, isn't it,' Mark said, swimming past her, pulling himself up and out in one effortless move.

Grace dripped dry on the climb up the valley. Halfway there, Mark led them off the main track to a rocky headland to admire the view below:

the ocean bounced the sun back into the blue; while below, Malibu sprawled the coast line. Grace found the mountainside even richer, with yellow broom scenting the air, its soft honey smell cut with sage and eucalyptus.

'Don't you love that scent when you step on the leaves,' said Grace, as they trekked back to the main path.

'Eucalyptus soaks up the water and isn't indigenous,' Sam responded, sounding like the teacher he was.

'Didn't you know, eucalyptus damages indigenous vegetation.' Serena pushed past Grace. 'Oh, sorry,' Serena said, 'accidentally' elbowing her.

'This way for the Ganesh rock!' Mark shouted, once again cutting into Serena's conversation, as he led them off the path. As Grace followed up the hill, Serena's bottom wobbled at her eye level, a plate-sized tattoo of the Hindu god Ganesh peeking over her low-slung sweatpants. Then, echoed in the red rock above, Grace recognized contours that could be construed as a trunk, elephant ears, and potbelly.

'The Hindu lord of success, the destroyer of obstacles,' Mark said, pointing to the Ganesh-like features in the rocky overhang. 'The god of education, wisdom, and wealth, his trunk represents om, the source of cosmic reality.' Mark made spooky eyes, earned a laugh, then trekked back down to the trail. Nobody lingered, or asked how an elephant had qualified as the god of education, which Grace stayed sitting to ponder. Whatever shapes and names had been imposed on the rock formation (this was Native American land and there surely would have been a few), Grace felt the place was sacred, and would be beyond time. She hummed 'om.' Even with only birds and insects to hear her, she felt ridiculous and stopped. But the sound of om vibrating in her body left her very calm. Grace tried again. She breathed in and let out a long, soft om, which set the blue jay above her squawking from the eucalyptus tree.

'Stand at the top of your mat.'

Garuda had come into the yoga studio unnoticed for the first class of the training. His command silenced the chatterers, who now stood stiff as soldiers on parade. 'Why not relax?' Garuda's features disappeared into a blink-and-you-missed-it smile. 'Don't go into this training expecting to quantum leap your practice and come out of here buffed up. Keep the long perspective. You've got your whole life. Let's start slowly with the Vinyasa flow series. Ujjayi breathing.' He told them to narrow their throats and suck air through their noses, to channel their breath to intensify heat and strength. The room filled with a Darth Vader sound. 'Ujjayi means master, victorious. Master your breath. For most of you right now that means don't forget to breathe.' While Rita and Mark closed all the windows, Garuda paced the strip between the two rows of students who faced each other down the length of the studio. 'We build heat so nobody gets hurt. Surya Namaskar,' Garuda said, and they were off.

At Swami D's, Grace was accustomed to three rounds of Surya Namaskar, the salute to the sun—it was the name for twelve flowing movements that went from standing, down to the floor, and back up again. After five rounds Garuda told his students they had five to go. Grace ignored her doubt that she might not make it. By round eight, even younger students were lying down to rest, but she did not succumb. She was determined to be youthfully strong and not flounder with the oldies and the unfit. By the time all ten rounds had been completed, windows had steamed over, mats were slippery with sweat, and everyone was soaking, most of them in a trance induced by movement, music, and conscious breath.

Back bends revealed that Stephanie was the elasta-girl of the training: her head hit her heels with such ease her vertebrae had to be hinged. Aware (or at least hoping) that such extreme flexibility is genetic, nobody tried to compete. Other rivalries were rife and eyes flicked the room to gauge agility, body shape, the coolest yoga clothes, and the most original tattoos. Paul, who had practiced yoga for forty years, kept his eyes down, in and out of the studio; he was a quiet man though his body spoke volumes. With sculpted shoulders and a flat stomach, in his black leggings and fine grey vest, he looked like a dancer. Nobody believed he was sixty. Olga, the slender Russian, a Jivamukti devotee, was the blondest of the blondes in the training, and her white acrylic nails were decorated with diamanté hearts. Watching other students was an absorbing distraction but the yoga studio

—an unadorned rectangle, twenty feet by forty—offered no other. After a few days, when everyone had been duly scrutinized, the students had nowhere else to look, apart from inward, where observations would take longer to surface, and evaluate.

As Garuda dictated their movement and breath in sequences that were unfamiliar, Grace felt once again a beginner. 'Vinyasa means connection,' he said. 'Vinyasa flow implies breath, concentration, going with the flow, and what's right that day. Make sure that's what you do, on and off the mat.' Going with the flow off the mat at the Bodhi Tree meant giving up makeup, coffee, alcohol, meat, and men. The focus was yoga for six hours each day in the studio, and for several hours a day out of it, working in study groups on the Bodhi Tree Yoga Handbook. Sam, Stephanie, Kirsty, and Fantasia were in Grace's group and, while they joked with each other, there was much vying for authority.

With one flight, and in one night, Grace had changed her world. She was immersed in the Bodhi Tree, and, in those early harmonious days, it was a mystery to her that the whole world didn't live in peaceful yogic communities. Each hour was allocated, every meal a feast with a social scene and music from Garuda's well-stocked iPod. The training was hard work, but easy living. Garuda and Rita had refined the schedule over many years, and along with everyone in the course, Grace was happy to follow it. The only decision she had to make each day was how much intensity to apply, which was no real decision at all. Grace was committed, and gave all the energy she had. Perfect sleep was the sweet reward: she could not remember sleep so profound, nine or ten hours, straight through her dreams, waking in the position in which she had lain down.

By default, Miss Messenger had given Grace the perfect cabinmate to share 'the Bodhi Tree experience.' Stephanie, the intellectual girl from Los Angeles, loved literature, language, and every cool Hollywood hangout, but was united with Grace by a passion for yoga, and Jewish blood—'on the father's side.'

'The side that fucked me up,' laughed Stephanie. 'Mind you, there's a theory that twenty years after blaming one parent, you realize it was the other one who *really* fucked you over.'

Grace nodded, but said nothing. Memories of her mother were too precious to be sullied. Resenting her father was easier, particularly since he was still alive and still drinking.

During that first week, personalities and personal history were secondary to the yogic purpose, but gossip was the sign that good behaviour only lasts so long. Secrets soon filtered beyond the fragile confines of new friendship, but throughout training the yoga studio unified them, whatever trouble brewed outside it.

Only Derek was consistently late to class, padding in ten minutes after the rest to pick a prime spot, blithely asking whoever occupied it to move aside. 'I need to see Garuda's mouth,' he would say, pointing to his own. Nobody turned Derek down, so he kept arriving late. Displaced students squeezed compliantly into remote corners of the studio while Garuda stopped the lesson, squeezed his lips between his teeth, and stared down the room. Rita, opposite Garuda at the far end, would laser him a look: 'Don't even think about it.' She may have acted tougher than her husband, but she was the compassionate one. Derek's yoga wasn't great and never would be. 'Give the guy a break,' was her attitude. Garuda went along with this but Grace could tell he didn't like it and neither, in truth, did she. Deaf or not, if Derek wanted a place at the teacher's feet, Grace thought he should get to the studio in time to claim it, like anyone else, and the morning he asked for her mat, Grace said 'no.' Later, in the lunch queue, convinced that she wouldn't turn him down twice in one day, Derek asked Grace if she and Stephanie would swap their cabin for his tent.

'For how long?' Grace asked.

'A couple nights, if you're feeling generous.'

'No need to do that,' said Garuda, walking by. 'Lookout Cabin's been repaired. Derek, you can move out of your tent anytime you like.'

Derek beamed. 'Thanks, Garuda. I've missed my creature comforts.'

It turned out that that night Derek got more creature than comfort: the smell of a decomposing skunk trapped beneath the cabin kept him awake all night.

It was unusual for Garuda to intercede in student conversation. He was usually aloof, a mysterious source of wisdom, which he would share, without wasting word or breath, only when the whole class was gathered. Under no illusion about how far teacher training would take them, he made no grand promises. 'We can give you an education, but it's up to you to be enquirers, to open your minds and hearts. Teaching yoga is the art of seeing. You'll learn that, over time, from your own practice and watching those you teach. Don't wait to be perfect. Start straightaway. Grab people from the parking lot if you have to—just don't hurt them.'

Jokes there were, but never during *pranayama*. *Prana*, the Sanskrit word for breath and nerve energy, was paramount and led to Garuda's preferred subject: the energy body. 'Within the nervous system are currents that yogis equate with the sun and moon, *ida* and *pingala*. That they haven't been scientifically explained doesn't make them less valid. In my experience these currents open the chakras, the energy centres of the psychic body, and alter consciousness.'

'Like an altered state on some kind of drug?' asked the pixie-girl Sara.

'I'm thinking of a dreamlike state, or the state of mind you get when you're walking on the beach. You don't need drugs to experience altered states.'

Garuda believed that the purpose of yoga's strenuous physicality was to open the chakras, each chakra a source of *prana,* the fundamental energy of life; he claimed there were many indications of when the chakras were activated, or waking up. A physical sensation in any one of the seven centres along the spine was considered a clue, as was the perception of colours behind closed eyes, whether pure light energy or the darker tones associated with the lower chakras.

Grace had seen swirling colours while resting on her yoga mat after class at Swami D's, but Swami D was wary of discussing the energy centres. Garuda was also cautious, but pushed by the class, he hinted at the chakras' potential. 'They hold secrets and, the yogis say, answers to the religious mysteries. One thing I know for sure is that working with your chakras is a way to know yourself. When you can see other people's, that's when you're really on to something.'

Garuda's psychic experience was balanced by his application of yoga's more visceral practices, among them the 'big six' purification techniques:

the appropriately named *shat kriyas.* All were familiar with *neti* (most had poured warm salt water up one nostril and blown it out the other), but none had ventured into *vasti,* an activity not for the squeamish, which required a bucket of warm water and a hollow bamboo tube. 'Mind you, if you go down to the garden centre and buy a garden hose, it's a darn sight more comfortable,' Garuda said, straight-faced. 'The big seventh' was his personal addition to the purification techniques: the elimination of television.

Garuda had traveled India in search of the great yogi masters and consulted many, but when students asked him to name his favourite guru he would say, 'The tao that is explained is not the Tao. He who knows, knows not.' Garuda was not in awe of the East or the esteemed yoga authorities, whom he enjoyed bringing down to size, sometimes two at a time. 'Desikachar's solution to make the asanas more spiritual was to chant the sutras of Patanjali during his practice. You could try that,' he chuckled. 'See if it works for you.'

Grace was not dismayed that Garuda did not revere Patanjali and doubted his authorship. She admired Garuda's indifference and respected his scholarship. He was clear when he said that all he could say for sure about the sutras was that they had been translated to death from Sanskrit and extrapolated every which way. 'In the entire writings, whatever the translation, never once have I found the word love, and, if you ask me, that's a state of grace we can't live without.'

Love. Everything came down to it. And at the Bodhi Tree those with love in their lives, or simply a love for life, shone out from the rest. Garuda and Rita had it. Always professional in public, Rita had quietly admitted to Grace that she and her husband saved their loving, and their fighting, for later. 'We've all got a shadow side and the sooner we face it, accept it, and lose shame about it, the better.' This made Grace think how much easier it was to see the dark side of other people, rather than one's own. As a child, she had turned dizzy circles trying to glimpse her own shadow, but at the Bodhi Tree, walking back to the cabin one night from the outside showers, she had jumped at the sight of her shadow, cast ahead of her like a dark, thin stranger.

Grace appreciated the balance that Garuda and Rita had found between love and work. In business Garuda deferred to Rita and in the yoga studio she deferred to him, but when the balance tipped, it added spice, and not just for them. One afternoon, teaching warrior pose and how to adjust it, Garuda called for silence. Low voices continued. Garuda called again, irritated at being ignored.

'No, Derek, the knee *above* the ankle,' Rita continued.

'Miss Gold, I said silence! See me in the principal's office after class,' Garuda called down the studio, eyes ablaze, face stern.

'Yes, sir.' Rita blushed, confident all the same that her husband appreciated how she stood up to him. Twenty feet apart, twenty-five years married, the couple's mutual desire, the love they had, was there for all to see. If they offered a course in that, Grace would have enrolled straightaway.

Chapter Six

PASCHIMOTTANASANA—forward bend

Paschi *means the West. It suggests the back of the body from the head to the heels. In this asana the whole of the back of the body is stretched, hence the name. It is also known both as* ugrasana, *which means powerful and noble, or* brahmacharyasana. Brahmacharaya *means religious study, self-restraint, and celibacy—qualities to which the yogi aspires. Forward bending is meant to be a passive process, utilizing gravity to stretch the back of the body. It also provokes introspection and helps to release both physical and emotional pain.*

Every morning and hot afternoon, Grace went skinny-dipping in the swimming hole. No other students ventured there, and she cherished the peace and the sense that for those few weeks at least, the place was hers. When she found Serena and her fellow yurt resident, Cindy, lost on the path, clutching towels, she reluctantly showed them the way. As soon as they were there, Grace plunged topless into the water, staking a claim to her territory.

Gasping against the cold until it numbed her body, she observed the girls' reluctance to remove their bikini tops. Serena stared into the distance as if absorbed by nature, delaying the revelation of her cupcake breasts. Once she had, she clamped her nose between thumb and forefinger and with a puppy yelp, jumped in feet first. She swam in urgent circles, her head above the water like a frightened turtle, calling, 'Cindy, come on! It's awesome.'

Cindy hopped from foot to foot, arms wrapped around her perfect torso. Grace wondered how many hours of yoga she was doing to get her Barbie body.

'You'll love it,' trilled Serena.

California Cindy tweaked her bikini and the delicate knitted top dropped to the ground; her breasts stayed up, though, even as she sprang into the pool. Grace had wanted yoga to account for Cindy's physical perfection but now suspected it was the consequence of cosmetic surgery the likes of which her own father would have been proud.

Within minutes the women were frozen, and clambered out, goose bumps all over. Beneath a violet blue sky, they lay on the smooth warm rock, the cold edging out of their bodies. A cloud floated by. It was a perfect afternoon.

'I didn't know you had a husband,' Grace said, noticing the ring on Serena's hand.

Serena twisted the gold band on her cold white finger. 'Yes, we're so blessed.'

'Why don't you wear your ring all the time?'

'I make it a conscious choice to put it on. That way I always remember the first time Ed slipped it on my finger.'

'That's soooo sweet,' said Cindy. Grace had the Generation Xer down as an airhead and was tuning out when Cindy said, 'The day I graduated Stanford my professor gave me this ring. I've never taken it off.'

'You went to Stanford and married your professor?' Grace asked, impressed.

'I studied electrical engineering one semester with him, so it hardly counts. And we've been married three years now. How long have you been married, Serena?'

'A year.'

And already so flirtatious with the single Sam, Grace thought, but said instead, 'Where did you meet your husband, Serena?'

'Fine dining.'

Turned out Serena was a waitress with a passion for yoga and her husband was a chef with a passion for golf, 'which means we don't see each other much.' Serena was wistful and Grace sympathized, until Cindy asked if she was married. It was important to smile at this point, and Grace smiled extra. To every question other students had asked in the descending scale of commitment—'Children?' 'Married?' 'Living with anyone?'—Grace had replied 'no.' She held up her ring-free left hand, smiled once again, then closed her eyes to rest in the warm sun.

Acting as if she were content had the strange effect of making Grace feel it—apart from the itch between her breasts right above her heart. She supposed this could be a sign of an awakening at her *anahata* chakra, 'the wheel of the unstruck sound,' as Garuda had translated it. She scratched the itch; it moved down to the soft part of her belly just below her ribs, to the *manipura* chakra—the place where the yogis claim the emotions reside. Convinced her psychic body was revealing itself, Grace tuned in to her energy field, quietly observing the sensations.

'Ow, that hurt!' Serena squealed, puncturing the silence as she jumped up to slap her bottom hard.

Grace sat bolt upright. 'Ladybirds,' she said flatly, disappointed that her psychic musings were down to the tiny creatures that had landed in squadrons on their bodies.

'Ladybugs bite. How come I didn't know that?' Cindy cried, brushing them from her defiantly immobile chest.

Giggly shivering ended the tension between them as they plunged back into the freezing water, the ladybirds overhead, a dark swarm in the bright sky.

Of all the women at Bodhi Tree, only one was a self-declared lesbian. A petite French American, she was hardly predatory but enjoyed saying, with apparent pride, that men didn't interest her. She seemed to regard women who loved men with pity, and no little disdain. In her own way, Grace was proud that, of the five women on the Bodhi Tree training without a man in her life, she was the only one who genuinely didn't mind. Stephanie was single and had enrolled in the yoga training with the expectation of a little sexual ecstasy. She was tormented that there were no prospects. 'I should have gone to Hawaii,' she complained to Grace. 'There's a yoga school there and my friends say it's packed with guys. If you wake up one morning and find me gone, don't send a search party. You'll know where to find me.'

Grace sympathized. 'We're so far from civilized temptations, men are your only source of trouble—and they're in short supply.'

In the privacy of the cabin, Stephanie had considered her options: Mark, fit and thirty-three, was an appetizing danger in theory, but he was such a dedicated teacher and so respectful of the girls that he didn't flirt with any of them. Reluctantly—some of them very reluctantly—all of them left him alone. Garuda, self-contained and very married, wasn't remotely available, but that didn't stop Stephanie, and all of the women, from appreciating him. Paul, the acrobatic yogi of physical perfection, was shy, married, and sixty—qualities that excluded him from the girls' musings. Derek was Derek (although even he had acquired a certain charm), which left Sam. Skin and bone he may have been, but with political savvy, smooth talk, a wide smile, and humanitarian ideals, some thought Sam was near perfect. 'If only I did,' Stephanie said. 'I'd soon prize him away from that bland Vegas chick, which I might do anyway, from sheer boredom.'

That evening, as they waited for the kettle to boil for their last cup of yogi tea, Mark was in the kitchen. Stephanie deliberately raised her voice. 'The trouble is, Grace, the more I do yoga, the more I miss men.' Mark was boiling milk for a mug of hot chocolate and, with Stephanie talking as if to include him, he felt comfortable to join in—which was what she had hoped.

'It happens every time,' he said, and went to sit at the kitchen counter. Stephanie sat beside him and picked up his mug—that had 'yoga kills' written in repeated lines around it, like a school punishment. 'So, yoga's a dangerous business?' she queried, teasing.

'Can be. About day fourteen I stop wearing my grey Lycra shorts,' he laughed.

'Which aren't the greatest colour,' Grace said, pulling up a stool on Mark's other side.

'Those shorts are tight, and it didn't take me a week to notice that,' Stephanie said.

'You think I should ditch the shorts?'

'For your own safety,' Stephanie said. 'They're a reminder of what we're missing.'

'We never have more than ten men here, and I don't know why more haven't cottoned on to that.'

'There are six in the whole place, if we include the gardener, and I'd like to. Not usually my type, but I saw all sorts of gorgeousness in him this afternoon,' confessed Stephanie.

'He's married,' Mark said.

'Darn it.' Stephanie hit the counter like a cartoon character, with clenched fist and a wide arm swing.

'Predatory women. It's a role reversal,' Mark reflected.

'Honey, get off the compound, go find out who's chasing who in the big wide world.'

'Is being desired so tedious?' Grace asked.

'At first it's flattering, but by week three all of you are fitter, building *prana,* and your chakras—and I mean *all* your chakras—are open. Some girls flirt with nuclear intensity, and you're all so sensitive, the slightest touch can set you off.'

'Set us off?' Stephanie laughed. 'Like how?'

'You know.'

'No, I don't.' Stephanie rested her chin on her fist, ready to be told.

'Helping with adjustments, it can happen. One time I was adjusting this girl in forward bend, and she had an orgasm.'

'In class?'

Mark nodded, and looked down embarrassed. Now Grace was laughing. 'That's a joke, right?'

Mark shook his head, and looked at Grace with such penetrating eyes she had to look away.

'If you could teach whatever you did to that woman, you'd be rich,' Stephanie said. 'My God, she must have wanted you bad after that.'

'It didn't have much to do with me. She was open, that's all, her chakras were open. It was a spontaneous release. Sex doesn't have to be a personal thing.'

'Really,' said Stephanie, 'is that a new idea?' Her sarcasm was so subtly expressed, Mark fell for it, and was on the point of giving her an answer—until he saw Grace's face. Later, Stephanie scolded her for spoiling the fun: she'd been curious to hear the Hampshire boy's take on impersonal sex. Instead, she made the most of Mark's being off guard and slipped in the kind of question nobody would have normally dared ask him. 'Did a student ever seduce you?' she inquired, innocent-eyed but horny as hell.

'Once.' Mark drained his mug.

'And?'

'Trade secret.' He winked at Stephanie but a deep sigh—close to a shudder, Grace thought—disclosed his hurt.

'So, what's the gossip on your side of the fence about Sam?' Stephanie asked, tactfully moving on from Mark's unburied memory.

'I'd say he's feeling the heat, but for a young guy getting a lot of attention, he's handling himself well.'

'Yeah, but who's handling him?' said Stephanie.

Mark chuckled, held up his palms. 'None of my business.'

'Oh, come on. You teachers talk about us, of course you do.'

'We're all in a goldfish bowl, baby, and don't you forget it. Time to turn in. Sleep tight,' he said, and disappeared through the kitchen door.

Stephanie dangled her tea bag. 'I'd say that was tantra.'

'What, the spontaneous orgasm thing?'

'Yep, and just what I need. I'm going to check it out when I get back to L.A.' Stephanie had cheered up. 'Okay, let's see what the wisdom of the yogi tea tells us tonight,' she said, studying the inscription on her tea bag tag. 'Live from your heart, you will be absolutely effective,' she read aloud.

'Not sure Mr. Yoga Kills would agree with that. Got a feeling he don't do love,' said Grace.

'His trade secret, what would you suppose that is?'

'A broken heart, after—'

'—he fell in love with a student,' Stephanie completed Grace's sentence, and they clinked mugs.

'How much do you fancy him?' Grace asked.

'After that story, plenty. You know, he lives just 'round the corner from our cabin, above the kitchen?'

'Knock on his door.'

'He's a tantric god, no doubt, but I won't risk rejection. He's got strong boundaries—unlike some. Guess who I saw earlier this evening, heading down the path to the waterfall?'

For the past few days Stephanie had given Sam and Serena's friendship tabloid treatment, analyzing and, in Grace's opinion, overestimating the significance of their discreet gestures. But the following morning, when Sam and Serena faced each other in the yoga studio, moving and breathing in unison, eyes fixed on, yet beyond, each other, Grace guessed the California girl had got it right.

After so many days in accordance with the Bodhi Tree schedule, even Grace craved a little profane distraction, and found it lying in the shadows after a late night sauna, listening to Stephanie and her young crew chatting in the hot tub. Stretched out nearby, beneath the stars, she enjoyed the chatter without being part of it.

'If Rita says flexibility isn't yoga one more time, I'll spit,' said Stephanie.

'Rita's cool,' said Kirsty.

'I love Garuda,' said Fantasia, the sweet-faced teenager in pigtails. 'When he helps me into a pose, his hands know exactly where to go.'

'You wish,' said Stephanie.

'Give me Garuda over Sam anytime,' Kirsty said, blind to the forty years between them.

'Forget Sam, Serena's got him, and I wouldn't mind about that if she didn't act so prim, while all the time angling for sex.'

'Sam's such a know-all, and that ain't sexy,' said Fantasia.

'He's skinny and inflexible. I mean: gross. Like going to bed with a stick,' Kirsty volunteered.

Grace found the insight impressive for a girl on her first trip away from home. It pulled her in. 'Sam's youthful beauty holds no appeal because you have so much of your own,' she said from the shadows.

'Grace?' Stephanie called.

Grace walked toward them.

'Come join us,' said Kirsty.

It was the perfect night for a confessional, but Grace was not tempted to sit naked in chlorine. Wrapped in her black towel, she perched on the corner of the tub.

'You're from London, right? There must be all sorts of trouble to get into there,' said Kirsty.

Since Grace's parents were hardly 'the shining example' but rather the 'horrible warning' Shaw had professed was best, she had never been tempted by trouble. It had found her anyway. Her mother and Ted, the two people she loved who had loved her back, were both gone by the time they were forty-two. It seemed to Grace that whenever she loved, death followed close behind.

'So, Grace?' Stephanie coaxed.

'So, what?'

'What kind of trouble do you get up to in London?'

'Love as strong as death,' Grace said, which stopped the hot tub banter, and stars fifteen million light years away seemed a little closer.

II:7 *sukhah-anusayi ragah.*

II:8 *duhkha-anusayi dvesah.*

Patanjali's Book Two, sutras seven and eight, are concise: attachment is caused by pleasure, says seven; aversion results from sorrow, says eight. Grace had memorized sutra seven in Sanskrit believing she had no need for eight. Aversion, by its nature harder to detect, did not concern her. Then, one afternoon, studying in her cabin with the door open, she

overheard a student say, 'I love you, Daddy.' One-sided telephone conversations were a feature of Grace's afternoons because the area in front
of her cabin was the only place that picked up a signal, though only for
those on the Verizon network. This afternoon's overheard words made
Grace abandon her study to see who would say such a thing. Frances from
Seattle was sitting on the wall. 'Daddy, I'll come over to see ya as soon
as I get back. I love you.' Twice. In one conversation. Grace had heard
enough and shut the door.

But Grace's memories of her father were not so easily dismissed and
were triggered the following morning when she stood in the studio facing
Cindy's enhanced breasts that recalled the sketches and paintings on the
wall of his study. If her father hadn't been a surgeon he would have been
an artist, and what he liked to draw, and drew best, were women's bodies
—breasts in particular.

While Garuda guided them through the Vinyasa series, Grace followed mindlessly, staying in turtle pose, all the time thinking she would
ask her father for a picture that had always been her favourite. It occurred
to her then that she had never asked her father for anything, or expected
anything from him. He had never told her, 'I love you,' and she had never
said those words to him. Still in turtle, her arms locked to the floor beneath her knees, her nose pressed to her yoga mat, Grace experimented
with how 'I love you, Daddy' might sound.

'Are you okay?' It was Mark, his hand lightly on her shoulder. Grace
extracted herself from the intense forward bend, and looked up with red-
rimmed eyes. The rest of the class had moved on to *parsva bakasana,*
toppling cranes, and were all uneasy on one leg; Grace was less steady,
sitting on the floor.

'Take it easy, and let me know if you need anything.'

'What I need . . .' Grace started, and the Hampshire boy with the
California rings and California ways waited. 'What I need, Mark, you
can't give me.'

After class Grace walked to the water hole and sat. She wanted to want
to see her father. The humiliation of telling him she had separated from
Harry, of whom he had never approved, didn't trouble her. Finding him

drunk was what she feared. Whiskey had always been his poison and his passion, and had kept him from her as much as his work. The last time he'd tried Alcoholics Anonymous he had followed the steps for one full year and Grace, who had long ago stopped wanting him to be the good father, had dared to hope he would be sober when she saw him. When her father wasn't drinking, she appreciated his bittersweet take on life, and enjoyed his stories about the famous women whose breasts he'd enhanced. And then there were the tales of the women who had sat for him, many of whom, she assumed, had been lovers. Grace encouraged her father to take up drawing again, to give his days of sobriety purpose, but he resisted. 'Who would sit for me now? I'm nobody,' he'd say. Grace had bought him the easel, the paints, the paper, the pencils anyway. The easel was up, untouched, but Grace kept faith that as long as her father stayed sober, it was simply a question of time. And then one afternoon, early that year, after a sales meeting at the Lister hospital, she had called by her father's Harley Street flat. The lights were on so Grace knew he was there, but she had to ask the porter to let her in. They found her father asleep in his chair, three empty bottles of whiskey at his slippered feet. The slippers were blue velvet, embroidered with 'Mr. Happy' and a yellow smiley face, obliterated by stains best not investigated. Grace had cleaned the room, and her father, and then prepared hot food. Tired of a pattern repeated, she kissed him good-bye. 'Thank you, Caroline,' he said.

It hurt that her father had failed to recognize her, but it hurt more that he called her by her mother's name. That afternoon, Grace decided she would not see him again unless he was sober. She had passed the flat once, hoping for progress, for him and for her, but a glance at the bottles in the bin outside was all she needed to know and she had walked on. That's when Grace had memorized sutra eight: *duhkha-anusayi dvesah.*

Aversion. Caused by sorrow. No kidding.

Chapter Seven

VYAGHRASANA—tiger pose

Vyaghrapada, which means tiger-footed, was an adept of the Nandinatha lineage who was understood to be a disciple of Patanjali. Vyaghrasana emulates a tiger stretching as it wakes from sleep. Practicing this pose loosens the spine in both directions and tones the spinal nerves. Other physical benefits include improved digestion and blood circulation. It can also reduce weight from the hips and thighs.

Well into the training, no dark secret was off limits: childhood traumas, eating disorders, divorce, lovers, ex-lovers, lesbian affairs. But for those over thirty-eight, age was the final frontier and beyond discussion. Most of the younger students were curious to know Grace's age; the midnight hot-tubbers were desperate.

'Grace, how old are you?' asked Kirsty. The bubbles, shared nudity, and the clandestine night made her bold.

'Most secrets are revealed in time,' Grace answered cryptically.

'We think you're thirty-four,' said Fantasia.

'Forget age. Just remember I'm too old for your cheek.'

'Yet young enough to tell us how old you are,' Stephanie persisted.

'Steph, I could be your mother, though thank God I'm not.'

Stephanie was so assured, nothing fazed her, not even Grace's mock insult—and she laughed with the rest of them. Grace's place in their affection was intact, and her secret along with it. At the next practice session, tired of further questioning, she capitulated. 'I'm forty,' she admitted.

Stephanie's eyes bulged at Sam. Grace's age had apparently inspired conversation beyond the confines of the hot tub, and she didn't like how that felt; she bowed out from the youthful crowd. It was time to frequent the suitable companions Miss Messenger had identified and meet the residents of Yurt Six. The women were all science graduates of Grace's age, which was, she discovered, all she had in common with these working wives and mothers. Age and old science degrees did not justify new friendship. So, open to new alliances, Grace did not spurn Frances when she took the empty seat beside her one suppertime. She could overlook Frances's 'I love you' twice in one conversation to her father, and would concentrate instead on what they had in common, which was work. Frances, who had celebrated her thirty-fifth birthday at the Bodhi Tree, had quit a career in banking to train to be a yoga teacher, giving up a large salary in much the same way Grace had. But unlike Grace, Frances's yoga future was organized—back in Seattle her solicitor was working on the purchase of a building she would be converting into a small yoga centre. Grace panicked. Swami D's offer to give her classes to teach was the only thing she had to go on.

'Did he give you that offer in writing?' Frances asked.

'No, but I trust Swami D.'

'Really? You trust a guy called Swami D? At least drop him a line, if only to remind him.'

That afternoon, Grace sent Swami D a postcard.

Once Frances and Grace had discussed the world of work, they turned to the world of men. Having banned Harry from her head and heart, Grace preferred to listen to Frances tell of her surfer boyfriend in San Diego, and chose not to warn her. It seemed unfortunate that Frances could afford a pretty boyfriend (Grace had seen the photographs), and the weekly West

Coast commute to see him. With Frances making all the effort, her surfer had nothing to do. Grace sympathized. It turned out that pretty, penniless boyfriends weren't the only thing they shared. Both their fathers were in medicine.

'My father was critical,' Frances said.

'Mine, too,' said Grace, thinking there was more to this than mere coincidence. 'My father really could be quite demeaning.'

'No, I meant my father was critical, critical to my childhood, to the woman I've become. He has always believed in me. He's even investing in my yoga centre.'

'Funny how we hear things.'

Grace refrained from saying that her father was currently a drunk and had always been an addict. One thing she could assume was that Frances's father hadn't been struck off the register for consuming the contents of his medicine cabinet—another secret which, Grace felt, was better left unsaid.

'Call your dad. I bet he'd love to hear from you.'

'My phone doesn't work here. No signal.'

'Use mine.'

'Thanks, but it's the middle of the night over there,' Grace said.

Frances was brand new in love with a sweet young thing and planning her yoga future with her father: she deserved enthusiasm but Grace couldn't muster any for the tales she had to tell. It was easier to return to the speculative enquiries of the cynical nighttime creatures of the hot tub, where the conversation had moved on—but not much.

'Sam's bossy like a teacher, but he sucks up to the teachers,' said Fantasia, sticking out her tongue, its silver stud clicking her front teeth.

'It's a contradiction Serena can't resist,' said Stephanie.

They took a vote: those who believed that Serena and Sam had got together, or would, and those who thought he was inclined to somebody else—like Grace for instance.

'Come off it, I'm far too old for him.'

'A woman of forty, a man of twenty-eight. My mum did it, and she's a Presbyterian pastor. It was perfect. He had such cute friends,' said Fantasia.

'How long did it last?' Grace asked.

'Two years. He got confirmed and everything. After they split he met this cool woman, an ex-nun, ten years older than him. They married and adopted a kid.'

'I propose we bet on Sam getting off with Serena of the dark eyes, which is why he'll go for her. She reminds him, if he'd care to remember, of his girlfriend back in Paris,' said Stephanie, getting back to business.

'Girlfriend?' said Grace.

'Half Hawaiian, half French and his screen saver until two days ago,' said Fantasia.

'He thinks he's attracted to somebody new but it's familiarity that draws him in,' analyzed Stephanie. The child of divorced divorce lawyers, she understood the subtleties of infidelity.

'It must help that Serena is impressed by his opinions,' Kirsty said.

'Cos she doesn't have any of her own,' said the pastor's daughter.

'She might not have opinions, but with Sam in tow *and* a husband, she must know something,' said Grace.

'Like what?' said Kirsty.

'What men want,' Grace replied.

'And what's that?' said Fantasia.

'Adoration?' Grace inflected, California-style, uncertain herself.

'Yeah, or a blow job,' Stephanie said with conviction.

Grace was grateful for the girls, whose exuberance helped her to forget the past. The future never came up in conversation: they were too young to think of it. This left the present. The Bodhi Tree yoga exam was given some consideration but nothing absorbed them quite like Serena and Sam's love affair—or the possibility of it. By week three the hot tub conversation was quite specific, fueled by the stakes the girls had in the affair as much as any progress the couple were (or were not) making. The consensus was that Serena had not yet cheated on her husband but would. Stephanie had thirty dollars on it being the night of the exam. 'They'll study together madly, then make a proper go of it, lemon squeezy.'

'Lemon squeezy?' asked Fantasia.

'Lemon squeezy, easy,' Stephanie clarified.

'You didn't pick that up in Cadogan Square,' Grace said.

'I learned my cockney in L.A. It's so multiculti.'

Fantasia was sure the lovers would 'do it lemon squeezy' in the comfort of a hotel. 'Serena's car will be the getaway vehicle and they'll escape in the dark without saying good-bye to the rest of us.' Fantasia's thirty-five-dollar stake was the highest. So far Grace had refused to gamble.

'Come on, even a modest stake will heighten your interest. Get involved, Grace,' insisted Stephanie.

'It's like we're willing Serena to deceive her husband,' Grace said, still sensitive about her own deception.

'Sure, it sucks,' Stephanie grinned. 'So, girlfriend, in or out?'

Grace settled on twenty dollars.

'For what?' Fantasia asked.

'That they will.'

'But when?'

Grace entered into the game. 'Serena will make the initial move, two nights before we leave, so they can do it again, if it's good.'

Theories were rapidly revised when Sam appeared the next morning, clean-shaven for the first time in two weeks. Stephanie and Grace caught each other eye-to-eye: tonight's the night.

'Had to do it,' Sam said, joining them to eat his bowl of oatmeal, stroking his smooth white chin. 'Didn't want a tan line when I shave back in Paris. Not a good look.'

According to that night's hot tub gossip, the only mark that concerned Sam was the one his beard would have left on Serena's alabaster complexion.

'It's a shame,' said Fantasia, unexpectedly moralistic. 'Serena's going to cheat on her husband to have sex with a man she'll never see again. What's the point?'

'Maybe that *is* the point,' said Stephanie.

By then the girls' skin had turned as florid as the gossip; it was time to get out of the hot tub and they were off to the side, toweling dry, when to everybody's excitement, Sam appeared.

'Evening, Sam,' Fantasia said, excessively polite.

'Evening, ladies. How is it?'

'H-o-t,' one of the girls drawled.

Keeping his baggy shorts on, Sam sucked through puckered lips as he lowered his narrow frame into the steaming water. 'Ahhh, that's good,' he said, sinking in, shorts ballooning, the hot tub lights reflecting on his long white chin.

'Let's get back in,' Fantasia said.

'Didn't you have enough already?' Sam asked, pushing the air out of his shorts.

'Enough? Naked in hot water beneath the stars?' Stephanie dropped her towel; Fantasia and Kirsty followed her lead. Sam was boggle-eyed as the naked girls stepped up to the tub.

'Any room for me?' Serena interrupted from the top of the wooden steps, her black Speedo a modest contrast to the young girls' nudity. She may have seemed like a coy kitten at the start of the training, but Serena prowled down the stairs now like a hungry cat. She picked up a towel and, holding it out to Stephanie, hissed, 'Cover up, sweetie. We don't want you catching cold.'

Confident that she reigned supreme in the eyes of the man who had entertained them all, one way or another, for the past few weeks, Serena balanced on the edge of the hot tub. Grace observed that, whether inspired by love, lust, or Sam's zero percent body fat, Serena had lost weight. Her legs were almost slender, her generous bottom firm and lifted.

'How is it, Sam?' Serena asked through the rising steam.

'Hot,' was the answer.

Serena bent down to test the water. 'That *is* hot,' she said, shaking her hand. A flash of gold arched away from her like a shooting star and fell into the undergrowth.

'What was that?' Sam asked.

Serena held out her hand and howled, 'My *wedding* ring. Ed'll kill me.' The supposed lovers jumped from the tub and leaned over the balcony, willing the ring to reveal itself within the tangled hillside scrub.

Grace went to bed. She had seen enough but was still curious to know where the couple would go from here. As it turned out, not far. Early the next morning they searched in vain, and again the following night, but no gold glinted in Sam's flashlight. Desperation mounting, they drove to Malibu to rent a metal detector. One bleep of hope led them into the scrub, where they found a rusted key ring in the shape of a cross, 'Faith' engraved down its centre. Serena's treasure was lost. The land had claimed the ring, and if it had a lesson to teach, Sam and Serena seemed to have learned it: they abandoned their search, and apparently each other. Sam's beard was back by the end of the week.

Stephanie kept up her late night vigil with the girls, but Grace now tended to avoid the tub, studying instead for the Bodhi Tree exam. She was usually asleep by the time Stephanie got back, their agreement being that there'd be no unsolicited conversation if the lights were out. This evening Stephanie overlooked the rule.

'Grace?'

'Mmm . . .' It was late, too late to discuss much with meaning. The days were long, and compounded by Grace's anxiety about their final exam. She wanted sleep, and was almost there.

'What's it like without kids or a husband,' asked Stephanie, tucked up in bed but wide awake.

'And no job. Get it right,' Grace mumbled.

'Isn't the desire to have a child biology?' Stephanie said.

'I've never felt I *should* have a kid, and Harry already had Lucy.' It was the first time she'd said his name since he'd moved out. Grace sat up, folded her arms, and closed her eyes again.

'You never wanted a kid with Ted?'

'I wanted *him*,' she said, eyes wide open. 'He actually wasn't consistently around, which is what I would have needed.' A beat. Then: 'Ted didn't want kids.'

'Did you?'

It had never occurred to Grace that she may have denied wanting a child with Ted to suit him, and to keep him. She spoke slowly. 'From the start, Ted was clear he didn't want a child, which makes sense now. I suppose I didn't want one enough to convince him. And you know, I always thought we'd have time.'

'You still have time, and if you're meant to have a child, I believe you will,' said Stephanie. There was silence in the absolute stillness of that windless night. 'I wish you'd meet a really great man.'

'Thank you. I'll let you know.' Grace rolled over to face the wall.

'And I wish I knew how I felt about having a kid of my own.'

'You're young enough to find out.'

'That it feels like a choice is scary.'

'It should be a choice.'

'Right now, I can't imagine it. Then again, I could see myself at thirty-eight dashing out to get pregnant.'

'Motivated by fear that you're missing out. The compulsion to have something before you can't have it anymore. You're better than that.'

'I hope I am. I'll let you know.'

'That could be a long time for us to keep in touch.'

'I'm down with that. You're a keeper, you are. Good night.'

Stephanie threw a brown padded envelope across the cabin. 'I knew you had somebody in the wings,' she said. Grace caught the package and checked the stamps. From London. Posted a week before.

'I *so* knew it. A woman like you, without a man, not possible, honey pie. You're good at secrets, I'll say that for ya.' Stephanie watched Grace take out the contents of the envelope. 'Socks?' she said in disbelief.

'And just about the best present.'

'I was hoping the package was from an admirer.'

'I think he might be.'

'A guy who sends socks? Is that an English thing?'

'Cashmere socks, I'm not complaining. It gets cold here at night.'

'Is there a letter?'

Grace waved a small, white envelope. Opening it, she admired the blue-lined interior. Stephanie stood patiently while Grace read:

> *Grace, not wanting to pursue an unavailable woman, I resisted contacting you but couldn't hold out. Hope you don't mind me tracking you down at Bodhi Tree. I keep thinking of all the things I should have asked, and wish I had, when we met. Like when you're back, for instance.*
>
> *I've booked my flight to Vietnam and will study there for the next three months, possibly longer. I hope we meet when I return. The socks are to wish you luck, and keep you warm when it gets cold in the mountains. Let's keep in touch on our alternative paths.*
>
> *David*

Grace passed the letter to Stephanie. 'Use my cell. Send him a text right now.'

'Maybe later.'

'You like him, right?'

'I do, but I'm not ready to do anything about it.'

'The guy's heading to Vietnam. You wouldn't be able to do something even if you wanted to. I think it's safe to send a text. It's hardly a commitment. And you should tell him you're available.'

'I know, but I'm a little scared by love that hasn't worked out. I'll wait, think what to say . . .'

'It's an absolute, demonstrable fact that the person who really practices love rises so high above fear it can no longer touch him,' Stephanie said.

Love conquers fear, of course it did. 'Who said that?' Grace asked.

'I did, quoting one Norman Vincent Peale. A weird guy who was right about some things.'

At half past four the next morning, Grace was awake. She had slept nine hours every night of the first week; by the second, five was all she needed. Lying in bed, she had Dr. James on her mind, particularly the way he'd pulled her to him the last time they'd met. She got out of bed, crept to the apothecary cabinet where Stephanie kept her phone, and, consulting her own, punched in Dr. James's number. Then she sat on the cabin step to compose her text.

Watching dawn light slide down the dark mountain, thinking of you. Thank you for the socks & the note. Let me hear from you in Vietnam.

Chapter Eight

MAHA VEDHA MUDRA—the great piercing attitude

Maha *means great and* vedha *means piercing. The purpose of the asana is to channel* prana *generated through the practice of related poses,* maha mudra *and* maha banda. *This pose stimulates introversion of the mind, which is one of its purposes. It awakens psychic faculties and stimulates the kundalini energy, which is said to lie dormant at the base of the spine in the* mooladhara *chakra. The pose balances the pituitary gland, regulates hormonal activity, and slows the aging process.*

In London, Grace had sensed danger on the street without feeling afraid. At Bodhi Tree, even noises in the night could unsettle her. Shuffling sounds outside the cabin filled her with unease, no matter that it was the wind whipping up the long grass, or an animal—one thing in the lab, quite another burrowing in the earth—possibly beneath her bed. Ashamed at her childish fright but unable to suppress it, she repeated the chant Rita had taught them, '*Lokah samaska sukinau bhavantu.*' 'May all beings on all planes of existence know peace and harmony,' was the mantra's meaning, a kind of prayer that Grace repeated softly, over and over. If that didn't calm her, she picked up Stephanie's Jim Harrison book and, by torchlight beneath the bedclothes, whispered aloud fragments of his poetry.

O lachrymae sonorense.
From the ground
paced the stars through the ribs
of ocotillo, thin and black
each o'clock till dawn,
rosy but no fingers except
these black thin stalks
directing a billion bright stars,
captured time swelling outward
for us if we are blessed
to be here on the ground,
night sky shot with measured stars,
night sky without end
amen.

'Are you all right?' Stephanie, who slept through howling winds and coyotes, was roused by the sound of Grace's whispering and the dull torchlight.

'Sorry to wake you,' Grace said, and turned out the light.

Grace's solution was to learn a few verses that she repeated, silently, in darkness. The poet's words about the nature of man and beast and earth offered her an insight into the surrounding landscape and, perhaps, she reflected, into her own nature. Living in her head, thinking, always thinking, the words helped her step out—to this. This.

Primed by yoga, her body responded to nature's rhythm with less resistance. It was as though the hard-edged effects of the city where she lived had been countered by the soft form of yoga she practiced there. In the slower paced natural world, Rita and Garuda's structured, dynamic yoga made sense, although Grace wasn't prepared for the physically aggressive practice. Seduced by the teachers and the centre they'd created, Grace overlooked Garuda's interpretation of 'going with the flow,' and pushed through the daily three-hour Vinyasa practice. After years of London living, breathing exhaust fumes, she was proud to be up early, claiming the day. She would run down to the swimming hole and, on the climb up the valley, she would dismiss the tightening in her toned gluteal muscles as they worked ligament and bone.

If going with the flow, as Garuda put it, meant sometimes taking it slowly, Grace was incapable of it at the Bodhi Tree. Ripe for a lesson to learn, she received it at six o'clock that morning, reaching into the old apothecary cabinet for Stephanie's cell to see if Dr. James had responded to her message from the night before. He had not, but if Grace was disappointed she didn't have time to feel it: a fierce pain ripped through her hip, nerves jangling in her pelvis. The pain was unbearable, even terrifying. Instinctively, Grace kept moving and hobbled to the sauna in the hope that heat would melt the pain away.

So much for her determination to be youthfully energetic at the Bodhi Tree. Grace moved like a ninety-year-old. The short walk exhausted her, and by the time she reached the sauna, she longed to lie down. It was still so early, she expected to wait while the temperature in the sauna reached therapeutic heat, but there was no need. Olga, the Russian model who now dreamed of being a West Coast yoga teacher, was lying on the top shelf, a white turban protecting her blonde hair, sweat pooling in her tummy and streaming down her thighs. She had to have been there for hours for the temperature to be that high. She ignored Grace. Garuda, upright in the corner in regulation black shorts, grunted hello. He wasn't sweating at all. Grace lay on the lowest shelf, her face screwed up in agony.

'What happened?' asked Garuda.

'I leaned and twisted and something snapped in my pelvis.'

'Have the massage therapist check out your *psoas* muscle when he comes later today, and take three painkillers. There's a packet at the back of the first aid shelf. Let me know how you get on.' Garuda stood slowly.

'Painkillers?' Grace said.

'Used wisely, I don't have anything against them. Remember, they're drugs like any other, and will get you high. Take it easy in class.' Garuda walked out, the wooden door thudding shut.

'Class? I can hardly stand.'

Olga pulled the edge of her turban over her eyes. No sympathy there. The Bodhi Tree painkiller was a Suprafarma anti-inflammatory.

Grace swallowed three, then went to the yoga studio long before class. The pain ebbed and she was ready for the challenge of the Vinyasa series. Relief was short-lived, and pain defeated pride. With a blanket pulled up to her shoulders, she watched Garuda teach, freedom from pain all she wanted. Lying still, she noticed Garuda's eagle eye on each student as he paced the room, hobbling discreetly. The painkillers had to be his.

'Stay within your limits,' he said, as the yogis powered on. 'If you are at the edge of your flexibility, chances are you are at the minimum edge of pleasure, possibly on the edge of pain. Pain, like doubt, is your friend, a feedback system that defines limits—whatever you're doing.'

His words sounded familiar and Grace wondered how often he had said them without her properly listening.

'Try practicing asanas at the minimum edge of your flexibility; it might put you at the maximum edge of your enjoyment.'

All around bodies moved in varying degrees of sweaty ease through challenging sequences. Feeling humiliated, Grace called Garuda over. 'This is too frustrating. Can I leave?'

'It's about being part of the training, not doing the asanas. Stay if you can.'

Grace remained faithful to the yoga studio, learning to accept her limitations, the pain so bad she had no choice and no shame in moving slowly, if at all.

In their other lives most students nurtured children, husbands, or lovers, and in the absence of somebody to care for, the wounded Grace became their focus. It wasn't easy receiving sympathy, but she accepted hands-on healing from Rita, whose gentle conversation and even gentler pressure, applied to Grace's gluteus maximus, eased the agony. Pain made Grace humble. She had no choice but to ask for help and accept it: her peers collected her dirty clothes and laundered them; Stephanie dressed her, and at meals Sam lifted her from sitting to standing. Grace declined a massage from Derek.

Whenever she felt killed by kindness, Grace could count on Olga for a dose of schadenfreude, delivered in the sauna or on the hot tub deck, where she was dedicated to tanning and sweating in a way only somebody from a cold, old country understood. Grace was the only student who still bothered to communicate with her. From the bubbling tub on a seventy-five-degree afternoon, she watched Olga smear her straight limbs with sun lotion, then settle in her yellow bikini. Its pink and silver graffiti—'sexy,' 'hot body,' 'lover girl'—contrasted with her reading: *This Light in Oneself* by Krishnamurti.

'Have you been to India?' Grace asked.

'The pawverty, the disease. India not for everyone.'

'Isn't Krishnamurti Indian?'

'So? Everyone read Chekhov but they not go to St. Petersburg. I passionate about Krishnamurti. He Indian and he very interesting,' Olga said and went back to her book.

'I've never read Krishnamurti,' Grace confessed, ashamed to admit she'd never read Chekhov either.

Olga peered disdainfully over the white-framed sunglasses that covered her face. 'Krishnamurti say know yourself, or what is word? Chaos? Know yourself, or you chaos, world chaos.'

This was the longest conversation Olga had had with anyone all training and, apparently bored, she retired to the silence of the sauna. Abandoned by the Russian, Grace wasn't alone for long. Sara stood on the edge of the hot tub, arms raised as she sang, 'hello.' Grace tried not to mind, and tried not to stare at Sara's hair-matted legs and the longer hairs that darkened her armpits. She focused on the tattoo circling Sara's navel. 'Love your lotus flower.'

'Actually it's a cactus—sixteen petals,' Sara said, sliding in. 'Getting my tattoos has been a pilgrimage. I wanted a tattooist who thought of herself as an artist, and she had to be a woman.' Sara raised one leg, then the other, showing patterned thighs. 'She did this one on December seventeenth, and this one on June seventeenth; the equinoxes are important dates to remember. What's your tattoo?'

'I don't have one.'

'I thought everyone had one.' In many ways, Sara was right. Everyone under thirty-five at the Bodhi Tree was indelibly marked with a design of some kind.

'Did they hurt,' asked Grace.

'Not as much as other things. This one,' said Sara, twisting to reveal her left shoulder blade, 'is for my moon, which is in Scorpio, and unites with the symbol for my sun in Aquarius, and this one,' she said, turning to the right shoulder blade, 'is for the Greek myth that goes with my birth sign.'

The air at the Bodhi Tree was clear and Grace gazed down to Malibu, where mist descended on the shore. In that instant, sitting in the hot tub on a California afternoon, Grace was able to accept everything, from a conversation about astrological tattoos, to not knowing how her yoga future would unfold.

With pain framing her perspective, Grace slowed down. She had no choice. No longer able to bound around, she was the resident invalid, and a captive audience. The most unlikely person to seek her out was Sungli, the tiny Vietnamese woman who called her family every afternoon from the hill outside Grace's cabin. Of all the overheard conversations, Sungli's carried with the most intensity and Grace would groan when 'helloww' heralded another excursion into Sungli's world—excursions that Grace sometimes truncated by covering her head with her pillow, which is how Sungli found her when she walked in.

'Helloww, invalid!' she laughed.

'Hi, Sungli,' said Grace, pretending to have been asleep.

'Oh nice. Soo nice. It brand new. Cabin sooo nice. Lucky you. Oh dear, my son, his soccer tomorrow.'

Grace had heard about the soccer the day before.

'If he get draw in next match, he go through to finals. He win cup *and* medal. I got to call him tell him he got to win. He want me call at three tomorrow.'

'Isn't that when we have our exam?'

'I know. Exam. I never done exam. It terrible. I leave exam, run call my son, run back. Hope exam okay. Did you study for exam?'

'I have.'

'Lucky you. English easy for you, you English!'

'Let's hope it helps,' said Grace, who planned to use Sanskrit as much as possible in her answers.

'My English lousy, I not know nothing.' Sungli's laugh ripped through the cabin, making the sweet rest of her impossible to bear.

Grace had prepared for the exam with Frances, sharing the Seattle woman's yoga encyclopedia and her methodical approach. While both women had given countless presentations to medics or financiers, the practical part of the yoga exam terrified them. They drew and redrew stick figures of asanas for the twenty-minute sequence in which each student would teach their teachers and peers. Using her body as a test case, Grace had devised a class for people with back pain. This wasn't the time for her to show off; she'd be lucky to get through her miniclass still standing. Frances had come up with a lesson for five-year-olds, giving postures animal names, and planned to ask her students to invent postures of their own. Grace would ask fellow students to imagine pain that prohibited movement; Frances required them to make animal noises. Imaginations rather than bodies would be stretched.

The papers for the written exam—an hour of furious scribbling at the dining room tables—were returned that evening. Everyone gathered for a public analysis. Garuda, Rita, and Mark had selected certain answers that were read aloud. Grace saw that some of her well-informed attempts at accuracy had missed the points communicated by the haphazard answers of others. It seemed that right answers were broadly constituted. Nobody failed; Grace was glad the teaching certificate would be harder to come by, awarded only to those Bodhi Tree graduates who submitted case studies of one hundred teaching hours for Garuda's and Rita's scrutiny.

Now that the training was almost complete, a celebration was called for, and one had been scheduled: the Bodhi Tree Leaving Party. Invited to look their best, the women applied makeup to faces that had been fresh for weeks, and all looked a little false, a little less beautiful. With apple juice to drink and mostly girls to dance with, it felt like a lesbian gathering of

Alcoholics Anonymous. When Rita appeared—rock 'n' roll glamorous in boots, designer jeans, and gold jewelry—Garuda's hand on her waist, roaming to her bottom, was her enviable accessory.

The party put Grace on edge. She went up to the cabin, pulled a warm jersey over her thin dress, and put on a pair of Dr. James's socks. Sitting on the step overlooking the mountains, she picked up Stephanie's mobile. She thumbed a text: *Have learned plenty but feel complete beginner. Wearing your socks. Thinking of you in Vietnam. x.*

Grace sat with the black mass of the night mountain. She had been right to forsake superficial certainties to come to this place and meet these people. An incoming text made her jump. *I'm discovering being a beginner is what the refinement of any art is about. Will write soon. Safe home if you aren't already.* Dr. James was thousands of miles, yet seconds away. Grace leaned against the cabin door. The night was quiet. The music had stopped. It was time to walk back to the party.

In the main hall, the lights were up and attention was focused on a small sofa draped with orange and purple, decorated with flowers and set upon a dais surrounded by a semicircle of cushions. Garuda and Rita assumed the elevated position, an indulgence Grace found at odds with their philosophy of equality, to address the students at their feet. Rita was gracious when she thanked them for what she called their dynamic of willingness. Then it was Garuda's turn. 'In twenty-three years of holding this ceremony, we've never put the seat here, which worried me this afternoon when I saw that it's in sight of the toilet door. Thinking it over, we decided the location is good. It's a warning that wherever there's a guru, or a teacher, chances are there's a fair amount of shit around. Be aware of duplicity and hypocrisy, not only in others. Celibate gurus, by the way, are usually the worst. Just about every so-called celibate yogi I ever met wasn't just having sex, but plenty of it. I've yet to be convinced that it's possible to turn off the most powerful life force that exists. Remember to check out the light in your guru's eye, and when it's your turn to teach, don't worry about impressing your pupils. An old teacher once told me, "Pupils, I only need two." As a teacher all you want to do is pass on some light; you know what happens to pupils when the light's too bright. Don't try to outshine anybody—and never fear your students. We all ride the crest of high and low points, and wherever you are on that curve, you can pass something on. A teacher, or guru, is a transformer, amplifying and reflecting the light received from those around him. Tonight we want to give you a taste of that. So come up here, and bounce the light back.' With that, Garuda and Rita sat on the floor among the students, as each one took their turn in the light.

Olga was first up and in her long white dress she was abundantly beautiful. 'I love California. I will be yoga teacher in Santa Monica. I am sorry for language. I had here, and this proper English, I had here fabulous good time.'

Sungli was next and so small that, when sitting on the sofa, her feet didn't touch the ground. 'I didn't want to come here. Now I don't want to go home. I was frightened to leave children, and husband. I thought without me they big mess. But they okay! And at Bodhi Tree, I okay. I like it. Soo nice. Next time, I have cabin!' Her braying laugh changed into a silent sob, the fine creases in her face wet with tears. 'I so scared, you know, to go back?' In spite of her Californian inflection, nobody doubted her.

When Grace took the guru's sofa, from its elevated position the faces around her looked brand new. 'If it took me too long to figure out what was important at the Bodhi Tree, and if I've seemed remote sometimes and too English, forgive me. Thank you for caring for me as I've hobbled around. And to the keepers of this land, Garuda and Rita, thank you for inspiring me to treat daily actions as sacred. To believe . . .' In love, she had wanted to say, but couldn't. Grace bowed her head—a sign of respect that conveniently hid her emotion.

'Don't you just love that accent,' said Stephanie, stepping up to the hot seat. Her words were short and sharp, until she hesitated. 'Oh my God, I'm going to cry. And I'm going to enjoy it.' After a second her streaming tears made Stephanie laugh. 'I can't remember the last time I did that.' She rocked back on the sofa. 'You know, this is the business. Sitting here is the real deal.'

When it was Sam's turn he directed his words to Garuda and Rita, a teacher to teachers; he wasn't sitting in the light so none bounced back. Serena followed him. 'Every early morning I have walked the trails, across my path the fragile but strong threads of spiders' webs reminding me how fragile but strong I am.' Apparently it did not remind her of the web we weave when we deceive. Grace felt ashamed for participating in all the hot gossip; Serena would not, surely, talk about spiders' webs if she were deceiving her husband.

All the students had taken their turn except Derek, who was slumped beside Grace and snoring. 'Derek!' Garuda shouted. Derek had escaped that afternoon for happy hour in the local tavern, a few glasses hitting hard after three weeks of clean living. Grace nudged him awake. He bolted to the dais, where he sat scratching his hair like Stan Laurel. 'Nobody in normal life knows I'm here. If something had happened, where would you have shipped the body?' Turned out Derek was a very funny man, and even Garuda howled with laughter listening to him describe his night with a skunk, learning to love a pit bull terrier, and the impossibility of shavasana with groin strain—which was nowhere near as hard as being the only man in a hot tub with six naked girls. 'Shouldn't have stayed in, couldn't get out.' When the slightly drunken monologue ended, Derek kissed Grace's cheek and slumped beside her.

That night, Grace couldn't sleep and crept out of the cabin. Certain it was the full moon's light that had awakened her, she stepped out into the garden and was glad. She never wanted to lose the connection and sensitivity to nature that the Bodhi Tree had given her.

'Hello. Is that you?' It was Mark, on the terrace outside his flat, staring into the shadows of the garden below. Grace froze, certain she was out of sight. Perhaps he had arranged to meet Stephanie—although it was unlikely she could have kept such a rendezvous secret.

Mark leaned over the edge of the balcony. 'Grace, is that you?' He sounded as though he expected her.

She was compelled to answer. 'Yes, it's me. What are you doing?' He asked the same of her, their overlapping words a gentle echo.

'Couldn't sleep.'

'Me neither.'

'Come up,' he whispered.

Grace walked up the wooden stairs and sat beside him. They stared ahead at the mountains and didn't speak. Sitting still and close to him she was aware of the magnetism between them: was it possible that this was the energy that had roused her? The corners of Mark's mouth curled up slightly, and his eyelids closed for a second when he said, 'Strong, isn't it?'

Grace nodded and looked at him.

'Shall we go inside?'

As they stood, he took her hand and led her to his bedroom. He took off his clothes. There was such ease and confidence in his movements, Grace was suddenly unsure. She had expected some kind of conversation, a polite negotiation, but Mark didn't need that, or offer it. He reclined, naked, waiting for her.

'I feel fifteen,' she said, still dressed, kneeling beside him on the bed.

'It's good to feel fifteen sometimes,' he said, resting his hand on her knee. Mark had the supreme assurance of an athlete who knows his body and how to use it. He made no attempt at seduction. His body was the fact—and so was hers. Grace removed her clothes. She knew that for them to lie together would mean nothing beyond this moment. Grace embraced that freedom, and in the half dark of her last Bodhi Tree night, Mark showed her things he hadn't learned in Hampshire. She responded, the energy they call kundalini rising, making her belly jump. 'I like it that you're natural with me,' he said, and kissed her.

After he had made love to her the first time, she shook with laughter at the pleasure of it, of the surprise of being here with him like this. They lay still a while. 'We're the only English on the compound,' Grace said.

'I'd been missing home without even knowing it,' he said, and squeezed her.

The purity of their attraction was untainted by any idea of what it should be, or should mean. In that moment it simply was.

They made love several times, at ease with each other as they moved around the bed. Their intimacy was natural, and possible, she later reflected, because they were both so comfortable in their own bodies—and because the next day she would be gone. They looked at each other for a long time. His dark brown eyes slanted slightly at the corners and were beautiful, almost delicate, in his face. 'I'd like to spend more time with you, if you didn't live on the other side of the mountain . . .' She pressed her mouth to his warm lips. He breathed in her exhalation and she copied him, completing a circle that was hypnotic. There was gentleness and sensitivity and raw power, their balance of opposites so complete, all difference between them dissolved.

The next day, the pain in Grace's pelvis had almost gone away. When she said her farewells, everyone remarked how recovered she was. She and Mark smiled at each other across the room: it wasn't sad to say good-bye to him, or to anyone. Grace happily lost her $20 stake to Kirsty when it was discovered that Sam and Serena had indeed disappeared the night before in her getaway vehicle.

On the plane back to London, the feelings of her last night with Mark stayed with Grace. It couldn't be love but if she had to name it she would have said that is what it felt like. But it couldn't be love, could it? That physical sensation wasn't love, yet sitting in economy, the seat in front reclined to her knees, Grace felt a peace deeper than any she had ever experienced in meditation. Peace that passes all understanding were the words that described it best. Grace didn't try to hold onto it, or concentrate on it. It was just there all around her and inside her like an atmosphere that she could push a little at the edges, before withdrawing into herself again—which was not herself but a beautiful void. She felt like an astronaut, suspended in space. Then, for some reason she recalled being in the yoga studio and crying and telling Mark that he couldn't give her what she needed. She laughed out loud at how little she knew herself, and the bubble popped. Back in the world of airplane food and in-flight entertainment, one heard the repeated mantra of the cabin crew: 'would you like wine with dinner?'

Grace pulled her blanket over her head and, sitting cross-legged in her airplane seat, floated on Bodhi Tree memories all the way home.

Chapter Nine

SALAMBA SIRSHASANA—headstand pose

Salamba *means with support and* sirsa *means the head. Headstand is one of the most important yogic asanas and mastering it gives the practitioner poise and balance, both physically and mentally. It takes time to feel oriented to surroundings when balanced on the head. Beginners can feel unfamiliar, and fear of falling can make it an effort to think clearly and act logically. But toppling over while learning the headstand is not as terrifying as we imagine.*

When Swami D saw Grace, California-tanned from the Bodhi Tree retreat, he urged her to take a photograph of herself to remember the moment and how she felt. 'You are refreshed and new, Grace, and the city will rob you of it.'

Grace doubted the concrete jungle could steal her high spirit. Delighted to be back in the neighborhood and to see her name on the studio timetable alongside his, she hugged Swami D's skinny frame in gratitude. He resisted, but settling his bony hands on her shoulders, said, 'Grace, I'm proud of you. You did what you set out to do. My only request is that you are patient with your students, and yourself.'

'I will try,' she said, instantly impatient when she realized that she wasn't on the timetable to teach for another two weeks. 'Swamiji, I'm ready now!'

'Grace, there's no rush. Surely you have things to sort out.'

'Like what?'

'Your pelvis for a start.'

'Is it that obvious?'

'You have a slight limp. Did you overdo the yoga?'

'I did, but I'm almost better, and tomorrow I'm seeing an acupuncturist who has promised he can fix me, so I'll be able to teach. And Swami D, when it comes to . . .' Grace stopped to search for a way to say 'money' without sounding crass.

'Consider your classes karma yoga, your pay the reward of teaching.' Swami D forestalled discussion.

Walking home down Ladbroke Grove, Grace felt dejected that Swami D needed to test that yoga was central to her life, rather than a money-making diversion from it. Perhaps she'd been unreasonable to expect to be paid. She chose not to think that Swami D was mean. Satisfied that it was enough for him to demonstrate faith by giving her classes to teach, Grace looked up from the pavement. An old Volkswagen was parked on the corner of St. Helen's Gardens, a 'for sale' notice in the window. It wasn't the retail therapy Grace was used to, but she did need a car, and this one was solid—in fact, that's all it was. Grace made herself like it. The dark blue colour helped, and the winter weather played its part. The price was irresistible. Half an hour later the car was hers.

Grace had never not worked. Freedom from nine to five, or the nine to nine it had sometimes been, was not the liberation she had imagined it would be. Her life stalled as she waited for her pelvis to fully heal and her work at Swami D's to start. Tai, the master acupuncturist of Notting Hill Gate, saw what her pelvis needed and stuck six pins directly into her bottom; instantly the pain went away. Convinced Tai was a genius, Grace made another appointment for three days later. By that time the pain had edged back in but one more treatment was all it took for it to disappear for good. During the second session, Tai addressed more than Grace's pelvis when he asked her where her friends were these days (tactfully implying she had some), then less tactfully adding, 'and what about nooky?'

'Nooky? Why?'

'I think that's what your pelvis needs,' he said, serious. 'You're yang-deficient.'

Taï's comments made Grace think: there was no question that yang, the male energy, was lacking in her life. Sex with the Calvin-Klein-cutout Harry had not realized the full promise of their first loving nights when she had opened to him, body and soul. And however much memories of her one night with Mark lingered, it did not make up for the deficit of the past four years. As for friends, Grace had always kept few friends, which had never bothered her. She had made the mistake, if that's what it was, of counting on the man she lived with for friendship and love. Now, Grace recognized that friends were what she needed. Suprafarma colleagues had never been more than coworkers, and while she loved and respected Swami D, respect put distance between them—which should not preclude friendship. Respect was good, she reasoned, but all her friends were somehow distant. She had stayed in touch with her friend Claire, from their Cambridge days, even when she had moved to New York for Goldman Sachs and an American man, but after her marriage and two children, their points of reference had diverged. The past had not sustained their friendship.

Grace traced her reluctance to form friendships back to prep school, where all she'd wanted was to fit in and be like everybody else, which was impossible because all the other girls had a mother. It seemed unfair that some had two. Ashamed not to have a mother of her own, Grace had kept her distance from the girls who did. The futility of Mother's Day, the fated weekend leave when children returned to parents and the headmistress decided with whom Grace would stay, and school parents' day when her father failed to appear, were all bad days. The mothers' running race on school sports day was worse. Grace had ached to be out there cheering her mother on, and at the end of the afternoon, when the crowds had gone, she would return to the abandoned sports field. Staring down the straight white lines painted on the grass, Grace would wait, and keep on waiting, until she could see her mother so clearly she would reach out as if to touch her as she ran in the outside lane, running for the tape, her arms raised and laughing.

This is what lived with Grace as she rattled around her house, aware of every sound and thought. Swami D had imposed waiting on her. She supposed he wanted her to be still, to be with herself for a while. Grace knew how to be alone, but in these days she was lonely. At the start of the Bodhi Tree training, she had cynically dismissed Rita's claim that they were creating a yoga family, but back in Ladbroke Grove, she recognized that they had. Grace missed the girls of spirit, wit, and wickedness, and cabin conversations with Stephanie. She longed for the big, American vistas, for her connection to nature. For the first time in months, she walked around her garden. Forty walled feet in London in December did not match the magnificence of the Bodhi Tree land, but this was her garden and it needed attention. Without Harry to tend them, the plants were overgrown, and apples rotted in the long grass around the fruit trees. Last year, she and Lucy had gathered the apples and made apple pie. 'Forget Lucy,' Grace said aloud, desperate to forget last year, and all the years.

Before she'd lived with Harry, Grace had employed a gardener, but would not do so again. Wrapped in old clothes, she worked in the garden as the London light came up, the smell of earth and plants strong in cold air. Grace was attuned to the world beyond the confines of her head and house: bird calls, the low-slung hum of airplanes, church bells, sirens, skateboarders' wheels over paving stones. The sound of traffic streaming along the A40 was her distant waterfall and by the time she had finished working in the garden, hundreds and hundreds of children were playing in the caged tarmac of the local school.

Date:	November 16, 2006
To:	stephanie17@gmail.com
From:	yogagrace@hotmail.com
Subject:	quiet in the house

At first I was excited to be in London again, but I'm missing the enforced routine, even the forced company at the Bodhi Tree.

I'm waiting to start teaching. Waiting for my life to start is what it feels like.

Are you teaching? Are you writing? Are you ever coming this way?
Love,
Grace

Date: November 17, 2006
To: yogagrace@hotmail.com
From: stephanie17@gmail.com
Subject: shrinking allowance

just made a scrapbook of B Tree and have already forgotten half the names. how should i feel about that? the only thing I miss about bt is you. am teaching in venice at this studio where serious yogis from all over the world come for flying visits. the pay is bad but I tell myself the experience is good, specially since this american yogi, diane who lives in rome, gave a workshop here. she spent thirty years in florence, studying with vanda scaravelli. i think her yoga is the one for me. mind you, inspired by that spontaneous reaction mark told us about, i've signed up for a tantra workshop next month.

writing articles for a freebie yoga magazine. no pay there at all and i don't care about that, i love it so much. getting through my allowance, which is kind of scary. moved into a little house off abbot Kinney near the ocean, sharing with an old school friend, but plan to come to europe anyway. i'm thinking rome late spring. a perfect excuse to see diane and the pantheon.

signing off. adios! did you tempt the sock man back from nam?
s
ps sent you package this afternoon

Two days later Jim Harrison's *The Shape of the Journey* arrived—by FedEx. No wonder Stephanie's allowance was shrinking. Grace held the book like a friend as she read the familiar poetry. At the Bodhi Tree the book had been Grace's nighttime companion and she thought she knew it from cover to cover. She saw now that she had missed Harrison's 'Cabin Poem,' around which Stephanie had ringed four lines:

> guilt & grace
> cabin & home
> north & south
> struggle & peace

Grace had intended to cancel Vince the builder but put it off until one morning he was standing on her doorstep with two men and a truckload of machinery on the street. Grace led them up to the attic and asked them to give her a smooth oak floor and two wide windows in the roof. 'I'd like to see a lot of sky,' she said.

'Not great for a bedroom,' Vince responded.

'It's not going to be a bedroom after all,' she said, and climbed down the ladder.

Thoughts of Lucy could still make Grace sad, no matter how many times she told herself to forget the five-year-old. No more Loobiloo. No more Harry was another matter. Grace still couldn't believe her capacity to be used by him, which had been matched only by his capacity to use her. Grace wanted to forgive him, and even herself for being that terrible thing: a fool in love—a poetic way, she thought, of saying a codependent idiot.

In an attempt to change her thinking, every morning Grace practiced a variation of *kumbhaka,* a breathing trick the old yogis use to alter consciousness. She would lock the bathroom door, lie in a bath that was full to overflowing, turn off the tap with her toes, take a gulp of air, and then submerge. Many seconds would pass before the first wave of resistance; she'd release bubbles of air through her nose one at a time until her ribs expanded, her diaphragm was drawn up, and her throat pulled down. In underwater silence Grace slipped into that place where not breathing at all becomes a seductive possibility. Playing with her oxygen intake, depriving her brain of even miniscule amounts, changed Grace's perspective. By the time she was propelled to the surface for air, she was indifferent to Harry and how they had been together. One morning she actually felt compassion for him—submerging six times was all it took.

At night she would rest her mind in the white noise of the distant traffic and imagine she was back at Bodhi Tree, listening to the waterfall. Lying in bed, she felt as if her body was suspended, floating on the sound. Such sensations didn't make sense to her scientific brain but she didn't question their validity, or their meaning—even the night she watched a tunnel of fine waves like compact streams of silver light emanate from the soft part of her upper belly. While the light was coming from that place the yogis call the *manipura* chakra—'wheel of the jeweled city'—it didn't seem to have anything to do with her. She stared down the channel of light that extended six feet from her body and saw Ted's face. He was there, as he had been when he was well, and they were happy.

'Love you,' Grace said.

'Then set me free,' he said.

'Go,' she whispered, wanting him to stay forever. He was still there. Without thinking, Grace repeated the chant that Rita had taught them: '*Lokah samaska sukinau bhavantu.*' The flow of light dissolved. Ted was gone.

That night, deep sleep gave Grace a dream of Rudra, the adept of *manipura* chakra. In her dream, Rudra, famous for wakening from the dream of conventional life to the reality of himself, played catch with the four-armed goddess, the dark-skinned Lakshmi, who lived with him in the jeweled city. Rudra accelerated the game and threw more, faster still: a rose quartz, Patanjali's sutras, a Barbie jeep, a condom, car keys, a packet of Procent. The goddess caught them all, until Rudra had nothing else to throw. 'The jeweled city is yours,' he said, and left Lakshmi alone with her many hands full. Grace slept in the following morning, and it took Vince and his builders banging on the front door for five minutes to wake her.

She let the men in, then took a bath. She submerged and knew that today she would do what she had avoided for so long—and she would need help. In Ted's toweling robe, her wet hair wound inside a white towel, she headed for the attic and was on the new staircase when she stopped.

'Look what I've found,' one of the men was saying.

'That's gold that is,' said another.

'I reckon that's a diamond in the middle.'

'I found a diamond once, in a bidet. What about you, Vince, did you ever find anything tasty?'

'Peanut.'

'You what?'

'A peanut.'

'A peanut ain't worth nothin'.'

'It was when I got a call from this woman. "Me hamstas stuck. I carn't get it out," she screams down the phone. So I goes over and there's her hamsta down the back of the radiator. She goes out for fags and I take a look. I got no idea how to get it out, till I find this peanut in me pocket. I put it down, and it come out. When the woman gets back, she screams it's a bleedin' miracle and asks how much. I tell her one hundred and fifty quid.'

'You didn't?'

'I did. She paid an' all. Ain't been nowhere without a peanut since.'

Vince's peanut had the men in stitches and, sitting on the stairs, Grace laughed with them. Laughter was infectious and soon her sides ached. When finally they'd calmed down, and so had she, she stood in the frame that was not yet a door. The banging, the sawing, and the banter stopped, the builders surprised to stillness by her lack of dress.

'We found somethin' you might want,' Vince said, businesslike to hide embarrassment. The youngest of the three held out his hand. Grace tiptoed over the loose floorboards and around scaffolding, trying to ignore the 'I wish it could be Christmas every day,' blaring on the radio.

'Thank you,' she said. 'We lost this years ago.' The cuff link had belonged to Ted's grandfather; she slipped it in her pocket. Standing there, she was suddenly self-conscious. She was hardly dressed for a work inspection, or to ask them to help her take down the lovemaking painting from the bedroom wall.

Vince turned the radio off. 'We'll go for lunch. Give you a moment.' It was eleven, and about lunchtime given their breakfast was at six. At the top of the stairs, Vince turned, 'Shout if you need anything.'

Grace could hardly ask to join them, although company—the builders' inane chatter—is what she desperately wanted. She had seen them squeezed in the front seat of their red van sharing a Tupperware container of white sandwiches and a huge bag of crisps. But Grace had no desire for food, for filling up. *Facing* up was her mood and it called for emptiness. Her yoga studio was taking shape; finding private yoga students to fill it would take a while—time she would need to gain experience teaching for Swami D. Her first class for him was only days away. The future was edging closer and to properly begin it Grace had to finish with the past.

That afternoon, the builders helped her lay the lovemaking painting facedown at the foot of the bed. She gathered all vestiges of Ted, things that had belonged to him or reminded her of him. Thick cotton socks, comfortable for walking, a hole in the heel now. His pyjama top. An old pipe from Afghanistan. His camera. The 'bloodshed paintings,' as she called them, from the hall. A last notebook, the small black kind he always used. Two jerseys, one white shirt. She loved him. She loved him and she had to stop. She took off his bathrobe and the initialed towel that wrapped her hair, then showered, dressed, and called her storage company.

Grace kept a photograph of herself and Ted together in Cornwall and the cufflink from the attic to remind her of how she had laughed with Ted, and the promise it held that she would laugh like that again. Everything else was taken away.

Once Ted's things were gone, Grace felt how much they had claimed her. Her house felt cold and unfamiliar. She needed to escape it for a moment, so she walked to St. Helen's Gardens for the clatter of the café, and had her first coffee in six weeks. It tasted so good she had another. Zinging from caffeine, she went to Orlando Hamilton's to buy herself some flowers. His shop, on the corner where the Laundromat once stood, had brightened the block and heralded its refined times. The vibrant colours, the scent of gardenias and lilies were heady, but Orlando's fingers lightly touching hers as he handed her the flowers was more astonishing to her senses.

*   *   *

Spending time in the house, Grace slowly changed the atmosphere of it. It was no longer a shrine to Ted, or the place she had wanted to make into a home for Lucy, or where she and Harry had shared flawed dreams. The house was hers and hers alone. Big and light, with clear rooms and space, she began to like it that way. During these quiet days, as she settled in, images of Dr. James played in the corners of her mind. She didn't have butterflies when she thought of him. She didn't long for him. He was just there. A man she liked and liked to think about. So when a letter arrived from Vietnam, butterflies surprised her.

> *Dear Grace,*
>
> *I have been at the Institute for a few weeks, staying in Saigon first. It's a pretty city, quite run-down, but I enjoy the mess. People I have met here have been old-fashioned in their manners and generosity. There is a seedy side, not unlike Bangkok, though less sophisticated. The food's wonderful. Every day at the Institute, the head doctor, Dr. Kim, cooks for ten of us. We've never had the same thing twice. We junior doctors (and we're all Western trained) have to cook, too, which requires getting up at five a.m. and going to the market to buy the produce. At seven thirty we eat together and practice Qigong. I am getting better at it. Before outpatients arrive we practice a daily activity: gardening, sculpture, calligraphy, flower arranging, or poetry. I usually choose calligraphy, which I hope you appreciate. The art, or this daily practice, apparently not related to our work, does affect my approach to it—and most things. Linear thinking isn't encouraged here.*
>
> *The first patients arrive at a quarter to ten. Whatever the sickness and severity of it, people here seek traditional Chinese medicine. Some choose to treat the most severe conditions exclusively with TCM; there is a tremendous level of success. Others combine Western and Eastern approaches for a truly complementary intervention. Certainly nobody considers Western medicine superior, or the source of accurate diagnosis. During my clinicals two doctors sit in with me. It was a little intimidating at first, to be observed. All*

doctors who teach us are trained in Western and Chinese medicine and speak Spanish, Russian, Chinese, French, Italian, and English. I am acutely aware of the limitations of my training! Early days, I know, but I have no regrets about giving up my consultancy and all that went with it.

What of you? I imagine that you have just got back from Bodhi Tree. It is probably quite a daunting time. One thing to be training, quite another to be confronted with building a career. Having said that, I don't think of teaching yoga (or what I'll be doing) as a career. These pursuits are fundamental, a way of being and, ideally, without ambition. Hope I still believe that once I leave here, where I am protected from the realities you now face, and the pressure of living in London.

Hope you still believe in the ancient art of letter writing; to receive one from you would be a pleasure. No e-mail here yet as resources are pretty tight and my mobile signal is in and out.

I'd love to know how you are, rather than simply imagine— which I do often.

Yours,
David

Grace wanted to reply; the tone to take was the sticking point. She remembered how Dr. James had waited for her to get inside when he'd dropped her home. She remembered the socks, the text messages, the way he'd tugged her hair. She had fancied him every time they'd met, which was twice. She should be reasonable, but 'Dear Dr. James' wasn't right for a sexy man who was writing her letters from Saigon. She put a line through it. 'Dearest David' she didn't like either and scored it through darkly. His description of Saigon had captivated her, but she had nothing exotic to relate. The Bodhi Tree training was a distant nirvana, the pain in her pelvis too personal, and while she wanted to tell him about receiving acupuncture, it didn't justify a letter. The converted attic, the builders; where was the romance in that? Best to take careful steps toward friendship and familiarity but when Grace composed those lines, she rejected them. She would wait until her first class at Swami D's; at least then she would have something uplifting to relate.

Grace and Swami D had agreed that he would not be at the studio when she taught, and he had planned his first midweek night off in years. Grace arrived too early, full of nervous energy, which Swami D suggested she dissipate by vacuuming the carpet. It took an hour, but there was still an hour to go, so she prepared the trays for the postclass tea. Swami D had instructed her how to fill out the studio book, where he noted who attended and how much they paid, but the entry for the seven o'clock class was empty. Grace looked through the book: if nobody showed up for a class that night, it would be the first time that year. Unsure why anybody would want to be taught by an absolute beginner when for the same price they could have the master, Grace went to the centre of the room and stood on her head. She was still upside down when three young people arrived at the door. 'Hi. We've come for yoga.'

Grace was so grateful to see them she took their money reluctantly. That they were brand new to yoga was the best news; they had nobody to compare her with.

'Turn your head slowly to the left,' she began, and for the rest of the class fought the impulse to copy Swami D. As hard as she tried to find her own words, his were lodged in her head. That night, she filed her comments for the Bodhi Tree teaching certificate and confessed, 'My style is not my own. This evening I was a Swami D impersonator, and when that didn't feel right, I mimicked Rita, and sometimes Garuda. I was a parrot, a parody, and not in the moment. I wasn't even responding to the people in front of me. I resorted to the words of others through fear of saying the wrong thing, or hurting people when I adjusted them. In a word, my first-ever class sucked.'

Grace went to bed downhearted the whole of her first teaching week. When she confessed this to Swami D, he refused to indulge her fears. 'Of course. At first it won't be easy, but the *Bhagavad Gita* says, "It is better to do your duty badly, than to perfectly do another's. You are safe from harm when you do what you should be doing." And I believe this is what you are meant to be doing. Grace, you are a yoga teacher, and no doubt, just like the rest of us, you will teach best what you need to learn.'

These words gave Grace courage and the next morning, before the builders arrived, she was in her yoga studio. She cleared a space on the yet-to-be-sanded floor and experimented with a class of her own invention. She spoke to imaginary students and, in anticipation of forgetting the sequence, penciled her moves in stick figures on the floor.

To be inspired by her teachers was one thing, but Grace would no longer copy them. She shared instead the things she discovered in self-practice. That Grace's classes at Swami D's were small was no bad thing: it gave her the opportunity to slow the pace, to have time to place her hands where people needed to rest the tension out of their bodies. The word got out. Grace was good. Within weeks, the numbers increased. Yoga had always connected Grace to a deeper sense of herself, but now it was also a road out and she was committed to follow. She arrived at Swami D's early, no longer from nerves but because she loved the anticipation before teaching class. Knowing the pleasure of a sweet thing after class, whenever the studio brownie tin was empty, Grace baked more (guarding Swami D's secret additions of chili and cardamom that gave his Martha Stewart recipe an Eastern twist).

Every night at home, she documented what she had seen in her students and herself. She analyzed her mistakes, and thought about how to correct them, all the time unconscious of her students' admiration, which was part of a self-forgetting that came when she taught, and stayed with her long after she'd left the studio.

Karma yoga was working in Grace the way Swami D had intended, but it did not pay her bills. The cost of converting the attic had dented her savings and while she lived frugally, the debits in her bank account weren't offset by a single credit. One evening, optimism high after teaching, she stopped off at Whole Foods with a poster advertising private yoga classes. 'It's too close to Christmas,' the manager warned. 'Stick it up in January. They're all abroad now, you know how it goes.'

Grace took the woman's advice about promoting her private classes, but resolved to follow Garuda's edict to teach straightaway. She would wait for the residents of Notting Hill to return from their winter warmth, but she would not grab people from a parking lot as Garuda had joked. What she wanted was to be referred to teach yoga by a doctor, a general practitioner, and overlooking their tendency to skepticism for any discipline not their own, she determined to find one. Instinct and prejudice led her to Dr. Damodaran.

With seven thousand residents, asylum seekers, and refugees on their register, Drs. Norton, Peters, and Damodaran were in a position to refer Grace more students than she could handle. She had met the doctors years before, assisting at a Suprafarma Phase One presentation at their surgery. Damodaran, an Indian national, was the doctor Grace set her sights on. Getting an appointment was easy when the receptionist assumed a Suprafarma connection that Grace had not denied.

The surgery was a converted mews house in South Kensington, its attic studio the perfect place to teach yoga. Grace sat in the waiting room, decorated with posters for flu jabs and nicotine patches, and strung with silver tinsel. At her feet, crawling babies sucked Santa Claus–shaped biscuits from a plate in the middle of the floor while their mothers were absorbed by well-thumbed copies of *OK!* and *Hello!* magazine—effective palliatives long past their sell-by date. 'All right Kylie, ready for your massage?' A cuddly nurse scooped Kylie up, and, gathering their babies, the mothers followed her to the studio in the rafters of the mews house.

Accustomed as she was to waiting to meet doctors, Grace understood that Dr. Damodaran was running late, but feared she was about to lose her prelunch slot to the insistent old man threatening the pretty, young receptionist. 'Nincompoop! Get me Dr. Damodaran right now!' he screamed like a spoiled child.

The receptionist shook. 'Mr. Kramer, I'm sorry—'

'I'll deal with this, Kelly.' Tammy, the olive-skinned head receptionist in tortoiseshell glasses, her black hair back, positioned herself between fat Mr. Kramer and the teenage Kelly. 'Mr. Kramer, please take a seat.'

'Does my doctor know I'm here?' he snapped in a thick Mancunian accent.

'I've left a message on Dr. Damodaran's screen.'

'Screen? Tell the doctor I'm here in flesh and blood!'

'Mr. Kramer, take a seat!' Tammy's insistence matched his, but the raised reception desk gave her the edge.

'Don't tell me what to do, young lady. You don't know my predicament.'

Outside, an elegant woman had parked a polished Rolls-Royce at the curb and stepped from the car into the surgery seemingly without touching the ground. She was followed by an ancient King Charles spaniel wheezing like an asthmatic.

'Darling, can the doctor see you?' The woman's French accent softened the correct clip of her English.

'This child 'ere is waiting to find out. Kiki, you tell her.'

'Tammy, please ask Dr. Damodaran to see my husband—even if he doesn't have an appointment,' she appealed.

Obliged as they were to look up at Tammy, the imposed deference made the Kramers uneasy. They forgot their King Charles, who wandered over to Grace, sniffed her shoes, licked up the babies' biscuit crumbs, and then peed on Grace's chair leg. Grace jumped to miss the splash and Kelly ran out in miniskirt and high heels, clutching the antiseptic wipes.

'Get that dog out of here! Only blind dogs in the surgery,' Tammy shouted.

'Frankie's half blind,' chuckled Mr. Kramer, happy with his little joke, happier still that Tammy had lost her cool. 'Come 'ere, Frankie. Get over 'ere.'

'I said get that dog—get Frankie—out of the surgery.'

Above Frankie's barking, Mr. Kramer wailed, 'I want my doctor!'

Grace sympathized with the irascible old man—particularly when heels tapping on the wooden floor announced Dr. Damodaran. 'What *is* going on?' she scolded.

Mr. Kramer quivered as if in the presence of a goddess.

Patients falling for their doctors is a well-known professional hazard, but most are restrained by a gentle reminder of the therapeutic relationship. Codes of conduct, however, did not interest Mr. Kramer.

'If you come to this surgery again without an appointment, I will call the police,' the doctor threatened. Mr. Kramer whimpered like a whipped dog. The doctor turned to Grace. 'Shall we?' she said, and linking Grace's arm, quick-stepped to her office.

Behind closed doors the doctor sank into her chair, gripped the edge of her desk, and rolled up to the computer, her habit to consult the screen rather than the visitor beside her. Grace's name was not accompanied with an explanation. Dr. Damodaran looked confused. 'I thought you worked for Suprafarma?'

'You're right . . .' Grace was evasive.

'Have you got something to subdue Mr. Kramer?' It was a joke, but only just.

'I might be able to subdue him, but not with anything from Suprafarma.'

'You've switched firms?'

'Not exactly. I've retrained. I'm a yoga teacher now.'

'Yoga?' said Dr. Damodaran, not because she didn't know what it was.

'Yes, you know, yoga . . .' Grace said reluctant to explain to Dr. Damodaran her country's heritage.

'Grace, I am familiar with yoga. As a very small child, before my parents took me and my sister away from Tamil Nadu, yoga was part of family life. Squeezed between the low clouds and the tarmac of Southall, all that was mystical beneath India's translucent sky seemed to me unreliable trickery. The certainty of science was more seductive.'

'I've gone the other way,' Grace said, enthusiastic. 'I'm ready for the mystery, Dr. Damodaran. I'm here to ask if I could be the practice yoga teacher.'

Dr. Damodaran swiveled in her chair, then got up to pace the blue carpet, thumbs hooked beneath her chin as she bounced her index finger against her lips. Grace sat on her hands, not sure where to look. So much for embracing uncertainty: she felt like a schoolgirl waiting for the headmistress to decide her fate.

Dr. Damodaran faced her with folded arms. 'Grace, I do not approve of the Western notion of yoga. It is a facile interpretation inspired by aspiration and celebrity. Yoga is not this. Yoga is an esoteric Eastern practice few Westerners are predisposed to understand. Grace, even I don't understand it, and my grandfather was a yogi.'

Dr. Damodaran sank back into her chair, apparently disturbed as much by her unexpected burst of nationalism as the yogic aspirations of incompetent Westerners. Dr. Damodaran continued, admonishing that Western yoga was an abomination, a merchandising phenomenon, and a deception, yet Grace was steadfast. She could see that the doctor was too worn down not to take a chance. 'I still believe I can help Mr. Kramer,' Grace asserted.

Dr. Damodaran stopped swiveling her chair to look straight at Grace. 'If you teach Mr. Kramer yoga, and he stays out of my surgery, I will refer you patients for years to come.'

'I would like to try.'

'Grace, you know who I'm talking about?'

'The man in the waiting room.'

'Exactly. The seventy-five-year-old obsessive depressive with a heart condition, prostate cancer, bowel problems, kidney malfunction, and an acute romantic infatuation with me.' Mr. Kramer's maladies prompted what seemed a hysterical giggle from the petite GP. Her features twisted, and she hid them behind elegant hands; only then did Grace realize that Dr. Damodaran was crying. It did not come naturally. The doctor quickly pulled herself together, an Indian trait as much as an English one, wiped her nose on the back of her shirt cuff, sniffed hard, and sat up. 'My therapeutic relationship with Mr. Kramer was never easy, but it veered right off track when he gave me a Porsche.'

Grace had heard about the Porsche. All the medics and sales reps who worked the area had. Not so many knew that the car came from Mr. Kramer, or that Dr. Damodaran had refused to look at it, let alone drive it. A year later the Porsche languished in the office garage, gathering dust and avaricious gazes from Drs. Norton and Peters, who were waiting for a diplomatic time to pass, and surely it had, before proposing that the practice adopt the car.

'Dr. Norton advised me to refer Mr. Kramer out,' said Dr. Damodaran. 'My first referral was to a psychiatrist at the Chelsea and Westminster.'

'Which one?'

'Perhaps you know him. Dr. James.'

An anxious pang hit Grace's stomach; she nodded.

'I liked him. He was good. Didn't stand for nonsense, which didn't impress Mr. Kramer. He wanted a woman, so I sent him to our practice counselor, who is, how shall I put it . . . motherly and competent but out of her depth treating him. He has since seen a dietician and a physiotherapist —both women—in addition to the nephrologist and oncologist, male specialists he is required to see given his cancer and his kidneys. Grace, I have referred Mr. Kramer so completely, I've run out of options.'

'Please let me teach him.'

'Would you teach him at home?'

'If that's what you want.'

'I'm afraid it's required. I've got to keep him out of here. And he would pay you himself. Perhaps you should think about it.'

'I don't need to,' Grace said.

'Then I shall tell him to expect you in the New Year, and if he stays out of the surgery until his next appointment, I promise to refer you patients.'

The women said good-bye, each one believing the other had answered a prayer.

Finally, Grace had the permission she felt she needed to write to Dr. James.

Dear Dr. James,

I am sorry it has taken me so long to reply. Saigon sounds exotic. Your joy at being there reminds me of how I felt at Bodhi Tree, which seems very far away now.

Nothing prepared me for teaching real students at Swami D's. I was underwhelmed by my performance, which was disheartening and why I waited to respond to your letter. I wanted some positive news—and now I've got it. Today I was offered my first paid job as a yoga teacher—referred through the National Health Service, with

whom I assumed I would never work again. I convinced Dr.
Damodaran that I could help her patient Mr. Kramer. You have
a better idea than I how likely, or not, that is. She told me that
you were her first referral after the Porsche. I am the latest, pos-
sibly the last as she has run out of other ideas. Do you remember
him?

If all goes well with Mr. Kramer the doctors will refer more
suitable patients for me to teach—a strange prospect. I was eleven
years in the lab and never met one patient. Rats and smaller crea-
tures were my specialty and I met tens of thousands of those.

Swami D is taking his family to India for Christmas and shut-
ting up the studio so we will have to go without his Christmas Eve
party—a modern tradition in West London. About thirty of us get
together for homemade apple cider, Indian food, and mince pies,
followed by singing in a circle—bahjans and carols. It's Christmas
with a Hindu twist. He has asked me to open the studio in Janu-
ary. I will give one class a day until he gets back. It's all without pay,
which I don't mind as long as paid work comes in from somewhere—
soon. Trying not to panic about that.

I will let you know how I get on with Mr. Kramer. What about
your patients? And your practice?

She searched for a way to sign off that fit her feelings, words that fell
between the cordial and the affectionate, words for a new friend and possible lover. Nothing seemed right.

Grace was all she put.

Dr. Damodaran called the next day with a quavering voice. 'Mr. Kramer
came into the surgery *again* this morning. I saw him on the condition that
he sees you tomorrow. Forgive me, I took a terrible liberty. Please tell me
you're available.'

Grace drove in pouring rain to Mr. Kramer's Knightsbridge penthouse
in a red brick mansion block squeezed beside the Albert Hall, overlook-

ing Hyde Park. The doorman directed her up. In the elevator Grace stared at her reflection in the metallic white light. Mr. Kramer had been coerced into the yoga class and doubting she could help him, a wave of insecurity hit.

Holding a long-stemmed rose and a pair of scissors, Kiki greeted Grace, and led her into a red drawing room decorated for Christmas: a tree filled the far corner and extravagantly wrapped presents cascaded around its base. A simple menorah in the window paid tribute to Mr. Kramer's past. The exclusive view of Hyde Park confirmed it was indeed a miserable day. Grace turned back to the rich warmth of the room to study the framed photographs on the grand piano. There was a picture of Mr. Kramer beside Prime Minister Harold Wilson at Chequers, in synagogue with the chief rabbi, and with Jimmy Carter at a dinner in Washington. He was pictured on the steps of Chelsea Registry Office beside Kiki (looking like a young Audrey Hepburn), with children—Grace presumed from his previous marriage—standing on the step below. Grace was leaning in to look at a young Mr. Kramer outside the Houses of Parliament with Aneurin Bevan, the man who initiated free health care in Britain, when old Mr. Kramer appeared.

'Do you know who that is?' he asked, leaning on his Zimmer frame.

'The father of the National Health Service.'

Mr. Kramer lumbered farther into the room. 'You're off to a good start. Nye Bevan was my political hero. If I were that young man today, who would stand beside me now? That comedian Bush? I don't think so. And who cares about Mr. Blair now? Gordon worries me, but Bill Gates would do. I've got a lot of time for him. And Victoria Beckham. Gutsy girl with great legs.' He lowered his bulky frame into the pile of cushions on his chair.

A smaller chair had been positioned opposite Mr. Kramer, facing the park so that even on this lacklustre day, Grace's face was illuminated. Overwhelmed by beauty he could not possess, tears splashed from Mr. Kramer's short white lashes.

'Dr. Damo . . .' He waited for the tremor to leave his voice. 'The doctor says you can help me. What do you do?'

'I'm a yoga teacher.'

'Yoga. What's that?' Instant scorn overcame his vulnerability.

'Yoga is a way of living, a form of exercise, a way of thinking.'

'I live like a king, I'm too fat to exercise, and I'm too old to change my thinking. So you can't help me, and that's a pity. From the look of you I thought we might get on.'

'I'd like to help you. We could look at your breathing.'

'Nothing wrong with my breathing. I'm breathing now.'

'We can all improve our breathing.' Grace's deep inhalation was a sign of her anxiety rather than a demonstration, but Mr. Kramer showed promise by spontaneously breathing deeper himself.

'And we could look at your diet,' Grace said.

'I'm not on a diet.'

'If you were lighter, yoga would be easier.'

'Darling!' Mr. Kramer shouted.

Kiki reappeared, still holding the scissors and a controlled smile.

'She wants to know about my food.'

Kiki recited the menu, like an efficient waitress. 'Breakfast: two poached eggs, one slice of grilled bacon. Lunch: vegetable or chicken soup.'

'Chicken *kreplach*,' nodded Mr. Kramer and sucked his bottom lip.

'Yogurt, low fat, no sugar. *Et pour le diner*.' Kiki paused as if to confess a sin. '*Le diner*: boiled chicken, vegetables, no potatoes.'

It was a sign of loving devotion that a French woman was prepared to serve such a meagre menu.

'So, no sweets, or cakes, or fried food?' Grace asked, trying to find the calories.

'*Non*. Everything is low fat.'

'So why the weight?' Grace said, bluntly.

Mr. and Mrs. Kramer stared at her, as though they too were mystified by the riddle of his fat. 'Sometimes I sits and thinks, and sometimes I just sits,' Mr. Kramer said, as though quoting *Winnie the Pooh* would get him off the hook.

'Movement is life. Perhaps to get you moving is the answer,' Grace coaxed.

Not one to be cajoled unless he was in love, Mr. Kramer snapped, 'Darling, have you got a question for our yoga teacher here?'

'No, I haven't.'

'Good. Neither have I. We'll meet again on Friday, young lady, same time,' said Mr. Kramer, his raised hand a signal for Kiki to help him up.

'Mr. Kramer, we haven't done any yoga,' said Grace.

'You're right, we haven't. But I'll be thinking about it and that's a start.'

As though he were royalty, the women waited for Mr. Kramer to Zimmer out of the room, then they walked together down the hall.

Grace had got off lightly. The old man had dismissed her but wanted to meet again. Sixty pounds for half an hour wasn't bad—if only Grace had asked for it. She was about to request a cheque from Mrs. Kramer when she was gripped by the arm and led firmly into the kitchen. Mrs. Kramer held the scissor tips to her lips, calling for silence. '*Excusez-moi*. Please, follow me.' She checked that the corridor was clear, then showed Grace to the master bedroom, where they stood by a vast bed covered with cream silk that matched the silk-covered walls. Grace looked at the paintings on either side of the bed—then looked again. On presumably Mr. Kramer's side was a northern factory scene by L. S. Lowry, on Mrs. Kramer's a rural idyll by Constable.

Mrs. Kramer cleared her throat to attract Grace's attention and, raising the heavy brocade on the night table, revealed a minifridge. 'Open it,' Mrs. Kramer mouthed. Grace did as she was told and three boxes of Entenmann's chocolate fudge cake fell out. The fridge was a chocolate heaven, crammed with everything from chocolate-covered donuts to Mars Bars.

'He's a secret eater,' Kiki whispered. 'Panzer's delivers when I'm out with the dog and I haven't the heart to stop it. It's his only pleasure, especially because he thinks I don't know.'

'Now that we both know, what are we going to do?'

'Precisely nothing.'

Date: December 14, 2006

To: yogagrace@hotmail.com

From: stephanie17@gmail.com

Subject: *Maithuna*

Sanskrit for intercourse, which ain't such a sexy word. Neither, by
the way, is tantra. Okay, so I shouldn't have enrolled in the advanced course. At least if I'd read the tantras I'd have known that
the '*panca-tattva*' I signed up for is group sex in a circle. No bigger
turn off let me tell you. That it's all ritualized and meant to be
sacred, and the men call the women 'divine Shakti' didn't do it
for me.

The guy I was partnered up with wasn't bad looking and had a
great body, but we had zero chemistry. For the first day, the teacher
went on about tantric sex being a meditation and not lustful; no
kidding. In an attempt to connect us with nature ('as rain penetrates
the earth, and oceans plunge the sands, etc. etc.'), he talked about
male and female energies. We had to do these exercises, mostly
breathing and swinging our bodies about. Dancing naked in front of
each other—in broad daylight—was the worst. We were meant to
focus on our partners, but I couldn't help checking out the room.
Of all the things that cracked me up, and there were plenty, droopy
testicles really got me. What's that about?

These preliminaries were meant to harmonize us with the universe,
and ourselves, before the harmony kicked off with our partners on
day two. Oil, candles, penetration, suppressed orgasms, the lot.
The idea is that instead of losing it all in one big glorious sexy bang,
we can diffuse that energy in our bodies, hold onto it, and live
longer, but really who would want to?

After my partner and I had caressed each other's necks with a
feather, 'softly as a mountain breeze,' we had to sit naked,
cross-legged—yep—facing each other. We touched hands,
gazing into each other's eyes, breathing. 'Course I got freezing
cold, and laughed whenever it was serious. In the end the teacher
told me if I couldn't stop laughing I had to leave. I was glad to.

The guy I was with was welcome to his withheld ejaculation. I certainly didn't want it.

If ever I fall upon a tantric master that I happen to fancy, I'm sure I won't complain, but otherwise, tantric sex feels contrived. If my kundalini Shakti is gonna rise, I want it to be one-on-one with a man who doesn't need to consult a tantric sex manual.

What are you doing for Christmas?

S

Chapter Ten

Kashyapasana — Sage Kashyapa's pose

Sage Kashyapa was the son of Sage Marichi, who was said to be the son of Lord Brahma. Kashyapa is often called Prajapati, the creator of the universe, the progenitor. While practicing the pose, focus on the manipura *chakra, and to help with balance, keep the eyes fixed on a point in front of the body. The asana will improve the practitioner's equilibrium, both physical and emotional. It will strengthen the arms, shoulders, and spine.*

Grace was prepared for a quiet Christmas. She did think of spending it with her father, but couldn't see the point when all he would do is drink. She didn't even bother to buy him a Christmas present, and had bought only one—for Lucy. It took courage to deliver it. When the cleaning lady answered the door, Grace regretted leaving her visit so late. She had missed one of the few excuses all year to keep in touch with Lucy, who wouldn't be back for a while. 'They're all in the Maldives,' the cleaning woman said, pointedly. Grace suspected that Harry had gone, too. It made sense even for a broken family to spend Christmas together, and to go somewhere hot to do it was very Notting Hill.

Grace's Christmas plans were modest: she would teach Mr. Kramer yoga on Christmas Eve morning, and go to *The Seagull* at the Royal Court in the evening. She had failed to own up to Olga that she didn't know Chekhov's work, and had promised herself to put that right. The other promise she had made at Bodhi Tree, to get in contact with her father, she had let slide. She knew she would call her father one day, whether he was sober or not, but would wait until it felt right. To wait forever occurred to her. Catch up with him in another lifetime. Why not?

The Christmas Eve yoga class for Mr. Kramer had been her idea—an exercise in damage limitation rather than any other kind. It would be Mr. Kramer's last chance to stalk the surgery offices before Dr. Damodaran disappeared for the holidays, and a Fortnum & Mason hamper was his fine excuse for a visit. The wicker basket had been in the hall for a week, Mr. Kramer adding his seasonal favorites to Fortnum's own: Beluga caviar, vintage champagne. A ham from John Robinson in Hampshire. Cheeses from Shropshire and Gloucestershire. Sloe gin. A box of Charbonnel et Walker's heart-shaped truffles. The £1,000 Christmas gift was a modest expression of Mr. Kramer's love, but Grace had to prevent him from delivering it. She could not risk him jeopardizing Dr. Damodaran's promise of patients to teach.

With this goal in mind, Grace tolerated Mr. Kramer's moods and accepted that he didn't want to be taught anything, least of all yoga. What Mr. Kramer liked to do was theorize and it was pointless trying to stop him. As a young man, Mr. Kramer had believed in himself and luck's role in the life of even the most determined men, but illness was his way of life now and he concentrated considerable acuity upon it. Sickness assured that his wife, his housekeeper, and his secretary fussed as much as they ever had. Granted the audience was small, but for all the attention he could muster it seemed to Grace that Mr. Kramer was not reconciled with himself. He sought consolation in Dr. Damodaran, his music, the American men of letters, and on a good day, his children—although the unreliability of his flesh and blood in all its forms was a source of sadness. That his children would not be home for Christmas had tipped Mr. Kramer into depression.

'What would you like to do today,' Grace asked, wondering if she could ever be this patient with her father, who was equally brilliant and impossible.

'I'd like to go for a spin in the Rolls-Royce. You could drive. You'd like that.'

'Where would you like to go?' Grace responded, although she knew.

'I want to see her smile,' he said.

It was such a simple, honest wish that Grace would have offered to drive him to the surgery, if she thought it would help. 'Mr. Kramer, the hamper won't elicit that response. Surely you know that? Remember the car.'

'The car was a mistake.'

'I think the hamper could be, too. Would you like me to deliver it on your behalf?'

The compromise agreed on, Mr. Kramer cheered up and Zimmered to his study to write Grace a cheque. This run for the money was the most active part of his yoga class, and returned him, however briefly, to a power he understood.

The doorman was called to carry the hamper to Grace's car, and Mr. Kramer handed her a sealed white envelope. 'Please give the doctor this,' he said, the poor, love-struck boy.

At the surgery Tammy helped Grace carry the hamper to reception, where Dr. Damodaran was behind the console, searching for a patient's medical records.

'Grace, you shouldn't have,' she said, bewildered but delighted.

Peering at Dr. Damodaran above the red-ribbon-wrapped cellophane, Grace confessed, 'I didn't.'

Dr. Damodaran didn't need to open Mr. Kramer's Christmas card. 'Get that hamper out of here,' was all she said.

'Please take the caviar, take anything. I'd like to tell him that he gave you something for Christmas.'

'I won't encourage him, and you shouldn't indulge him.'

Tammy and Grace struggled with the hamper back to the car, wide-eyeing each other above the delicacies. 'The course of true love . . .' Grace said, which set them giggling so hard they had to put the hamper down before they dropped it.

'What am I going to do with all this? Why don't you take something?'

Tammy shook her head. 'Mr. Kramer may be generous to Dr. Damo-daran, but it doesn't go further than that. You'd better give it back.'

The doorman looked confused to see Grace again, but without question or complaint helped her take the hamper to the top floor. She rang the bell, the hamper pushed out of sight so that she could break the news gently.

Mr. Kramer was eager for news. 'She liked it did she? Did she see the champagne, did she see the year?'

'Mr. Kramer, she thanked you, but couldn't accept it.' The words crushed him. As kindly as she could, Grace asked, 'Where shall I put the hamper.'

Mr. Kramer shriveled to meanness. 'Keep the bloody thing,' he stormed, and slammed the door. Not even a 'Happy Christmas,' but then again, Grace wasn't expecting one. She stared at the hamper, her burden of bounty.

The doorman had first pick: he took the ham and the Christmas cake. Grace got back to the surgery just as Tammy was shutting up for the holiday and signaled to her from the mews. Tammy tiptoed out, and made a delicate run for the car in the fine rain. She filled her arms with treats to take home to her family. 'Dale loves marzipan,' she said, 'and red wine.' She grabbed the claret and the sweets, the chicken pie and the cheese. She didn't even look at the champagne, or the caviar. Finally, Grace drove to Piccadilly, to Fortnum & Mason itself, to offer its mince pies to the tramp who spent his days in their doorway. His hands were caked in dirt from a lifetime on the street. His beard was matted and a black beanie hat was yanked over his rank hair. Grace bent toward him, holding out the mince pies.

'Don't like 'em,' he said, without looking up.

By evening the rain had stopped and after the theatre Grace walked around Sloane Square. The blue magic of the Christmas lights captivated her and she would have liked to have talked with somebody, like Dr. James for example, about the intricacies of the performance, and then take him home to share the excellent remains of Mr. Kramer's hamper. Grace preferred to bear pain alone, but when life was beautiful, she longed to share it.

Grace had prepared for her solitary Christmas Day by finding a church—St. James on Piccadilly. The seventeenth-century church was the only one designed by Sir Christopher Wren still standing outside the city's square mile. St. James's claim to accept all denominations seemed remarkable but from the look of the congregation, it did. As if inspired by Wren's sparse brilliance, there was no pomp here, but plenty of heart. The sculpture above the altar by Grinling Gibbons was the building's only ornate detail and put Harry's old headboard to shame. Bach had once played the church's organ, and William Blake had worshipped here.

Grace sat between a family from Canada and a Japanese couple; a homeless man was comfortably asleep at the end of their pew. A Nigerian family occupied the row in front. Visitors from around the world had gathered with members of the resident congregation to celebrate the birth of their Saviour. 'Welcome to our ragged but cheerful clump of a Christian community,' said the vicar, Hugh Valentine, whose sermon on the essence of Christmas and its promise of infinite love didn't sound like a sermon at all. It seemed to Grace that what Mr. Valentine said made sense, and not just that. What he said made sense of life.

Grace stepped out into London's Christmas Day, the church bells ringing as she turned right on Piccadilly. She had meant to turn left for Hyde Park and the long walk home, but found herself heading to the West End, toward her father's flat. Jewish he may have been, but it was Christmas and she wanted to celebrate with him, her only family.

A tall woman with silver hair answered the door. Grace's heart contracted; could her father have died without her knowing? But the woman called out, 'Terrence,' and then opened the door wide to let Grace in.

It was no secret that Grace's mother had not liked her father's name. She had called him T, or Terry, when she teased him. But here was Terrence in clean pyjamas, receiving the full entitlement of his name from a good-looking woman holding a wooden spoon and wearing an apron. The apron was her father's joke of old and showed fantastic breasts and the outline of a naked maiden's form. Ginny was wearing it to make bread sauce from scratch; Grace liked her straightaway.

Terrence had met Ginny two months before when he'd returned to Alcoholics Anonymous to take the Steps for what he promised would be the last time. If he failed this attempt, he had sworn never to go back. Grace was encouraged that he had finally made it all the way to Step Three and had not been defeated by the effort of turning his will and his life over to the care of God, 'as he understood him.' Every other time, it had been easier for him to surrender to the bottle. Ginny was seventy-five years old and ten years clean. With Ginny beside him, Grace held out hope for her father, who was clean himself today. Today was a word Ginny used a lot. And Ginny seemed to know all about Grace, which was strange because she had assumed her father knew her not at all, and yet he was Ginny's only source. An extra place was laid and they sat together for lunch. Grace ate turkey and did not tell her father that she had left medical health care to be a vegetarian yoga teacher because today her father was happy. He smiled. He'd had his teeth fixed. He called her Grace and said he was sorry. His abstract apology drifted down the table and landed.

'I'm sorry, too. Forgive me,' Grace said, unsure what for but knowing that an eye for an eye leaves the whole world blind.

After lunch, they walked the Harley Street block, her father still wearing his Mr. Happy slippers, pyjamas, and old plaid dressing gown. Much had changed, but Grace was grateful that her father's eccentricity was intact, and that Ginny was willing to preserve it. As a young girl her father's inability to conform had embarrassed her, but now she enjoyed it, admired it even. They walked down the street, Grace linking arms with her father and Ginny; another threesome, she thought, that looked like a family and perhaps, this time, would be.

Later, when it was dark and past seven, Grace prepared to walk home. Ginny protested. 'It's dark, sweetheart, and a long way.'

'I'll jump on a bus.'

'If there is one, and if there isn't, avoid that Bayswater stretch of Hyde Park,' her father cautioned from his armchair.

'Right, Daddy. Thanks.' Grace sounded dismissive but the latent activation of her father's paternal gene moved her to kiss his deeply grooved forehead. 'I love you, Daddy,' she said. The words came out without her planning to say them, as though they'd been waiting for the moment. In the silence that followed, she wondered why she'd said them. She supposed she loved her father for being sober, and for remembering her name. Being her father at all was justification enough for loving him and saying that she did. She was at the door, her back to him when he called, 'I love you, Grace.'

Hesitation at the door was her only acknowledgement. To turn back would be sentimental. Her father's 'I love you' had slipped out, much as hers had, but his sounded as though he'd said it a thousand times. She told herself it was an everyday exchange and nothing extraordinary but out in the night, walking home, life seemed to her different and she felt different in it. She could have gone on pretending forever that she didn't care about her father, that she had no sense of belonging, but perhaps now she wouldn't have to.

Alone at home, wrapped in an Elle Macpherson robe—a Christmas present to herself and about as far as it is possible to get on the bathrobe spectrum from Ted's white toweling—Grace took Mr. Kramer's champagne, opened the night before, and went upstairs intending to finish it. Stretched out on cushions beside the fire, she found the champagne easier to drink than when the bubbles were hard and fresh. A letter to Dr. James spontaneously formed.

> *David, it is two and a half months since I have seen or spoken to Harry and I find myself free to think of you, which I do often. I wish I could come right out and tell you I'm single. I suppose I haven't because it's a leading thing to say, as if you'd have to do something about it, which of course I'd like . . . I wonder if my growing affection for you is linked to the fact that you are far away and unlikely to return to claim me anytime soon?*
>
> *Today my father told me that he loved me for the first time in memory. Me forty, he eighty-five. No rush there, then. It was sim-*

pler than I'd expected to say that I loved him. And I do. He has a new girlfriend, an excellent woman who sees the best in him. To see them together was the greatest Christmas present in a long time.

My yoga work expands exponentially. I will soon be London's first yogi mogul, earning one hundred and twenty pounds a week. Seriously, teaching yoga is a joy. And how much I like it that you like me.

With love on Christmas night.
Grace

Grace folded the letter she would never send and placed it in the drawer of her dressing table. But to let Dr. James know that she was thinking of him, she sent a text. *Happy Christmas. x.*

She didn't mean to wait for a reply but couldn't help it, and lay in bed, Radio Three for company. The station was playing only Bach between Christmas and New Year, twenty-four hours a day, never once a piece repeated. With her mind settled in the music Grace fell asleep and woke the next morning to a Bach cello suite and Dr. James's reply. *Sleep beautifully. With you in spirit. Letter on its way. Happy Christmas.*

When his letter arrived she could not have been happier if Dr. James had walked in himself.

Dear Grace,

I received your letter today and I have come to the meditation garden to reply. Quite a coincidence that Mr. Kramer has been referred to you. Expect a challenge. I recall he was sentimental (probably a side effect of minor strokes), and monstrously successful. He keeps quiet that he revolutionized the textile industry and initiated changes in business practice that are apparently considered commonplace today. He is an unusual combination of intellect and intuition, and preferred to observe me rather than let me observe him. He is quickly bored, which triggers depression, the origin of which he was not remotely interested in uncovering in his sessions with me.

He attended no more than three. I expect you to have greater success. Too many studies show consistent physical exercise reduces depression, in some cases more effectively than antidepressants. Of course, lack of exercise is what's depressive. We were made to move.

You asked how I think you should deal with Mr. Kramer—I think the key is be firm. Take none of his bullshit! Here they say meet yang patients with yang, yin with yin. Sounds simple, and perhaps it can be.

You couldn't be with a better practice by the way. Back in the days of fundholding, before Primary Care Trusts, Drs. Norton, Peters, and Damodaran were used as a case study for how they budgeted their funds and the treatment of patients—sadly in that order. Norton and Peters go back a long way. They have always been forward thinking, as demonstrated by what they are offering their patients through you—I know they also refer to an acupuncturist and a homeopath. Damodaran is relatively new to the team. She started a rehabilitation centre for kids in the East End, was working there and as a general practitioner. I think joining the Norton practice was, initially, seen as a way of cutting down.

Next week we increase our hospital rounds, visiting one every afternoon under the watchful eye of Dr. Huang—one of only two doctors in the whole of Vietnam permitted exemption from the Communist Party. That's how good he is. He has an extraordinary gift, but does not like to call himself a doctor as he says he had no 'formal' training. An apprentice from sixteen, he can tell just by looking at a patient what's going on. When I first met him I stood before him and challenged him to tell me how I was. All he said was, 'okay, you can carry on smoking,' which I haven't, as cigars aren't easy to come by here. Huang watches the outpatients walk in, which is all the information he needs to verify our diagnosis. He is a laser-eyed healer. I don't know if it's possible to learn his uncanny art.

The hospital wards are like dormitories. They have beds but there isn't the money for equipment. They have little but do very well with what they have. I have chosen to work with pediatrics, geriat-

rics (dealing with mobility and what they call tremors—a term that embraces Parkinson's, MS, and most neuromuscular disorders), and addiction.

The coincidence that you are working with Dr. Damodaran made me feel the world is small, even though you feel impossibly far from me as I write this.

Let me know how you get on with everything. No Christmas here, of course, but a big buildup to Tet, the New Year, which starts this year in mid-January, on the first new moon, and ends on the full moon. Fourteen days of feasts and families gathering, and we students have all been invited. That, plus the study to get done, I'll be busy.

Happy Tet!
David

Immersed in yoga teaching at Swami D's, Grace's appointments with Mr. Kramer required other skills. She still dressed as though she were teaching him yoga, and took her mat as if to remind him, but that was as close as they got. Mr. Kramer was equally consistent: he was never interested in yoga, and he was always late.

This morning Grace waited while he finished his bath. From behind the door a nurse counted down, 'three, two, one.' Whooshing water announced that Mr. Kramer was up and out. He appeared with a vast towel barely wrapping his middle. 'Kiki, show her to the sunroom,' he called, eyes down, scuffling in leather slippers to his dressing room. His wife appeared from her study and winced when her husband's towel fell. Naked and shameless he shuffled on, followed by the dog.

Grace waited in the so-called sunroom, a simply furnished glass-domed extension at the back of the apartment. She recognized the symphony that was playing, but not the composer.

'Mahler's Third,' said Mr. Kramer, waddling in with Frankie. 'Mahler died of heart disease, aged fifty-one. Left a beautiful young wife.' He stared into the urban distance and humphed. 'I miss my house in the country, the animals, the meadows. I miss so much of my life.'

Mr. Kramer's red Adidas tracksuit was stained down the front with egg yolk and the unmistakable sludge of Entenmann's chocolate fudge. 'The fated Ninth. I'll play you that next week,' he said, turning off the symphony. 'Always switch off at the mains. Over a lifetime you'll save a first-class airfare to Paris.' Mr. Kramer sat heavily, dropped the dog a treat from the bowl on the table, and then took one himself. 'I've tasted all the slobbery dog treats. They're fat-free,' he said, biting in.

That Mr. Kramer was sharing the dog's chocolate drops in public hinted he might confess to other eating habits. It was the kind of development Grace hoped for when she asked, 'How are you, Mr. Kramer?'

'The privates,' he gestured over them.

It was not the response Grace had expected.

'My privates are in constant pain. Can't pee without pain, can't walk without it, can't talk without it. The dog's got prostate cancer and so have I. Can't judge how far I can go without having to go.'

'Have you been out this week?'

'I saw Dr. Damodaran.'

'How was she?' Grace reined in anxiety.

'She said we're making great strides, and she wants me outside, breathing fresh air.'

Perhaps they would get to yoga after all. 'Shall we make a start by walking a few steps down the corridor without the frame?'

'I don't feel like it,' he said. There was no arguing with that. 'My heart's the thing. I've got heart problems. I fall in love with all the people who care for me, and if I don't, I don't want to see them.'

'But you're married,' Grace said, to divert him from a loving declaration, or from firing her.

'I certainly am married. Twenty-five years, never once unfaithful. My wife doesn't mind me falling in love every now and again. It gives us something new to talk about.'

'Shall we do some breathing?' Grace suggested, keen to get off the subject of love and marriage. 'Try to expand your back ribs if you can,' she encouraged.

'My back ribs? Where are they?'

Grace placed her hands on Mr. Kramer's back. 'They sit somewhere here,' she said, searching the fat above his waist.

'I like the feel of your hands. Very sensuous. Can't concentrate on me breathing.'

'Think of this as work, Mr. Kramer.'

'I haven't worked for years.'

Grace leaned heavily on his shoulders so that when he breathed in they would not hike up. Mr. Kramer's ribs were obliged to expand. 'That's it!' she said, excited. 'Now you're using the intercostal muscles rather than postural muscles. What did that feel like?'

'A breath,' he said, unimpressed.

'A beautiful, strong breath.'

'You're an evangelist for the breath. Are you married?'

'No, Mr. Kramer, I'm not. Please try another conscious breath.'

'A girl like you not married. The world's changing.'

Date:	January 20, 2007
To:	stephanie17@gmail.com
From:	yogagrace@hotmail.com
Subject:	The myth . . .

How do you like teaching yoga? Trying to pass on some of that light Garuda talked about isn't easy in cold, wet January. I'm currently on trial to teach at a doctors' practice where the idea of passing on some light would make them laugh.

Even at Swami D's the light burns less brightly. Last week he got back from India and brought this guy, Ryan, with him. They go way back, apparently, to Swami D's ashram days, although Ryan must have been a child then. Ryan is teaching a few classes at the studio, which makes sense as we have so many girl students, but I don't like him. The other night he said to Swami D that it was a normal response for a (male) yoga teacher to walk into a class and want to 'fuck the women on the mats.' Apparently it comes down to seeing a line of women lying on their backs, legs slightly apart, eyes closed. Trouble was, Swami D didn't contradict him. Do the manly yogis you know see yoga as an excuse to get laid?

Ryan has a yoga centre in Ibiza. Swami D told me it's closed for the winter cos R's got a recurring groin strain and needs to take things easy. Ryan has since confessed to me that he got a local girl pregnant and when her father insisted he marry her, he flew to Goa for Christmas—where he bumped into Swami D. He's biding his time in London teaching a few classes at the studio, waiting for things to 'blow over' before going back to Ibiza in the spring. The kid is in utero, quite why he thinks things will blow over once it's born, I have no idea. Blow up, more like. My guess is the kid's maternal grand-father will torch Ryan's yoga centre if he doesn't get back soon . . .

Cheer me up, girlfriend. This yoga scene is getting me down.

Grace

Date:	January 22, 2007
To:	yogagrace@hotmail.com
From:	stephanie17@gmail.com
Subject:	Nothing's perfect . . .

First, Swami D is a good person in your life, so overlook the flaws in his otherwise acceptable nature. As for Ryan, is he getting paid? That's what I want to know.

Of course the best, and worst, male yoga teachers in the world come to California. ALL the men fuck their students, or try, as far as I can make out. Perhaps not a whole class at a time, but certainly picking them off, one at a time. Makes Garuda exceptional . . .

I did a workshop last weekend with this Ashtanga guy who's famous for doing this trick with trucks—balancing between them in the splits. Perhaps you've heard of him—Chuck Shmizer. Anyway. At the end of the workshop Chuck was talking to one of our star teachers (male), and I heard him say, 'we've got the best job in the world. We fly to beautiful places and fuck beautiful women.' For the record, I think Chuck's had a face-lift.

I'm sticking to yoga with Diane, and only wish she didn't live the other side of the planet. At least there is no confusion when she teaches that we are doing yoga. We are not trying to get into each other's pants. She says her yoga is like a journey inside yourself to a surprising place and it is like that: the asanas aren't rigid at all, and each time I work with her, I go deeper. Doing the asanas with her requires such concentration it's impossible to think about anything else. It is a complete mind body discipline and requires real effort, although to watch her class you wouldn't think so. It really is yoga from a feminine perspective (only took a few thousand years to get here), developed by an Italian aristocrat, Vanda Scaravelli. She never charged anybody to teach them yoga—a luxury few teachers can afford, and it probably wouldn't occur to most of the famous yogis who can.

I am coming to Rome this spring. Can I come through London and stay a while?

S

Date:	January 23, 2007
To:	stephanie17@gmail.com
From:	yogagrace@hotmail.com
Subject:	As long as you like

Grace feared that Dr. Damodaran's request to discuss Mr. Kramer's progress was premature. In the past six weeks she couldn't get him out of his chair (unless it was to write her a cheque), he didn't like breathing exercises, and wouldn't contemplate meditation. Yoga with Mr. Kramer was a failure and Grace did not look forward to a dressing down from the doctor.

'Excellent results,' the doctor beamed when Grace walked into her office.

'But didn't you see him recently?'

'For the first time in a month. For a scheduled appointment. Grace, this yoga is powerful stuff.'

'It's hardly yoga.'

'Don't worry about that. My colleagues and I have already referred you patients and they are expecting you to call.' Dr. Damodaran handed Grace a list of fifteen names and telephone numbers. 'The word *class* makes it sound hard work, so your intervention will be called a yoga *workshop*, and free at the point of entry. We will provide the mats, the studio, and pay for your time. Your job will be to persuade seven patients on that list to show up, and keep showing up, for eight weeks.'

It all sounded remarkably easy. 'If the workshop is free, won't it be oversubscribed?' asked Grace.

'I admire your optimism. If only our patients were that predictable,' said Dr. Damodaran.

> *Dear Dr. James,*
>
> *You asked me to tell you everything, so you have been warned. Well, I kept Mr. Kramer out of Dr. Damodaran's surgery and the partners have asked me to teach yoga to other 'heart sink' patients. Being an NHS practice, the yoga course is free and I had expected to turn patients away. Having met them, I'd be surprised if any turn up for class. All the patients they referred were classic 'heart sinkers,' persistently visiting the surgery while failing to comply with their prescriptions. They weren't easily persuaded that something other than drugs could help their symptoms, either. No wonder the doctors' hearts sink at the sight of them.*
>
> *An eclectic group has signed up. Mrs. Moore is my favourite, and at seventy-nine by far the oldest. She's hardly an obvious candidate, but none of them are. I was asked to assess the patients' suitability, but had decided not to turn anyone away if they were willing: Mrs. Moore was, on condition I didn't ask her to give up smoking. She*

said I was unlikely to succeed where lung cancer had failed. A belligerent, die-hard smoker, I really like her.

Harriet Manslip is on steroids and huge. About thirty-eight, she's obsessed with taking calling cards out of phone booths. No doubt a worthy job, it's the only one she's had for ten years. She has been on benefit all that time. Of the people I met today, over half of them didn't work and the others were stressed from overwork. Ms. Manslip's records show countless consultations for minor ailments—heartburn, eczema, aching muscles—and a tendency to make calls for house visits whenever the young Cuban locum, Fernando Perez, is on night duty.

Another big lady, Gladys with hypertension, blames her obesity on hormone replacement therapy, but Emily Daze is a hormone-replacement creation, skinny and, she admitted, hungry all the time. With her mass of blonde hair, narrow hips, and long legs, from across the room, Emily looks like a model. Up close, there is no doubt she is a man—a straight man, as it turns out, in the process of becoming a gay woman. All her symptoms relate to anxiety about the final operation in her gender reassignment—quite literally the cut-off point, about which I didn't feel qualified to reassure her. She called her offending member, 'a bit of skin shriveled as a slug in salt,' but how can she know for sure that one day she won't miss it? Assuming there are all sorts of drugs that could save the slug, I told Emily to stay open in case she should change her mind—the prerogative she has surely earned. She smiled when I said that, and was crying, too. I was trying not to.

I promised Emily, as I promised them all, that yoga could help. What else could I say? 'Go home, you're doomed'? Although Maud may be. She had electric shocks as a child and a lobotomy at twenty-five. She wants to feel better but equates this with being able to remember the first twenty-five years of her life, 'even if they're worse than the last twenty-five,' and she suspects they were. I told Maud yoga could make a difference and she said, 'what kind of difference, that's what I want to know?' A very level-headed response. It's sad that such a person has slipped between the tracks. She lives in a *bed-sit in diminishing hope that doctors can put right what doctors before have put wrong. She sleeps during the day and eats food straight from tins at night so as not to wake the Albanian family of five living in the room next door to hers. She calls herself a human experiment and, sadly, I think that's what she has been.*

Single mother Sally Moleslide is the kind of patient I'd expected in terms of age and general fitness. She's thirty-seven and has four children aged from two to twenty-two by four different men, which qualifies her for council accommodation and state benefit. Sally's got 'gut ache' and is scared she's got cancer, although tests show nothing wrong. I think her pain is connected to a diet of vodka and frozen pizza. She sounds bad but she's spirited—in fact all the ones who signed up for yoga are. Even Maud. They see the humor, in spite of the hardships—although Sally has it made with a four bedroom council flat in Chelsea that has balconies overlooking the Fulham Road, and hundreds of pounds a week from benefit for all the children. She even has a cash job on the side.

The only bona fide male patient willing to sign up was Davis, who suffers from migraine and first-class problems. A retired financial wizard, he has a house in Switzerland, one in Launceston Place where he lives with his wife, plus a flat in Pimlico where he keeps his mistress. That list right there would give anybody a headache. He dreams of ditching the lot and going to live in Venice in an apartment by the Accademia Bridge, a plan I did not discourage, as long as he completes the workshop first.

Dr. James, forgive me. All I've done is talk about the patients I've met, as though you've never had the privilege, but I can't stop thinking about them. Writing this has helped to get them out of my head. Listening to patients all day drained me as surely as a pulled plug drains water. Their willingness to tell me intimate details bordered on desperation. Mrs. Moore was the only one who was circumspect and didn't seem lonely, even though she lives alone. In them all, including Mrs. Moore, I caught a look in their eye close to chaos.

To deal with rats was easier. I felt less in the lab; didn't feel at all in fact.

Dr. James, thank you—I was going to write thank you for listening, but of course I mean for reading this, and for being there.

Have a great Tet. I like the idea of it coinciding with the cycle of the moon and that families travel from miles around to eat together and celebrate. I am feeling part of my own small family, thanks to Ginny—my father's elegant old-new girlfriend. She makes it possible for me and my father to spend time together without resentments from the past getting in the way. They came for supper the other night—the first time he's been to my house in three years. My father was standing in his overcoat, hands in his pockets, in the middle of the room I've built for yoga at the top of the house. He thought I was going to take up painting, so I confessed that I was a yoga teacher and planned, one day, to teach at home. He shrugged, then told me my mother did yoga in the sixties with Iyengar, and even went to India. It made me think that perhaps she had looked to the East for answers, seeking some truth or solace she couldn't find at home. Of course, it made me want to talk to her. I still have so many questions I long to ask her. I wonder if this wish to speak to her will ever leave me? And here I am, so many years later, seeking answers in a discipline that she also explored. Genetic patterns play themselves out . . .

How are the hospital visits? Does it mean you are officially a Barefoot Doctor? What of the patients? Do you have a translator, or can you tell everything about them from taking their pulse? It still bemuses me that the pulse contains the secrets. Perhaps one day you'll read mine—and I'll give you a yoga class.

Much love,

Grace

Dr. Damodaran and Grace had agreed that if fewer than five patients attended the yoga workshops, the trial would be abandoned within the month. Grace intended to have a full house from the start and the night before rang her patients to remind them. Inspired by Rita at Bodhi Tree, she had also rehearsed a rallying talk on the power of the yoga family, but lacked the pep to deliver it when only six patients showed up.

Those who arrived showed willingness by wearing their interpretation of the 'soft, loose comfortable clothes' Grace had recommended. Emily's fitted black pants with the diamanté belt were identical to Russian Olga's at Bodhi Tree, and Davis's white shorts and white T-shirt were on the tight side of loose, classic exercise clothes that hadn't changed since his prep school days. Gladys's tent dress was the perfect excuse not to do headstands. 'I won't go upside down in this,' she insisted, rolling out her brand new mat, then picking it clean of invisible fluff.

'Gladys, don't worry, lie down. We won't get to headstands for weeks, if at all.'

The big woman carried on sipping from her small bottle of Evian, sneaking Maltesers, one at a time, from her fake Birkin bag; these prissy movements irritated Grace. 'Come on, Gladys. Put the sweets away. It's time to get to work.'

Gladys huffed in protest. With chocolate melting on her tongue and her eyes fixed on the ceiling, finally she lay down on her mat with all the relish of a patient on a surgeon's table.

Holding out for Sally, Grace took her time to relax the rest. 'Let go of the day,' she said, her voice so soothing Davis nodded off. Ten minutes later most of the patients had joined him. To see the patients sleeping at her feet made Grace feel humble and she was uncertain where to begin to teach patients who spanned forty years and every physical and social divide. Sally was a welcome distraction when she burst in with enthusiasm borne out by pink track bottoms, 'yoga' inscribed down the leg, and 'yoga babe' swirled across her crop top. 'Sorry, Grace, sorry, everyone!' She held up her open palms. 'Oops,' she said, too late aware of the stillness and the snoozing. Across the room she whispered loudly to Grace, 'Had to wait for me oldest to get back to look after me youngest.'

Sally had stirred the snoozing class, and finished the job by plonking her mat beside Mrs. Moore, who looked peacefully demure dressed in loose navy slacks and a jersey.

'God help us through this yoga malarkey,' Sally sighed. The patients grinned like tired old cats that had no intention of moving. To get them up and standing would be an achievement, and take a while. Then Grace noticed only Davis had bare feet. 'Socks off' was a standard request. The patients protested.

'Nobody gets away with a lesson wearing socks. Socks restrict your feet, which need to be free to work. Don't worry, they'll soon warm up,' she encouraged.

The group was resistant for reasons that went beyond the cold. Feet were private (Maud), feet were ugly (Emily), feet were fetishistic (Harriet), feet sometimes smelled like cheese (Sally), the patients joked, removing their socks.

'Is this *truly* necessary?' asked Gladys.

Grace was losing patience with Gladys. She was also aware that she now had less than an hour to inspire the patients to return for the next class, and all they'd done so far was snooze. 'Come on, Gladys, get your socks off.'

Scratching the back of her head, Grace watched Gladys's extraordinary effort to stand.

'In twenty years my husband is the only person who has seen my feet. If I can't leave my socks on, yoga is not for me.'

Grace saw that she was guilty of assuming the patients were at ease in their bodies when all the evidence before her was to the contrary. It was a terrible assumption, and the sign of a bad yoga teacher. 'Gladys, please forgive me, and please leave your socks on.'

For a second it wasn't clear whether Gladys would stay or go, then her shoulders slumped forward and she sank back to the floor.

More than the maladies and the obsessive comfort found in food, it was Gladys's bobby socks that revealed to Grace the realm she had entered, courtesy of the National Health Service. So, they had gathered— the lonely, the old, the inflexible, the flexible, the neurotic, the needy: the Introduction to Yoga Workshop could begin.

'I would like to call you students rather than patients, if that's okay?' said Grace.

They nodded. Mrs. Moore smiled.

Grace had planned to lead them in the sun salute, but thought better of it. Far better to keep the movements slow and simple, rather than confront them with aches, pains, and resistance. She wanted them to enjoy being in their bodies, rather than burdened by them. With their feet slightly apart, slowly raising their arms, they breathed in. It wasn't quite what Grace thought of as yoga, but as nobody could agree what yoga was, she decided that didn't matter.

By the end the patients' moods were transformed by collective pride at coming through their first yoga class. They were so exuberant it took Grace half an hour to get them out of the upstairs room. Only Mrs. Moore slipped away without a word.

Grace stayed at the doctors' to fill in the patient records (another of Dr. Damodaran's requirements), and by the time she'd finished the building was empty. She had been instructed to turn out all the lights before locking up the surgery, but passing Doctor Norton's floor, noticed a low light had been left burning. Grace turned in to Dr. Norton's office and froze: the fifty-eight-year-old senior partner sat at his desk facing the teenage receptionist, Kelly, who perched before him, her feet balanced one on either side of his chair. Dr. Norton's hand was inside her skirt for an inspection that looked far from routine. Kelly and the doctor looked at Grace. 'I'll leave you to set the alarm,' she said, and fled.

Grace drove in a haze to Whole Foods. Surrounded by people who shop organic, happy to pay more in order to be chemical-free, she couldn't get her chemically addled patients—or Kelly's position—out of her mind. She tried to expunge Dr. Norton's antics from her memory but when she sat at a corner table to her eat supper, she was taunted by the look of pleasure on Kelly's face. Intent on forgetting, Grace retrieved from her bag the postcard she'd bought that day for Dr. James. Her last letter had been dedicated to describing her patients and she needed to let him know that she thought of him in other ways, too. He had been in Vietnam for almost five months, and she had hoped he would have returned to London by now.

To remind you of what's best in London. Albert Bridge is my favourite and at night, with all its pretty lights, the most romantic—but fragile apparently, given the sign that warns marching troops on exercise to break step when they cross. Grace's romantic notions extended far beyond the structure of the Victorian bridge but to express them seemed absurd. Sometimes, in her fantasies, Mark and Dr. James melted together, even though nothing in the doctor's correspondence justified such sexy thoughts. She returned to safer ground.

Have just finished my first yoga class with the heart sinkers. After this evening, I expect Dr. Norton will refer masses of patients just to keep me quiet about discovering him and the teenage receptionist playing in his office, after hours. His secret is safe with me. The guy's married and Kelly is young enough to be his granddaughter. Mind you, they both looked enraptured. Norton does have charisma. Could he be the South Ken medical fraternity's Bill Clinton? Everybody seems to love him—obviously Kelly a little more than most . . .

Even though my chance encounter this evening has probably just made my job a whole lot more secure, I want to convince the doctors about yoga's healing power. I certainly had the feeling today that as long as my intervention keeps the patients out of the surgery, the doctors don't care what I'm doing. Meanwhile, I've got to believe that yoga will help, otherwise how can I expect my pupils to believe it?

I hope, Dr. James, that you are enjoying the rounds in Saigon. Perhaps you have written and our words will cross in the post. Wish you were closer.

Much love,

Grace

Chapter Eleven

VRISCHIKASANA — scorpion pose

*Vrischika means a scorpion, and the posture resembles a striking scorpion
as it arches its tail to strike its victim over the head. The psychological significance of Vrischikasana is very much associated with the head, the seat
of knowledge, but also of the emotions pride, anger, hatred, jealousy, intol-
erance, and malice, more poisonous than the scorpion's sting. In the pose
it is as though the yogi stamps on his head to destroy these emotions and to
develop humility, equilibrium, and tolerance. Subjugating the ego in this
way leads to harmony and happiness. It is best to practice the pose near a
wall until confidence and strength permit balance. Make sure the surrounding floor area is clear of furniture or other obstacles in case one falls. The
pose increases blood flow to the brain and pituitary gland and alleviates
piles and varicose veins. It stimulates the reproductive organs.*

Grace was right that being referred by doctors would establish her as a
yoga teacher, but what she had not counted on was the kind of patients
they would send her; failure to inspire Mr. Kramer and slow progress with
the doctors' heart sinkers wore Grace down. At least at Swami D's she
didn't need to convince anyone that yoga was a good thing—but there were
other challenges. Ryan's Notting Hill fan base assured that his classes were
instantly packed and there was even a waiting list for his one-on-one medi-

tation class. Ryan's popularity, and the extraordinary ability of some of Grace's ultraflexible students at Swami D's, could sometimes dent her confidence. Many were so familiar with the postures they seemed to follow along without thinking—a theory Grace tested one evening. 'Raise your right arm and bend your right elbow,' she said. They all obeyed. 'Now put your thumb in your mouth.' Some students were sucking their thumbs before suspecting.

'Why is it that as soon as somebody gets on a yoga mat they want to be told what to do? Try to stay conscious of what you're being asked to do— on and off the mat.'

Privately, Grace wasn't convinced she had the right to ask more of people if 'switching off' was what they wanted. She had once appreciated Swami D's warm candlelit studio and the luxury of having each movement and breath dictated by a trusted guide. Grace decided to be that generous with her students, and stay attuned to those moments when she could ask more of them. Absorbed by the teaching, striving to be the best she could be, Grace no longer associated working at Swami D's with earning, or rather not earning, money. She forgot the Vedic claims for self-transcending action, which is when karmic justice took care of itself.

Jackie and Rosie were very English women, groomed in ways that reflected age, vanity, and immense wealth. Their look was Camilla post marriage to Charles, Joanna Lumley anytime. Both were glamorous, however old they were (and probably they had forgotten), standing out at Swami D's even from the latest Notting Hill immigrants whose wealth, and ways of spending it, had eroded the neighborhood's diversity. Five years ago Jackie and Rosie wouldn't have ventured north of Hyde Park but since a designer clothes shop had replaced the post office, and 206, a lifestyle emporium with a lunchtime restaurant, had replaced the pub, Jackie and Rosie were Westbourne Grove regulars. On their first visit to 206 they had sat on a street-side table next to Bono. 'We can't be the only ones who recognize him,' whispered Rosie when nobody had bothered him for an autograph in the half hour he'd sat in the sun drinking tea.

'That's Notting Hill,' said Jackie, who'd been told by her daughter, Plum, a Notting Hill local, that Westbourne Grove was full of Celanthropists.

'Celanthropists?' asked Rosie.

'Philanthropic celebrities, very W11,' disparaged Jackie, who wasn't the type to dispense cash downward unless in her own cause. Paying tax was bad enough.

The ladies had found Swami D's flier in Whole Foods, so were a little surprised when the journey to his studio took them far beyond the familiar territory of Westbourne Grove. The women arrived in Jackie's blacked-out Range Rover—away from SW1's clean streets to the mean streets of NW5, where, as visitors in a foreign land, they stuck together and declined Swami D's vegetarian supper. Not content to lie on his standard blues, they carried their deluxe black mats in £500 Gucci mat bags. Their 'meditation shawls' were Chanel, and they sat in lotus, stiff but still, their faces as tight as their yoga pants.

'Grace, do you travel?' asked Jackie, the apparent leader of the two, approaching at the end of class.

'Travel where?' Grace said.

'Knightsbridge,' was the response, as though it were a distant nirvana rather than seven squares on the *A to Z*. 'What we want is yoga at home.'

'I can come to Knightsbridge,' Grace said.

'For sixty pounds?' asked Jackie, who had researched the rate.

'For you and Rosie?'

'Seventy pounds then,' said Jackie, misunderstanding in a way only the rich can.

'Sixty for two is fine,' Grace said, wanting to do the right thing.

'So let's do twice a week,' said Jackie, delighted to have met somebody who wasn't milking her for extra cash just because she had it in buckets.

On her way to teach the Knightsbridge ladies Grace stopped at the zebra crossing on Colville Road. Harry passed in front of her old car, which was new to him and not the kind to catch the eye. His gaze was to the ground and he was in a hurry. A mat bag was slung across his back and he carried a silver Nick Ashley crash helmet. Evidently the boy had a motorbike and had got his look down.

After her first sighting of Harry since their split, Grace breathed deeply all the way to Knightsbridge but was still on edge standing outside Jackie's house. In the late winter sun, waiting in front of a row of uniformly perfect, white stucco houses, Grace watched a woman in a black dress and white apron scrub the black railings of the house opposite. Steam rose from a red bucket that was the same shade as her red rubber gloves. Matching accessories have always mattered in SW1. Down the street a chauffeur in a black cap polished a black Bentley. In this black-and-white world, servant activity was the only life on the street, and it was too soon for Grace to imagine this might include her.

The harmony of classic columns and pilasters, the curving stone pavements, the mature trees of the communal garden, all induced calm. Grace was no longer anxious, or in a hurry, and nobody else seemed to be either. She rang the bell again and this time set a dog yapping from behind the door. A Filipino woman in the outfit apparently all the rage in this part of London opened the door. The buttons on the maid's short-sleeved black dress strained at the chest and a yellow duster was stuffed in the pocket of her white apron. She wore yellow rubber gloves and dropped a plastic dog bone (yellow), to distract the terrier from Grace's ankles. 'Sorry, so sorry you wait. Lady Larchmont, she downstairs. She expect you,' and the woman indicated the stairs with her feathers.

Barefoot, Grace went down to the wood paneled den: sofa and chairs had been pushed aside but even with a full-size snooker table at the far end, there was plenty of space. On a pink sofa Jackie and Rosie sat beside a Jane Fonda look-alike, dressed like her, too, circa 1982. The white Lycra tights, black headband, and striped leotard were bold choices for a woman who had to be at least sixty-five. Grace stood in the doorway, waiting for them to finish talking. Waiting seemed to be part of going to other people's houses to teach private yoga classes.

'Olivia's house is crammed with Impressionists,' Rosie was saying. 'I've never seen so many outside a museum. Did Plum tell you I saw her? She looked splendid, by the way, with this absolutely charming young man.'

'How old is Plum? Thirty-four, thirty-five?' asked the Fonda look-alike.

'Thirty-seven,' Jackie corrected.

'Really?' said Rosie, surprised. 'But how old is he?'

'Twenty-five.' Jackie's facial nerves, deadened by Botox, helped to communicate an impression of indifference.

'Goodness. She's done *every*thing, and now a young beau.'

'She wants to settle. It's the only thing she hasn't done,' said Jackie.

'With the boyfriend?'

'I suppose so. Malcolm—'

'Malcolm?' interrupted Rosie. Nobody in their circle would name an inanimate object Malcolm, let alone a son.

'Malcolm,' Jackie emphasized, to prove she was reconciled, 'Malcolm is frightfully keen. Calls himself a portrait photographer and is absolutely, absolutely lovely. His parents are something else. Salt of the earth.'

'Salt of the earth! How jolly,' said Rosie.

Grace stepped into the room. 'Excuse me, I'm here for the yoga class.'

Jackie jumped up as if seeing Grace was an unexpected surprise. Introductions were made. 'Princess Elizabeth, Grace. And you remember Mrs. Shawfoot-Jones?'

Of course Grace remembered the woman; she'd seen her days before at Swami D's, but there, Mrs. Shawfoot-Jones was Rosie. Put out by the name game, and the ladies squeezing in a princess on their two-for-one deal, Grace did not sweet-talk them into rolling out their mats. Grace was mean and the ladies loved it.

She lifted their feet and extended their legs with a tug firmer than usual but when it came to holding their heads to release their necks, Grace was reminded of the healing potential in every touch. She softened her hands and gently said, 'Don't exhale with cigarette lips. Breathe in normally, then hold your breath for a second or two before exhaling. It will shift your mood.'

Grace thought *hers* had shifted, but extending Jackie's blonde bombshell head she envisioned it detaching from her neck, veins and arteries neatly sealed so that no blood spilled onto the taupe carpet. Grace blinked Jackie's body back together and moved on to Princess Elizabeth, who was on her back, clutching her mobile. It was not a good time for it to vibrate.

'Hello, darling, hello.' The princess's accent was part Spanish, part English, with a hint of Rhode Island thrown in. 'Darling, that's impossible. He can't have,' she said, looking around, impatient for her neck tug.

'Either you're in the class or you're on the phone,' Grace said, fixing the princess with a cold stare. Rosie and Jackie stopped breathing. Not only had Grace declined to use their friend's esteemed title, she had actually been rather rude. They expected the princess to pull rank, but she mutated into an attentive student who sat with such composure at the end of class, Grace asked where she had learned to meditate.

'I studied with Maharishi, you know . . .'

'Yes, The Beatles,' Grace said.

The ladies said that they had loved the class and wanted another. What they really wanted was a body like Grace's and if doing yoga was what it took, that was what they were prepared to do. Princess Elizabeth, aware of yoga's esoteric possibilities, placed her hands at her heart and bowed *namaste*. Jackie and Rosie mimicked the gesture with sincerity. Grace *namasted* in haste, willing to enter into the spirit, but not if it would cost her a parking fine. The class had gone over the hour and waiting for Jackie and Rosie to decide how to split her payment had delayed Grace further still. Clutching their cheques and her shoes, she sprinted down the crescent, just in time to beat the traffic warden to her car.

Parking tickets would not be the only hazard of teaching in London SW1. As charming as Jackie and Rosie appeared in the half-light of Swami D's studio, in the hard light of Knightsbridge, Grace saw they were boot-tough. But she had enjoyed giving the class, and the ladies had soaked up her touch and her teaching, leaving her depleted in a way that didn't happen at Swami D's, or even at Mr. Kramer's. Grace suspected the ladies were predisposed to treat her like a yoga maid. The irony did not escape her that dressed in black and white she already had the outfit.

Coming home and finding a letter from Dr. James restored Grace. She was back in her world, and better for it. She forgot the ladies to concentrate on the doctor.

Grace, my favourite bridge in London is Tower Bridge. Our preferences conform to type. Yours more yin and best by moonlight, mine functional and solidly yang. A good balance.

How are you, and what of the yoga patients? Are they taking to it? You are right to say that you need to believe in what you're offering them, at least as much as they do, if not more. Double blind trials, as you know, always work best—even with placebos, which I hasten to add, is not how I classify yoga.

Interacting with patients as you do on such a physical level (and, I believe, an emotional one, even though it's less apparent), it would be good practice to protect your energy. I don't mean to sound prescriptive and perhaps you do this already but, if not, try sleeping for half an hour during the day. We actually have that scheduled at the hospital here. I don't see Chelsea and Westminster implementing the policy anytime soon. The Qigong is tremendously helpful, its effect similar, I imagine, to self-practice in yoga.

From seeing so many patients over the years I learned the hard way the value of putting them out of your head—and heart—as soon as they are out of your sight. Be empathic, sympathetic, treat them with respect, and give them the best care you can, but leave them to live their lives. Best not to think about them when they are not there. I wasn't always able to do that—as you may recall. A patient can stay with you long after they've stopped being your patient. Sometimes long after their death.

You asked about the mind in Chinese medicine: there isn't one, which was worrying at first for a shrink, and then liberating. Emotions are attributed to organs but they are less like emotions, more like temperaments, and the organs are those of the meridian lines, which don't equate to our physical organs although they share the same names. If a person is anxious, for example, it could be that treating the spleen meridian, or the stomach, will help. Generally, in TCM it is said that if a person is disturbed, the spirit in the heart is displaced. The five so-called spirits recognized in the body equate to the five elements. *TCM is an empiric method that has taken four thousand years to evolve although all of the recommendations in the Yellow Emperor's* Basic Questions of Internal Medicine, *the bible of TCM, were tested in ways that make our clinical trials look speculative.*

The Emperor had at his disposal the proletariat of China on whom to test his theories—and it was a vast number even in those days. Testing substances for longevity (the Yellow Emperor wanted to live forever), he suspected mercury had the necessary properties, and fed it to half a million subjects who promptly disproved his theory by dying. Half a million people, by the way, was considered a controlled test, a quarter of a million a random test. Forget the three thousand recruited for our phase-two trials and the years it takes to recruit the required number of volunteers (particularly males) to try a new drug. I am tempted to believe that Viagra was an exception; is it true three thousand volunteers signed up within three hours? Normally it would take three years for that many men to step up. The Emperor didn't worry about volunteers: he commanded his subjects to swallow whatever took his fancy, which is how we know the herbs in Chinese medicine are safe. Barbaric then, but four thousand years on, we benefit.

The work here is intense: in addition to seeing patients I have hours and hours of study. Dr. Huang advised that if in doubt, we should always treat a patient for heart fire, which is yang, and kidney water, which is yin. As an experiment, I spent one whole day treating thirty patients exactly that way, regardless of their symptoms. Twenty-six patients came back with improved or cured symptoms. Once the body is balanced, healing seems to take place naturally—but this is no excuse not to learn about the herbs and all the pressure points.

I often study at a monastery not far from here where herbs are collected from the wild, then prepared, dried, and packaged for different apothecaries. The monks and nuns have individual retreat

huts where they sit among the fruit trees in the orchard for medita-
tion. Life is simple; sitting, eating, praying, gardening. Beautiful
bonsai and miniature gardens, lotus ponds, frangipani, scented
gardens, shady coconut and bamboo groves. Blissfully tranquil,
timeless. Would love to show you this place one day.
   David

Grace thought it safest to think of Dr. James as a friend but could not ignore the threads of desire that infiltrated her reading of his lines, and hers when she wrote to him. She didn't want anything to ruin their connection, yet she didn't want to want it too much, either. To name what they were to each other, to categorize it, would have suited her, but a category eluded her. All Grace knew was that hearing from Dr. James made her glad in ways that could get complicated.

Grace soon understood that teaching people privately at home conferred upon them a sense of ownership. Essentially, Grace's wealthy students thought she was their property and existed for their convenience, which she tolerated, simply because she needed the money. But wealthy clients were rarely a source of other clients, preferring, as they did, to guard their trusted help—whether manicurist, massage therapist, chef, yoga teacher, dog walker, or whoever else might feature on what is, for some, an endless list. It seemed the wealthier the individual the more likely it was that everybody they knew was, in some way or another, on their payroll. There could be nothing worse for such a person than calling their valued yoga teacher to discover she was squandering time teaching a friend and rival, too busy to invest in them. Hence 'don't refer your best help'—the unspoken code by which London's elite live.

   Princess Elizabeth proved the exception when she asked Grace if she had room for an extra client. The following week she told Grace to expect a text from Carl, which duly arrived, inviting her to what turned out to be one of the finest houses on Chelsea's Cheyne Walk. That Princess Elizabeth's friend lived in such a house was to be expected; Carl was the surprise. The graceful black man of six foot three had a stunning presence and looked far too hip to be a friend of the European royal. Grace's only regular male clients were Mr. Kramer and Davis. Carl was different, and how he was different made her nervous.

Standing with him in the black-and-white tiled hall of the Cheyne Walk house, Grace was conscious of a warm flush filling her cheeks. She spoke fast. 'If you need a yoga mat I've got a spare one in the car, and perhaps you'd like to change. Jeans aren't good for moving about.'

Carl stuffed his hands into his pockets and leaned back, smiling. 'As much as I like the idea of a yoga class, you're here to teach Collette. I'll let her know you've arrived.' Carl sent a swift text. Carl was not dressed like a housekeeper-cum-butler, and he certainly did not look like one, but Grace guessed that was his job. Collette was probably the model whose meteoric career and rock star husband, Mike Edge, made her last name superfluous. As famous as Collette was, teaching her was a less intimidating prospect than going one-on-one with Carl for a full hour. Being a yoga teacher had brought Grace many challenges, but desiring a student wasn't one of them, and she was grateful to be spared the pleasure and pain of working with a man as beautiful as Carl.

Within seconds a harmonious chord combination announced Collette's reply. 'The cabbala meeting's running late. She's invited you to join them,' Carl said. 'Do you have time?'

'This is my last appointment until this evening.'

'Good. This place doesn't run on Greenwich Mean Time. If Collette invites you back, I'll make sure you've got a parking space.'

Grace was reminded that she was on trial, a new teacher to a new student. There was no guarantee there would be a second class but she wasn't concerned about that: she was curious to meet Collette and learn a bit about cabbala. Grace's great-grandfather had been a rabbi and though secular, her father's family had always respected the scholarship of rabbinical law. That gentiles were buying into cabbalistic mysticism, deciphering the encrypted codes of the Old Testament, was her father's idea of a joke. 'Only Jewish scholars are worthy of cabbala. Even I know you can't cherry-pick the Old Testament.'

Grace supposed that cherry-picking was what Dr. Damodaran thought she was up to with yoga, and she felt guilty of it as Carl led her into Collette's mansion. He opened the doors of the subtle, sink-into-it-forever green drawing room where a gallery of faces from rock music and fashion were gathered around an old rabbi. Grace slipped into the back row, trying not to stare at this group who proved that fame, infinite wealth, and well-maintained beauty were not enough. Their quest had to be for something money can't buy.

The rabbi, hunched on a stool by the stone fireplace, was straight out of Central Casting, with a pasty round face, John Lennon specs, and a fluffy white beard. 'The alphabet,' he droned, 'embraces the wisdom of the world and of God. The individual letters I picked for each one of you last week must be displayed so you can absorb their meaning. We will recite the twenty-two letters to finish.'

Collette glanced at Grace with a guilty smile. 'Won't be long,' she mouthed as the gathering pronounced, somewhat hesitantly, the letters in Hebrew, reading right to left from a white card that reminded Grace of the periodic table.

The second the lesson was over, a younger guest pressed toward the front. 'Excuse me, rabbi, I need to know what to bid for a house coming up in closed auction,' she said.

'Write the highest figure you are prepared to offer on a piece of paper,' the rabbi advised. As the woman did so, the rabbi also wrote down a figure. They swapped papers.

'My God, that's incredible,' she said.

'That is the figure you must offer if you want the house.'

'Can we do cabbala and business next week?' asked another woman, her face distorted by plumped lips. 'My husband's cynical but I know he'd make better decisions if he listened to you.'

'Have him call me,' the rabbi said, handing her his card.

Collette led the cabbala guests into the blue dining room and made her way to Grace. 'So nice of you to come. Sorry we're running late. Do we have time for lunch before class?'

Seduced by Collette's sweet manner and American accent, another song of the South like Rita's, Grace agreed to meet back in the drawing room in half an hour.

'Darling, hey, Mags!' Collette called. 'Get that book, the one on manifesting, and the DVD. They're fabulous.' Collette was gone, forsaking food to promote the power of cabbala.

Grace sat with the bass player and the lead guitarist of Mike's band and tucked into roast vegetables from Mike and Collette's organic farm in Kent. Achingly thin, or desperate to be, most of the women preferred to savor the stack of books and CDs for sale alongside plastic bottles of sacred, calorie-free cabbala water. It could have been Prada, but this was cabbala, the season's must-have. Credit cards were held out to the young Jewish woman, modestly dressed in shapeless black, who, with pale equanimity, pressed platinum plastic into her portable charge machine.

After her food-free lunch, Collette rushed into the drawing room with a purple mat, wearing skimpy shorts and a skinny tank top. 'Where does the time go?' she sighed, locking the double doors, slinging her mobile phone at the sofa.

'Would you mind switching that off?' Grace said.

Collette, only mildly put out, did as she was asked.

The room was large but so tastefully cluttered there was room for only Collette's mat. Grace squeezed in between the sofa and a heavy low table.

'Boy, that feels good,' said Collette as Grace gently tugged her head and extended her legs. The usual trick seemed to be working—Collette was calming down, but then she raised her long arms above her head and twiddled the red wool cabbala thread around her wrist. Lifting her head she said, 'The rabbi's kind of interesting, don't you think?'

'I had no idea the Hebrew letters were so significant.'

'"For by thy words thou shalt be justified, and by thy words thou shalt be condemned." Matthew 12.'

'That's impressive,' Grace said, thinking Collette didn't learn that from her rabbi.

'I'm a Bible Belt baby. Down south they drummed it into us, which I resented at the time. Mind you, it's a pity the cabbala misses out on the sayings of Jesus.'

There was more to Collette than met the eye, which was saying something. Her radiant face was makeup-free, and with her long blonde hair splayed across the floor, her beauty shone brighter than from any magazine. Grace guessed she had to be forty, simply because she'd been a famous face for so long, but her tiny shorts didn't look remotely ridiculous and her legs were as endless as the luxury she lived in. Except that the perfection of her legs was 'ruined,' said Collette, 'by thick ankles.' Grace took a look. There was nothing wrong with Collette's ankles, although in relation to the perfect rest of her, they weren't her best feature.

'Collette, your ankles are fine,' said Grace.

'Fine doesn't interest me. My ankles are the bane of my life.' She flicked a smooth tanned leg in the air and turned her foot clockwise. 'I'd pay you double if you could slim them down.'

'Your ankles will elongate once your feet start working.'

'There's nothing wrong with my feet.'

'You're right,' Grace said, admiring the arched soles and long manicured toes. 'You just need to activate your ankles.'

'I've never worn an ankle chain. I'm hoping with yoga I will.'

Yoga for thin ankles was a new idea but Grace did not judge Collette's motive. If she were a good enough teacher, the motive would change. 'In time, Collette, with yoga your ankles, your body, and even your mind will be different.'

'We go to Cannes in May.'

'We can aim for that,' Grace said, thinking May was an impossible target unless Collette was committed to hours of yoga each day—unlikely given that Carl had come in to cut the class short. Collette's voice coach had arrived.

'I'm singing on Mike's next record. Backing mostly, but we're in the studio next week and I can't mess up. So let's meet in a few days. Carl will sort it out.'

* * *

Dear Dr. James,

Thank you for your letter. You were right to remind me of the importance of self-practice—I don't relish it as much as I did. No doubt teaching up to six hours a day has something to do with this.

In busy London, the essence of the world you described in the monastery sounds appealing. I'm sure it's what the group I met today is searching for—Collette, the model, and Mike, the musician, had friends over for a cabbala class. I met the rabbi when the day's self-improvement schedule got backed up. I felt as though the rabbi and I were traveling ministers, admitted to the world of the uber-rich clutching reliquaries, mine the yoga mat, the rabbi his Hebrew alphabet. It is as though we were exchanging spiritual secrets for money—and rather medieval. As you know, selling pharmaceuticals eventually made me uneasy. I suspect selling asanas won't sit too well with me either.

Devotion to the discipline of yoga has to be the thing, otherwise what I'm doing doesn't make sense. Any spiritual path, regardless of the religion that veils it, requires a commitment for which nothing else compensates—although Mike and Collette's paintings by Bacon, Poussin, and Picasso are, as compensations go, about the best. And it would be nice to have their organic farm in Kent, where they grow vegetables and breed horses and edible animals. Everything served at lunch was produced on the farm and cooked perfectly. Ah, the luxury of having a chef, and a housekeeper like Carl. That everything they have is maintained or prepared by somebody else might be part of the problem. They're looking for something to complete them but they're going about it the way they go about everything else—buying it rather than . . . what? What should they do? At least they're searching. Maybe the more you have, the more money and fame and apparent abundance, the harder it is to see clearly.

I have been invited back to teach Collette, which is flattering, but the monk's life you described appeals. Do you think you could settle for it?

Last week I taught a Notting Hill couple who have taken up yoga to help his MS—a recent diagnosis that worried them. They expected one yoga class to cure him. I said it didn't work like that but they booked another class anyway. I turned up and rang their doorbell for ten minutes, then tried their mobile. They were having breakfast on their yacht, 'looking at St. Tropez harbor,' he said, and wouldn't want yoga in the future thank you very much.

I wish you were closer. I'd like a friend to remind me what's real. A walk along the canal—in the daylight—would be a nice thing to do with you, laughing at the ridiculous nature of humanity. It has to be the only response, although to retreat to the monastery might also be good.

Much love,

Grace

The next time Grace went to teach Collette, Mike answered the door. It was surreal to see such a famous face doing something so mundane, dressed for comfort as he was in sky blue sweat pants, thick white socks, and a thin white T-shirt of the finest cotton. He was nothing like his hot hard image and Grace liked him better for it. 'You're Rose, right?' he said, smiling steady.

'By any other name,' she said, walking in without waiting to be asked.

The rock star liked it that the yoga teacher was not intimidated. 'What's with this yoga thing, Rose?' He stood opposite her, closer than she expected. For a second she thought he was going to kiss her.

'Grace,' she said, holding still.

'What's that?' He came closer.

'I'm Grace,' she said.

'Oh, right. I'm Mike.'

'I know who you are.' Grace held his gaze but Mike was the same height and face-to-face, it was too much. Uncertain what was going to happen next, she stepped back.

'Grace! Come up, darling!' Collette's call was cheerful.

Mike and Grace looked at each other. Darling? So soon? Mike knew then that Grace was Collette's. 'She's upstairs—all the way up,' Mike said, watching Grace take the stairs two at a time. 'Perhaps I'll join you next time.'

Grace found Collette on her yoga mat on a bare mahogany floor beneath a suspended flat-screen television, singing along to Madonna's 'Ray of Light' on MTV.

'At least we've got room up here,' Collette called above the music.

'We should turn that off,' Grace said, rolling out her own mat.

'I like Madge and I like this tune. And I like her shape. Can I get a shape like that doing this?'

'I think Madonna prefers Ashtanga Vinyasa,' Grace said, shouting to be heard. She declined to mention that when Madonna practiced yoga, she surely did so without distraction. MTV at full pitch defeated the purpose of doing yoga, let alone paying for it, but if that's what Collette wanted, that's what Grace would give her.

'What is Ashtanga whatever-it's-called?' Collette said, looking up from her forward bend.

'A yang style that makes you sweat, and whacks the adrenals if you do too much.'

'Whacks the what?' Collette stopped her sun salute to listen.

'The glands on top of the kidneys that produce adrenaline.'

'Adrenaline's my problem. The doctor says I've got too much. Where were we?'

Grace showed her. 'Now left foot forward. No, left foot, Collette.'

'Shit, I'm all over the place.'

Collette was not at ease in her lean long body and Grace felt as though she were fighting to guide the mentally-willing-but-disembodied super-model through poses that should have been a gentle pleasure. The challenge of helping Collette to a Madonna-like physique, competing with MTV, the prospect of Mike joining in, *and* slimming the ankles was all too much for Grace. 'You know, Collette, Ashtanga might suit you. I could find you a teacher,' she said.

'If you don't want to work with me come straight out with it.' Collette was fast as a whip and nobody's fool.

'I'll never get your ankles the way you want by Easter,' Grace admitted.

The model popped up again in mid–sun salute, a sign, Grace feared, that she suffered from attention deficit, detrimental to yoga and most things. Collette zapped the MTV. At six foot, two inches taller than Grace, Collette slung out her hip so they could stand as equals. 'Whatever I said about my ankles, they're not why I'm doing this. Mike and I are trying for a baby even though, as half the world knows, I'm forty-six—that's no reason not to conceive.' Collette's eyes shone but accustomed as she was to holding in and holding on, there were no tears. 'Mike's sperm's still got a kick, I've got eggs, and the rabbi picked out the female letters for me. And prayers; boy am I praying. All I need is to see a lot of Mike, and calm down—which is where you come in, if you're up for it?'

'I am,' said Grace, moved by Collette's appeal.

'Fantastic. Elizabeth said you made her relax, so I know you can help me.'

After the confession, Collette concentrated and practiced the asanas without distraction. In lotus pose, the power of sitting to meditate was intensified because they were two, and when Collette stretched on her mat like a cat, Grace could tell that an essence, the tiniest drop of what was possible, had settled in her body.

'I think we'll work well together,' said Grace.

'Hallelujah,' Collette said, eyes shining with unshed tears.

Chapter Twelve

SHANMUKHI MUDRA—clearing the seven gates pose

Shan *means seven and* mukhi *means gates or faces. In* shanmukhi mudra *the awareness is directed inward by closing the seven doors of outer perception: two eyes, ears, and nostrils, plus the mouth. Close the ears with the thumbs, the eyes with the index fingers, and the nostrils with the middle fingers. The fourth and little fingers are placed over the mouth. To breathe, release the pressure over the nostrils and close them after inhalation. Retain the breath only while it is comfortable to do so. There may be many internal sounds, or none at all. This pose is best practiced late at night or early in the morning when there is quiet. People suffering from depression should avoid this posture, which is also known as* devi mudra, *the attitude of the great goddess.*

Yoga in London had been heading mainstream for years but spiritual materialism's transcendence of the merely spiritual was confirmed when Nigel Freyn invested five million pounds to convert a warehouse in Primrose Hill into a yoga centre.

While the construction was underway Nigel and his wife Chrissy, a yogini and one-time television weather girl, attended Swami D's for edification. Nobody suspected they were there for anything other than asana practice until Nigel asked Swami D about student turnover. 'Student turnover? Nigel, this isn't a grocery business,' Swami D chuckled, deflecting the need to reveal his figures, canny East Ender that he still was. The Freyns were interested in Swami D's business, but not his style. They planned to do away with the hippy and go straight for the hip, creating Europe's first nonstop yoga studio. Lifestyle yoga is what they were selling and the way they planned to make money. If it didn't, Nigel already had planning permission to turn the building into a restaurant and bar.

While Chrissy always went to Swami D's classes, Nigel would attend Grace's and had long hinted that he wanted her for his yoga centre. That he might also want her for other things seemed likely; he would hang around after class, often the last in the studio while she locked up. Grace didn't mind Nigel and put up with his flirting until the time she adjusted him in class and his fingers reached around and touched her high on the inner thigh with such gentle precision it could not have been a mistake. She did not touch him again.

That Grace now avoided Nigel only made him more persistent, and when he called to invite her to teach at his studio, he wouldn't get off the phone. 'We're ready for business, Grace, and we want you to work for us.' Grace declined.

'Grace, why are you loyal to that old Swami D when he doesn't even pay you?'

'How do you know that?'

'Ryan told me.'

Grace desperately wanted to know if Ryan was being paid but steered clear of trouble. 'What I'm doing at Swami D's is called karma yoga, Nigel.'

'Karma yoga. Very clever. I call it exploitation. We're paying top rate, linked to student turnover, and we've reserved two great slots for you. You could earn £500 a week.' Nigel paused to let her digest the figure: he had her attention, and knew it. 'You're the only teacher we know who's been trained by Garuda and Rita, you've got experience from teaching for that old hippy, you work on the NHS, and Grace, best of all, you're good to look at. We want to be famous for more than our beautiful interiors.'

Grace confessed to Swami D that the Freyns had invited her to the teachers' meeting and wanted to put her on their timetable. He gave his blessing. 'You are ready to earn money teaching yoga,' he said. Sadly, it seemed not from him. Grace had to go where the money was, which was a pity; once she worked for the Freyns she would be driving around London as much as when she had been a pharmaceutical rep.

The Freyns' yoga centre was a temple to contemporary interior design: Buddha heads, once sacred icons, added gravitas to leather sofas on faux skin rugs, the designer cushions were white, and the walls were whiter still, to complement the dark wood floor. Grace was reminded of Harry's yoga bible that had been put together by the fashion editor, who turned out to be a friend of the Freyns', and credited with the 'Primrose Hill yoga design concept.' The place was so far from the heart of yoga Grace felt defeated, and nothing changed that when she sat among the teachers in the big Ashtanga yoga studio.

The Ashtanga devotees, lean with concave bellies and a few dodgy knees from years of demanding poses done at speed, were the high rollers of the yoga world, confident in their physiology. The Iyengar teachers were softer with long, straight thighs and lifted chests, their similar shapes reflecting a precise rendition of the poses and, Grace thought, a more secure psychology.

At the close of the meeting, everybody received a copy of the timetable. As Nigel had promised, Grace had two classes at popular times. 'But what's this?' she asked him.

'We're confident if anyone can get people in on a Friday it's you,' Nigel said.

'At seven o'clock in the morning?'

Nigel didn't answer. His mobile rang and he disappeared to take the call, leaving Grace with a Friday morning class that she didn't want.

Grace's Tuesday and Wednesday classes were a hit, and the hourly flat rate plus the extra pound for each student soon added up. Meanwhile, Friday mornings were dead. In bohemian style, in Primrose Hill the weekend began on Thursday and lasted through Monday afternoon. Only Ashtanga students remained steadfast to yoga, whatever the day.

When Grace arrived to set up for her Friday class in the small studio the sound of Ujjayi breathing and the monotone commands of the notoriously alluring Frederick echoed down the corridor. At least fifteen of Frederick's students were fanatical enough about him, and their practice, to be there at half past six. Grace's class was busy if two people showed up. To get out of bed at dawn to return a couple of hours later only ten pounds better off felt like folly. Swami D and her students at his studio, the heart sinkers, Collette, Mr. Kramer, even her Knightsbridge ladies deserved Grace's devotion. Nigel Freyn did not.

After a few months, Grace had had enough. She called Nigel. 'I don't want the class, and you know I never did. Please give it to somebody who does.'

'Relinquish one, relinquish all. You should consider yourself lucky; people are desperate to work here. And we can't show favouritism by having certain teachers pick and choose their class times,' he said, although from looking at the timetable Grace guessed that's exactly what Chrissy and her teaching friends had done. Grace could not afford to drop all her classes at the Primrose Hill Yoga Centre, and so she backed down. And for that, a few weeks later, she was grateful.

The following Friday, parking her car on Primrose Hill's deserted high street, Grace was wary of a small dark-haired man in tracksuit and trainers pacing up and down the pavement.

'Where d'you get a coffee round here?' the American asked Grace as she got out of her car.

'The cafés open in an hour.'

'An hour? What kind of city is this? Where's the traffic? The people getting to work, where are they?'

The man's frustration amused Grace. 'Sorry, I've got to go or I'll be late for work myself.'

'Lynus, by the way. Lynus Shlossinger,' he called to Grace's departing back.

Lynus had been in London for less than a week and missed his native New York. At this time in the morning he would be in his local café, tucking into a double espresso, the *Post,* and what kind of pastry? What he wanted this morning was an almond croissant. He bet he could get one at that café he'd found in Chelsea that opened early—by English standards. Baker & Spice. He'd kept the card. There was one in Queen's Park. That wasn't so far away. Just as well there were no taxis on the street. Lynus had promised his wife that his belt would not go up another notch while he was on location. She'd prodded his tummy and told him it would be easier in England than anywhere else in the world, which was a sad reflection of how seldom she traveled with him these days. He had declined to tell his wife that the London eateries he frequented were among the best anywhere.

Lynus was a film producer, renting a house in Primrose Hill that was too far to be practical for his daily pilgrimage to Pinewood Studios, but he refused to live in the suburbs. Primrose Hill, people had told him, was the village in the heart of the city and village it most certainly was, but not in the way he'd imagined. Compared to the metropolitan villages he'd had in mind—Manhattan's East Village and Greenwich Village—Primrose Hill was a rural outpost. The name should have been a clue. Even so, he wasn't willing to forgo the small fortune he'd paid for his short-term lease. Instead, Lynus appreciated the fine houses in the neighborhood and the wealth that abided there, keeping his eyes open for Kate Moss, the Oasis boys, Patsy Kensit (Lynus had invested in her first movie), Sienna, and of course Jude. Lynus liked Jude. He had wanted Jude for his movie but the man wasn't available. Jude might not have liked the script, but Lynus was sure his response would have been different had he known that Jessica Bell would be his female lead. Miss Bell had signed Lynus's contract the month before she was nominated for, and subsequently won, the Oscar for Best Actress.

A week after their first impromptu meeting, Lynus timed his pacing to coincide with Grace's arrival on Primrose Hill. When he spotted her on the high street, he turned on his heel and quickened his step to follow her down an alley to an apparently abandoned industrial building. When Grace disappeared inside a wide metal door, Lynus didn't even hesitate: the white temple-looking interior was such a contrast to the exterior, he gasped—or perhaps it was the shock at finding himself in a yoga centre, where it was evident to all, and to his credit particularly to Lynus, that he was no yogi.

Lynus had reassured Jessica at five o'clock that morning that by the time she arrived from Los Angeles he would have appointed a group of health experts specifically for her. He had the fitness instructor, massage therapist, and nutritionist but the different styles of yoga, and its esoteric principles, confused him. He hadn't even attempted to find a yoga teacher. When Lynus told the receptionist that's what he wanted for Jessica Bell, Nigel and Chrissy popped out from their glass office behind reception.

'Hi, I'm Nigel and this is my wife, Chrissy. This is our centre. Why don't you join us for breakfast while we tell you about our fabulous teachers?' Nigel was so keen to meet Jessica he was willing to give Lynus his own coffee and almond croissant, picked up, as luck would have it, from Baker & Spice in Queen's Park. Jessica had been Nigel's fantasy since he'd watched her first film, *Take Me Home*. He'd wished, as had every other heterosexual male in the Western world. There was nothing about Jessica Bell Nigel didn't like and it would be a professional and personal triumph, not to mention a thrill, if he could arrange for his wife to teach her.

Lynus followed Nigel and Chrissy into their office behind the reception desk. 'Pleased to meet you, Chrissy,' said Lynus, biting into Nigel's croissant, casting crumbs and castor sugar over the floor. Unfortunately, this morning Chrissy was tired. Launching the centre had taken a lot out of her and she was suffering from the effects of too many caffeine breakfasts and high-powered Ashtanga classes. With her hair scraped back and dark circles beneath her eyes, she was not the best advertisement for anything, least of all yoga.

'I've heard about yoga, we all have, but what does it do, exactly? The last thing I need is for Jessica to lose weight and burn out on my movie.'

'You'll think I'm biased, but Chrissy is one of the best teachers in England. She'll know exactly what to do with Jessica,' Nigel enthused.

'So you're telling me to take your wife?' Lynus said, looking at Chrissy as he mopped his forehead, still sweaty from the exertion of chasing Grace down the street. 'How about you, Nigel?'

'How about me?' Nigel echoed, hoping to convey his distaste for Lynus's flip familiarity and the speed with which he had polished off the croissant without offering to share it.

Lynus reached for the cup of coffee and, sucking through the white plastic lid, studied Nigel. He certainly looked healthier than his wife. 'How about you teaching Jessica? Would you like that job, Nigel?'

Nigel twittered. 'I'd love nothing better, but I'm a solicitor.'

'Wadda you know? A lawyer. I sure as hell don't need another one of those,' Lynus sniggered. It was down to Chrissy then but Lynus wasn't feeling it with Chrissy, and with Nigel perched on the edge of his seat, Lynus wasn't convinced by him either.

'Jessica's a sweet girl, and I was hoping for a good teacher who might be a friend—not an instant friend, you understand.' Lynus shut up. He'd said enough. 'Thanks for breakfast, it hit the spot. I'll catch you later,' he said, wondering what it was about Nigel that so irritated him.

Lost in thoughts of Jessica, Lynus had drifted out of the yoga centre and was on Primrose Hill high street before he realized. He returned to the receptionist and in an uncharacteristically quiet voice asked about the woman who had led him there in the first place. 'Long dark hair, white top. Cute. Came through about fifteen minutes ago.'

'Grace.'

'Exactly. Where do I find Grace?'

'Upstairs.'

'Thanks,' Lynus said, heading off.

'That will be twelve pounds please.'

'Get outta here. I've never done yoga and I'm not going to start now.'

'Why not? You might like it.'

What with the jog down the street, and now the stairs up to the yoga studio, Lynus had done more exercise in the last twenty minutes than he had the whole of the year. He really didn't want to do yoga, it wasn't his thing and never would be, but his interest was piqued by the sight of Grace, bending over a CD player.

Grace wasn't putting on the Vedic chants, she was taking them off. It was quarter past seven, and with no students to teach, she was entitled to leave. Grace was looking forward to breakfast so when Lynus appeared, puffing from the stairs, her 'good morning' was a shade ambivalent. Lynus did not notice. All he wanted was to lie down and digest that croissant.

Lynus would have hired Grace on looks alone, which would have saved him the unlikely prospect of this early morning exertion, but he had to put her to the test for Jessica's sake. It was soon apparent that Grace wasn't the one being tested. She authoritatively encouraged Lynus's efforts, however pathetic, while being simultaneously sensitive—but what convinced Lynus about Grace was the discreet way she tucked his shirt into his pants to save him the indignity of exposing his round belly while he was on all fours in down dog.

Down dog, indeed. Lynus found himself faintly excited by Grace's domination of him. Later, curled in the aptly named child's pose—another compromising position that made him feel helpless (and remarkably stiff in the lower back)—Lynus felt incomprehensibly proud when his bottom touched his heels. Grace had applied pressure to his sacrum, which had surely helped, and he found it curious that the sensation of her hand remained on his back long after she'd removed it. Yoga, he reflected, had it all: sexy girls, kinky thrills, mystical touch, and just the right amount of pain to prove it was doing him good. At the end of the hour, Lynus was grateful that Grace had not humiliated him—although the thought that she might was the recurring fantasy of his weekend.

'I've never felt so good with my tracksuit on,' he said when it was all over. And then the line he'd been waiting to deliver. 'How would you like to teach Jessica Bell for the next three months?'

From his office window, Nigel Freyn watched Grace and Lynus walk out of his yoga centre, mobiles out, thumbing numbers. In a bid to prevent Grace getting the job with Jessica, he called right then to tell her they had revised the timetable and allocated her extra classes. Grace politely declined, and also let him know she would have to drop her Friday class. 'I've been asked to teach a private client. I hope you understand.'

'I do. And I hope you'll understand that if that's your decision, we will cut all your classes.'

'From when?'

'From right now,' he said, hanging up.

'Nigel Freyn is the unacceptable face of yoga I hope to never see again,' she said to Lynus, sticking her mobile in her pocket.

'He fired you?' Lynus knew he had.

Grace nodded; she looked downhearted.

'You're better off without that asshole. My job will pay better. Take me to Baker & Spice and I'll tell you all about it.'

Lynus climbed into Grace's old Volkswagen. 'The last time I got into a car like this, I was shooting in Eastern Europe fifteen years ago. If this is all you can afford, yoga is a fool's game,' Lynus scoffed. 'Don't worry, kiddo, breakfast's on me.'

They sat at Baker & Spice's communal table, Lynus attacking his second almond croissant of the day as though he hadn't eaten for a week. 'Exercise makes me hungry, and exercise is what I want you to give Jessica at seven in the morning, and before she goes to sleep at night.'

'Sounds as though she needs a nanny, not a yoga teacher,' Grace said.

'You might not be wrong.'

Lynus's movie schedule was demanding—a concern given the East Coast whispers that Jessica was falling under the influence these days. Quite what influence Lynus preferred not to say. 'To name anything gives it power,' he said, then toyed with possibilities. 'A slight addiction . . .' It was a dangerous word, so he rephrased. 'If sex is her thing, indiscriminate sex, that would be a serious problem.'

In Lynus's movie Jessica was playing the saviour of a world under siege from aliens, her character a master of every kind of lethal weapon but innocent of her own fantastical beauty, which proves to be her most lethal weapon of all. While nothing in the movie was credible, to have Jessica act a killer virgin on screen and be a 'ho,' as Lynus put it, in real life, would make a mockery of his movie and him along with it. A romance with a high-profile leading man was the only kind of influence Lynus would countenance for Jessica. To counteract other possibilities he planned to provide his star with so much physical exercise she would be incapable of any activity other than carrying his film. Which is why he had put together a compassionate group of helpers who would, if necessary, keep their mouths shut and carry her.

*　*　*

Lynus was confident he had found the members of what he now called 'Team Jessica,' and invited them, one at a time, to meet his leading lady at The Ivy. In the hope the girls would get along, Lynus saved Grace's interview until last so he could suggest she join them for dinner, which is what happened.

Jessica was impressed by Grace's references. 'Do Collette and Mike still live in Chelsea?'

'Yes, not far from your hotel.'

'Cool, let's invite her to my class.'

'Jessica will have individual tuition,' Lynus cut in, unwilling to hemorrhage money on Jessica's yoga classes only for them to descend into high-profile chats on a plastic mat. 'We want Jessica focused, don't we, sweetheart,' Lynus said, neatly dividing his star into object and subject. 'Yoga centres you, doesn't it, Grace? I sure felt centred after that class with you. We want you centred, Jessica sweetheart.'

Jessica, Jessica, Jessica, Jessica. On and on and on. So this was what it was like to be a Hollywood star. Grace admired Jessica for being unaffected by the frenzy that surrounded her. She certainly didn't seem to want it, or to be the one generating it.

'Lynus, don't worry. I've done yoga and I'm sure Grace knows her job.' Jessica held Grace's eye as if to say, let's tell Lynus what he wants to hear and get this dinner over.

'Jessica's right, don't worry. We'll work out a yoga routine to complement her—'

'—other exercise, and the acting. Let's not forget why we're here. Jessica darling, I've been thinking, it might be good for you to start and end the day with yoga.'

'Fine,' she said, appeasing her producer, until it registered. 'Grace, isn't two hours of yoga a day excessive?'

'It's the kind of excess to indulge, Grace, don't you think?' Lynus chipped in. 'I want you to feel looked after, Jessica. That's what matters.'

'Thanks, Lynus. I appreciate it. Excuse me.' Jessica's lassitude was tangible, her voice a weary trail of compliance. Picking up her palm-sized purse, she headed for the bathroom.

The restaurant fell silent as Jessica glided through. Lynus, who had heaved his frame one inch out of the banquette out of respect for a standing lady, slumped down, deliberately not gazing after her. He knew curious eyes would seek the identity of the star's companions and he preferred to look involved in his own business. He leaned toward Grace. 'I was going to offer you £150 an hour, but if you do mornings and evenings five times a week, I'll make it two fifty.'

'That's two—'

'—fifty an hour.' Lynus was a great sentence finisher. 'It would be worth it for me. I have a good feeling about you, Grace. I know I can trust you to keep an eye on Jessica. In fact, go to the bathroom, will you? She might need a hand.'

'In the loo?' Grace squinted at Lynus.

'Honey, do me a favour, get your ass up there ASAP. I need to know my star ain't doing a line of coke, throwing up her hundred-dollar entrée, or fucking the waiter.'

There was no sign of Jessica, although one of the cubicle doors was locked, no feet visible beneath. Grace waited. 'Honey, I miss you,' Jessica whispered. 'I wish you'd come over. Get on a plane and I'll be yours from 8 p.m. to 8 a.m. Shit, no I won't. Lynus wants me to do yoga at seven . . . yeah, and evening. I'm sick of him already. Why the hell did I take this ridiculous job?' She laughed. 'Yeah right, a Malibu beach house, but do I really need one? Yes baby, I know. I am being patient.'

Grace returned to reassure Lynus that his star was perfectly fine. Nothing to worry about at all, so if that *was* all, she would head home and see Jessica in her hotel room at seven the following morning.

'And nine in the evening,' Lynus said, standing to kiss Grace's cheek, his hand on her waist gauging the shape of her.

Leaving through the Ivy's revolving door, wiping away the moisture Lynus's lips had left, Grace was startled by the pack of burly photographers crouched on the pavement, waiting like wolves for Jessica Bell. In the taxi home, Grace was uneasy. To be offered a couple of thousand pounds a week to teach one woman yoga hinted at the possibility that as stunning as she was on that month's cover of *Vanity Fair,* as charming as she'd been over dinner, and as in love as she'd sounded on her secret telephone call, teaching Jessica Bell could be hell.

Date: March 5, 2007
To: stephanie17@gmail.com
From: yogagrace@hotmail.com
Subject: inside information—urgent!

It's all been a bit crazy recently: nights still quiet but days spent running around, teaching. My student profile is changing dramatically, and I need to know, Hollywood girl, all you know about Jessica Bell. Whether she's a prima donna is the kind of information I need, rather than the movies she's been in, which I'm sure I'll discover. I'm supposed to be her yoga teacher, starting tomorrow. Any information would be appreciated.

Are you still coming this way? I might come to Rome with you. If I take this job with JB and we get on, I'll be able to afford Rome and take a few weeks off. Diane sounds interesting. I am ready to try yoga from a feminine perspective, as you put it. What Diane said about her yoga being a strong journey to a surprising place sounds like life. Perhaps there is no separation between the two—and shouldn't be. You mentioned Vanda Scaravelli. I've heard of her, but who was she?

Love

Grace

Date: March 5, 2007
To: yogagrace@hotmail.com
From: stephanie17@gmail.com
Subject: Re: inside information

vanda scaravelli studied with iyengar when he went to switzerland, say fifty years ago, and stayed in her house where he taught her along with yehudi menuhin and krishnamurti. an elite bunch. of course, now i'm impressed that olga (funny i remember her and we didn't even speak) was reading krishnamurti at bodhi tree, which proves you can't judge a girl by her bikini—or her sunglasses. when iyengar gave up switzerland, vanda carried on doing yoga alone and made her own discoveries. she lived outside florence and noticed diane at some yoga gathering and asked if she could teach her. that was about thirty-five years ago and they studied together twice a week and became incredibly close, until vanda died aged 91.

i am coming to london. no date yet, but would be fantastic to stay between you and my uncle. at some point i'm supposed to use his contacts to hunt down an internship with a magazine. daddy's disappointed that his magna cum laude daughter ain't using her brain.

have thought of living in rome, to study with diane and eventually teach there. can't make a living from it in southern california. there are as many yoga teacher wannabes here as there are actors. to earn extra cash i hostess in this café on melrose where—and here's the scoop—jessica b is a regular. comes in no makeup, very normal. she's polite, low-key, not unlike sharon stone—another regular and fine lady. they sometimes sit together. i've actually seen j bell read a novel over breakfast. 'hollywood star reads novel' is a more news-worthy headline than the other crap they write about her. apart from serving her breakfast, and taking her five-dollar tip, i know nothing about your latest yoga client that hasn't come from a magazine. the only men she's come in with are her father and an ex-boyfriend, you know, the guy on that law show, who she lived with for two years about a hundred years ago, although she's only 32 and in her prime every which way, so make that ten. i like it that a woman stays in touch with her significant ex(es). oh yes, jb doesn't eat grapes. she has them taken out of the fruit salad. not such a

prima donna request. she won't be a problem to teach is my bet.
om *shanti, hari* om!
S
ps whatever happened to harry? do you ever see the insignifi-cant ex?

Date:	March 6, 2007
To:	stephanie17@gmail.com
From:	yogagrace@hotmail.com
Subject:	Om *shanti*—forget *hari*

Thank you for the information about JB, Scaravelli, and Rome. Am more confident now about teaching the actress.

As for Harry, I have seen him only once and from a distance, which was close enough.

You can stay here for as long as you like, just let me know when to expect you. Would you like me to ask Swami D if you can take some classes while you're here? Ryan left last week. Something to do with him getting an erection in his private meditation class. This girl had paid £50 to sit for an hour, one-on-one, facing him, being told how to breathe and which *bandas* to squeeze and for how long. All the usual. Anyway, that muscle work must have got Ryan going. Apparently he had the modesty to pull his shirt out to hide his excitement but his student complained to Swami D and he was asked to leave. Poor Ryan. He's a victim of his good looks and libido. The student who complained is incredibly pretty, wild hair, long legs, big boobies, and minimal yoga clothes. Ryan didn't stand a chance.

Much love,

Grace

Stephanie was right. Jessica was not a problem to teach. Grace had not seen her movies, so didn't treat her like a film star, and it helped that Jessica did not act like one. She was professional and polite, and always on time for class in her immaculate suite. Lynus had sent over deluxe yoga outfits from Harvey Nichols, but Jessica rejected them in favour of cut-off sweat pants and a white cotton tank top that proved her full breasts were, rare for her kind, her own. Jessica was delightfully normal. Lynus was the problem.

Every day he called for Grace's impression of Jessica. Late one Friday evening, Grace told Lynus he was wasting his time. 'There's nothing to worry about. Jessica is a perfect student,' she reassured him—again.

'The rumours are rife,' he mumbled.

'Don't listen to them.'

'I can't afford not to. Rumours like these don't make the papers, they're too serious.'

'Or not true.'

'You think she's okay?'

'I've seen nothing to make me doubt her.'

'What are you doing tonight?'

'I'm in. I'm tired. I'm teaching Jessica at eight tomorrow.'

'Saturday? We didn't agree to that. How much is that costing me?'

'Nothing. It's on the house. Good night.'

The following day Grace confided in Jessica about Lynus's late night calls.

'Not you as well. I'm sorry,' she said. 'Somebody is feeding him lies.'

'Who would do such a thing?'

'The short answer is who wouldn't. Next time Lynus asks, tell him acting is my drug.'

Grace was ambivalent about Lynus: he was a pest, but he also paid her invoice—a civilized arrangement that allowed Jessica's yoga class to be unsullied by money. The women were free to enjoy yoga and each other's company, and both had a vacancy for somebody to talk to and trust. Their conversations soon distracted from the yoga, so Jessica suggested Grace join her for breakfast in the suite. The high-protein affair, designed to build muscle, wasn't Grace's idea of delicious, but the food was healthy and eating together gave them time to get the things they had to say said.

'Do you have a man?' Jessica asked.

'Not at the moment,' Grace admitted, thinking that too many weeks had passed without word from Dr. James. 'What about you?' Grace pushed aside her egg-white omelet, all of a sudden not hungry.

'What about me?'

'Do you have a boyfriend?'

'I'm chilling in a situation.'

'Chilling in a situation,' Grace mocked. 'That's some phrase.'

When it came to money and men, Jessica was very discreet, and had timed her question to coincide with the arrival of her limousine; she left for the film studio without giving anything away. And Grace left for her next yoga class—or in Mr. Kramer's case her next conversation—where it would be her turn to dodge the questions.

Mr. Kramer stood in pyjamas, staring out of his study window. 'Good morning,' Grace said, although it obviously wasn't. He continued to watch his wife, a distant but distinct figure in a cream coat walking Frankie in Hyde Park. 'Most men think a young wife will make them happy. These days my wife's beauty makes me miserable. You know, I don't want to get a little bit better. Either I want to be one hundred percent or I want to die.'

'Few people are ever one hundred percent.'

Mr. Kramer sank into the leather chair. 'You saying that doesn't make me feel better.'

'What does make you feel better, Mr. Kramer?'

'Dr. Damodaran, but not her drugs. They're fighting inside me. She wants me to cut out Prozac but keep seeing you.'

Grace wasn't sure she was up for being the buffer between Mr. Kramer and his depression. 'Do you believe I can help you?'

'If you believe you can.'

'You need to have faith, too.'

'Faith is believing what you know ain't so. Mark Twain.' He pierced her with dark eyes, and she fixed him back, determined not to be worn down. The old man chewed the inside of his mouth, hardly breathing at all.

'How is your breathing?' she asked.

He stared off, bored. 'It's like I'm breathing through a straw.'

'Drop your jaw.'

'Drop what?'

'The bottom jaw. Open your mouth.' Grace opened hers, breathing until her tongue turned dry. 'Are you embarrassed to drop your jaw?' she asked.

'Why?'

'You're not doing it. You're watching me do it.'

Mr. Kramer stuck out his furry tongue. 'That white stuff, see that? It's from the pills. I'm all over with thrush.'

Grace knew about the thrush; it was in the records. 'Count one as you breathe in, one as you breathe out. Then two in, two out. If your mind wanders, return to one.'

'One,' said Mr. Kramer out loud.

'Quietly, to yourself.'

They sat together, breathing, Mr. Kramer's beady eyes locked on Grace.

'I can't reach two,' he moaned after a minute. 'The saddest thing in my life is I'll never play golf again.'

'Perhaps you will, if you concentrate on one step at a time—'

'One step. One breath. I'm Steinbeck's ancient baby. My wife married a man, and here I am back to one at a time and being a good boy. I wish you'd seen me in my young days. When I sit here listening to music with the dog on my lap, I think about you, Grace. I don't want you to miss out on the stature of a man.'

STATURE, *n* body height; eminence.

Grace knew Mr. Kramer well enough to appreciate that by stature he meant to suggest to her more than a man's physique. Not satisfied with the figurative, she searched the dictionary for specifics.

EMINENT, *adj* distinguished; exalted in rank or office; rising above the others; conspicuous. EMINENCE, *n* a part eminent or rising above the rest; a rising ground; a ridge or knob; height; distinction; a title given in 1631 to cardinals, previously styled Most Illustrious; advantage or upper hand (*Shakesp*).

An eminent man, a man of distinction, was what Kramer had in mind, and Grace thought she'd met one. Dr. James had stood out in her eyes, and she believed that she had registered with him, too, yet a month, or more, had passed since she'd heard from him. For no reason he'd stopped contacting her, which was disappointing because he had seemed such an adult. This childish vanishing, without even a text to say good-bye, confused Grace. How could she have got him so wrong? Had his letters meant nothing to him? And what about his offer to drive his Aston so many months into the future? Why had he said that? Grace kicked herself for being so literal. His comments were flip, mindless flirting that meant nothing.

She had resisted contacting him to find out if he'd been struck down by a virus even acupuncture couldn't cure, but prompted by Mr. Kramer's comment, couldn't hold out. She sent a text. *Thinking of you. Please let me know you're ok. x.*

Texts are tailored for instant replies. One was not forthcoming that day, or the next. By the end of the week when she had received no word at all Grace decided to forget Dr. James—if she could.

Teaching the heart sinkers had been an uphill struggle for weeks but by the time their seventh class came around, it was by far Grace's favourite. Diplomacy forbade her from revealing that she now thought of them as heart lifters, a name that made them sound like a group of seventies Motown singers rather than the bunch of NHS no-hopers they had once been. Even the doctors noticed that the patients referred to yoga weren't coming in quite as frequently, and when their computer printouts confirmed a 56 percent drop in their attendance at the surgery, Grace was no longer on trial. A list of new patients for the next workshop was compiled and Dr. Norton was even talking about a one-year contract, such was his willingness to keep Grace sweet, and his secret safe.

Dr. Damodaran was right, yoga had been bastardized, but as the NHS yogis proved, *something* was working. The heart lifters, converts to 'rolling around on a mat' as Davis put it, wanted to continue the classes beyond the eight-week trial and a sliding scale had been agreed on: Davis would pay twelve pounds, Maud only one.

Gladys had cut back her Prozac and said it was a revelation to stretch the muscles of her lower back, 'like a smile from the inside that leaves my mind shining.' Grace welcomed abstract comments, which were always easier to field than the personal ones. Harriet Manslip, no longer such an androgynous Ms., had planned a trip to India and taken a part-time job to pay for it. Sally had reduced the vodka, stopped the pizza, and lost four pounds and an aching gut in the process. Emily was learning to accept her masculine side now that she had connected more profoundly with her feminine, 'thanks to yoga opening my base chakra'—another abstraction Grace let fly. Davis was migraine-free one night a week after class, and Mrs. Moore was enigmatic as ever—so no change there.

Perhaps only Mrs. Moore could have guessed that she was Grace's favourite yoga student. She arrived promptly for class with a look in her eye that Grace read as ironic amusement, and she left with a nod, as if to acknowledge what she had received. Grace conversed with all her students but it was the taciturn Mrs. Moore with whom she most wanted to sit down and talk. So it was with delight that she received a handwritten invitation to tea in the Boltons.

Mrs. Moore opened her door to Grace, the sound of Bach's *Goldberg Variations* playing in a distant room. 'This is the most beautiful music,' Grace said, following Mrs. Moore down the dark corridor.

'Glenn Gould played it best, and it's what I play when I need to remember that life is perfect sometimes. "Life without music would be a mistake." Now who said that?' asked Mrs. Moore, puffing on a cigarette.

The flat, one of five in an imposing house converted in the fifties, was postwar austere. The square sitting room, necessarily nicotine yellow, had a huge desk and two armchairs covered with plaid wool blankets to hide threadbare holes. A slim, silver television—a gift, she said, from her grandson William—was a concession to modern times, as were pink Post-it notes stuck to the edge of the green baize card table, laid for tea with a very homemade-looking Victoria sponge.

'Prepared in a lucid moment,' Mrs. Moore said, indicating the table as she sat. She pulled a Post-it note and read aloud. '"Four thirty William to discuss yoga." He's curious to meet you. I've told him all about your class. We must seem a strange lot.'

'At first, but teaching you yoga has become a pleasure,' Grace said.

'My husband died years ago and by the time I was ready to take a lover, my body was hardly the vehicle for it. The yoga was surprisingly sensual and your class the longest I've been awake without a cigarette.' She hacked a splendid cough.

'Did it help your headache?'

'Not at all, which is why I asked for a brain scan. The results came back last week. Grace, I wanted to tell you myself. I have a tumor in the base of my skull.' She sliced into the sponge.

'Can they operate?'

'No. It's in an impossible place and frankly, I wouldn't want them to. I have long understood death as another experience, though I've adored being alive. Not that it's been easy, but I never was attracted to anything easy—a quality some would call perverse and one I suspect we share, which is why . . .' Mrs. Moore looked around the room, as if searching for the end of her sentence.

'Which is why?' Grace prompted.

'It's gone. Where was I?'

'Cutting cake.'

Mrs. Moore observed the embedded knife as if for the first time. 'There is nothing like losing your mind. You have no choice but to be in the moment. Everything seems new, which is tiresome, and when I'm tired, words vanish. Absolute hell for a writer.'

'I didn't know you were a writer,' said Grace, serving them both cake.

'Writing and smoking are what I did best.'

'When did you start?' Grace asked, quickly tasting the sponge before Mrs. Moore ruined its flavour in a tobacco puff.

'Smoking at sixteen, writing not much later. They went together for me. Words still go softly out toward the unsayable. Now who wrote *that*? Things I knew return partially. I forgot the sugar, didn't I?'

'It doesn't matter. The strawberry jam is sweet enough.'

'To be filled up; fulfillment is the thing. Not to be confused with happiness. Expectations of happiness insult intelligence.' Mrs. Moore lit another cigarette, then became irritated to discover one balancing on the ashtray. 'To die of pneumonia would have been dignified compared to this slow rotting of the brain. The oncologist should have left my lung tumor where it was. Exposed to oxygen, the cancer spread like wildfire. My head is riddled. Why did I let them take responsibility for my body?'

'People trust specialists.'

'I should have listened to Dr. Damodaran. She told me to do nothing. Doctors differ, patients die. All I'd wanted was to greet death with equanimity.'

'It's incredible they referred you to the yoga class to help with a headache.'

'A fortunate mistake. I met you.'

Grace wanted Mrs. Moore to herself for a little while longer. By the time William arrived, a half hour late, she was not in the mood for his youthful enthusiasm about his television production company. 'We're looking for a yoga teacher and Granny recommended you.' He winked at the old woman, who adored him.

'Where would you want the class? In your office?'

'On telly—it's for the BBC. Would you be interested?'

A class of virtual students would be the perfect antidote to the real kind. Grace gave William her telephone number, then left Mrs. Moore with her grandson and cigarettes and last days.

At the door to say good-bye, Mrs. Moore was energized. 'I have composed a list of things, things I believe and that have mattered to me, and in the end still do. Would you like to read it?'

Grace waited while Mrs. Moore went in search of her list. 'I know I put it somewhere,' she called from the far end of the dark corridor. She reappeared waving a sheet of white paper, which she pressed into Grace's hand. 'I won't forget you. I won't forget you, my dear,' Mrs. Moore said, and then shut the door without good-bye.

Grace framed Mrs. Moore's 'Personal Creed'—seven sentences that began, 'I believe in the communion of landscape, in an ultimate reality. Never and always,' and ended, 'I believe in hope, for without hope I am nothing.'

Chapter Thirteen

SIMHASANA—lion pose

Simha means the powerful one. In this meditation asana the lion sits, waiting. This is the attitude the mind needs to enter deep meditative states. Sitting in padmasana, *the practitioner leans forward with both palms on the floor between the knees, the arms straight, and the front of the neck stretched. With the eyes open, focus on the centre of the forehead above the eyebrows. Open the mouth and stretch out the tongue as far as it will go toward the chin. The pose helps to cure foul breath and cleans the tongue, and eventually even words will be clear, and flow with ease.*

If lying on a yoga mat made students submissive, it also encouraged them to divulge secrets. Even Collette let confidences slip from time to time, and confessed to inner turmoil that could bring her down to earth, and sometimes way below it. It didn't help that in Collette's world the slightest deviance from perfection was magnified, triggering gargantuan insecurities, which she then minimized by honing her strengths. Balancing between these poles, Collette was propelled along the tightrope of life.

The supermodel's ability to absorb new identities and champion new causes impressed Grace, who suspected it had less to do with the ability to detach than with a frenetic nature and the fortune at her disposal. Collette had shifted her allegiance from rabbinic law to Hindu mythology with apparently less soul-searching than she might give to switching from Valentino to Versace.

'Hinduism suits me better,' she said, by way of explanation. 'Those rabbinical texts can be dry, let me tell you, and the Hindus are so much more sensual than the Jews. Don't tell Mike I said that, he's half Jewish.'

'So am I,' said Grace, 'through my father, if that counts.'

'In my book, mother or father, half is half, but don't take it personally. I just like the way Hindus include the body in worship.'

Collette may have been fickle but she was also kind and did not abandon the rabbi. She still let him use her house for his weekly seminar; she simply chose not to attend. This meant that Mike didn't either, and the rabbi watched his numbers dwindle.

Collette loved yoga but craved the social scene that had come with spreading the cabbala word. The dilemma of wanting a public with whom to share her private practice was resolved by the *puja* party.

'*Puja* is an intricate, sacred ceremony,' Grace cautioned as they descended the stairs to the main hall.

'Honey, I know, and we've found this Brahmin guy who's going to perform it. We're devoting it to Lakshmi, the goddess of fertility, in the hope she'll kick-start my pregnancy. It's gotta be a whole lot more fun than IVF. As my yoga teacher, you're guest of honor, so bring whoever you like.'

'Can I bring Jessica Bell?'

'What, Jessica the actress?'

'Yes.'

'How do you know her?'

'I'm her yoga teacher.'

'Fabulous. We heard she was in town and meant to ask her over, so sure. How often do you teach her?

'Twice a day.'

'Holy moly she's keen. You know, I was thinking yoga twice a week isn't enough. Have you got your diary?'

Not for the first time it occurred to Grace that her livelihood would depend on her pupils' inability to roll out the yoga mat and practice alone. Self-practice, it seemed, was the thing, the dedication and the discipline.

* * *

When Collette greeted Grace for her tenth yoga class in twelve days she was full of enthusiasm for the changes she had made to the attic. The changes she had made to herself were evident. The minishorts, tight T, and red wrist thread had been discarded; Collette floated up the stairs in a pale orange cashmere vest and the softest pants of purple velvet, her wrist jangling with gold bangles.

'Shakti worship was all the rage about four thousand years ago. I thought it was time for a revival,' she said, opening the door at the top of the stairs. 'I've christened the attic the Shakti room.'

A vast carpet of pink, yellow, and orange, decorated with flowers and shells, covered the wooden floor. 'This carpet is the perfect texture for your yoga practice,' Grace said. 'It's the kind the first yogis would have used.'

'Pre–rubber mat, good. We're closer to the source. Check this out,' said Collette, tracing a cowrie shell with her big toe. 'These symbolize the yoni, our lovely little cunts, the conch shells are the cock, the linga, and that's Shiva and Shakti, lost in *sahaja,* which accounts for their pretzel position. Impossible, by the way. Mike and I tried.'

'What's *sahaja?*'

'You don't know tantra?'

'I'm not familiar with the terms,' Grace said carefully.

'But you're familiar with the feelings?'

Grace raised her right eyebrow and suppressed a smile.

'So, you know Mike and I are having a ball. *Sahaja*'s that spontaneous dissolving-in-unity thing. In our last session we lost our egos through divine sex, to reach *purusha,* as our teacher puts it.'

'*Purusha?*'

'*Purusha*—the lowdown of who we are. The tantras say we get to the true self through sacred sex, which beats analysis. You see what I mean about the Jewish-Hindu thing. Mike and I were in bed until three in the afternoon on Saturday.'

'Lost in *sahaja?*'

It was Collette's turn to arch her brow. 'Come, meet the girls.' She swept her braceleted arm one hundred and eighty degrees toward the broad windowsill that had been transformed into an altar to the divine feminine by figurines of the goddess in her many forms. 'André recommended the good girls, like, um, Uma and Parvati, but Mike wanted them all, good and bad, so we've got the lot. Kali, Durga, Chambla . . .'

'Chambla? I've never heard of her.'

'The thin one.'

'Most of them are pretty thin,' said Grace.

'Okay, Chambla's anorexic, bless her.'

Grace studied the figurines. 'This collection wouldn't look out of place in the British Museum.'

Collette ignored the comment. She did not like employees to refer to her purchasing power. Friends were another matter, and she was still undecided about where to position Grace on that sliding scale.

Aware that something she'd said or done had cooled Collette's mood, Grace cautiously admired a palm-sized figure with pendulous breasts and meaty thighs, formed from fragile clay and set in the middle of the altar. 'She's something. Who is she?'

'The Great Mother. We gave her pride of place, given the goal of our enterprise,' Collette said, stroking the Great Mother's pregnant belly.

'She's round and luscious. I like her,' said Grace.

'Really? I prefer this one.' Collette touched a delicate grey stone deity. 'Diana, goddess of the moon, the hunt, easy childbirth, and chastity—go figure.' Collette was animated, Grace back in favour.

'Where did you find them?'

'André. He used to be one of the curators at the Louvre. He sourced the painting and everything in two weeks.'

The painting, pre-Raphaelite and above the fireplace, was a sensual scene of a maiden, her auburn hair bound with ivy, submitting to a unicorn. 'Just look at that horn,' sighed Collette.

Evidently Collette could focus when it suited her, and with André's help had acquired knowledge and a priceless collection to celebrate, as she put it, 'the Devi who resides within.' All of which prompted Grace to

Google Devi as soon as she got home and download a chunk of information in the hope of keeping up.

Jessica sent her limousine to collect Grace so that they could arrive together for Collette's *puja* party. Unaccustomed to waiting for others, Jessica instructed Grace to call five minutes before she reached the hotel; it was another fifteen before the movie star appeared.

Jessica, always pretty, through sleight of hand and haute couture looked sublime. A mink stole, possibly fake, fell from her sculpted shoulders, and her long white Chanel dress was cut high in the centre to reveal legs—and particularly ankles—that would make Collette melt. Grace folded her arms, then unfolded them, struggling to be at ease beside the superstar. She tried not to mind that her dress was two years old, possibly three, and that she lacked the all-round glitter of Jessica Bell. To be affected by Jessica's physical transformation would undermine their friendship, 'the real wealth' as Jessica had recently called it. Grace told herself, and tried to believe, that Jessica was the same person in spite of her adornment, although she held her head at a haughty angle and wasn't inclined to talk. The short journey to Cheyne Walk was completed in silence.

As suggested on the invitation, they had brought fruit offerings, gifts for the goddess they were celebrating. Grace had three real pomegranates while Jessica held two solid-gold miniature apples from Tiffany. Carl, in blue jeans and a white Indian-style shirt, took their gifts with equal care; Grace thought he was the most regal person in the household.

Delicate lanterns cast magical light that flattered Collette, dressed as a mythical goddess in a long white dress with a plunging neckline, a gold asp bracelet snaking her arm. Her radiance was only slightly dimmed by Jessica's presence, which may have accounted for her delayed greeting. Grace and Jessica stood in the hall, waiting, while Collette fussed over decorative minutiae. 'Carl, put extra gardenias in here, would you? And keep an eye on the candles. We want the lanterns alight all night.'

Grace guessed that asserting authority over Carl was a tactic the older beauty used while composing herself to face the younger. Collette then approached with hands in *namaste* and bowed, waiting for her moment of insecurity to pass. By the time she raised her head it had, for she embraced Jessica with open arms and extravagant affection. Grace looked at her yoga students, first sisters in the Fame Family, and supposed the public display of extravagant affection was the way of their world. And if the Lakshmi evening was extreme, Grace understood that was also as it should be: Mike and Collette were rockocracy and in the new order it fell to them to create the life to which others aspired. From the gifts the gods bestowed, enhanced by ungodly ambition, they had ascended from the comprehensive ground of middle England and a trailer park in Memphis to sit at the right hand of those whose birthrights included Eton, invitations to High-grove House, and red carpet treatment just about anywhere.

Grace told herself that wealth was impermanent, that pride grants no equanimity, but standing in the shadow of Jessica and Collette her spiritual truths felt like clichés that didn't quite cut it.

'Trying for a baby. What a fantastic excuse for a party,' purred Jessica.

'We want everyone to have as much fun as we've had. We've gone along with the whole thing, even fasting. And I'm starving, let me tell you. The bath did it. We filled it with olive oil, or rather Carl did. How long did it take, Carl?'

'Two hours, Collette. Next time we should buy the oil in vats.'

'Great idea; look into it, would you? Waitrose can't have any organic olive oil left. Mike and I have never had such fun worshipping the goddess.'

'The atmosphere is like Christmas, New Year, and Thanksgiving rolled into one,' said Jessica, her pleasure childlike as they walked up the candlelit stairs to the Shakti Room.

'Not bad considering it's spring,' Collette laughed.

'The house is a temple,' said Grace.

Collette basked in approval. 'Vaastu Shastra for the heavenly home, feng shui Indian style. The Vaastu architect, an amazing woman from Colorado, said the house faces the wrong direction. I thought we'd have to move but she put a Ganesha in the bedroom with a bowl of milk and said we should conceive. Which reminds me.' She leaned over the balcony. 'Hey, Carl, remember to put full cream milk out for Ganesh.' She turned to Grace. 'You've got to meet the tantra teacher, and you'll love Siddhartha Shah, my Sanskrit teacher.'

'You're learning Sanskrit?' Jessica was further impressed.

'One class a week.'

'Collette, you're more of a yogi than I am,' said Grace, wondering on what grounds she qualified these days. She hadn't done self-practice for at least a week.

'All or nothing; it's the way I am,' Collette announced, and nobody questioned it.

In the Shakti Room the members of the cabbala group (sans rabbi), Mike's family, the members of his band, and their families all sat uncomfortably cross-legged around the *puja* altar, a low mahogany table decorated with the deity statues, the fruit offerings of friends, and delicate pastry tarts. Having got the hang of the dos and don'ts of step one cabbala, Mike's dad and sister looked bemused to be in at the deep end of Hindu ritual. Beside them was Collette's mum, flown in especially from Miami. Saved the indignity of the floor, she sat on a small padded chair, which made up for the thin gold tiara she had been asked to wear as the evening's Honorary Mother. Mike wasn't fazed by any of it and seemed to appreciate that it was all a little ridiculous. He'd go along with anything to keep Collette happy. She wanted a kid and why not? He already had six, and hardly needed another, but it was fun trying for the child he already called Lucky Seven. When Jessica walked in he winked, and then gazed steadily at Grace. Finally, Collette sat beside him and he kissed her softly on the lips, which was Dr. Kulkarni's cue: he stepped into the circle.

Dressed, or rather undressed, as a traditional Brahmin priest with bare feet, bare chest, and wrapped below the waist in lustrous yellow silk, Dr. Kulkarni greeted them with such solemnity that Grace and Jessica looked at each other and almost burst out laughing. Grace bit the inside of both cheeks, closed her eyes, and inhaled hard. In an attempt to keep the giggles in, Jessica followed her example, and those close by copied them, assuming this was an advanced meditation technique.

'On behalf of Mike and Collette, welcome.' Dr. Kulkarni's sincerity evaporated Grace's giggles and she opened her eyes. 'The *puja* is devoted to the propitiation of goddess Lakshmi. We will pray to the divine mother, Maha Lakshmi, the Hindu goddess of fertility, light, and wealth, to ask her to lavish blessings upon us.'

Mike's sister squinted 'whatever next?' at her dad, but he'd already nodded off.

'Now we prepare for *kum kum*,' Dr. Kulkarni said. The world-weary kids of Mike and Collette's celebrity friends snickered, but the mature guests followed Collette's example, brushing hair from their foreheads to be daubed with blood-red paste. After the doctor's earnest anointing, a hushed silence fell. 'All mothers are like the Mother Goddess,' he said. 'Protector, kisser of wounds, disciplinarian. The divine mother is the abode of dharma, or righteousness. She is not bound by Maya.'

'What's Maya?' whispered Jessica.

'Illusion,' Grace said, watching Dr. Kulkarni liberally douse the altar with supposedly sacred water, soaking the sweet pastries she'd had her eye on.

'In Indian philosophy, the birth of a child begins with music, so we shall chant invocations to Lakshmi. Listen, then repeat.' Undaunted by the presence of the world's biggest rock band, the doctor sat behind his harmonium and with eyes closed in bliss played the small keyboard with one hand, the other pumping its bellows, sucking air across its reeds. The hypnotic sound of the mystical accordion soon had the whole room singing devotional songs from Vedic scripture. By the time the *bahajan* had ended everybody was ready to party. Collette jumped up and clapped her hands—the only truly embarrassing moment. The doctor gently reminded her of other priorities. 'We shall sit a little longer to reflect on the prosperity we are praying for: the blessings of inner peace and prosperity that bring light to our lives and faith in abundance. We pray for spiritual wealth.'

Mike blinked at the notion and his sister nudged their father awake. Finally, it was time to eat from the platter of now sacred food, none of them forgetting to use their right hand. After more chanting and prayers, truncated by a discreet word from Mike, the party took off. Crowds arrived, there were fireworks, vast displays of light filled the sky, and blessed food and wine were served until two in the morning.

Jessica, stopped at every turn by members of the Fame Family, escaped with Grace to a small room at the back of the house. Like absconding schoolgirls they shut the door. 'Peace,' said Jessica, collapsing on a long sofa. Grace stretched out on another, perpendicular to Jessica's, and kicked off her shoes.

'Lakshmi is impressive,' said Jessica, 'but when it comes to archetypes, I'm ready for Shiva and Shakti.'

'Divine coupledom.'

'That's the one. I want my life to centre around something bigger than me and my next movie.'

'Tonight's the night to have a dream.'

'Mine's not so different from Collette's, although in her place I'd adopt. It wouldn't matter the baby isn't physically hers. She'd love it the same. I would.'

'Don't you want your own child?'

'Children in my life, but not necessarily out of me. I'd rather have an extraordinary man to share the day to day.'

'How is he, by the way?'

Jessica had recently confessed to a man, but declined to name him. 'He's figuring out the best way for us to be together, and I wish he'd hurry up.' She shrieked in frustration and gripped her hair by the roots. 'I'm a wreck, and now I've wrecked my hair.' She laughed. 'What about you?' She stared Grace down in a way nobody had.

'What about me?'

'Do you have a dream?'

Next to a master dream weaver, Grace was reluctant to express her tentative own. 'I think I have a dream,' she said.

'Either you have a dream or you don't. Are you brave enough to own it?'

Grace was about to say, 'I think I'm brave enough,' but instead said, emphatically, 'Of course I'm brave enough.'

'So what is it?' Jessica slung out a pale arm, dangling her champagne glass. Uncomfortable with the focus on herself, Grace's mind went blank. 'Come on, Grace. What kind of life do you imagine for yourself?'

'Being fulfilled in my work, and living with a man who appreciates me, whom I also appreciate.'

'What about love?'

'Love is the goal.'

'Both ways, cos that's the trick.'

'A two-way love is what I want.'

'Good. I presume you have the work dream down?'

'I do.'

Jessica paused, expecting Grace to fill her in. She was not forthcoming. 'Grace, come on. It helps to say out loud the kind of work you want.'

'In a way I'm doing it, and don't take this badly, I love teaching you and all my privileged ladies . . .'

'But?'

'I want to work with people, possibly with children, who can't afford a yoga class or even imagine one.'

'Free yoga classes for inner-city teenagers, abused kids, that kind of thing?'

'Don't sound so flip.'

'Hon, I can be flip, it's not my dream. But I can see it already: a centre in the East End, one say in Ladbroke Grove, and let's have a retreat in the country.'

Grace grinned. Jessica didn't think small, ever. 'Okay. Now for the *really* complicated bit. The man. Any man in mind?'

'I did have someone.' Grace cleared her throat.

'Did. That's not great. What's his name?' Jessica had warmed to the novelty of being the one to ask the questions, and to the challenge of getting an answer.

'Dr. James.'

Jessica sat up, digging her heels into Collette's sofa. 'In love with your doctor. Even I know that's not good.'

'He's not my doctor.'

'Then why didn't you bring him tonight? Don't tell me—he's married.'

'Why would you think that? Is your man married?'

'This isn't about me. Come on, Grace, where is your doctor tonight?'

'Saigon.'

Jessica laughed. 'Last thing I expected you to say. Let's go find him. I wouldn't mind a trip to Vietnam.'

'I don't think—'

'Stop thinking!'

'Actually, I don't know what to think. He hasn't replied to my last letter.'

'Which century are you in? You can't wait on letters for your love affair—'

'It isn't a love affair.'

'Why not?'

Grace stared at Jessica.

'Why isn't this a love affair if that's what you want?' the actress pressed on, obviously familiar with the interview technique.

With the focus on her, and Jessica demanding answers, it was as if Grace's mind had turned to glue; she was stranded without access to thought or feeling.

'Okay, you need to tell this guy that you love—'

'But Jessica, I don't love him. I don't want—' Grace heard the sentence complete itself inside her head.

Jessica pounced. 'You say you want love, but when it comes down to it, you can't imagine it, can you?'

'Love doesn't feel possible for me, that's all. However much I *have* loved and *have* wanted it to work, it always ends badly. Really badly.'

'We all dream of one love.'

'Perhaps one love is all we get, and I've had mine.'

'Grace, it's great that you're this caring person who looks after me, Collette, and God knows who else, but one day you'll look around and all you'll see is people who pay for an hour of your time, then say good-bye to get on with their lives. Meanwhile, what about yours?'

Unruffled nothingness was the kind of smooth future Grace had convinced herself she wanted but tonight, submerged in the realized dreams of her glamorous pupils, she saw how bleak her nothing looked. It was not the vision of an optimist, which is how she liked to paint herself.

Jessica swung her legs to the floor and drained her champagne like a cowboy downing a beer, but kept her focus. 'Can't you see that if yoga keeps you from being present to the whole of your life then it's no different from any other addiction on that list we know so well? Grace, you know what they say about seeing is believing? Well, sometimes believing has to come first. Why don't you call this guy and tell him?'

'Tell him what exactly?'

Jessica sighed. 'How about, you thought of him tonight when somebody asked about your dreams?'

'I can't say that,' Grace said quietly.

'What have you got to lose?'

'I know I can't say that. The words wouldn't come. But I wish I had told him I'd split from Harry.'

'Who's Harry?'

'A loser, let me tell you, and the man I was with when I last met Dr. James.'

'Grace, this doctor has stopped writing because either he has another woman at the moment—and, let's face it, Asian women are pretty irresistible —or he has the sense not to pursue a woman he thinks is unavailable.'

'I thought he'd assume I was single again. I've assumed he is.'

'Grace, clear this up, and not by letter. Can't you see, whatever happened in the past, however much it hurt you, you've got to believe in the something good meant for you—and it's time to find out if that includes Dr. James. What's his other name?'

'David.'

'Can't we call him that?'

'I've called him Dr. James since we first met, and I haven't got beyond it.'

'Well, here's hoping you do,' said Jessica, who stood and held out her hand to Grace. 'Come on, let's go join the party.'

Collette was on Mike's lap, surrounded by friends and her newly appointed faculty of Eastern specialists, plotting when they would hold their first weekly seminar. She pushed André, her French curator, at Grace and Jessica, as much for their entertainment as his, and they spent the rest of the evening listening to his explanation of the pictorial script in India's epic tradition.

'Indian theology is skeptical of words. They believe symbolic form—paintings, storytelling, and so on—better expresses the riddle of the universe.'

'Which is?' asked Jessica.

'To understand the purpose of life.'

'Isn't that the great mystery?'

'*Exactement,* but if we extract ourselves from maya, the creative world, the world *we* have created, perhaps it is possible to reach the ultimate truth. It is the purpose of yoga, *n'est-ce pas,* Grace? *La transmutation* of the mind to overcome *ahamkara.*'

'*Ahamkara?*' Jessica looked to Grace, but it was Collette who answered. 'Literally your I-maker, the ego.'

'Very good, Collette,' André said, not intending to patronize.

Mike smiled proudly. He really didn't give a fuck about the many thousands his wife had spent with André. He liked the guy, appreciated the education his wife had received, and enjoyed being on her spiritual tour.

'The thing is to become no longer egocentric but self-centred,' André continued.

'I thought self-centred was bad?' Jessica questioned.

'There are different kinds of self,' André clarified. 'Atman is the form of self that cannot be seen by the eye, and the one we aspire to. Once we achieve it, we are no longer in thrall to the false powers of the world.'

'Hello, Grace.' Harry slipped his hand around Grace's waist with such casual intimacy, for a second she couldn't speak. Grace turned her back on the group, as much to hide vexation as to avoid introducing Harry, which is what she suspected he wanted. Dressed in white shirt and black suit, he looked impressive in clothes not so unlike the aesthete André's.

'You ignored me,' he said, sotto voce, his hand still resting on the small of her back.

'When?' She stepped away from his touch.

'On Westbourne Grove.'

'I thought you ignored me,' she said.

'I waved,' he said.

'On the zebra crossing?'

'No, outside Whole Foods.'

'I didn't see you.'

Misunderstandings. They would always have them.

'How come you're here?' he asked.

Indignation, a familiar feeling around Harry, rose up. Grace said as lightly as she could, 'I'm Collette's yoga teacher. And you?'

'We came with Nick and Joe.'

'We?'

'Vicky—'

'You and Vicky? That's something.' Grace's smile was ice.

'Vicky calls it the new paradigm.'

'Paradigm. My, my. And what is it?'

'Once lovers, now friends, always parents. To be honest, she's a whole lot better since you and I split up. So, what's with this divine mother theme?'

'Celebrating the feminine,' Grace said.

'A tricky business.' Harry's jaunty reply was meant to amuse Grace but his phrase was unfortunate. Grace, already cold toward him, was reminded of her brief conversation with Tricksy and turned colder still. He was oblivious. 'You look beautiful. I haven't seen this dress before.'

'Why would you? We never went out.'

'And I'm sorry about that. Grace, I'm sorry I fell apart when I was with you.'

'Is that what you were doing?'

'Come on. Be nice. When I saw you I was glad I came tonight, for a chance to talk. That, and picking up a client.'

'What kind of client?' Grace's face crumpled.

'A yoga client. I'm a yoga teacher these days,' he said.

Chapter Fourteen

SIDDHA YONI ASANA—power pose

Siddha *means power and perfection.* Yoni *means womb or source. Siddha refers to psychic powers that include clairvoyance, telepathy, and even disappearing at will. Siddhasana, or* siddha yoni asana *for women, is the pose that develops these faculties. Sit cross-legged with the sole of the right foot against the left inner thigh, keeping the right heel firmly inside the labia majora of the vagina. Get comfortable while feeling the pressure. The heel of the left foot is directly over the righ heel so it presses the clitoris. Wedge the left toes down between the calf and thigh toward the floor. With the spine erect, place the hands on the knees, close the eyes, and relax.*

'That Harry doesn't look like a loser,' Jessica said when Grace turned up to teach the following morning. 'He looks like Zac Jones.'

'Zac Jones. He's not *that* good looking, is he?'

'I think so.'

'Well, he'd love you for saying that. When I was with him he longed to be a famous movie star. Probably still does. Sun salute?'

After the yoga class, teacher and student sat for breakfast, recently enhanced by the addition of a two-pint protein shake made with full fat milk and three bananas, a high-calorie bomb that Grace declined.

Hyperactive Jessica had no choice. 'I'm still not gaining weight fast enough,' she said, gulping the gloopy mixture as though it were medicine.

Apart from Jessica's luscious breasts and sensuous top lip, (just now sporting a milk moustache) the actress's lean frame lacked curve. 'That fuck Lynus is threatening me with steroids if I don't bulk up soon. My weight training isn't doing it.' Jessica raised her right arm and flexed. A very junior bicep popped up. 'Feel that,' she said.

Grace poked the mound of muscle that looked like a white marble threaded with blue—Jessica's veins. 'That wasn't there a few weeks ago,' she encouraged.

'Right, but I'm still E.T. with tits.'

Grace could not contradict her.

'Lynus wants an Amazon woman. He wants me looking like Raquel Welch in her fur bikini, by the end of the week.'

'You're burning too many calories to build muscle. Cut down your training.'

'There isn't time. I've got so much to learn. Karate, sprinting, acrobatics, firing ammunition. Shit. What was I thinking taking this part?'

'You set yourself a challenge.'

'No kidding I did. And I'll do it. I'll be great. I know I will.' Jessica's determination was as cold and precise as a blade. 'Sometimes I get nervous, that's all. Living in this hotel doesn't help. I can't settle, and my metabolism's racing. Room service ain't home cooking, that's for sure. Last night, seeing Collette's house made me want to be home somewhere, even if it isn't mine. Can we have class at your place tonight?'

So far Grace had failed to persuade a single student to visit her at home for yoga lessons, which was her goal. It would change her working world to have people come to her, rather than chasing down parking spaces and fighting the traffic as she drove around London to teach. Wealthy clients sensibly insisted upon the convenience of yoga in their own homes, the doctors' patients were perfectly content with the room above the surgery, and Swami D's students were loyal to his studio and its social scene—particularly since the number of men attending had tripled since Grace had started teaching. Students soon observed that Swami D failed to adjust his alpha males, choosing to leave them wobbling unsteadily, even in headstand, now giving unhurried attention to girls desiring special direction. Pretty girls were always first with Swami D. Having succumbed, as a student, to Harry's physical perfection, as a teacher Grace was wary of beauty. She had distanced herself from the most attractive male students until realizing that that was no better than Swami D's modus operandi. The solution was to look at her students with different eyes. Regardless of appearance, or gender, or where she was called to place her hands, Grace just about managed to treat her students the same—unless they smelled. Natural pungency was easier to stomach than a sickly scent, but for the malodorous few, her approach was to take a deep breath, hold it while adjusting the student's asana, then flee to breathe elsewhere.

Grace used her yoga studio at home for self-practice—a luxury she appreciated every time she took to the mat, left unrolled and ready in the centre of the room below the skylight. That evening it was a pleasure to prepare the studio for its first guest. She swept the floor, rolled out a second mat, and lit candles and incense. Filled by the trance-inducing chants of Tibetan Buddhists, the yoga studio was better by a thousand petals of a lotus flower than any hotel room.

'I could live like this,' Jessica said, walking in.

'What, in an empty room?'

'Sure, with space to breathe. That hotel room is tight, let me tell you, and I don't need another tight situation. Man, Lynus is killing me.' Jessica flopped onto the beanbag in the far corner of the studio.

'Let's forget Lynus,' Grace said. It was her sixth class of the day and she didn't intend to delay it. Jessica, who had spent the day weight training and fencing—and firing two machine guns at the same time—was equally intent on practicing the slumped position. Grace fought the temptation to collapse beside her. 'Come on, Jessica, don't get comfortable.'

'Why not? I'm shattered. I'd love a glass of wine.'

'No!' Grace said, fighting her own desire to end the day that way. 'Get up, Jess, before you can't. Follow me.' She fell into standing forward bend.

Jessica slid reluctantly off the beanbag and stood on her mat. She raised her arms, raised her head, and drew in a long breath. 'Look at that,' she said, gazing at the moon through the skylight. '. . . how slow this old moon wanes! She lingers my desires . . .'

'I don't suppose you're quoting from Lynus's movie.'

Jessica laughed. 'Midsummer Night's Dream, and how I'm feeling. I miss my lover.'

Grace stared at Jessica staring at the stars then returned to forward bend. Jessica followed. Yoga melted the actress's resistance, and restored them both. When the class was over, Grace rolled up her mat, almost overwhelmed by the prospect of a hot bath and an early night. Jessica rolled onto her side, resting her head on her hand for the postclass chat. 'I wanted to see how you lived before I asked you to come on location.'

Grace sat down. 'Location?'

'We go to New York next month. I've told Lynus I want to take you.'

'What did he say?'

'That I could have anything, as long as it's good for me. That you are is the only thing we agree on. So what do you say?'

'How long for, and where would we go?'

'New York for three weeks, then L.A.'

'Jess, I won't join you in L.A. but I can put you in touch with a teacher there,' she said, thinking of Rita. She was reluctant to disengage from London and the stability she had achieved since returning from California.

'What about New York? You can come there, can't you? I mean, it's only for a few weeks.' Jessica's pleading was new.

'How many weeks, exactly?'

'Three. Four max.'

Grace wasn't sure the actress understood what she was asking of her. To provide the multimillion-dollar star with security was all very well, but not if it threatened her fragile own. 'Jessica, I will only come with you if I find a replacement yoga teacher to cover my classes.'

'Grace, I *need* you to come to New York. I don't think I can face it otherwise.' Jessica found it unbearable to admit that she needed anything from anyone.

'Jessica, are you okay?'

'I will be when my fucking boyfriend makes up his mind. I hate this not knowing. I'm powerless, and I don't like it. Zac's thinking. Can you believe that? He refuses to make a plan to meet, and won't even talk on the phone until he feels clear about . . .' Her eyes loaded with tears.

It was safe to assume that Jessica was talking about *the* Zac Jones—beautiful actor, producer, and film director, famously married for the last ten years. Grace knew better than to ask Jessica what she hoped to achieve by loving another woman's husband.

Arm in arm, they walked down to Jessica's waiting limousine. The driver hurried out when he saw them approach. The door was open by the time they were five yards away. Every fundamental thing was taken care of in the actress's life, but Jessica craved challenges. These were becoming elusive since she'd reached the top of her profession and shed all the vices —almost all the vices. Everything was hers for the taking—apart from a curvy, strong body and another woman's husband. Zac was still the greater challenge. No wonder she wanted him.

'Take care of yourself. Try not to hurt,' Grace said, deliberately not specifying whom.

'She who lives in hope dies fasting. I don't intend to. By the way, did you call that doctor?'

'No. I've decided to forget him.'

'You can't kid me—or teach me again until you speak to him.' Jessica got into the car and from the back seat raised a threatening finger.

Grace waved her off, glad not to have a driver waiting, a studio demanding, an audience expecting, Lynus panicking, and love in the balance. She was grateful for a solitude that was bearable, and sometimes preferable. Jessica meant well, but Grace didn't take her threat seriously. She wouldn't call Dr. James. Why hurt more than you have to?

In the kitchen, she punched the button on her answering machine: 'Hi Grace, it's William Turner. Mrs. Moore's grandson. We're auditioning for the television yoga teacher next Tuesday at my office in Westway Studios. Black Cat Productions. Ten o'clock. Hope you can make it. And Grace, I didn't want to tell you this on the machine, but Granny died in the Isle of Skye, where she wanted, if not how. We had the funeral there last week, which ultimately wasn't sad. Thank you for what you did for her.' The machine clicked off. Dead silence.

Grace climbed the stairs to her yoga room and lay on the floor, where, through the skylight, she watched a ripple of cloud drift across the moon. 'Lingers my desires' was all she could remember from Jessica's quote. Right then, Grace desired to be held, and to tell somebody how much she missed Mrs. Moore. Dr. James. He could hold her. He had once, briefly, she still remembered. And he would have understood, she knew, how desolate it made her feel that Mrs. Moore had died. But Dr. James was in Saigon shopping for breakfast at the market, or asleep—or lying in the arms of a beautiful woman. Whatever the doctor may, or may not be, doing in Saigon, and whatever Grace had told herself about not calling him, she changed her mind.

Nerves worked the whole way through her but eased when the oddly reassuring automated voice on his mobile asked her to leave a message. It was easier to communicate with a disembodied voice. 'Dr. James, I've missed hearing from you,' she began confidently, but the confession made her hesitate. She was suddenly unsure. 'Well, I just want to know you're okay. Please let me know how you are and where you are. Where *are* you?' She hung up quickly. What good was instant communication when it allowed her to instantly communicate the wrong thing? Grace switched off her phone, regretting that she had sounded plaintive and mothering, rather than the alluring woman a man would be certain to call back.

Unease followed her to bed and she slept fitfully. In the morning she grabbed her phone. It was time for Jessica. Grace sped to Mayfair before breakfast, cursing the actress for encouraging her to reveal her feelings to a man who did not deserve them.

The Black Cat Production office buzzed with yoga teachers. Chrissy, revived and quite spectacular, was there with her Primrose Hill posse, along with a room full of other women, all dressed, like Grace, in black yoga pants. As they waited to meet the producer of the television yoga show, the camaraderie was almost genuine. In the time an audition allowed, on what could the producer base his choice: Hair colour? Body shape? Smile? Voice? Rivalry was pointless. The women could be reasonable with each other because they all stood an equal chance of being the television yoga teacher—until Harry walked in.

For the first time in his life, Harry had turned up for an audition to discover that he was unique. Accustomed to competing with men, and men only, he knew that, today at least, his sex gave him the edge. In whiter than white pants and a white T-shirt, with a tan (not obviously fake), toned muscles, and a professional smile, he was quite impressive. When it came to show time, Harry knew how to perform. He and Grace smiled at each other—he had smiled first—and Grace was about to cross the room to greet him when he was ambushed.

'Hey, Harry,' said a groovy *yogini* as she threw her arms around him. By the time Grace had recognized her from the Primrose Hill teachers' meeting, Harry had progressed to Chrissy for full, prolonged and—from what Grace could tell—moist contact. It was all so Fame Family that Grace regretted that she'd canceled her appointment with Mr. Kramer. For some misguided reason, she'd half expected William simply to give her the job.

When he entered the waiting room, the hierarchy shifted. He acknowledged her with a nod, Mrs. Moore–style, then introduced himself and the five guinea pigs who had volunteered to be taught by the aspiring television yoga teachers. 'The purpose of this morning is to see how you come across on camera, so we'll videotape each of you teaching for five minutes. Some of you will get a callback next week for a more intimate chat.'

As luck would have it, Harry was first up. He bowed his head in *namaste* and gave William a firm handshake. Harry had the wide shoulders, the narrow waist, the smile. He had the om *shanti* and the *namaste*, and that day Grace saw that Harry had confidence. The audition door closed behind him, and the women sat subdued, waiting their turn. But not Grace. She headed home.

Date: May 10, 2007
To: yogagrace@hotmail.com
From: stephanie17@gmail.com
Subject: jb, nyc, tv

hey hey hey
you were right not to compete for a job you don't want. how
glamorous is television yoga anyway, unless they're shooting in
hawaii, which I suppose they might. sounds a little trite whatever
the location. you're better off with jb and nyc.
thanks for the schedule, and commentary on your clients. can't wait
to cover your classes and would love to stay in ladbroke grove. have
ditched the yoga magazine but will wait to jettison the classes. it's
good practice for me to teach until i leave for england.
i e-mailed diane about rome. she's in london before you get back, so
i will see her in both places. will you join me in rome? i can't believe
how yoga with diane sorts me out. when i do my practice i feel at
one with myself. my gahd, i sound so yogic but this practice has
helped me to stop worrying—about work, finding my path in life,
finding a boyfriend. mind you i've been dating vigorously: an older
man who i think is close to perfection, and a much younger one
(thirty) who i've had my eye on for years. i'm not fooled by them, or
myself. kind of liberating. hell, exceedingly liberating, if a little cold.
i'm waiting for them to reveal themselves, and I don't mean physically, as I know you know.
yoga with diane would certainly help you put that doc in perspective. you're caught up on him. when i told diane that i got caught up
in my shoulders doing siddha yoni asana, she said, 'it's hard not to
get caught up full stop. that's life, as frank says.' she makes me laugh
and holds yoga so lightly, even though it's central to her life.
incredible how every question, every hang up i have somehow gets
addressed on the mat, through the body, in this strange way of
moving that grows deeper in me.

forgive enthusiasm, most uncharacteristic, but i'm feeling so fine
these days, and this practice is the only thing that can account for it.
nothing else has changed.

all of me.

s

Grace could see that New York with Jessica would be a useful distraction
from Dr. James, not to mention a lucrative one. All she had to do was convince her yoga students to release her for a month. Doctors Norton, Peters,
and Damodaran agreed to allow Stephanie to teach the heart lifters (all competent yogis now), but requested that the workshop for the next group
of heart sinkers wait for Grace's return. 'You promise you'll come back?'
Dr. Damodaran asked at their meeting.

'Of course.'

'Good. It would be a pity to lose you.'

Generous praise from Dr. Damodaran, who had finally accepted Grace's
offer of a yoga class upon her return from the States.

The Knightsbridge ladies were less accommodating. It may have been
frightfully hip, as Plum would say, to share a yoga teacher with the most
famous actress in the world, but it was also frightfully inconvenient. Jackie
knew she wouldn't stay hip for long if her aging muscles lost the strength,
length, and definition yoga had given them. The ladies refused to take 'this
girl' sight unseen—unless Grace went with them for a weekend in the South
of France before deserting them.

'Four hours of yoga a day for three days sounds intense, but it might
inspire us to practice in your absence. Grace, say you'll come and I'll book
the tickets today.'

She agreed. How bad could a May weekend be in Cap d'Antibes?

Grace was waiting for the right moment to tell Collette that she was
going away, and was put off yet again when the supermodel announced
her pregnancy. Receiving the credit was the last thing she expected. 'But
I didn't do anything Collette. It was you and Mike,' Grace protested.

Collette wouldn't hear it. As her yoga teacher, Grace was the jewel in the lotus flower. 'You brought me to the place where, for the first time ever, I feel complete.'

Grace was uneasy. If she was responsible for it all going right, she could be blamed if it all went wrong, which, of course, life being life, Collette being Collette, it did. The next day.

'My breasts are huge.' Collette was lying on the cushions in the Shakti room. 'My stomach's beginning to show, and look at my ankles!'

To Grace's eyes, Collette's breasts and belly were unchanged, but her ankles were rather swollen. 'It's only fluid retention and that will go down if you lie with your legs up on the wall.'

'After the scare I had last night, it's the only thing the doctor wants me to do. I've been told no exercise for three months.'

Grace dared to hope she was off the hook. 'The doctor is right, you should rest, which works well as I'll be away—'

'I'm going to be fat,' Collette said, her voice small, her face streaming with tears that she had held in for years.

'Not fat, Collette, pregnant.'

'Mike hates big breasts and fleshy hips.'

'What about the Great Mother, the symbol of fertility?'

'I can't bear to look at her,' said Collette, going to the altar. 'Take her,' she said, placing the figure in Grace's hands.

Grace cradled the chubby, priceless icon that so offended the skinny sensibility of modern celebrity. 'Collette, I can't accept her.'

Collette curled like a kitten on the cushions. 'Why not? You've got to admit she's fat. I hate fat. And when I'm fat I'll hate myself. Grace, the Great Mother is yours.' Collette smiled for the first time that morning.

'If only you could accept that a beautiful round belly—'

'I feel sick when you say that,' Collette said, not smiling now.

'Do you want the baby?'

'Of course I do.'

'Then stay in this room if you have to, and be thankful.'

'I *will* be thankful, Grace, but not today. Today I'm sad that everything is going to change forever. Perhaps next week I'll feel better. We'll do yoga then.'

'Collette, I'm going away—'

'Away? Where?' asked Collette, sniffing into a soggy tissue.

'Jessica's asked me to go on location.'

'What a drag. For how long?'

'A month, but a friend who trained with me is taking my classes—'

'I won't be passed around and as I really don't feel like doing a single thing, let's forget today,' Collette said with distaste at somebody daring to dictate her plans.

Things changed fast after that. Collette called Grace's mobile in the middle of the night, no doubt hoping it would be turned off, which it was. 'You were right,' she said. 'I do feel safe in the Shakti room, so I'm going to hide here and balloon in private. Thank you for everything.'

Grace called the next day, but Collette did not pick up her telephone, or respond to any of her messages. Grace dropped a note at the house, which Carl promised to hand to Collette the minute she got back from the country. Grace never heard from the supermodel again.

Collette's Great Mother was given pride of place in the yoga studio, along with Mrs. Moore's creed: objects Grace cherished in memory of two women she held in such affection that yoga alone could not account for it.

Every time Grace explained to Mr. Kramer that she was going away he would appear to have understood, but when she saw him next the details of her departure had ebbed from his memory. Grace had one class left to get the message across and was surprised to find him waiting for her, listening to music in the sunroom, which, for once was bathed in sun.

'*In a Summer Garden*. Do you like Delius? He was the son of a mill owner from Bradford.'

'I'd like to hear about Delius, but first we need to write in your diary the dates I'm going away.'

'Can you hear the bird song in his music? And the water? I can see the sunlight reflecting in the river.'

Grace gave up trying to drag Mr. Kramer into her reality, and settled in the world of the man and his music. When the piece finished, they sat in silence. After a long time he said, 'So, you're abandoning me. You women are all the same. Kiki was out for three hours yesterday walking Frankie.'

Not wanting to be drawn into the mystery that was Frankie's exercise regime, Grace interrupted to say that Stephanie was looking forward to meeting him.

'Stephanie?'

'A young yoga teacher from California.'

'Coming to London to teach me?'

'Yes, Mr. Kramer, if that's what you would like.'

He brightened. 'I'll play Gershwin for her, and Fred Astaire. What about the Beach Boys?'

'I'm sure she'd love them all.'

Mr. Kramer stared at Grace. 'Question for you: do you think love can turn to friendship?' They were back to his take on love and life.

'That would depend on the lovers who want to be friends,' she said, willing to humour him.

'But whoever the lovers, it wouldn't be easy, romantic love being selfish and demanding, which are qualities no friendship can survive. What about love and friendship flourishing together? Have you ever had that?'

Grace gave the question due consideration.

'You're taking too long. You haven't had it!' Mr. Kramer said, delighted. 'At first the friendship makes you think love can't be there, but if you're lucky, and patient, love comes. If you fall in love too fast, it ruins the friendship.'

'Very interesting,' Grace said, sneaking a look at the time. Only another forty-eight minutes to dodge Mr. Kramer's sideways investigation of her private life. 'Would you like to try walking down the corridor without the Zimmer frame?'

'I'd rather tell you a secret.'

'Okay.'

Mr. Kramer leaned forward. 'This secret is almost as old as my marriage.'

She waited, fearing she was about to hear a terrible revelation about the Kramers' relationship, which did, in fact, bemuse her. Grace found Kiki remote, beautiful, and far too young and genteel for the brutish old northener.

'Kiki's got no idea. If she had, she'd kill me.'

'Don't tell me. Some things are best left unsaid.'

'But I want to tell. Only Frankie knows, and he doesn't count.'

'As long as you're sure your confession won't cause harm—'

'The harm's been done. You're looking at it.' He slapped his stomach. 'I'm a secret eater!' He may as well have said he'd won an Olympic medal, he was that pleased.

'Mr. Kramer, I can't believe it,' she said, suitably astounded.

'It's true. The fridge in the bedroom. Go see if you can find it—and if you do, bring me something would you?'

'What would you like?' she said, standing.

'Surprise me.'

Grace returned with two Mars bars.

'That's my girl.'

'One's for me.'

'Even better.'

They peeled back the wrappers and bit in, Mr. Kramer dribbling as he gnawed. 'I'm trusting you not to tell my wife. After years of nonfat cooking, it would break her heart, which is the last thing I want to do. You know the deepest human desire is companionship. Freud went on about sex and sex sells, but companionship is the thing,' he said with a full mouth, happy to be sharing secrets and chocolate. About as intimate as it gets, thought Grace, whatever your age.

When she got back to her car, she glanced at her BlackBerry. A voice message was waiting. 'Grace, I've been away and just heard . . . you.' Somewhere in Saigon, Dr. James had paused. So, Grace wasn't the only one to feel a little nervous. She smiled, listening. 'I've spent the last few weeks discovering the country with two monks who wanted to improve their English. No mobile phones allowed, and no money required. It really is monkey business when you're traveling with monks in Vietnam. We were showered with gifts wherever we went, including a motorbike for our trip. Three men on a bike if you can picture that. Thank goodness they were a lot smaller than me. Will call tomorrow, if the time difference doesn't get in the way.' He paused again. 'I've missed you.'

Dr. James may not have been in touch with Grace for at least six weeks, but she could tell that if he had been loving another woman, it hadn't been for long. Something in Dr. James's voice told Grace that he hadn't forgotten her quite as completely as she'd feared.

At Jackie's London house the familiar upstairs charade with the maid and the terrier was underway. It would be followed, Grace knew, by the downstairs charade—ladies' chatter. This morning's subject was the yoga weekend. 'Retreat, not weekend,' corrected Jackie. 'Grace, we're counting on you to keep us in order. No cocktails, only water to drink.'

Princess Elizabeth frowned. 'But we will go to Juan-les-Pins for hot dogs?'

'Of course not,' Jackie admonished.

'Oh come on, darling, just one. I never eat them anywhere else. It's a tradition, and such fun taking the jeep,' said Rosie.

'One can't hurt,' said Grace.

'Not even one,' said Jackie, resolute.

Grace was to be their yoga guru. That's what Jackie called her on a good day, rather than the 'yoga maid,' which was how she treated her on others. Which whim would prevail in Cap d'Antibes? Grace decided not to invest too much thought in it.

At the end of the class, Jackie handed her a plane ticket. 'We're all flying out the day before, to settle in and get ready for you,' she said. Traveling on separate days, Jackie had decided, was the discreet solution to their first-class tickets and Grace's economy—a discrepancy that wouldn't have mattered to Jackie if Plum had not been flying with them. Plum had become disturbingly liberal since Malcolm had moved in and Jackie did not want to be chastized in public for sticking the yoga teacher in the back of the plane. Though being obliged to upgrade her would have been worse.

If Jackie had learned anything from her husband, Sir Leonard, it was where to take the cost advantage, although looking at her monthly expenses, he would have doubted it. That Jackie had saved £350 on Grace's economy seat—the cost of one day's teaching—was a matter of pride. 'Grace, we want to maximize our yoga time, so we'll have a yoga class before dinner the day you arrive.'

'Don't worry, Grace, you'll have time for a shower before we begin, won't she, Jackie?' Princess Elizabeth interjected.

'She can jump in the shower, why not?' said Jackie.

'Does Plum have a mat?' Grace asked.

'She has all the kit,' Jackie replied. Grace felt foolish for doubting it.

'A car will meet you at Nice airport. You will have no expenses,' said the princess, who had assumed responsibility for labour relations. Grace was grateful, and increasingly fond of the princess. In fact, on a good day, she could be fond of them all, and it was with excitement for the forthcoming trip, and with intimations of affection, that she bid the Knightsbridge ladies good-bye.

Chapter Fifteen

YOGAMUDRASANA—psychic union pose

Mudra *has many meanings in yoga, but in this instance it means the
seals, or physical locks, in the body that have curative and restorative
powers, like the asanas themselves. This asana is considered to be part of
the* padamasana *or lotus group of postures, which help to clear physical,
emotional, and mental blocks, awaken the charkas, and bring calm. The
ability to sit for extended periods of time advances meditation. Stay in*
padmasana, *bending forward with the eyes closed, with the forehead as
close as possible to the floor. Those with eye, heart, or back disorders
shouldn't practice for long, and those recently postoperative or postdelivery
shouldn't practice it at all.*

Jackie's Cap d'Antibes residence was on a modest lane, behind simple
wooden gates that did not prepare the visitor for the forty immaculate acres
that rolled down to the Mediterranean. Madame Vilpins, the housekeeper,
was a sturdy woman dressed in a blue housecoat and flat black boots.
There was steel in her handshake and her voice thought Grace. '*Laissez
vos bagages,*' she said, then led Grace to the first floor to inspect the weekend yoga studio.

'*Ca va?*' she asked, arms folded across her chest like an impatient
matron.

The room was empty, apart from yoga mats set in a star formation. 'It's perfect,' Grace said. Madame Vilpins grunted '*bon,*' and turned down the corridor. Grace followed. '*Votre chambre,*' the woman said, pushing the door open. Grace's bedroom was painted a delicate pink. It had a modern four-poster bed, and a bay window with a view through eucalyptus trees to the sea. 'This is beautiful. Thank you.' Grace was so delighted to be there, she kicked off her shoes and lay back on the bed. 'Madame, this is divine,' she said, but Madame Vilpins had thudded off without a word. Hearing a lighter tread approach her door, Grace jumped up as a young man wearing a black bow tie and a white shirt stepped inside.

'I'm Jacob, the Larchmont's butler.' Jacob was a sprite of an Englishman, with gold-framed spectacles and tightly cropped, curly blond hair.

'Hello. I'm Grace, the—'

'—yoga teacher,' he finished. 'Is there anything you need?'

'This room, this whole house, is perfect. There's nothing I need.' Grace checked her watch: less than an hour before she had to teach. 'Apart from a bath.' She edged open the bathroom door in the hope that Jacob would take the hint and leave.

Jacob had no intention of going so soon. Grace watched as he lifted her case onto the Balinese chest at the end of the bed, mild gratitude turning to disbelief as she saw his pale, slender fingers flutter with the zip, and hurry inside. With infinite care Jacob picked out her crumpled clothes, including three white lace thongs. Oblivious, Jacob folded them neatly in a drawer. Clothes that would have been perfectly fine slung over a chair were, within seconds, hung on hangers in the wardrobe. Jacob then went through to the bathroom. While the water was running he turned his attention to Grace's wash bag and, horror of horrors, arranged the contents on the glass shelf below the mirror.

Conversation opened with confession. Jacob, it transpired, fueled himself for duty with Twix and Procent. 'It's the only way I can cope with Madame Vilpins' bossing and Lady Larchmont's fits. Mind you, I try not to judge Lady L. Sir Leonard's such an arse. I expect you've heard he's got a three-year-old love child in the Ukraine, the old dog.'

'I had no idea,' said Grace.

'His mistress is twenty-eight. No wonder Lady Larchmont does so much bloody yoga. You and the massage therapist are probably the only people who touch her these days, have you thought about that?' Jacob sprinkled rosemary and lavender essence into the water. 'Your bath is ready for you now, Madame,' he said.

Alone, and grateful for it, Grace stripped and sank into the deep enamel tub. Facing the open window she propped her feet on the bath ledge to let the breeze tickle her toes. She rested back—but not for long. There was a soft tapping at the door.

'Yes.'

'*C'est* Brigitte.'

'Come in.'

Grace had not expected to see Brigitte quite so clearly. In a pink cotton dress and white apron, she was a thick-lipped young maid with shiny chestnut hair that was cut in a bob. She stood at the open bathroom door holding a tray with a fruit plate and a jug of elderberry wine. '*Pour vous*, Madame. Miss Plum say if . . . *si vous voulez un massage, elle* will uh . . .' The attempt at English expired.

'I'd love one, thank you so much,' Grace said, wanting most of all to be left in peace. But Brigitte was indifferent to Grace's nudity, and privacy. Grace knew enough of Jackie's world to know why: staff were constantly available and therefore invisible to employers and their guests. To acknowledge them would be too time consuming and defeat the point of having them.

'I close curtains Madame?' Brigitte inquired.

'Please no. I'll do it.' Grace wanted to watch the colours of the setting sun play across the bedroom walls.

'Is there anything else?' the girl asked, head bowed in submission. She was young, young enough to escape, thought Grace.

'Brigitte, you know what I'd like? I'd like you to take the night off.' She assumed that the girl wouldn't fully understand either her English, or the concept of a night off while Jackie was in the house and Madame Vilpins was watching.

Brigitte understood. '*Impossible* Madame,' she said, and fled.

Revived by the bath, and anarchy, Grace went to the yoga room, where a surprise guest—there would be one, of course—had arrived before her. India, a friend of Plum's and on the podgy side, stated she had never done yoga and wanted to lose weight. Candid analysis of these ambitions was postponed when Plum came in. Forthright, with long blonde rasta hair and a tattoo on her shoulder, Plum had seemingly devised her look to affront her mother, although she seemed too self-assured for pointless rebellion. Her chipped front tooth had been left that way—an acceptance of imperfection, Grace supposed, that made her doubly attractive.

During the first class, the Knightsbridge three enjoyed parading their flexibility before the relatively younger two women. Spirits were high at the prospect of a weekend of health and the resulting natural beautification that would hopefully occur. A timetable for the retreat, in which every waking hour was allocated, had been typed up and placed on each guest's pillow. There were walks and meditation, and yoga classes morning and evening, with massage once a day for everyone, including Grace. Lady Larchmont's schedule had left nothing to chance, but what had not been anticipated was the profound stillness that descended at the end of class. An atmosphere of peace filled the room, and everyone in it.

A little later, lying on her bed listening to the sea, an unexpectedly languid sound, Grace was distracted by a repetitive scratch in the corridor. It sounded as if an animal was caught somewhere. Grace opened her door cautiously. At her feet a wrinkled old woman, gnarled as an olive tree, was on her knees with a dustpan and brush, sweeping the carpet, which, as far as Grace could see, was already spotlessly clean. What to do? She shut her door, now feeling guilty for lying on a bed. A firm knock got Grace back on her feet. It was exhausting to be in a house so fully staffed, Grace thought. Madame Vilpins stepped inside and stood by the dressing table chair, instinctively dusting the back of it with her palm. 'Your supper will be served in the kitchen at a quarter past eight.'

Grace hadn't expected to eat separately from her charges, but didn't much mind. It would allow her time alone. 'Thank you for letting me know.' Madame Vilpins left, but then Grace realized that, released from the obligation of dinner, she was free to explore Antibes. 'Madame Vilpins,' she called down the stairs. 'I won't eat here this evening. Do you have the number of a taxi?'

'It's too late to call a taxi. I am making the dinner. You can have the jeep, but not tonight. *J'ai pas le temps pour l'arranger.*' The commander-in-chief had spoken.

Madame Vilpins was a year-round resident of the Larchmont house, and ran it as if it were her own. She negotiated with the staff and even smoothed tension among the guests—a far more frequent occurrence than reasonable people might expect—sparing Jackie from petty details, such as the dilemma as to where Grace should eat her meals. On the flight from London the Knightsbridge ladies had unanimously agreed that she should not join them, choosing not to communicate their decision to Plum, who had conveniently been excluded from the vote by two rows of first-class seats.

When Plum went to the dining room to pour herself an illegal absinthe before dinner, she noticed that only five places were laid. She drained her glass and ran up to Jackie's bedroom.

'How sweet,' Jackie said, delighted Plum had come for a mother-daughter chat before dinner—an intimacy she missed but remembered from her daughter's younger days. 'Be a darling, would you?' she said, indicating that she needed her daughter's help to fasten her diamond-and-emerald pendant.

Plum closed the clasp. 'Is India skipping dinner?' she asked, standing behind her mother.

Jackie nestled the stone at her throat, then lifted her eyes to meet her daughters' in the glass. 'India not eat? From the size of her, darling, I doubt it. We've only had raw food all day and one can assume she's not accustomed to that.' Jackie was the kind of woman who found fat a personal affront.

'So who isn't eating?' asked Plum, throwing herself onto her mother's enormous bed.

'Darling, the pillows.'

Plum fluffed them up and lay back, hands behind her head. 'So?'

'So what, darling?' said Jackie, distracted by a strand of blow-dried blonde hair that refused to lie flat. 'What am I going to do without my hairdresser for another *three* days?'

'Mum, why only five places for dinner?'

'We *are* five.'

'Not if you count Grace.'

'I didn't.'

'Why not? I'm going to set her a place.'

'You will do no such thing!' Plum got off the bed and was at the door by the time the command was given.

'Grace is going to eat with us tonight, or I won't.'

'Darling, Madame Vilpins has already told the yoga teacher she's eating in the kitchen.'

'You're a coward, Mum, getting old Vile Pins to do it.'

'Darling, don't be childish.'

'Fine, I'll eat with Grace.'

'Don't you dare. One is not friends with the staff.'

'Grace isn't staff. She could be a friend of mine.'

'I pay her to do a job, which makes her staff.'

'Mummy, she went to Cambridge and St.M—' Plum stopped. She was using her mother's criteria to justify her argument. 'You can't stick Grace in the kitchen. It's not evolved.'

'Evolved.' Jackie laughed. 'There's nothing wrong with the kitchen. One of Daddy's friends actually prefers it.'

'It's his novelty night and you know it. Mum, you've got to invite Grace to join us.'

'Shall I invite the gardener and Madame Vilpins while I'm at it?'

'Now you're being ridiculous. Invite Grace. It's right.'

'Darling you sound like David Cameron.'

'At least he's shaking things up.'

'He talks poetic nonsense neither you nor he has thought through.'

'I'll be eating in the kitchen, then, just so you know,' Plum said, heading for the door.

'Darling. Be reasonable. If I befriend the yoga teacher it's the thin end of the wedge.'

'Not inviting her to eat with us creates a divide.'

'A divide is what I want. There *should* be one. *Imperium in imperio.*'

'Oh, get a life.' Plum hated her mother's motto and walked out, but in an effort to be evolved, was careful not to slam the door.

Jackie, Rosie, and Elizabeth were in the dining room when an irritated Madame Vilpins appeared. 'Where do you want me to serve dinner, Madame?'

'In here, and tell my daughter to hurry up.'

'Lady Larchmont, Miss Plum *est dans la cuisine. Elle bouge pas.*'

The boycott confirmed, Jackie marched into the kitchen, one of the prettiest of all the pretty rooms in her house. Candles, flowers, and a linen covered the table laid simply for six: it was an inviting scene. 'Mummy, we were waiting for you,' said Plum.

Jackie's performance matched her daughter's. 'What a treat, supper in the kitchen. How *intime.*'

Rosie, entering behind her, pulled out a chair. 'If we're not allowed a glass of wine, at least let's have a giggle, which is always easier in the kitchen, *n'est-ce pas?*'

Plum had won round one. There was a long way to go, though, and Jackie was quick to reestablish authority. 'Sorry, everyone, my French confused Madame Vilpins,' she said, her smile fixed on her daughter. Without modifying her Queen's English accent—that even the Queen had learned to soften—Jackie fired French words at the timid Brigitte. *'Dites à Madame Vilpins, des maintenant nous allons manger ensemble.'*

Dinner was delicious. Jackie employed a French woman from St. Lucia, who she'd poached from a neighbour two winters before. Members of their London society were still traumatized by this audacious move, but, under Jackie's supervision, the chef was now considered to be among the best on the Côte d'Azur. She had skillfully prepared six vegetarian dishes using produce from the Larchmont's garden and, to the delight of the sweet-toothed Jackie, a pudding had been created for the healthy diners: pineapple and blueberries with chickpea pancakes.

Wary of abusing her employer's reluctant shift toward enlightened times, Grace retired early to bed but before the kitchen door swung shut she heard Plum say, 'See, that wasn't so difficult.'

Grace stood completely still.

'Nobody said the yoga teacher wasn't intelligent,' Jackie acknowledged begrudgingly.

'And rather good company. Grace would be welcome to eat with me anytime,' said Elizabeth.

'Thank God she's not a dolt like that Brigitte. There's no law against staff having wit and charm, though that doesn't make them one of us.'

'To be honest, Mum,' Plum said, 'I'm rather tired of people like us.'

The rest of the Cap d'Antibes weekend passed peacefully enough, with yoga classes interspersed with long walks, short meditations, light suppers, and lighter conversation. Grace knew better than to be offended by Jackie's posturing, but she was human: when it came to downward facing dog, she let her mistress hold the pose until she panted from the strain, and Grace felt cruel for keeping her there.

The afternoon Grace returned from Nice, her father called. The habit of a lifetime had been broken that last Christmas, and father and daughter now spoke to each other almost every week.

'We want to see you,' he said now. 'We're coming over.'

'When?'

'This evening. We won't stay long, don't worry. We just want to say good-bye before you leave for the States.' We. Grace had never heard her father use the term. This was seismic. She guessed the shift was down to Ginny—and the program, his triple A, as he called it: the Addictive Alcoholics Anonymous.

Grace rushed to unpack her South of France bag. New York with Jessica would require a different kind of wardrobe, one that Grace realized she no longer owned. Disappointment in her limited choice of clothes was forgotten when Ginny and her father arrived. Grace welcomed them in. As she did so, her father thrust a wrapped package at her with an awkwardness born of unfamiliarity. 'Ginny and I talked about your studio. It's too plain.'

Grace could feel the frame through the wrapping paper. She waited until they were all downstairs around the kitchen table, having a cup of tea, before she opened it. Cutting the string and lifting the brown paper away, Grace recognized the abstract shape of the beautiful woman—the painting she had meant to ask her father for when she was at the Bodhi Tree.

Father watched daughter hold the painting at arm's length. 'That's the first painting I did of your mother,' he said.

Grace drove to Cadogan Square on a rescue mission to release Stephanie from her uncle and Noel Coward. Grace was glad for her own sake as much as Stephanie's. It was a relief to be with the young American, who was untainted by the ways of the old country, although seemingly at home in London, SW1. She wouldn't need long to acclimatize to the life she was inheriting. Grace had intended to warn her about the tactics the Knightsbridge ladies might use to keep her in her place, but thought better of it; Stephanie would instinctively know how to finesse her way through trouble. After introducing her to the doctors, Mr. Kramer, and the heart lifters, their day ended at Swami D's, where they taught a class together and had the vegetarian supper. As they said good night, Swami D suggested that Stephanie teach Grace's classes. Things were going according to plan.

Later, at Grace's kitchen table, Stephanie laid out the weekly timetable of where and when she'd be expected, alongside a large-scale map of west London, each location highlighted in fluorescent green. 'Anything else I should know?' she asked.

'Be yourself,' said Grace, 'and enjoy it.'

The following morning, just before Grace left for New York, a letter arrived from Vietnam. She waited to open it until she was sitting calmly in a black cab on the way to the airport.

Dear Grace,

It's 1:30 p.m. Everyone is resting in their rooms before our 2 p.m. clinicals. I've just had a bath and I'm sitting at my favourite spot in the covered part of the garden. It's raining again, gently; fine drops elicit small circular ripples on the pond and there is the slow, heavier sound of rain falling from the huge leaves. All the plants are clean of the Saigon dust, everything is fresh.

Saigon after rainfall in the night is colourful. Everyone rides their bikes with plastic ponchos draped over the headlights so the traffic is multicoloured as it streams along. But the noise! Puddles splashing, half-flooded roads, the smell of humidity, the dampness of your clothes sticking to your skin, and the never-ending din of horns. The senses are assaulted, but if I don't get caught up in it all —and don't mind being wet and a little shocked at the madness—I can accept the noise at such levels of discord that all the sounds merge into a sort of harmony.

My plans are to go to Chinatown again before I leave. I hope to get to the Gulf of Siam for sun without rain, to watch the world go by before returning to London. I have written to a few treatment centres: two have replied, sounding keen, so I'm hopeful. A far cry from Harley Street, which is what I used to want.

Your text just landed! How lovely that you're thinking of me while I'm thinking of you. So, you're off to New York with Jessica, who sounds adorable, but spending so much time with one client could get intense. Do you consider yours to be a therapeutic relationship, as the saying goes, or are you beyond that? I suppose there could be hazards however you choose to define it.

You'll probably still be in New York when I get back to London. There have been so many changes in both our lives; I can't wait to hear all your stories, and <u>see</u> you. It keeps occurring to me how wonderful it is that you're now working closely with patients: such a change from the pharmaceutical rep I met—who, as you must know by now, got to me. Sometimes I picture us working

*together! In these peaceful surroundings I often find myself think-
ing of you.*

    Safe travels.
    Much love,
    David

Grace folded the letter carefully back into the envelope, her feelings for
Dr. James temporarily suspended. She was filled with dread. His declaration of affection was very much what she'd hoped he'd write—but now that
he had, she was terrified.

Chapter Sixteen

Hanumasana—monkey pose

Hanuman was a devotee of the Hindu god Rama, the seventh incarnation of Vishnu. Hanuman's extraordinary strength, devotion, and flexibility are qualities required in the pose that bears his name. The pose also refers to the monkey god's great leap, according to the yogis the greatest leap ever taken. Very few people will be able to lower the body completely to the floor while keeping the legs straight in the final position. Those who attempt this posture should do so slowly. Benefits include improved flexibility and blood circulation in the legs and hips. Hanumasana massages the abdominal organs, tones the reproductive system, and prepares the female body for childbirth.

Grace was glad that she'd have only one student to teach, especially since it was Jessica. Living in the same hotel, working only two hours a day, teaching classes an elevator ride away, would simplify her life. She hadn't seen Jessica for four days and had missed her. When she stepped into the Paramount plane their reunion was not the celebration she'd imagined. A commercial seat at the back of economy would have been more comfortable than sitting in the atmosphere that prevailed between Lynus, his director, and their Oscar-winner.

Lynus and the director were shouting about their film, now so over-budget they would have to shorten it by twenty minutes to save three million dollars. According to Lynus this was the director's fault and he was reluctant to pay a scriptwriter $500,000 to spend a week rewriting the script. Jessica said the film was way too long and, as far as she was concerned, the script could be halved. Tired of being caught in the cross fire between producer and director, she unhooked her seat belt and went to sit at the back of the plane beside her driver-cum-bodyguard. Her new best friend, Grace supposed, as so far her presence had been ignored.

Jessica perked up when they got to the hotel, where nobody could have cared less about Grace's healthy glow from the Cap d'Antibes regime. Jessica was the star, and the manager had done his impressive best to make sure she knew he knew it. Jessica's suite was filled with her favourite candles, Jo Malone everything, and a row of shopping bags from boutiques across the city. It was enough to initiate recovery. She called Grace to suggest a yoga class in her suite, her mood evidently improved. Grace was grateful. She didn't see the point of teaching a sullen student.

'What I'd like to do today,' Jessica said when Grace arrived with the yoga mats, 'is meditate.'

'For the whole hour?'

'Sure. You can talk us through it.'

'Talk through what?'

'The meditation. I want to meditate on Zac coming to New York and for everything to work out between us. Can we do that?'

Grace felt a current of incredulity surge through her, and hoped it was not broadcast on her face. 'I've never conducted that kind of meditation.'

'But you believe in the chakras and in something more than the grand illusion, or whatever that French guy called it?'

'Maya.'

'Exactly. You believe there's something more than all this, don't you?' Jessica said, holding out her hands to indicate the material world of her hotel suite.

'I do, yes.'

'So, let's get to work.'

While Jessica placed the candles in a circle around two cushions, Grace jotted down things she hoped she'd be able to say with conviction. She didn't know Zac, and she didn't approve of a woman borrowing another's husband, let alone stealing him. And yet she composed words to console Jessica, even if their power to manifest a male sex god in the suite by the end of the week might be in doubt. When all the candles had been lit, Grace and Jessica sat in lotus, facing each other.

'Wait,' the actress said, after Grace had led them in a second om. 'What about you?'

'What about me?'

'I think we need to manifest something for you. Like that doctor. Have you heard from him?'

'I received a letter today.'

'Go and get it,' Jessica instructed.

'Is that really necessary?'

'To have something he's given you will make this more powerful.'

Grace obeyed. Jessica knew a thing or two about manifesting, and it seemed she'd undertaken some independent research into meditation techniques. When she got back, Jessica was holding a small silver handgun.

'Where did you get that?'

'Zac. First thing he ever gave me.' She kissed the pearl inlay, then stuck it under her cushion. Very Bonnie and Clyde, thought Grace, sticking her letter from Dr. James under hers.

The women sat on their meditation cushions in candlelight, facing each other. Grace began slowly and ended every wish with the words, 'for the highest good of all concerned,' just in case the words did have the power to realize Jessica's desires, along with her own. When the hour was over, Jessica opened her eyes. 'That was absolutely fucking weird. He was right here. Did you feel it?' she whispered, as if in fear of breaking a spell.

Grace stared back at the actress. It was bizarre; she too had felt that Zac was in the room with them. The power of sitting together to concentrate with a clear mind, open heart, and a strong intention, had surprised her almost as much as Jessica.

'He was here, wasn't he? My God, he was right here.' Jessica was standing in the spot that Grace had thought she'd seen Zac's ephemeral likeness. She tried not to mind that the movie star was the man they'd manifested rather than the doctor. She had dedicated nearly as many words to Dr. James, as Jessica had insisted that she should, and yet he seemed remote, as far from the room as it was possible to be.

The virtual encounter had revived Jessica. Struggling to contain her excitement—but not struggling too hard—she invited Grace to rifle through her multicoloured shopping bags.

'How about this?' Jessica pulled out a Dolce & Gabbana dress.

'That's stunning,' said Grace, resisting the impulse to touch it. Since giving up Suprafarma she had averted her eyes outside every designer shop.

'It would suit you.' Jessica slung the orange silk dress at her. 'And you can have the Max Mara,' she said, pushing three bags in Grace's direction without bothering to look. 'But this is mine,' she said, pressing a Hermes skirt to her waist to check its length.

Seconds later cream silk—a Hermes shirt—fluttered at Grace's feet. Jessica picked through the clothes as though at a jumble sale, scattering the gifts that had come with handwritten notes from fawning sales people, welcoming her back to New York City. 'Let's have dinner uptown. I feel like steak and a glass of red wine. Then we can come downtown to see a movie. We could go bowling, or to a club if you want. We should definitely wear some of this stuff. Or you can.'

Grace wore the Hermes shirt with jeans, Jessica her regulation black T-shirt and jeans, which was a mistake. The pictures in the papers the next day did not flatter her.

'You look good, though,' Jessica said, wrapped in a bathrobe, scrutinizing the tabloids as she worked through her bodybuilder's breakfast.

Confused that her student was eating before class, Grace dismissed the compliment. 'I've got a tan. I'm out of focus. Anybody would look good,' she laughed. Jessica did not. She didn't even look up from her boiled egg. 'Book me a tanning session.' Grace waited for the follow up line. There wasn't one.

'Jess?'

'Grace.' Jessica sighed heavily.

'You shouldn't be eating all that just yet. What about yoga?'

'What about it?' She scraped the egg white out with her teaspoon, then squashed the shell. 'Shit, I'm late.' Jessica got up from the table. 'No time for yoga. Sorry 'bout that.'

'I'll see you this evening, then,' Grace said.

'Maybe.' Jessica disappeared into the bathroom and shouted from the shower, 'Don't call me, I'll call you.'

It didn't occur to Grace to book the sun bed for the pale star. She walked out of the hotel, and picked up the *Post* for a closer look at the photographs. If Jessica had scowled once all evening, Grace hadn't noticed, and yet that was her expression in the picture on the front page. Grace flicked through the paper, and stopped at page three, where a picture—taken with a long-range lens and slightly out of focus—showed Zac Jones on a private beach in Malibu holding his wife in his arms. It was impossible to tell whether it was a romantic scene, or a good-bye forever embrace, but either way, however close Zac had seemed to Jessica in yesterday's meditation, there was no denying that he'd been a hell of a lot closer to his wife. Grace dumped the newspaper.

Grace did not hear from Jessica that evening, or the following morning. Waiting for her call, Grace explored New York. It was late spring, the city was at its best, and she enjoyed the liberation of a day to herself and the luxury of hotel living. When Jessica hadn't contacted her three days later, Grace was on edge. She left a message on the actress's phone. In the Museum of Modern Art, at the Frick, jogging around the reservoir, walking through Central Park, even in meditation, Grace counted off the days until she could fly home. She pushed a written note under the actress's door. There was no reply. It seemed that a vanishing act was standard in a diva's repetoire. Both Collette and Jessica had admitted her to their inner circle, only to eject her the minute she'd stepped out of line. The famous beauties were stars around whom others were meant to revolve—and if you didn't revolve properly you were put out. Jessica had put Grace out, no doubt about that. What wasn't clear was why. Obviously the actress hadn't appreciated her yoga teacher outshining her in the *Post*, but Grace knew that wasn't reason enough. Could it be that Jessica was simply humiliated to have confessed to Grace that she loved a man who appeared not to love her back?

Given that Jessica was shooting in a studio on the outer edge of Queens, scenes that required her to thrash about in a tank of water with a plastic monster, Grace did not expect the film star's mood to improve soon. She did, however, expect to teach her yoga. Every morning she went up to Jessica's suite to do just that, only to find a note stuck to the door: 'Not today, thanks,' the actress had scrawled. 'Sleeping in. Have a nice day,' was the other note she'd leave. It seemed friendly, although Grace didn't rule out sarcasm.

Meanwhile, Grace received countless calls from Lynus, who was desperate to discover why Jessica was being so goddamn difficult. 'Aren't I paying her enough?' he said. The *Post* had claimed Jessica was getting $15 million for the movie, which seemed enough to Grace, though her loyalty was to her student rather than the man who paid for the yoga classes.

'I can't say I've noticed anything different about her,' Grace said, ignoring the fact that she hadn't actually seen Jessica for six days.

'She ain't moody with you then?'

'A little. Perhaps she needs a break—'

'Sure. How about I send her to St. Barts? Is that the kind of break you had in mind? I know what, let's all go.' Lynus stopped, hoping Grace would let something slip. She kept quiet. In the silence, Lynus breathed down the phone. 'Okay, Grace. Call me, please, the minute anything seems off. Or, hell, let me know if things improve. They couldn't get much worse.'

Grace tended to agree. Waiting for Jessica to deign to have a class wasn't why she'd come to New York. She didn't like Lynus, but felt guilty for cheating him, charging for classes she wasn't teaching. It was time to stand up to the actress. The next day, clutching her yoga mat, she waited in the corridor outside Jessica's door. At half past seven exactly, a waiter rolled up with a breakfast trolley. He used his pass to open the door. Smiling politely, as though she were expected, Grace slipped in behind him.

The room was a disaster, strewn with bags of new clothes, old newspapers, and random pages of script. The waiter pulled a chair up to the linen-dressed trolley. 'Your breakfast, ma'm,' he called, then slipped away. Grace thought of following him. She had no right to be there, and was about to leave when Jessica appeared from the bathroom wrapped in a white towel.

'What the *fuck* are you doing here?' she shouted.

'Jessica, I can't just not teach you. Lynus is expecting me—'

'*Fuck* Lynus.'

'He's paying me a lot of money—'

'Grace, you do what you need to do to have a good day, and I'll do what I need to do. Now, get the *fuck* out.'

Grace left and quietly shut the door behind her. *Fuck, fuck, fuck, fuck, fuck, fuck, fuck!* Things, as Lynus had said, couldn't get much worse.

Grace decided to wait one more day before offering to teach Jessica again. If her offer were declined she would abandon the woman she had once thought a friend, and take the next plane back to London. It was Saturday. Eleven o'clock in the morning. A civilized hour. Time enough for Jessica to have slept in. Grace dialed the suite.

'Hi, Grace,' Jessica said, in a sweet sleepy voice.

About as relaxed as if she were poking a snake with a stick, Grace offered, 'Would you like a class this morning?'

'I'd love some yoga.' She sounded warm and cuddly, then moaned a little as if she were stretching. 'I'm with somebody who wants to join in. Is that okay?'

Zac Jones, looking remarkably like Harry, sat at Jessica's breakfast table. Grace felt she'd entered a film set: *Breakfast. Morning after the night before. Zac politely greets the yoga teacher. Jessica seems shy, yet proud of her man's manners.*

Zac wasn't just polite; during the yoga class he proved that he was flexible and strong, and so caring of Jessica that she was putty in his hands. When the class was over, Grace was ready to leave the couple to their day, necessarily confined to the hotel room unless they planned to court the whole world's press along with each other.

Back to her pre–prima donna self, Jessica showed Grace the door. 'Nobody knows,' she said in a low voice.

'I won't tell a soul.'

Jessica kissed Grace's cheek, partly as an excuse to say, without Zac overhearing, 'Sorry. For the whole week I wasn't sure he was coming.'

'I'm glad he did.'

'So am I. And let's forget evening yoga while he's here, just between us.'

This was Jessica's code for Grace to bill Lynus for a few thousand pounds worth of yoga classes, thereby keeping a secret he would have paid her many thousands more to reveal.

After several days of teaching Zac and Jessica (mornings only) Grace went up one day to such shouting from behind the door that she hardly dared ring the bell. She was still deciding whether she should or shouldn't, when Jessica appeared. 'Don't just stand there. Come in. We're waiting.'

Jessica's putty days may have been over, but her leading man was obligingly on the mat, his arm slung over his head partly concealing a fine red gash. He winked at Grace. They both knew that Jessica was adorable and terrible in equal measure. The couple behaved throughout the class, but as soon as it was over and Grace had closed the door, there was a percussive smash, a scream, then silence. Either they had killed each other, or desire had reasserted itself and driven them back to bed. Assuming the latter, Grace took the elevator down to her suite, where there was a message on her mobile from Dr. James. 'I'm getting closer. Back tomorrow. Hope New York is treating you well. Please call when you're home.'

New York was one thing. Jessica Bell another.

After Zac left for Los Angeles, Jessica spiraled downward, picking Grace up like a rediscovered toy. They went shopping on Saturday and to lunch on Sunday, with yoga classes back to twice a day. Most evenings they ate dinner together in Jessica's suite, on the terrace, their conversations last-ing long into the night.

Tonight dinner was sushi, sent not from the hotel kitchen but deliv-ered by Jessica's favourite Soho restaurant. Grace could see that for all the problems posed by fame, the advantages, if you were clever, could add up. Not that it made fundamental things like love any easier. Jessica had no doubt that Zac was the Shiva to her Shakti, and believed they were closer than ever to getting together. 'He wants to wait before going pub-lic, but I've run out of patience,' she said. 'We've never been outside, not even for a walk in disguise. He won't risk it. Can you believe we've never breathed fresh air together? And he wonders why I won't keep waiting.'

'Hand it over.'

'Who to?'

'Some people call it God. But whatever word you use, the discipline, the practice, is the same. It's about letting go. If I've learned nothing, I have learned that.'

'To want this relationship, to want Zac as much as I do scares me.'

'You were the one who said that to have a dream takes courage,' said Grace, slightly distracted by brilliant lights across the street, where men dressed in overalls scaled the wall of the building opposite.

'The consequences of my dream will be tough for a while. That's why I want you in L.A. And I won't disappear the way I did last week. I'm sorry about that. Retreating from the world is what I do when things get diffi-cult. I've done so much growing up in the public eye. The press picks over all my mistakes, every relationship I've ever had, and plenty I haven't. I don't trust easily, which means I test everyone, too much sometimes. You didn't deserve the way I treated you.'

'Don't do it again.' Grace's mock solemnity amused Jessica.

'I won't, not to you anyway. Listen, Grace, please come to L.A. We'll have fun there. And as soon as this monster movie is over, you can go back to London and I'll join Zac on location.'

'Then the whole world will know.'

'And the press will have a field day, as you Brits say, which is when Zac and I risk falling apart. It's the kind of pressure that can kill a relationship.'

'You'll hold it together,' Grace said, distracted by what looked like Jessica's frail arm going up on the billboard behind her. 'Jessica, is that you?'

The women leaned on the terrace railing watching as a vast poster of Jessica was assembled. 'They're slowly putting me together,' said Jessica. The men worked their brushes back and forth, diminished by the expanse of Jessica's thirty-foot naked torso. A commercial for jeans emerged, and jeans were all she wore, her bottom to the camera as she twisted to look behind her.

'I'd say that poster proves my body *has* changed. I mean look at my ass now,' she said, slapping her rump.

'Your waif days are numbered,' Grace agreed. 'It must be strange to see yourself fifty-feet tall.'

'Especially when you don't particularly feel it. That image makes people think they own me, or know me, but the truth is, they don't and never will, however many interviews I give, or pictures they take.'

'Thank you for trusting me, Jess, and for being so generous with all those clothes.'

'Clothes are nothing, but your closed mouth is everything. Thanks for keeping my secret.'

The poster magnified Jessica's power so that the image was greater than the woman herself; she seemed impenetrably perfect. 'Nobody but the gods were portrayed on such a scale,' Grace said.

'That's the paradox. Models and actors are notoriously insecure. You know, to take in the power of that image would destroy me. But if I can turn it around and put the power it brings into the service of others rather than myself, then I've got a chance.' Jessica stared at the huge photograph of herself.

'Have you thought how you're going to do that?'

'Remember what I said at Collette's *puja* party, about you seeing people who pay you for an hour and then get on with their lives, leaving you with nothing. I was wrong to say that. You're helping others, you're being of service, which is what I've decided to do.'

'Teaching private yoga classes in one of the world's most expensive cities; who exactly am I helping?'

'Honey, don't knock classes that pay the bills. At the doctors' you must be doing good. You're certainly lightening their load. What about your dream to help the kids?'

'I'm saving the money from this job for that. It's a start.'

'I bet children who've been through hell could learn to feel safe doing yoga with you. I have . . .'

'Jess, thanks for saying that.'

'I believe in you, Grace.'

'To set up the kind of place I have in mind will take a whole lot more than just me. I'd need to find experienced people—'

'Start looking. I want to help kids who've been through the worst kind of bad times. I'd willingly put up money for an inner city yoga place.'

'Are you serious?'

'I am. Let's work on it together—well, you do the work, I'll do the money. But right now, let's go inside. I can't face that picture anymore.'

They stepped off the terrace and Jessica closed the curtains to block out her image.

Grace was careful not to repeat the mistake she'd made with Collette, and the next day made sure Jessica understood that she wouldn't join her in California. 'It wouldn't be fair to my students—and Dr. James is back from Vietnam.'

'When did you find that out?'

'He left a message.'

'What did he say?'

'He's asked me to let him know when I'm home.'

'Is that all?'

'We can take it from there. See what happens.'

'So he didn't meet anyone new?'

'I don't think so. I hope not. Seeing you with Zac made me really want to—'

'Want to what?' Jessica's eagle eye was on Grace again. 'Did that doctor kiss you yet?'

Grace shook her head.

'Oh boy,' said Jessica. 'You're gonna have a wild time, I can just tell. I hope he deserves you.'

'We'll see if I deserve him—and if we get that far. You're lucky. Zac is absolutely adorable *and* he adores you.'

'He holds me close and sets me free, the first man I've met who lets me be. That didn't feel like love at first, let me tell you.'

'Sounds very grown up,' Grace said.

'Yeah, and sexy as hell.'

The last time Grace had flown across the Atlantic she'd been heading back from the Bodhi Tree, floating on memories. Now her future was more certain, and it was one that excited her. She had a clear purpose, and felt closer to what she was meant to be doing, closer to the heart. After the heady world of Jessica Bell, she was ready for the reality of Ladbroke Grove, teaching at Swami D's and the doctors'. Her other yoga students she had decided to let go. She'd be too busy searching for a project team, recruiting people who cared about the same things she did, who would help her build a yoga centre. 'Free everything for inner-city kids up to seventeen,' was the first condition of Jessica's investment.

Stephanie had insisted on driving to the airport to meet Grace, and seeing her standing in Terminal One arrivals, Grace recalled Mrs. Moore's creed: 'I believe in the affection of the extended family, and the compassion of the young.'

Stephanie was a bright light and proud of her knowledge as she drove Grace into London. 'I had a blast. I love your students. Emily's a riot. Maud's cray-zee but I love her, and Jack's wicked.'

'Jack?'

'Mr. Kramer. What a guy. Love him. And Swami D's classes were fantastic.'

'So you liked the karma yoga.'

'No karma yoga for me, sweetheart. He paid twice what I asked.'

'How much was that?'

'Twenty bucks an hour. Breakfast's on me. I'm dying for bagels and smoked salmon at this funky Jewish place in St. John's Wood.'

'Harry Morgan's. My dad took me there when I was a kid.'

'Let's go before class.'

'Class?'

'Diane's been giving a workshop nearby. Today's the last day. I signed you up.'

To have breakfast straight off the plane followed by yoga was an order that didn't seem right, but Stephanie wouldn't let Grace change the plan. 'Breakfast first is the only way to fit everything in, and you can't miss Diane. I promise, you'll love her yoga.'

Grace found Stephanie's confidence endearing; commandeering her car, and her day, the girl had what her father called *chutzpah*. 'Am I allowed to stop at home to change?'

'Excellent idea.'

After a quick shower, and pulling on yoga clothes (a lovely outfit from Jessica and just about the most comfortable thing Grace had ever worn), they drove to St. Johns Wood.

Stephanie had picked up the Saturday papers, and they sat at her regular table. 'I've really got into coming here.' She stopped turning the pages of the colour supplement. 'Cute. Check him out,' she said, turning the magazine towards Grace.

'That's Harry,' said Grace, staring at a beautifully lit photograph of Harry in *Supta Virasana*.

'What, that's your Harry in reclining warrior?' Stephanie snatched the magazine back to scrutinize the photograph, and the article. 'You're right. He got that TV yoga job and he's about to be very famous,' she said, pushing it away in disgust.

Grace read aloud, 'Selected from hundreds of applicants to teach on television, Harry is determined to use the public exposure to demystify the ancient art of yoga. "People think yoga is too esoteric, or too trendy, or simply too difficult unless they're flexible" he says. "I want them to tune in to my show and see that yoga is for everyone. Yoga for the masses is my goal."' Grace yawned. 'I think his reclining days are over,' she said, which made them both chuckle. 'What the hell. The guy deserved a break.'

'Well he got one—thanks to you, which he isn't honest enough to mention,' Stephanie said.

'Gratitude is not the angle of the piece.'

Amused about the inaccuracies of the article (apparently Harry had forsaken a fantastic media career, 'to join the peaceful world of yoga teaching,' which was proof enough he didn't know what he was talking about), they finished breakfast. On their way to the St. John's Wood Healing Centre, Grace observed that after years of trying to help Harry, the best thing she'd done for him was kick him out. 'I've felt free of him for ages, but seeing that article has proved to me that I'm over him completely. In fact, I'm glad he's making it in the world. And he'll be famous, which is what he's always wanted.'

Stephanie linked arms with Grace and leaned her head on Grace's shoulder. Grace hesitated to accept such easy affection, but softened. Stephanie was a girl without inhibitions, a girl who was herself. They ran upstairs, lightness descending, lightness ascending—in spite of the breakfast—to stand in line for Diane's yoga class.

'I wonder what you'll make of this,' Stephanie said. 'Diane doesn't even call this practice yoga.'

'What does she call it?' asked Grace.

'A way of being and moving, like a dance deep inside yourself. She says yoga is a path, not a method.'

'I'll go for that,' said Grace.

'Yesterday she told us that if you do yoga in the right way, it's never what you think it is, and that you don't want it to be because real freedom is always one step beyond what you know.'

'So knowing what's going to happen next isn't freedom?'

'Something like that. And that's good, right?' Stephanie looked uneasy all of a sudden.

'Don't worry, Steph, I'm open to discovering what this yoga dance is all about.'

Stephanie leaned toward Grace. 'There's a man looking at you.'

'Is that a good thing?'

'Grace?' said a voice behind her.

Keeping her eyes on Stephanie, she said, 'Dr. James?' Still she dared not turn around. She had no idea how she'd react to seeing him again: she might throw her arms around him—or run. Holding on to the image of him she'd carried within her was safer than turning to face him, so she didn't.

Even Stephanie was self-conscious when Dr. James stepped in front of Grace, who had no choice but to look at him.

'Grace, do you think you'll ever call me David?'

And there he was, better than she remembered, closer than she'd dreamed he'd be quite so soon. She smiled and in that instant everything around her disappeared, apart from him. He opened his arms to her. 'So, you'll call me David from now on?'

'Yes Dr. James—I mean David. Yes, I will, I promise!' She blushed as he hugged her. 'Are you doing yoga with us?'

'I'm working,' he said, indicating his jeans and well-pressed shirt. 'I'll leave the yoga to you, but we could meet after class.'

'This isn't a coincidence is it?' Grace said, directing the question at Stephanie.

'It is—and it isn't,' she said.

Dr. James winked at Stephanie. 'I'd better go. I've got a patient waiting.'

Stephanie had rushed to the changing room; when Grace caught up with her at least she had the humility to look a little guilty. 'Tell me I didn't do wrong?'

'That depends,' Grace said, pretending to be put out.

'Oh damn. It's just that—'

'Just that what?'

'Well, I wasn't snooping, but I found a letter in your dressing table. One you wrote to David—'

'You didn't show him?'

'No! I've never seen him before. He's gorgeous by the way. Why didn't you tell me he's mixed race?'

'It didn't occur to me.'

'All this time I've been putting the wrong face to your David James. I was picturing a waspy, doctorly guy.'

Grace grinned. 'At least now you can feast your mind on the reality.'

'Honey, it will be a pleasure.'

'How did you know he was going to be here?'

'This was the most interesting thing in your mail all month.' Stephanie handed Grace a postcard. 'After reading the letter you never sent I knew I had to speed things along. I still had his number on my mobile from when you texted him from California, so I called, because I didn't trust that you would. Not in time anyway. After seeing him, I wasn't wrong. That man could get snapped up any second. Do you forgive me?'

'Nothing to forgive,' Grace said as they walked into the studio.

Lying on her mat Grace read Dr. James's postcard.

Grace, this picture of Tower Bridge tells you I'm in London. Can't believe the back and forth between East and West and us will soon be over. I didn't know if we could keep in touch with nothing to go on but letters and texts and two (rather strange) meetings. Seems we have! In the hope that nothing has happened in the last few days to make you change your mind, I look forward to seeing you very soon. David.

Watching Grace read, Stephanie's confidence returned. She fell into a backbend from standing, which was her idea of a warm-up, the tricky little acrobat that she was. Without even a catch in her throat, folded backward, she went on to explain, 'When your doctor told me he was working at the centre where Diane was teaching, I was inspired to take the guessing out of it.' She kicked up into a handstand.

'Somebody had to,' said Grace, appreciating her friend's good intentions and remarkable agility. Grace told herself she would have called Dr. James within the week. But who knew what would have happened in those intervening days? At least the meeting had happened. Grace and David would walk and talk together and . . . Grace's imaginings were cut short. Diane was in the room.

'Hi everyone,' she said. Her accent was another song of the American south. Grace slipped David's postcard under her mat. 'Anybody here new today?' Diane asked.

Grace raised her hand, along with a few others.

'Well, take it easy and don't rush. Don't try to make something happen,' Diane said. 'Remember, this way of working is about finding a rhythm deep inside yourself, and taking time to rest.'

'I can't believe I've introduced you to Dr. James *and* Diane in one day. You've gotta love me,' whispered Stephanie.

'Okay Steph, I love you. Now shut up,' Grace smiled.

'Seriously, this is the day. This is the one to remember,' she said, completely convinced that Diane's yoga was a good thing, and Dr. James, too.

Grace looked over at the lean, long-legged yoga teacher with her rough-cut hair and shining eyes. 'And if you were in yesterday's class, forget it,' Diane said. 'Don't try to repeat the good things, those poses that came easily to you, or avoid those that didn't. Be a beginner. Bring quality to your attention, and awaken to the deep alive strength in yourself. Okay. Enough talk. Where shall we begin?'

Acknowledgements

I would like to thank Tai and Viv for generously letting me use his letters to her from Vietnam and for sharing so generously their memories of that time. Thank you, Marcus, for inspiration, constructive criticism, and words of comfort; and Jim Harrison for his poetry. Huge thanks to Morgan and all at Grove/Atlantic, particularly Lauren and Elisabeth, and the art department for perfecting the asanas. My thanks to Dr. Jamie Arkell and Dr. John West for their insights, and to Stephanie, Charles, Bobby, Charlet, Pete, Tony, Nicole, and gml for support when I most needed it, and friendship always. If I could I would thank Philip Lebon for his tremendous spirit; thank you, Mark, for allowing me to try to capture it.

I am forever grateful to my mother and sisters, and Jim for his presence in the Force. Lastly, to my yoga teachers over the years—Fausto, John Stirk, Ganga White, Tracey Rich, Sophey Hoare, and Diane Long: thank you. And thank you to those who asked me to teach yoga in my turn, most fondly Arabella and Dorothée.